OF SEA & SHADOW

Will Wight

Books by Will Wight

The Traveler's Gate Trilogy

House of Blades

The Crimson Vault

City of Light

The Traveler's Gate Chronicles

The Elder Empire

Of Sea & Shadow

Of Shadow & Sea

Of Darkness & Dawn•

*Of Dawn & Darkness**

**forthcoming*

OF SEA & SHADOW

THE ELDER EMPIRE : FIRST SEA

WILL WIGHT

Of Sea and Shadow

Book and cover design by Patrick Foster Design/Chris Arnoldus

Cover illustration by Melanie de Carvalho

ISBN 978-0-9896717-2-9 *(print edition)*

www.WillWight.com

will@willwight.com

twitter.com/willwight

To Mom, who taught me to Read.

Welcome, Reader.

Right now, you're reading the first book in The Elder Empire series.

But it's not the ***only*** *first book.*

Of Sea and Shadow *was written in parallel to* ***Of Shadow and Sea****, which takes place at the same time from a different perspective.*

You can begin with either book, and you will find that they each tell a complete story. Upon finishing ***Of Sea and Shadow****, you will be fully prepared for its sequel,* ***Of Darkness and Dawn.***

But I wrote these first two books together, and their stories intertwine in a way that I think you'll enjoy. I invite you, when you're through with this book, to check out ***Of Shadow and Sea.***

Until then…

Welcome to the Elder Empire.

CHAPTER ONE

Calder Marten stood on the deck of his ship, sailing into the wall of black clouds and rain. He clamped his hat down, holding it tight against the slashing grip of the storm.

"No more need for sails, Andel!" Calder shouted. "We go against the wind!"

Quartermaster Andel Petronus stood next to him, clutching his own hat. "What do you expect me to do about that, sir?"

"Nothing! I simply enjoy shouting!"

Calder gripped the wheel, Reading the Intent bound into the wood. His mind flowed through the bones of the ship, sensing every inch of The Testament as though it were his own body.

He sent a simple, silent order to his Vessel. Behind him, the sails furled.

They looked more like a bat's wings than ordinary canvas sheets; *The Testament's* sails were nothing more than stretches of membranous green skin that seemed to grow from the mast and yard. When they folded, the ship resembled a Nightwyrm bunching its wings to dive.

As the ship began to slow, Calder sent another mental command. After a moment they continued moving, jerking forward a few dozen yards at a stretch, as though an invisible giant tugged them along behind.

"Is my wife secure?"

The Quartermaster shook his head. "I'm afraid she's dead, sir. A fever took her in the night."

Calder spared a glance from the upcoming storm wall to catch a look at Andel's face. Andel Petronus was a Heartlander, dark-skinned, and his white suit and hat stood out against the black wood of the deck.

The man, as usual, wore no expression. He pressed his hat down with one hand and clung to the railing with the other.

"One day you're actually going to have bad news for me, Andel."

"Then I'll try to smile, so you know something's wrong." The man in white strode off across the deck, shouting orders. "Raise the thunderlights! Ready the cannons!"

Calder silently persuaded the ship to release its four captives: thunderlights, huge alchemical lanterns with copper spikes that unfolded almost as high as the mast. Thick ropes hauled the devices out of the hold through a hatch on deck, until a glass lantern big enough to hold a man rested on each of the four corners of the ship.

The lines tightened themselves, tying each thunderlight to the deck, but

Andel had to release the copper spike by hand. As the first drops of rain began to slap the ship, Andel turned a crank on the lantern, slowly raising a copper limb into the sky.

An Imperial Navigator could sail the Aion Sea with a light crew thanks to the Captain's control over the ship, but even Calder couldn't handle everything. The storm was a dark slice of night in front of them now, flashing with lightning and rolling with wind-tossed waves. As the ship slammed down into a valley between two waves, sending spray rolling over the deck, Calder looked to his gunner.

Dalton Foster straddled one of the cannons, a hammer in one hand and an alchemist's spray-bottle in the other. He was leaning out over the railing, his head practically stuck inside the cannon's mouth.

"How's it coming with those cannons, Foster?" Calder shouted.

Foster pulled his head out and turned. His wild hair and beard were soaked through until he looked like a cat that had escaped the bath. He tore one pair of spectacles off, letting them dangle from a cord around his neck, and lifted a second pair to his eyes.

"That depends, Captain! Do you want to *hit* our quarry, or do you want a face full of shrapnel when the cannon explodes?"

"Must I choose, or can I have it all?"

Calder squinted up through the rain, scanning the ceiling of dark clouds and jagged light. The Kameira they hunted wasn't particularly dangerous on its own, but it only flew during lightning-storms. They'd been tracking this one for weeks, and if it got away this time, he might decide to mutiny against himself. Those thunderlights had cost him a hundred goldmarks apiece.

Andel finally finished setting the lights, their copper poles stabbing into the storm.

Normally they would be risking their mast in a storm like this, but those copper poles were invested to attract lightning. Calder had Read them himself, checking and strengthening their Intent. He only hoped they would work soon, so they didn't spend any more time in this weather than necessary.

Even as the thought occurred to him, a spear of lightning stabbed one of the copper spikes. There came a blinding flash from the starboard thunderlight, and then the liquid in the glass container ignited, glowing with the bright yellow of a cheery summer noon.

In essence, thunderlights worked the same as quicklamps: they were glass containers of alchemical formula that produced bright, steady light. But unlike quicklamps, which glowed for a few years and had to be replaced, these thunderlights would work as long as they had lightning to recharge them.

They were essential equipment for any Navigator that meant to hunt Stormwings, but Calder was missing something even more critical.

Namely, his prey. Normally a Stormwing would show itself on the storm wall, drifting over the tops of the choppy waves, but *The Testament* was still charging through air thick with slashing rain. All with no sight of the Kameira.

Calder was about to call for more drastic measures, but then a song drifted over the detonations of thunder and the crash of waves against the hull. It sounded something like a pod of whales singing in chorus, somehow keeping harmony with the percussion of the storm.

"Port side, Andel!" Calder shouted as the Stormwing blasted through a wave.

He caught sight of it in flight. The Kameira soared over their ship, a line of pure white lightning with wings of shadow stretching off to the sides. It sang in triumph and exultation as it passed over, its volume piercing even through the storm.

The wheel fought him as he forced the ship to starboard, lining up with the Stormwing as it vanished behind a wave. A bright detonation marked the creature's passage, sending up a towering spray.

Andel's white suit was already soaked through, but he didn't let that affect his dignity as he marched across the deck. "We have a shot, Mister Foster. Load the redshot."

Foster clung to the cannon like a monkey to a tree branch, furiously working on something that Calder couldn't make out through the rain. "What do you think I'm trying to do? Hmm? You think I've picked just this moment to polish the iron?"

The Quartermaster's response remained as even as ever. "I don't care what you're polishing. I want a red ball in that cannon *right now*."

The Stormwing passed in front, and by the creature's own luminescence, Calder caught a better look. It resembled nothing so much as a manta ray the size of their ship, with a bright rippling luminescence rolling up the tip of its tail and all the way through its spine. It glided on the wind, lashing the peak of a wave with its tail. A bright flash of light exploded from the point of contact, sending up another plume of water.

Calder leaned forward, trying to angle his three-cornered hat so that it kept more water out of his eyes. It didn't help. A second bolt of lightning lit up the thunderlight on the bow, giving them a better glimpse of the Stormwing as it vanished behind another wave.

He shoved the wheel to one side, sliding past the wave in the Kameira's wake. "Where's that shot, Foster?"

Foster shouted something that was swallowed up by the thunder, jamming a red ball into the cannon. He fumbled around on the end of the cannon as Calder tried to keep the ship as steady as possible, working as much through Reading and his Intent as through any manipulation of the wheel.

Finally, a flare of light came from the back of the cannon. The gunner yelled in triumph, hauling his weapon around to point at the storm-chopped horizon.

At that moment the Stormwing blasted up from the waves, exposing its belly to the ship, the core of its body rippling with luminescence. It howled a song of triumph.

Calder forced his Intent down into the wood. *Hold steady*.

But there was nothing the ship could do against the forces of nature. *The Testament* began to slip down the other side of a wave.

When the cannon fired, its shot tore a strip of skin from the edge of the Kameira's wing instead of taking the creature in the head.

Redshot, a special ammunition used by Kameira hunters, was designed by the Alchemist's Guild to prevent the powerful creatures from striking back when injured or dying. Simple tranquilizers had been used since time immemorial, but Stormwings were among those Kameira breeds that managed to escape as soon as they felt the pain of the shot. They would simply dive beneath the waves to flee from the pain.

With that in mind, a round of redshot was actually a hollow ball containing an alchemical paralytic, tranquilizer, and hallucinogen. The compound was designed to work in concert, confusing and subduing the Stormwing before putting it to sleep.

In its confusion, the creature would settle down and float on the surface of the waves to get its bearings. The paralytic meant it couldn't get far, and as it rested, the tranquilizer would have its time to set in. Calder and his crew would catch the Kameira in their invested steel nets, hauling it back to port to sell fresh.

But if the shot wasn't a direct hit, the whole plan died a fiery death. Now they had a confused, pain-enraged, *hallucinating* monster striking at them with a tail that caused explosions. And they had to fight it in the middle of a storm.

If they made it back to port, drinks were on Foster.

The Stormwing screamed, lashing its tail at the ship. The deck exploded in a blinding flash of light, sending splinters, torn rope, and one of the spare cannons hurtling into the storm. Calder felt the broken wood like a physical pain, and through the smoking hole he could see a slice of his hold.

He couldn't help worrying about his wife—she was supposed to be in a different part of the ship, but what if fate was unkind, and she had found herself impaled on a piece of debris? Then again, he was relieved that the Stormwing's strike hadn't shattered any of the thunderlights. They had enough to worry about without adding an alchemically fueled fire on top of everything else.

Foster clung to the back of his cannon, trying to swing it around for a clear shot as the Stormwing banked around for another pass, screaming as it thrashed its deadly tail in the air. Andel hurried over to the hole in the deck, kneeling and gazing into the hold as though he could fix it in the middle of the storm.

"Look what it's doing to my ship!" Andel shouted.

As he watched the Stormwing come back around, Calder realized that he was wasting his time. If they kept at it, they would be flopping around until they got in a lucky shot or the Kameira tore them apart.

He abandoned the wheel, hopping down to stand beside Andel. He unbuttoned his sleeve, rolling it up to the elbow.

It was about time for extreme measures.

Calder knelt beside his Quartermaster. "Pardon me, Andel, but this is *my* ship."

Then he pressed his palm to the deck and Read the ship. Visions flashed through his mind—*Calder nails one plank to another, begging them to stick; Calder's mother places her own hands on the wood, persuading them to repel water.*

He called on the bond between him and *The Testament*...and the bond between the ship and something far older.

A six-fingered hand rose up from the ocean.

The hand—webbed, dark blue, and big enough to rip the belly out of the ship—lifted out of the waves like a sunken tower cresting the surface. Dull, algae-spotted metal encircled the wrist: a manacle made of enough iron to recast every cannon onboard. Links of chain, each thicker than an anchor, trailed from the creature's arm to vanish in the dark water beneath *The Testament*.

Reaching up from the storm-tossed surface, the hand closed in a giant fist around the Stormwing's tail, jerking the Kameira to a halt in the air. The Stormwing screamed, thrashing and beating its wings, even turning in on itself to sink its fangs into the scaled hand.

From the shadows beneath *The Testament*, a cloud of bubbles rose. A hiss of pain sliced through the storm, and the giant arm flexed. It whipped the Stormwing against the water with a crack that deafened the thunder itself. Water rose in a rolling wave away from the impact, a wall of the ocean rising for them.

"Brace yourselves!" Calder shouted, and the Quartermaster echoed him.

Calder dove for the lines, wrapping himself in fistfuls of coarse rope. When he saw Foster still scrambling to control the loose cannon, he sent a simple mental signal to the ship. Ropes snaked over to Foster, grabbing him by the wrists and ankles and holding him fast.

"Light and life protect us," he muttered to himself, as the wave loomed over them.

A weight settled onto his right shoulder as if a cat had suddenly landed there. Something tickled his cheek, and a deep baritone echoed him. "PROTECT US," it chuckled.

Calder turned to glare at the creature perched on his shoulder. It was a squat little monster with a dark green, leathery hide and stubby little bat wings. Its eyes were solid black orbs, its mouth hidden behind a mass of squirming tentacles.

"Shuffles, what are you—"

Then the icy water of the Aion Sea crashed down on them both.

Darkness and cold rushed over Calder, trying to tear his eyes open, drowning his ears in a rush of sound. The water clawed at his body, trying to pull him out and away. His wrists burned where the ropes cut into him, but he didn't dare loosen his grip.

Finally, the wave subsided. Before the water had completely washed over the ship, Calder was untangling himself from the lines, hurrying back to the wheel.

The Stormwing was still alive, but it wouldn't be for long. Each of its wings was caught in the grip of a giant hand, and it struggled uselessly to escape.

As the Kameira writhed, a true monster rose from beneath *The Testament*.

Both of its arms were bound in shackles that terminated beneath Calder's ship, but the rest of its body was unbound. It stood like a man, with a row of ridges running down its spine like sails. Its head belonged to a predatory fish, though it bore three black eyes on either side of its face.

It drew the Stormwing closer as though to get a better look at its meal. The Kameira still struggled, but the towering monster's grip was unbreakable.

The blue lips parted, revealing a mouth full of shark's teeth. It hissed, a sound sharper than a knife's blade, and gills flapped on either side of its neck.

Then the Lyathatan, the Elderspawn bound to the bottom of *The Testament*, tore its prey apart.

One wing came off in each hand, spattering the ship's deck with droplets of luminescent blood.

Calder's heart sank even as Foster fought his way free of the lines, sending a futile kick at his own cannon. "You couldn't wait? You could not wait *one* more second for me to line up another shot?"

Calder sent his Intent through the ship, running down the invested chains, to the Lyathatan itself. The Elderspawn was old beyond imagining, but it did tend to listen to its captor. Most of the time.

Into his Reading, Calder poured his need for the Stormwing, his desperation to bring back something to sell, and his determination to extract the Kameira's precious fluid.

Usually that worked, though sometimes he had to throw in a bribe.

Andel walked below deck, presumably to check on the rest of the crew, but Foster was still going. "Now we're locked in the middle of a storm with nothing to show for it, and we won't find another one this late in the season—"

He was cut off when the severed tail and spine of the Stormwing landed on the deck, leaking glowing yellow-white fluid. It was big enough that it crossed *The Testament* from stem to stern, and bright enough to drown out the illumination of the thunderlights.

Calder heaved a sigh and let his whole weight rest against the wheel. "Foster, get Petal and Urzaia up here. We need to preserve as much as possible."

Foster marched down the ladder. "Petal! Woodsman! Get your buckets and get on deck before I make you bleed!"

Shuffles chuckled in Calder's ear, tentacles waving. "BLEEEED."

Calder ignored it. The Bellowing Horror liked to imitate the most disturbing words it heard, but the creature was entirely harmless. He'd begun to treat the thing like a parrot. Ship captains were supposed to have parrots.

It didn't look like they'd get the full payoff they'd hoped for, but they could probably retain sixty or seventy percent of the Stormwing's luminescent liquid. Two-thirds of a fortune was still a fortune; the Alchemist's Guild would pay in hundreds of goldmarks for vials of this fluid.

He grinned, settling his hat back on his head, and bowed in the Lyathatan's direction.

The giant was slowly settling beneath the waves, hissing as it disappeared under the water.

Disconcerting and reassuring at the same time. As Sadesthenes said, *"The worst enemies make the best allies."*

Calder wasn't sure he could count the Lyathatan as an ally, exactly, but certainly as an asset. It had agreed to serve him for a short time, but 'a short time' to the ancient Elderspawn could extend into the lives of Calder's grandchildren.

He turned the wheel, sending his Intent down, and the Lyathatan obediently dragged the ship along. Away from the flashes of lightning. After weeks of chasing this Kameira, they could finally leave storms behind them, and Calder had never before looked so forward to sunshine.

Boots pounded back up the ladder, and Urzaia Woodsman appeared, a bucket dangling from each of his huge hands. He gave his gap-toothed smile when he emerged, staring up into the rain with his one remaining eye. "I never get tired of the rain. No matter how often I feel it, you hear me?"

"Well, I've felt it *too* often," Calder called down. "We're heading out to smoother seas."

"That is a shame. The monsters here are much bigger."

Petal slid out behind Urzaia without a word, her frizzy hair hiding her face. She sank onto the deck beside the severed Stormwing spine, crooning as she milked glowing liquid into her bucket.

Calder didn't bother saying anything. When the ship's alchemist was lost in her own world, nothing so mundane as human speech would get her attention.

The next person onto the deck was a surprise: his wife, Jyrine Tessella Marten.

Jerri wore a bright green raincoat that matched her emerald earrings. Bracelets flashed on her wrists as she hurriedly pulled her hair back, tucking it under her waterproof hood. She wore a wide, eager smile that instantly worried him.

It had taken him days of pleading to get her to stay below during the confrontation with the Kameira. There was nothing she could do to help, and the more people they had on deck, the greater the risk. She had finally agreed, but she wasn't happy about it.

If she thought there was something in the hold more interesting than two giant monsters fighting, he needed to see it.

She rushed up to him, pecking him on the cheek and wrapping him in tanned arms.

Alarm bells sounded in his head.

"You would not *believe* what I found down in the hold!" Her eyes sparkled as though she had heard wonderful news.

Calder leaned back, examining her expression from arm's length. "What did you find?"

She pulled on his wrist, tugging him away from the wheel. "You'll have to come see!"

The last time she'd had a surprise for him, it had ended up being a clawed Elderspawn that he'd been forced to nail to the inside of the hull. "Should I bring my pistol?"

"Only if you plan on shooting Andel, which I would wholeheartedly support. It's not a monster this time, but I would have sworn it was *impossible.* Maybe a Reader could tell me how they did it."

That was entirely too intriguing to pass up, so he let her guide him down into the belly of the ship.

The hold had been packed with barrels, crates, and packets of gear, though most of the space was unoccupied. They had planned to return with a new load of cargo, after all. Now, raindrops and thin rivers of luminescence flowed in from the fractured deck above, through the hole that the Stormwing had blasted. Some of the crates had cracked open, leaking salt or wine, and a loose barrel rolled around on the wood.

Calder stopped the wild barrel with one foot, looking around for anything unusual.

Jyrine picked up a quicklamp, shook it, and raised it to one side.

In the splash of yellow light, Calder saw a message burned into the inside of the hull, as though someone had scorched a letter onto his ship. Thin wisps of smoke still rose from the charred wood.

Calder kicked the barrel aside, walking up to examine the lettering. "Petal didn't do this?"

"I came in here after the explosion to survey the damage, and I saw it being written. It burned itself into the wood as though someone was writing with an invisible pen." She clapped her hands eagerly, like a child at a show. "Now read it!"

He did, his own excitement growing by the word.

Calder,

Hope this mysterious message finds you well! I just learned how to do this, and it's going to blow the pants off certain people back in the Capital. If you see it first, show it to Jyrine. She appreciates a good touch of theater.

The Guild has a new client. A pair of Witnesses wants to hire you to take them to a certain island, and withdraw a certain relic.

This could be huge, Calder. Not just for you, but for the Empire. And for the Emperor.

Calder stopped reading for a moment, shooting a glance at his wife. "The Emperor?"

Jerri's smile widened. "Keep reading. It gets better."

Whatever else this letter said, the Emperor had been dead for over five years. What did the Witnesses hope to find on the island? A way to bring him back from the dead?

With the Emperor, they might even be able to do it. That was a disturbing thought.

And by the way, this will be big for you. This was the Chronicler in charge of finance in the Imperial Palace. He wants me to tell you that if you're successful, you will "sleep under sheets of golden silk in the cabin of your flagship. At the head of your brand-new fleet." His words.

So I suggest you get your leaky tub and your flea-bitten crew back to port before he comes to his senses and hires somebody else.

-Cheska

Captain Cheska Bennett, Head of the Navigator's Guild, was prone to exaggeration. But if she'd taken the effort to burn an entire letter onto the wood of his ship to get his attention, then this must be big. And if the reward was half as generous as promised...

He felt his mouth go dry. Sadesthenes once said, "*The wise man is not blinded by gold, but only a fool turns it down.*"

Calder rushed back up to the deck, Jerri following close behind him.

"Andel! I'm raising the sails! I find myself suddenly homesick."

CHAPTER TWO

Everyone has Intent. Even you!

You use your Intent every day: when you use a pillow to sleep, a brush to straighten your hair, or a coat to protect you from the wind, you are lending some of your Intent to an object.

Over time, your Intent builds and builds, helping that item get even better at doing its job! You will fall asleep faster on your pillow, your brush will never snag, and your coat will stay warm year-round!

What an amazing world we live in!

– FROM CHAPTER 1 OF THE BEST-SELLING CHILDREN'S GUIDE,
READING ABOUT READERS!

THIRTEEN YEARS AGO

Calder walked through the wood-paneled halls, over carpets soft as an owl's whisper, and tried to look bored. When he passed an urn with delicate gold filigree worked into the edges, he moved his eyes over it, as though he took in such sights every day.

One hundred silvermarks, he guessed. Then he spotted a collection of pocketwatches, hung on the wall and arranged in a tasteful display. *At least fifty silvermarks apiece. Maybe a goldmark for the frame.* The snarling head of a Kameira, something like a lion with a head of sterling silver, mounted over the coat-rack.

A hundred goldmarks? More? Who could you hire to stuff a Kameira, anyway? Is that legal?

Altogether, the house positively reeked of *money.* Walking beside him, Calder's father adjusted his fake glasses and blew out a fake moustache. He was trying to appear nonchalant, but Calder could all but feel his excitement.

Their host, Mister Karls Dunwood, led them to a spacious office walled in polished logs to make it resemble something like a hunting lodge. A stonework hearth against one wall enhanced the effect, and an array of more stuffed heads—black bears, twelve-point bucks, and even what seemed to be a young Nightwyrm—completed the impression.

Mister Dunwood had a seat at his desk and gestured for his two guests to do the same. He had to use his left hand, as his right had been replaced by a blunt silver hook. An accident at sea, they'd been told.

"Before we begin, can I offer you anything by way of refreshment?" Mister

Dunwood asked, his smile revealing several gold teeth. "I received six bottles of the Shiftapple Ninety-six from Nathanael Bareius himself. You'll never taste another like it, I assure you."

Calder's father, Rojric, chuckled politely. "Perhaps if my son weren't with me, then I would accept, but he's a bit too young. It would be rude of me to exclude him so."

Their host gave Calder a gold-speckled grimace. "He is more than welcome to wait outside. Business meetings are no place for children, I've found."

This was all part of the plan, and Calder had rehearsed his part. He drew himself up, indignant. "Excuse me! I am twelve years old, and I have been attending such meetings with my father since I was nine and a half. We are *partners* in this endeavor, sir!"

Mister Dunwood laughed, trying to appear amused, but he rubbed the base of his silver hook with his one remaining hand. His eyes shifted between the two of them.

They had selected their appearance carefully: two matching blue suits, immaculately tailored. Their red hair was slicked back with grease in precisely the same manner, and they even sat with the same affected posture.

After trying once to get the child out of the room, Mister Dunwood would realize that he could not separate the pair, and continue while ignoring Calder as much as possible. That was the plan.

And, indeed, matters proceeded as they expected.

"Of course, sirs," he said. "I would not hope to separate the noble family of Fairstreet."

'Fairstreet' was the name of an alley through which they had happened to pass a few weeks earlier.

"It's unusual, I know," Rojric allowed. "But where else would I send him? His mother, may her soul fly free, was taken by drink. I did what I could to save her from her fate, but when one is set on the road to self-destruction...alas, her liver failed her only two winters past. If he does not learn the family business, then where is he to go?"

Calder's mother lived not an hour's walk from this very building. He could barely remember her face.

Mister Dunwood bowed his head solemnly. "Fate can be cruel. But let us not linger too long on the past. It is the future that concerns us today, is it not?"

Rojric smiled beneath his orange mustache. "It is indeed, Mister Dunwood. I have a buyer who is willing to secure the future for *all* of us if you can produce what you claim. Pending the verification of a Reader, of course."

"I have taken the liberty of securing such verification myself, in fact. The document will be provided along with the object itself."

Calder shifted in his seat, letting his posture slacken, resuming his facade of boredom. In fact, he was scanning the decorative firearms mounted on racks behind Mister Dunwood's head. *Fifty silvermarks, sixty silvermarks, thirty-five silvermarks...*

Rojric cleared his throat and glanced from side to side, as though checking for observers in this windowless room. "Regarding the object, sir, would you be so kind...?"

Dipping his hook into his jacket pocket, Mister Dunwood withdrew a ring of keys. After fumbling one-handed at the metal for a moment, he found what he was looking for and leaned under his desk.

Surreptitiously, Calder brushed his hand against the heavy wood of the desk.

The tree is a little girl's favorite hiding place. She tucks her favorite toys into its roots, where her brothers will never find them.

The lumber is solid, sturdy. The laborer thinks it will go to a fortress wall, maybe, or a vault door.

The carpenter places his hands on the desk, feeling the wood. He's finished bolting metal plates to the inside of the wood; it has enough armor to stop a pistol-shot, and stands more than sturdy enough to hold a safe.

It took longer to sort through the impressions left in the desk than it had to Read them. This desk was not terribly significant—it hadn't been through any momentous events, at least none that had made their mark in its wood—but it was invested with enough Intent to reinforce the grain, keeping it sturdy and solid. It would be hard to saw through and steal the safe; much easier to take the key.

Good thing that's the plan, then.

From somewhere beneath the desk, a safe door squeaked open, and Mister Dunwood withdrew a polished wooden box. He set it carefully on the surface of the desk, as though it contained an explosive that would be set off by the slightest wrong movement.

"Gentlemen," Mister Dunwood said, in a reverent whisper. "I give you the oldest Imperial artifact not currently in the Emperor's possession."

With the tips of his fingers, he levered open the lid of the box, revealing...a worn, and somewhat ragged, quill pen.

The feather itself must once have been beautiful, as a lustrous rainbow sheen still clung to the pen like a thin slick of oil. But the intervening years had worn it down until the feather looked sickly, bedraggled. More like a relic of a strangled chicken than a Kameira-quill pen wielded by the Emperor himself.

Rojric gave a low whistle. "I can practically see the aging. Five hundred years, you say?"

"You have a good eye, Mister Fairstreet. Yes, I had my Reader date it back at least that far. The Emperor used it to pen the documents that led to the end of the Scullery Wars."

"Truly a shameful moment in our history." Calder's father rubbed his hands eagerly. "Well, whatever the provenance of this item, I can tell that you have some impressive contacts, Mister Dunwood. Where, for instance, did you manage to procure the head of a Nightwyrm?"

Mister Dunwood shifted to look behind him, at the black-scaled draconic head baring its teeth from the wall. He grew a proud smile as he started to launch into his story.

Calder's moment had come.

He hopped up, snatching the pen from its case as soon as Dunwood's attention was distracted. "It doesn't look like much," he said loudly.

The Windwatcher glides through the air, eyeing the currents that shift like rivers of blue smoke through the sky. It nudges an updraft of hot air closer, and the wind obeys, bending the warm column toward the Kameira. The Windwatcher catches the draft in its wings, letting the wind lift it higher. It needs all the help it can get, for its passengers are heavy and want nothing more than speed.

The craftsman works at the end of the feather with his penknife, desperate not to make a mistake. This quill should never spill ink, never smudge or break. It has to write flawlessly, smoothly. For all he knows, his life might depend on it.

The Emperor sighs, holding his quill over the inkwell. A servant-girl rushes forward, rubbing his shoulders, and he leaves her to it. Tonight, he needs anything that will help him relax. With one letter, he could condemn a group of merchants to poverty and probable starvation. With another, he might damn his loyal servants to execution. He needs to be eloquent now, to phrase the perfect message that will save them both.

Or else he might be tempted to kill them all, and let Kelarac sort out their souls...

The visions faded as Mister Dunwood grabbed the pen back, red-faced. "This is *priceless!* What do you think you are doing?"

"How do we know it's even real?" Calder replied automatically, his mind still swirling in a spiral of Intent.

"I'm so sorry, Mister Dunwood," Rojric apologized. "He's been an Elder-spawned nightmare since his mother passed, that I can tell you."

Mister Dunwood replaced the pen in its case as though lowering an infant into its cradle. "Then why don't we let him be someone else's nightmare for a time, hmm?"

Rojric sighed. "Would you wait outside for me for a while, son?"

Calder huffed and marched outside, slamming the door for good measure.

It was hard staying in character while still in the grip of a Reader's trance, but he kept it up until he was safely outside the office. Then he slumped into a chair, gasping for breath, trying to separate his own thoughts from his alias, from an ancient craftsman, from the Emperor.

At least they had their answer: the artifact was real.

Rojric followed his son out only a few minutes later, wearing a broad smile. "We've finalized the sale. A bit more than I was hoping for, but he negotiates like Kelarac himself!"

The second reference to Kelarac, the Collector of Souls, almost sent Calder spiraling back into the trance. He shook off the visions, following his father out of the building.

Only when they were outside did Rojric mutter, "It was real, then?"

Calder grinned.

Later that night, Calder and his father returned, but without the props.

They were dressed in the simple clothes and apron they had stolen from a local delivery company, and carried empty boxes over their shoulders. If they were caught, they could claim that they had received a late-night delivery that required a signature, and had found the door unlocked.

They wouldn't be caught, though. This was the Capital: the city that night could not conquer. No one would even notice a couple of deliverymen and their packages.

Rojric set his crate down with a huff, knuckling his back as if he'd been freed of a great load. His mustache and glasses were gone, his red hair loose and hidden behind a cap. Calder had adopted the bulk of the disguise this time, having dyed his hair black and slipped a bandage over his left eye like an eyepatch.

He put down his own burden, a box of flowers, and placed a hand to the door. Nothing but a faint echo; the door held no Intent or significance enough to bother them.

"No traps on the door," he whispered.

His father jiggled the doorknob as if testing it. His left hand slipped into his pocket and pulled out the greatest treasure they'd ever found.

An old, dented, corroded copper key.

He palmed it, tapping it once against the knob.

Instantly, Calder heard the tumblers unlock. The door swung open.

"They left it open for us," Rojric said loudly. "Must want us to leave it inside."

The house was less impressive at night, and more frightening. The mounted heads seemed to be trying to shoulder their way through the walls to get him. The guns on their racks pointed straight at him, their muzzles yawning like bottomless pits.

All that Calder noticed with half his mind, while the rest was focused on all the riches they were leaving behind.

They had a schedule to keep, so they were passing up the fifty-goldmark urns and hundred-silvermark watches, even though they could easily stuff enough into their flower-box to keep them for a year.

But the quill could see them in silk suits and cigars for a decade.

They rushed to the back office, where another tap of the key let them right in. The ordinary-looking copper key was the only genuine Imperial artifact they'd found to this point, and the only bounty they'd kept for themselves. It was too valuable to sell, Calder's father had said, and Calder believed him.

When they reached down for the safe, they found it already empty, the door hanging open.

That was when Calder knew they were caught.

He bolted for the door while his father stepped up to the wall, as though trying to find the quill's new hiding-place. Both of them were too late.

A squad of monsters marched through the door.

One of the men looked ordinary except for his arms, which were covered in fur like a bear's. Claws tipped each of his fingers. Another, a woman, grabbed Rojric and forced him against the desk. She hissed in his face, revealing fangs like a snake's.

The parade of horrors spread out over the room, a display of human and Kameira melding. One of the men lashed a tail, and another stared straight at Calder with the too-wide eyes of a giant owl.

That was when Calder realized what they all had in common: they wore the same uniform. A red-and-black pressed uniform, tailored to meet their unique anatomical requirements, and marked with a crest.

The crest stood proudly on the breast of each uniform, the size of a man's spread hand. It was a golden shield, marked with the Imperial Seal: a crescent moon tucked inside a blazing sun, to represent the breadth of the Empire. "My dominion shall stretch from the sun to the moon," the Emperor had once said, and he had proven himself right.

Only one Guild had the right to bear the Seal. And if the Imperial Guard were here, that meant the game was well and truly over.

As everyone in the Capital knew, no one escaped the Emperor's Guard.

When the Guardsmen had Rojric secure, with his arms tied behind his back and a pistol to his head, one of them let out an unnaturally high whistle.

On cue, their leader entered the room. He looked like a strict grandfather—bone-thin, with only a brush of white hair on his head, and the pinched look of someone who consumed food only as fuel for his body. He wore his Imperial Guard uniform as though it had been glued to his skin.

And a set of gills rode on either side of his neck, flapping in the air as though gasping.

"Mr. Marten," the Guardsman said, nodding to Rojric. "Mr. Marten." He nodded to Calder. "I am Watch-leader Fitch. You are hereby under arrest for attempting to purchase the stolen personal property of the Emperor."

It did not escape Calder's notice that the Watch-leader had not called them 'Fairstreet.'

Rojric panted in the chair where the Guardsmen had shoved him, glancing around the room and soaking himself in sweat. "You have to understand! We thought it was a Windwatcher feather! There's a big market for them overseas, and we had no idea the Emperor had ever touched it!"

Fitch flourished a piece of paper, gills flaring. "That's not what this bill of sale says. We received it from Mister Dunwood not an hour ago."

"A bill of *sale?*" Rojric repeated, incredulous. Calder understood his confusion.

Who wrote out a bill of sale for stolen goods?

"Karls Dunwood is not the greatest criminal mastermind this Empire has ever seen," Fitch said dryly.

Rojric changed tactic. "What about Mister Dunwood?" He latched onto the name like a drowning man to a log. "Get him in here, and I'm sure we can straighten all this out."

Watch-leader Fitch reached onto the mantelpiece and pulled down a pocket-watch, popping it open. "I have extracted a penalty from Mister Dunwood once before, on the understanding that I never hear from him again. I refuse to repeat myself."

From somewhere outside, a shout rose, followed by a pistol-shot.

Fitch snapped the watch closed. "Right on time. Now, Mister and Mister Marten, you must have built a substantial network of information to make it this far. I will have the names of your confederates from you, and then you will be incarcerated in the Candle Bay Imperial Prison for the foreseeable future."

Rojric lunged forward, grabbing his son by the shoulders as if to protect him. "You can't take him! He's too young for chains, please! I'll serve his sentence!"

The Imperial Guards pulled Rojric back without any trouble, but not before Calder felt a slight weight drop from his father's hand into his shirt pocket.

Watch-leader Fitch remained expressionless. "I have come to a different arrangement regarding the boy. Rest assured that he will remain secure."

Rojric didn't look assured by that at all, any more than Calder felt. He could sense walls closing in around him, penning him in.

Were they going to send him to an orphanage? He'd heard horror stories about such places all his life, how the children were abused and then sold to black alchemists for experiments.

Would he ever see his father again?

Calder felt tears welling up at the corners of his eyes, and he decided to use them to his advantage.

"Please, Mister Fitch," he said, looking up at the Watch-leader with wet eyes. "We'll work for you! We know people, we can give you names! Let us off with a warning, just this once!"

Rojric closed his eyes.

Fitch, by contrast, looked absolutely unchanged. "The last time I let someone off with a warning, it cost him his hand. And he still didn't change his ways. Now, I'm afraid you must be searched."

Two Guardsman marched Rojric out of the room. "Please, don't take my son! Don't take my son!"

The door shut behind them, leaving Calder alone with the rest of them.

Watch-leader Fitch's gills flared. "You too, boy. Off with your clothes."

Calder obeyed, unbuttoning his shirt. He pretended to fumble at the second button, working at it hard enough to tear.

All so he could keep his hand close to his shirt pocket.

He could feel the significance of the key even through the fabric, but he focused on the pocket around it, silently chanting, Hide it. Hide it. Hide it. Hide it. Calder bent his will entirely on concealment, focusing his Intent like a scalpel.

He moved his fingers down to the next button, but kept focusing on the weight of the key through his shirt. He imagined the Guards overlooking the pocket, and the key inside it. *Hide it, hide it, hide it.*

When he stripped down to his undershorts, shivering more out of awkwardness than cold, the man with the bear arms patted him down. It felt like having a dog walk up and down his sides.

Meanwhile, the owl-eyed man ruffled through his clothing, calling out everything he found. "Small knife. Delivery order to this address, likely fake. A small river-stone, possibly invested." His hands moved to the bundled-up shirt, and Calder made his sniffles louder, trying to draw attention away from the shirt.

"Nothing else," the Guard declared. "We'll need to get a Reader to check it all out, of course."

"I suspect that will be taken care of by his new guardian," Fitch said. "Go on, boy, put your clothes back on. If there's nothing suspicious about your belongings, they'll be returned to you at your new address."

A fresh wave of tears struck him through the shivers, and he was ashamed to admit that they were anything but fake. "Where am I going?"

Fitch placed a hand on his back and guided him over to his pile of clothes. "To your mother."

CHAPTER THREE

Repairing *The Testament* was a relatively simple matter, involving nothing more than three hundred planks of purchased wood and an afternoon of Calder's attention. Once he placed the boards where he wanted them, he simply invested them as part of the ship, Reading the whole to make sure that the ship accepted its new addition.

When he had finished nailing the boards more or less in place, he placed his hand against the deck and sent a command to his Soulbound Vessel.

The Testament grew together, merging its deck with the new planks into a seamless whole.

His work done, Calder leaned back against the deck, massaging a nascent headache. He hadn't pushed himself into a full-blown case of Reader's burn, not yet, but he still felt like someone was throwing bricks at the back of his head.

Andel stood over him in his white suit, surveying the deck. "That's convenient."

"I'd hate to hire a carpenter. We'd have to split our fee seven ways."

Thanks to the Captain's control over his ship, a Navigator's crew was incredibly small. This was one of the reasons why the Guild remained the only force capable of crossing the Aion Sea at will. And why its Navigators tended to amass huge personal fortunes.

One of the reasons.

Ignoring his aching head, Calder pushed himself to his feet. "Since you're here, I imagine we've heard from Cheska's mysterious passenger."

Andel handed him a folded sheet of paper. "You might say that."

Prepare to receive us at sundown, the paper read. *We depart at dawn.*

Calder tried to look into the paper's past, not just reading its words but Reading the Intent behind them, but he got nothing more than faint wisps of emotion. Not surprising—such a small slip of paper would not have retained much Intent, especially for an innocuous note. But you never knew what Reading might show you.

He winced as his headache increased; even an unsuccessful Reading put a strain on him. "I guess he wants to spend the night on the ship."

"Why wouldn't you? Clever company, romantic atmosphere, the lingering aroma of dead Stormwing."

"Did you get this straight from the source?"

"From Cheska's messenger. The girl with the evil eye."

Andel rubbed his silver amulet as if for luck—it was carved with the White

Sun crest of the Luminian Order. Some believed that wearing such a symbol would bring the blessing and protection of the Unknown God.

Of course, the amulet hadn't landed Andel anywhere better than a ship exiled to the Aion.

"So we still don't know anything about our mysterious Witnesses." Calder placed his three-cornered hat back on, gazing out over the Candle Bay harbor. The water was busy this time of year, with Navigators, merchants, and fishermen jockeying for position along the docks.

Calder had many memories of this place, and most of them still showed up in his nightmares.

Andel tossed a loose nail into the bay. "They didn't even tell us how many passengers to expect."

"Knowing Witnesses, almost certainly two."

"Nor were they very specific about our pay."

"If it was enough to get Cheska to pay attention, it will be enough for us."

"I'm not entirely certain I can return the crew in time." Nevertheless, he didn't seem like he was in any particular hurry.

"Jerri's visiting her mother, which means she'll come back furious within the hour. You'll find Urzaia in the closest establishment that will serve him a drink, Foster at the gunsmith up the hill, and Petal...if Petal's left this ship, I'll commission that life-size statue of yourself you've always wanted. In gold."

"I've always pictured myself in marble." Still, Andel didn't move.

At last, Calder sighed and turned to face his Quartermaster. "Mister Petronus, what seems to be the problem?"

Andel drummed his fingers on the rail, eyes shadowed by the wide brim of his hat. "I know you remember what happened last time Cheska Bennett promised us an unusually large reward."

Calder tried not to. "We did receive the money. She honors her word."

"Was it worth it? If you had known what you were signing up for, would you have agreed? Even for five hundred goldmarks?"

He liked to think that he would do *anything* for five hundred goldmarks, but the truth was that he didn't know. Cheska's last assignment had almost killed him, and had been even worse for Jerri.

"We're not working for her this time," Calder said with confidence. "It's a real, legitimate Guild assignment for an independent client. And it could be for much more than five hundred goldmarks."

"I don't get out of bed for 'could be.' And I would never agree to a voyage sight unseen."

"I haven't agreed yet."

Andel fixed him with dark eyes. "Haven't you?"

Calder's gaze traveled past the bay, up a hill to the west and into the sprawling Imperial Capital. "This could be a moot point very soon, Andel."

"Why is that, sir?"

"Because if I'm not mistaken, that's our client right now."

Down at the docks, two people moved against the crowd. A man in a bright red suit strode in front, with his wavy hair blowing in the breeze behind him. The figure that followed him stood out even more: Calder thought it was a woman, wrapped in bandages like a body prepared for burial. Wisps of black hair stuck out of the bandages over her head, and she wore an overcoat two or three sizes too large for her. In one hand she carried a gilded wooden case, and in the other a full-sized traveler's chest.

The man had his eyes locked on *The Testament,* a confident smile on his face.

Andel turned to look at the two of them, adjusting his hat to block out the setting sun. "What makes you think that's them?"

"Because they're the only two people in the crowd strange enough to be hiring a Navigator for a mysterious, sudden mission."

The Quartermaster let out a breath. "I'll gather the crew. But consider walking away, Calder. At least consider it." Then Andel left, brushing past the two strangers on his way down the ramp and across the dock.

Calder took up his position at the top of the ramp, wearing his best smile. He bowed, sweeping the hat from his head.

"Lady and gentleman, honored members of the Guild of Witnesses, please let me be the first to welcome you aboard *The Testament.* I am Captain Calder Marten."

The man in the red suit extended one hand, and Calder took it.

"Naberius Clayborn. Guild Chronicler, and onetime keeper of the Imperial Palace treasury. This is my Silent One, Tristania. Ah, are you familiar with the traditions of my Guild?"

Calder smoothly relieved the woman in bandages of her luggage, setting it to the side. She was carrying a smaller case as well, but when he tried to take that one, she bowed and stepped to the side. "I was fortunate enough to have Witnesses as tutors in my youth. Though one brother never spoke, he managed to deliver his lessons nonetheless."

Naberius smiled as though he were trying to show off each one of his teeth. "You will find much the same here. Tristania is no tutor, but she does make herself perfectly clear without speech."

From Calder's past experience with Witnesses, the Chronicler would be a Reader of impressive skill, and the Silent One a warrior and bodyguard. Though Tristania bowed politely, and kept her eyes lowered through the gap in her bandages, Calder had not a single doubt that she kept weapons in that coat of hers.

The Chronicler, Naberius, looked like an actor hired to play an ancient Imperial hero. His dark brown hair rolled down to his shoulders in rippling waves, and his bright red suit—while eye-catching—was high quality and closely tailored.

Naberius clapped his hands together. "Now, would you kindly show us to our cabin?"

Assuming I'll take the job. He wondered what Cheska had said to them—it wouldn't be unreasonable if she had accepted on his behalf.

"I don't mean to be disrespectful, Mister Clayborn, but I wonder if I could hear a few more details about the voyage first."

The Silent One widened her eyes in surprise, turning to Naberius.

For his part, Naberius adopted a look of exaggerated shock. "Did Captain Bennett not tell you? I should have realized, forgive me. She didn't strike me as the type to see her work through to the end."

"You are an excellent judge of character, sir."

"As I have said, I was the Chronicler in charge of financial records in the Imperial Palace. Since the Emperor's death, may his soul fly free, my partner and I were the only ones remaining with the knowledge to access the treasury. We have used those resources for a few essential tasks: keeping the Capital running, funding the Imperial Guard, the list goes on. But soon, that will not be enough."

The Chronicler's smile broadened. "The Emperor's personal finances were much more interesting than simple piles of silvermarks and goldmarks. They included the location of several items of value. Including, you might say, buried treasure."

Calder's eyes filled with visions of ancient chests, filled to overflowing with Izyrian gold coins. He took an involuntary step closer, suddenly much more interested in the story. "I'm sorry if this seems rude, but...do you have a treasure map?"

Naberius tapped the side of his head. "It's more accurate to say that I *am* a map. Now, I know that you and your crew are not treasure hunters—"

"Let's not rush to any conclusions. If you hire us, we'll hunt whatever you'd like."

"Well, Captain Bennett recommended several crews in your Guild that were more experienced in the detection and removal of valuable items, but that wasn't the crew I asked for. I asked for a ship crewed by those who could handle themselves in dangerous situations. She directed me to you."

"The fool seeks out combat, but the wise man stays at home." One of the most well-known sayings of Sadesthenes. Calder found himself in fights depressingly often, but he prided himself on never seeking them out.

Except when he had to. There were exceptions.

"So you expect dangerous situations to arise, then?"

"I simply find myself prepared for the possibility. And for ten thousand goldmarks, I believe that you should be prepared as well."

Calder's smile stuck. He couldn't seem to wipe it off.

Quickly, he ran through the math. For day-to-day expenses, most people dealt in marks. For larger expenses, they could use silvermarks, and for monumental investments—like hiring a Navigator to sail across the Aion—the prices were most often measured in goldmarks. Ten thousand goldmarks meant *one million* marks.

Once, Calder had fallen into debt to the Emperor. That debt had since been cleared, both by his own efforts and by the Emperor's death, but this *single* voyage could have covered what he owed twice over. With some to spare.

Cheska hadn't exaggerated. He really could buy his own fleet.

"I..." He choked, then cleared his throat. "If you have a heading, I have a ship."

Dalton Foster shoved his way up the ramp and past, seeming not to see their passengers. He held a lumpy sack over one shoulder, and his mane of gray hair stuck up in all directions. Two pairs of spectacles hung from cords around his neck, and he squinted forward in the sunlight.

"A crewmember of yours?" Naberius asked, sounding amused.

"My gunner, don't worry about him. He doesn't care where we go." Calder raised his voice to address Foster. "Andel found you, then?"

The old man sat down cross-legged on the deck, swiveling a cannon around to face him until he stared it down the barrel. "He cost me a deal on a Tedoria Sixty-Six. I expect compensation."

Calder turned his smile back to the Witnesses. "See? He's eager to serve you."

Naberius peered around the deck. "I was told your wife would be traveling with us. Surely you would like to consult with her?"

"She is visiting her family, actually, which means I should be able to see her..." Calder turned to the west, to the crowd at the docks, until he spotted a woman in a simple blue dress pushing through a crowd as though each and every person had offended her. "...right now. She'll be here in a moment. Until then, shall I show you to your cabin?"

He heaved their luggage onto his shoulder, taking them to the furnished cabin at the stern. It was designed as the captain's cabin, but whenever Calder had a passenger, he preferred to give them the room. *"Generosity pays off when the final bill comes due."* That was Hestor, not Sadesthenes, but no less true for that.

Naberius stood a head over Calder, and he had to lean down to look into the cabin. "Very cozy. Truly, better accommodations than I expected from a Navigator's vessel. But this is where you sleep, isn't it?"

Some passengers liked to make a show of reluctance before they accepted. "For this voyage, it's where *you* sleep."

Naberius shared a glance with the bandaged Tristania, who bowed and walked back to the ship's bow.

"I appreciate your generosity, but we have not spent our entire lives in the Capital." He gestured for Calder to bring their luggage back out. "While we are here, you may treat us as cargo. Take us where you and your wife were planning to sleep."

If they really wanted to ride like cargo, then they'd be down in the hold, but Calder said nothing. Instead, with many a protest that they were more than welcome to sleep in the cabin, Calder led them to the space beneath the bow.

It wasn't another cabin; in the original plans for *The Testament,* this space was designed to hold extra supplies. The boards were so low that Naberius was bent over almost in half, and there were no amenities except two rolled-up hammocks and a candle next to a box of matches.

"Charming. We'll take it."

A little reluctantly, Calder set the luggage down between the two hammocks. He couldn't help but wonder why they were turning down the cabin. Would this be an excuse to skimp on their payment? How much money was this going to cost him?

But they had made their wishes clear, so he bowed to the both of them. "As you please, Mister Clayborn."

"Naberius, please." He stuck out a hand, and when Calder shook it, he found a paper crumpled up within. On further inspection, it seemed to be a crisp yellow-printed bill: a goldmark.

Maybe they wouldn't skim money from the contract after all.

Jyrine marched onto the deck now, eyes still burning, but she smiled when she saw the passengers. "These must be the guests in Cheska's letter. Have you come to an agreement?"

"Ten thousand goldmarks," Calder said.

She curtsied politely. "How very generous of you both."

"And he suspects there might be danger."

Her smile grew wider, and the anger vanished from her eyes. "Gentleman, gentle lady, welcome aboard *The Testament.* How may I serve you?"

That night, when everyone had returned to the ship, Calder introduced his crew. Now that the sun had set, they had all gathered around a quicklamp on the deck, eating roast quail and spiced chickpeas. This might be the only decent meal they had for the next two months, so Urzaia had stretched himself.

"First, let me introduce the man who crafts all the meals we will enjoy onboard *The Testament:* Urzaia Woodsman!"

Urzaia rose to his full height and thrust both fists in the air, as though he had been called to fight in the arena. He had pulled his blond hair back into a tail today, and his broad smile held a few gaps where teeth had been knocked loose. His sun-tanned skin bore a network of scars, and he wore patches of fabric all over as though he sliced up all his clothes before wearing them; a stretch of golden hide wrapped around his right arm, and dull snakeskin covered his left. A worn leather breastplate protected his chest, below a woolen scarf that must have been unbearable in the heat. He wore his pants underneath a patchwork kilt straight out of an Erinin legend. Even his boots didn't match.

"Every meat we eat onboard, I made sure to kill it myself." He stuck his chest out proudly and jabbed a finger at the plate waiting for him on the ground. "This quail, it gave me more trouble than most. It almost took an eye."

Andel gestured at him with a drumstick. "Then you too almost became the prey of the deadly Aion Quail. Armies have fallen to its might."

Urzaia laughed broadly and clapped Andel on the shoulder so hard that he almost lost his plate. "I don't think that is true, but this quail troubled me nonetheless."

Naberius chewed, his eyes resting thoughtfully on the big cook. "You are Izyrian, correct? An arena fighter, if I'm not mistaken."

Urzaia settled down, returning his plate to his lap. "I was meant to die there. The Captain saved me, and now I will die aboard his ship."

"Of old age, hopefully," Calder said, trying to steer the conversation away from death.

The Chronicler in red smiled. "Surely, that is the death we should most seek to avoid. Tell me, Urzaia, why are you called Woodsman?"

The cook reached to one side, pulling out a bundle of two hatchets. They looked as though they had been burned in an oven, with scorched wooden hafts and smoky gray blades. "In the arena, I killed with these. Those who saw me in action, they said I looked like I was chopping wood. Over time, that became my name. Woodsman." He hefted a hatchet in each hand, proudly. "There are many worse names."

Naberius looked as though he was about to ask another question, so Calder moved on. "That's Urzaia, the ship's cook. And of course you know my wife, Jyrine Tessella Marten."

Jerri inclined her head and gave a suggestion of a curtsy. It somehow managed to look graceful, even though she was seated on an upturned crate and her mouth was stuffed with peas.

The Chronicler's eyes flicked from her face, to the hand holding her plate, and back to her earrings. Calder knew exactly what he was looking for, but he waited for Jerri to answer the inevitable question.

"Jyrine, is it? I wonder, where does your family hail from?"

She took a swallow of wine before speaking. "As you guessed, my father and mother came to the Capital from Vandenyas before I was born. I know very little of the southern parts of the Empire."

He pointed to her hand—or, more accurately, to the script tattooed on the back of it. The lines of symbols covered most of the left side of her body, from the top of her foot all the way up to the side of her neck, flowing down her arm like a tributary river. If he looked closely, Calder could glimpse the symbols terminating below her jawline.

"They must have been somewhat important, if you carry the lines."

Jyrine smiled politely. "And you? Surely 'Naberius' is a Vandenyan name."

It wasn't much of a guess—the Chronicler also bore the same caramel-tan skin as Calder's wife, though his was a shade lighter.

"Half-heritage, I'm afraid," Naberius said. "My father came from Erin, and my mother was an Imperial clerk from Vandenyas."

Calder cleared his throat and spoke again, to draw attention from the fact that his wife had dodged the question. "Next, we have our resident alchemist, Petal."

Petal wore a drab gray dress and hunched over her meal, her frizzy black hair hiding her expression almost entirely. She twitched when she heard her name, but said nothing.

"Introduce yourself, Petal," Andel ordered.

The alchemist shook her head, her hair shaking like a tree in high wind. Her fork slid from her plate and tumbled toward the deck.

It never made it. Suddenly Tristania was there, the fork in one bandaged hand and her coat settling behind her like a bat's wings.

The whole crew jerked back, including Petal. Urzaia raised a hatchet on instinct, then laughed and put the weapon back down.

Tristania placed the fork carefully back on the other woman's plate. She reached out, smoothing Petal's dress, and with a few quick strokes tamed the alchemist's hair. Petal's eyes stared out as if from a cave, wide and blinking.

The Silent One took a few steps back, bowed to Petal, and then sat down in her seat. It might have been Calder's imagination, but he thought she looked somewhat proud of herself.

Naberius gave no indication that anything out of the ordinary had happened. "An alchemist. Was she trained in Kanatalia, then?"

"You might say she was self-trained," Calder answered. "But don't worry. She has enough experience to match any three Kanatalia alchemists."

And paranoia to match any twelve, he thought, but elected to stay silent.

The Witness nodded to his partner. "Tristania was self-taught as well, in a manner of speaking. And in a Kanatalia laboratory, no less."

Tristania ate her meal calmly, her bandaged hand lifting a fork to her mouth. The strands of hair sticking out from behind her bound head made her look even more like an asylum inmate than Petal, and her high-collared coat belonged on a battlefield.

Perhaps because she wore such a strange outfit without a hint of shame or self-consciousness, or perhaps because she was a member of the Guild of Witnesses, he got the impression that she would make a solid, dependable ally.

Naberius, on the other hand...he was too handsome, his suit too bright. He showed up without a proper introduction and rushed them into departing quickly. Either something was rushing him or he was trying to keep Calder from looking too closely into his business.

Though that, on its own, didn't particularly bother Calder. Many travelers hired Navigators for less-than-reputable business, and as long as this treasurer kept throwing money around, Calder would be willing to show him far more trust than he'd earned.

Jyrine had picked up the introductions, waving to Andel. "Please, allow me to introduce you to Andel Petronus, our Quartermaster and our oldest traveling companion."

Andel pressed his wide-brimmed white hat to his chest as he executed a seated bow. "A glorified babysitter, really."

"A Luminian? Really? On this crew?" Naberius shrugged, holding a forkful of quail in one hand. "How did a man such as yourself end up in such company?"

Slowly, Andel returned the hat to his head. The sun was long down, but a white suit was not appropriate attire for working on the ship at any time. Andel wore what he did for reasons other than practicality.

"I found myself at odds with the Order," Andel said. "I turned to another Guild. It's as simple as that."

Naberius held one hand out in a pacifying gesture. "Truly, I meant no insult. Quite the opposite. Very few have the courage to turn against the Luminians and their beliefs."

"I don't think I said anything about their beliefs."

"True enough, true enough." He turned to face the last member of the crew, only to find Foster's seat empty. "And what about your gunner?"

Foster had returned to sitting in front of a cannon, scrubbing out the insides with a long iron rod. He had finished eating and left without a word, even to their guests. That was very much in character for the man, but it left Calder in the awkward position of having to explain.

He chuckled, trying to lighten the insult. "Don't mind him. He was a gunsmith, once, and something of a hermit. He doesn't talk to anyone unless it's about iron and powder."

Naberius opened his coat, revealing for the first time a pair of pistols, one on each hip. He pulled one out, holding its polished handle up to the steady light of a quicklamp. "That's a pity. I have two pieces here I would have liked to discuss with him."

"Is that so?" Calder asked. "Have you had them long?"

"Since before the death of the Emperor, may his soul fly free. They're Dalton Foster originals, you know. Some of the last."

A sound rang out, like a muffled bell, as Foster hit his head on the inside of the cannon.

Petal buried her face in her hair again, muttering something. Urzaia laughed out loud, and Andel looked down so that the brim of his hat hid his expression. Jerri and Calder exchanged a glance.

It only took a moment, but Naberius couldn't help but notice. "Have I said something amusing?"

Jerri cut in quickly. "No, sir, no. A private joke among the crew. Our gunner was once an admirer of Dalton Foster's, that's all. But his opinion changed, and now we try not to mention that name at all."

Naberius looked somewhat put out. "I see." He holstered his pistol once more. "I apologize for bringing it up, then. Your gunner, what is his name?"

"Duster," Calder said quickly.

Andel snorted a laugh.

Jyrine took over before the Chronicler could ask any more questions. "Now that the introductions have been dealt with, shall we turn to business? You implied that we might see some *danger* on this journey?"

From her tone, you would have thought she'd said "excitement" instead of "danger."

Naberius sobered up quickly. Even Tristania set her plate down and rested her hands inside the pockets of her coat.

"I will admit to you, there are political ramifications to our actions," Naberius said, eyeing each of them in turn. "The Empire has held together remarkably well these past five years, thanks especially to the efforts of the four Regents. But cracks are beginning to form at the seams. Elders stir in the Aion and beyond, along with those who worship them. Izyrians have quickly begun to revert to the old ways, and some of their arenas feature blood-sport once more."

Urzaia rubbed one of the scars on his cheek. "Is that so?"

"Even worse, there are those in Erin—and elsewhere—who begin to talk of independence. Secession."

Calder and Jyrine had spoken of the idea before, usually out of dread, but it was Petal who responded this time.

"You mean...little Empires?" she whispered.

"You're half right. They want small, self-governing states, each of them ruled by separate rulers with separate goals. If it falls to men to govern separately, then war is an inevitability."

"You know Sadesthenes," Calder said in approval. The actual quote was, "*When men govern according to their own petty concerns, rather than for the good of all mankind, then war becomes an inevitability.*" But at least Naberius had paraphrased, which was more than most bothered to do.

Naberius shook his head. "I'm not as familiar as I should be, sadly. But his words remain as true today as when he first spoke them. The Empire is falling apart, as should be expected without someone to hold it together. We need an Emperor once again."

This time, instead of reacting, his whole crew froze. Even Foster's scraping against the inside of the cannon stopped. Calder could feel Jyrine's dark eyes boring holes in his head, but he couldn't afford to look at her.

How much does Naberius know? he wondered. *How much can he know? Did he really hire us because of Cheska's recommendation, or is there some other reason? How much does Cheska know?*

"You expect to install another Emperor?" Calder asked, raising a bite of food to his mouth to make himself look as casual as possible.

Tristania shifted in her seat, looking between Naberius and the crew. It was obvious that she sensed something off about their reaction, but she didn't seem too nervous yet.

The Chronicler, it seemed, noticed nothing. "It is not an expectation of mine, but a necessity. With my knowledge and resources, as well as the treasure we look to find, we can raise a second Emperor. If we do nothing, this Empire will tear itself to pieces inside a decade."

The crew and Calder relaxed, Urzaia letting out a heavy breath.

"What is it we'll find on the island?" Calder asked.

This time, Naberius hesitated. "I would like to keep that to myself for now, if you don't mind. Other ears than yours may be listening."

Calder glanced around. There were other ships nearby, but none within easy earshot, and no one on the docks. The bay itself, of course, was empty. "I've trusted my crew with secrets before, Naberius."

"I do not refer to your crew," the Witness said grimly. "Where we seek to preserve the Empire, there are others who would prefer it to fall apart. Those who profit more from its dissolution, or who simply oppose me. I believe they may have hired the Am'haranai."

Calder scratched his head. "The Consultants?" It was well-known that the Consultants could answer any question or give you advice in your business, but he wasn't sure he'd ever heard of them as objects of fear.

Jyrine smiled at Naberius, an invitation to share the joke. "Are you so afraid of a well-informed opponent, then?"

Tristania locked eyes with Jerri and slowly shook her head. In front of her grim silence, it was difficult to take anything lightly.

"Do not underestimate the Consultant's Guild," Naberius said quietly. "Let me tell you a story. A man once believed that he would be driven out of business, so he hired the Consultants. Within a year, his opponents all filed for bankruptcy."

"I beg you, don't tell such terrifying stories before bed," Andel said drily. "Petal still needs to sleep."

"Let me tell you another story. A man was outnumbered two to one in a battle, and he feared that his troops would lose. So he hired the Consultants. The enemy general surrendered in a week."

Urzaia hefted one of his hatchets. "It would not take me a week before my enemy surrendered."

Naberius went on, undeterred. "Let me tell you another story. A woman was cornered by a gang of killers. With no one else to turn to, she stumbled into the Consultants' chapter house and pawned everything she owned to hire their services. Her attackers were found dead the next morning, deposited inside a cemetery and prepared for burial."

The pattern was clear, but these still sounded like myths to Calder. The other Guilds operated more or less openly, but the Consultants seemed like they were prone to theatrics.

"Let me tell you one last story. Roughly twenty years ago, a man began kidnapping children around the poorer areas of the Capital. He continued, uncaught, for years before the parents of the missing children hired the Consultants. The *very next day,* he was found murdered in his own home, and the children were recovered."

"I take your point," Jyrine said. "But even according to your many stories, the Consultants are advisors only. Even if they have been summoned against you, they can't sail the Aion without hiring a Navigator. And we're on official Guild business. Captain Bennett would never allow two competing contracts."

Naberius ran a hand down his long hair. "Many stories...there are thousands of stories like these, Missus Marten, stretching back before the Empire was founded. Much rarer are the stories that tell of one side *losing* after having hired the Consultants. Indeed, I have never been able to locate a single example of such a tale."

That seemed absurd to Calder. The Consultants were a Guild like any other, and not even so powerful as some. If the Champions had been hired against them, for instance, he would be heading for the horizon even now. The Magisters could likely find a way of setting their boat on fire from a distance, and the Alchemist's Guild would be even more terrifying than that. They would find themselves frightened to breathe for fear of some exotic poison.

So, in his personal threat estimation, the Consultants did not rank high enough to justify any paranoia. Naberius' obvious caution seemed...unnecessary, at best.

"Well, if they're that good, then why not give up now?" he asked. "There's no point in opposing an enemy who can never lose."

Naberius rested his hands on the hilts of his pistols. "I did not mean to imply that they never lose. Only that when they do, they have ways of making sure that no one ever hears about it. To me, Captain Marten, that is plenty frightening."

When he put it that way, they did sound relatively frightening. "If that's true," Calder said, "then we'll only be safe at sea. Why did your message say to depart at dawn?"

"In your estimation, Captain, should we leave now?"

"Absolutely not." The tide was against them, his crew could use the rest, and the Lyathatan was exhausted from pulling them back to land with such speed. Well, not exhausted precisely, because Calder wasn't sure the Elderspawn ever got tired as he understood it. But from Reading the giant creature that pulled their ship, Calder was sure that it would find a way to retaliate against overwork. Forcing it to pull against the tide could be a straight route to the bottom of Candle Bay.

But if it was a choice between trying to persuade the Lyathatan and fighting off assassins, then Calder would pick the "flee to open ocean" route anytime.

Naberius nodded. "I agree. Tristania and I are also tired from our journey here, and we would welcome a night of rest before we headed out into open ocean. To be fully honest with you, we do not expect to be pursued this early, and we have set other precautions in place to be sure. But in case our preparations come to nothing, this is why we hired you." He leaned forward. "It may be improper to ask, but...is it safe to say that you have a Soulbound among you?"

Calder tried not to do anything that would draw the Chronicler's attention to Urzaia. Or Foster. Or, for that matter, himself.

"That would be safe," he said at last.

"Then I am relieved." He held up a hand. "Again, I do not expect any trouble tonight. But in case of a mistake on our part, it is a relief to know that there is at least one member of your crew who can stand with Tristania in our defense."

"For the amount you're paying, Naberius, consider the lives of my crew completely expendable. If you'd like to kill one to relax, I have a pistol you could borrow."

Andel took a swig of wine. "That offer is good for the next ten minutes, until our inevitable mutiny."

Calder jerked a thumb in the direction of his Quartermaster. "Andel will be first in line to take a bullet for you. I can tie him to a shield, if necessary."

With a crash like thunder, the trap door to the hold burst open, and a dark figure soared out.

Naberius had a pistol out and aimed before the sound faded. Urzaia rose to his feet with a hatchet in each hand, Petal shoved herself behind a barrel, and Andel drew a pistol of his own. Tristania reached a hand inside her coat, Calder's hand tightened on the grip of his cutlass, and even Jerri pulled a dagger.

Then the dark figure flapped into the light of the quicklamp, its black eyes glaring, working stubby wings to stay afloat. "MUTINY," it bellowed, and then hopped up onto Calder's shoulder. It leaned over, reaching out with the nest of tentacles on its mouth to clean the last bits of debris from Calder's dinner plate.

The rest of the crew relaxed, but the Witnesses kept a tight grip on their weapons.

"What is *that?*" Naberius asked in disgust.

They normally kept their pet Bellowing Horror sealed up when they had passengers onboard, but it seemed that this time the cage hadn't held.

Oh, well, Calder thought. *He was going to find out sooner or later.*

"Naberius, Tristania, meet Shuffles."

CHAPTER FOUR

When someone charges an object with their Intent, we call that process 'investing,' and we say that the object has been 'invested.'

Why? Are we nothing more than slaves to ignorant tradition?

The early Empire knew nothing of finance, and thus nothing of true financial investment. I think you'll find that our proposed term, 'empowering,' really captures the modern spirit of today's Empire.

– FROM THE (REJECTED) PROPOSAL OF THE AURELIAN BANKER'S UNION TO THE GUILD OF MAGISTERS

THIRTEEN YEARS AGO

Rojric rarely spoke of Calder's mother at all, and Calder thought he was beginning to understand why.

"He took you with him on a *burglary?* You're lucky the Guard knew to take you to me, or you might be in prison right alongside him!" She did not shake her finger at him, as Calder had somewhat imagined mothers would do, but remained seated. Her back stayed straight as a poker, even as she stared down at her son with disapproving eyes.

His mother, Alsa Grayweather, was everything Rojric pretended to be. She could trace her family line back to the dawn of the Empire, she wore only the latest in Imperial fashion, and she owned her own three-story home in one of the Capital's wealthier districts.

In Calder's mind, she needed more flaws. She was *too* perfect; like an Elderspawn stuffed into human skin. And, of all the Imperial Guilds, she had to work for the worst one.

The family line was mostly confidential, the Imperial records of her family sealed for security purposes. Her high-fashion dresses came in only one color—tar-black—and her home was stocked with more curios and deadly artifacts than a museum.

A curving tusk sat on a rack next to a pair of dueling sabers, all of them polished and oiled for immediate use. When he had first asked her about the tusk, she'd seemed shocked.

"If a Whispering Gaunt finds its way in my back door, how do you expect me to defend myself? With a sword?"

And, worst of all, that crest she had embroidered into her dress, woven into a tapestry, and displayed in the stained glass of her sitting-room window: a squirming mass of tentacles with six eyes overlaid.

The Elder's Eyes, symbol of the Blackwatch.

"He needed me," Calder insisted. "Only I can tell him what's fake and what's worth taking."

"Worth taking! You have too much talent to waste on someone like your father. You'll be better off with me, that's for certain."

Calder decided that honesty had gotten him as far as it could. It was time for persuasion. "I've always wanted to meet you, Mother. To think you had a house like this...I'm sure even Father would agree that I *am* better off with you."

He smiled up at her, watching a brace of ornamental pistols out of the corner of his eye. *Eighty silvermarks.*

One side of Alsa's mouth curved up. She was a pretty woman still, with rich brown hair running down her back.

"You have your father's tongue as well as his hair," she said. "Flattery can serve you well, or it could end with you in the cell next to him."

That didn't sound too bad to Calder. If he wound up in a cell next to his father, at least they could see each other every day.

"Do you have horses here?" he asked. He'd wondered about that ever since he'd arrived here. Big houses were supposed to have horses.

"We do. And you will learn to ride, as well as several other skills important to your future."

"What future did you have in mind, exactly?" he asked hesitantly. His father's idea of a future had always been 'earning a fortune and retiring to our own private island,' but Calder doubted his mother would see things quite the same way.

Idly, she touched the Blackwatch Crest embossed into the table. "Among the Guilds," she said, as if it were the most natural thing possible. "You're too old to find a place among the Consultants or the Champions, thank the Fates, but riding will be important if you find yourself with the Witnesses or the Greenwardens. You seem surprisingly well educated, despite Rojric's influence, so you might enjoy a life with the Magisters."

Working in one of the ten Imperial Guilds? He'd have more freedom in a prison cell. He turned up his smile like a quicklamp, resolved to change the subject before she decided his future for him. "Oh yes, Father made sure I was educated. I have read all the classics, and I've been told I could pass for a governor's son."

"Can you, now? I had no idea your tutors were so well-rounded." She leaned back in her chair, pulling a knife out of her pocket. Without preamble, she began trimming her nails right there at the table. It was so contrary to how he had imagined her that he could scarcely reconcile the picture: the proper, well-to-do, Guild-trained Capital woman, sitting at her table trimming her nails with a hunting knife.

"In what year were the Greenwardens established?"

"The Greenwardens, then known as the Brothers of Peace, were originally founded to counteract the spread of weaponized alchemy and a sudden increase in the worship of Othaghor. They were established in the...eighth...century, and remain one of the most influential Imperial Guilds to this day."

He brushed off his shoulder, as though he answered questions like this every day.

She nodded to him, conceding a point. "Very good. I'd only correct a few bits, here and there: they were originally known as the *Sisters* of Peace, as the first generation of Greenwardens were all women. They were meant to counteract the worship of Ach'magut, *not* Othaghor, established in the seventh century rather than the eighth, and they are among the *weakest* Guilds in terms of both political power and available capital."

Alsa stowed her knife without looking at him, flushing in shame. The heat spread down almost to his shoulders before he managed to choke back his embarrassment.

One question. That was one question, and I could have answered it had she given me more time.

But she didn't seem inclined to give him any more time at all. "It will be important for you to know the history of the Greenwardens should you choose to join them. Kameira are fascinating creatures, and you would work quite closely alongside them in the Greenwardens. In fact, Imperial history is a critical subject for any of the Guilds."

"I'm not sure I see myself as a Guild man," he said. "I had thought about boarding a ship for Izyria and connecting with my culture, perhaps as a sailor or a hunter."

He tried his best to make those sound like viable career paths, and not boyhood dreams born of travelers' stories.

Alsa went on as though he hadn't spoken. "If you do want to pass as a governor's son, for some reason, then you should familiarize yourself with the fundamental philosophers. Penmanship, too, is crucial in more professions than you would expect."

Penmanship? He didn't want to learn penmanship.

"Listen, Mother. I understand that you think Father was irresponsible in bringing me along on an…artifact retrieval...and you're probably right. That's inappropriate for a boy my age, and I understand that." He understood that *she* thought so, and that was what mattered. "But I'm as intelligent as any rich Guild son, and I'm quicker, and I can think on my feet. I could do quite well outside the Guilds, because I can get along on the streets. In the real world, not the cozy drawing-rooms of the Magisters or the alchemists."

Calder had taken that speech point-for-point from an angry rant his father often brought forth when he'd been drinking. Not word-for-word, of course, because he thought his mother would appreciate eloquence more than passion.

But he did believe it. The ten Guilds acted as though they were part of some private world, running the Empire while everyone else simply benefited from their expertise.

Let's see how a Greenwarden does without money to buy his food. He won't have the spine to steal a loaf of bread, not to mention the hands to do it without getting caught.

A voice in the back of his mind mentioned that the Greenwardens were supposedly all Soulbound, capable of healing wounds and miraculously restoring blighted crops. Even if they were kicked out of the Guild for some reason, they were unlikely to starve.

He shoved that voice away.

Alsa looked as though she was having a great deal of trouble restraining her laughter. "The real world, you say? I see. And you think I don't live in the real world, do you? Is that what your Father said?" There was an edge to her humor now.

Come to think of it, his father hadn't ever listed Alsa among those Guild privileged who leaned on their fortunes.

"Father spoke most highly of you," Calder lied, "and I'm sure you're an excellent Watchman. Watchwoman. Watchlady."

"Watchman. The founder of our order was a woman, and she took the name 'Watchman' upon herself because she 'Didn't want to set herself above her male counterparts by flaunting her superior gender.' That's a quote from her biography, which you will know after your courses in Imperial history."

That was an incredibly useless bit of trivia, and he thought about pointing that out, but there was still an edge to her voice that he couldn't quite place. Best to put out the fires. "Be that as it may, you have to admit that a Guild lifestyle is somewhat...insular." 'Insular' was a word he had learned from the news-sheets last week, and he was determined to use it as much as possible. "Wouldn't I be better trained if I continued to take on the broad world as it is, facing all its dangers with eyes wide open?"

While he spoke, Alsa had walked over to her mantelpiece, drawing the tip of her finger along one of her mounted pistols as though checking for dust. "You would say you've lived a dangerous lifestyle, then?"

Too late he realized that saying his life had been dangerous might be calling his father irresponsible or abusive. "I had Father to look out for me, of course. But I have faced my share of dangers."

She pulled the pistol down, cocked it, and pointed it at him.

"How would you face this one, then?" she asked.

He didn't believe she would pull the trigger, not really, but staring down the barrel of a gun still turned his backbone to dust.

Unconsciously, he raised his hands like a hostage during a stickup. "I would do my best to avoid situations like this."

Alsa nodded, expression serious. "Very wise. And if, despite every precaution, you found yourself in this scenario? What would you do then?"

He tried to look as confident as possible without lowering his hands. "I do have other talents, you know."

"Please elaborate."

Now he had her. Laymen tended to be superstitious about Readers, ascribing them abilities they did not actually possess. When the Emperor flaunted his overwhelming powers publicly, it went a long way toward establishing Readers as superhuman.

They were not, of course. Only the Emperor could display that level of obscene control, levitating wagons or creating doors in blank walls. But most people did not know that.

Calder cast his glance around him for something he could use, spying a small decorative pillow on the edge of his chair. He picked it up, smiling.

"If I were so inclined, I could invest this with enough Intent to stop a pistol-shot. If I had some more time and the proper equipment, I could even Awaken it, but that..." He shuddered theatrically. "Who knows what powers that could unleash?"

Alsa's eyes widened. "Really? You could make this pillow bulletproof?"

She lowered her pistol and moved a few steps closer, running a hand along the pillow. "This right here? Without changing a thing?"

He had her. "I would need a little time, of course, but in an actual situation of—"

She pushed the pillow against his chest, pressed the barrel of her pistol against it, and squeezed the trigger.

A noise burst in his ears as though a horse had kicked him on either side of the head, and a flare of light and smoke blinded him. The cloud of gun smoke filled his nose, choking him, and for a moment he was torn between a gasp and a hacking cough. He was afraid it came out more like a wail.

He was shot! She'd shot him! His own mother!

Desperately he shoved the pillow out of his lap, scrambling to locate the wound. If it was a gut-shot, he might live until they got him to a doctor, but he would need something to staunch the bleeding. The pillow! He shouldn't have dropped it after all, now where...

It occurred to him after a few seconds that he was not actually wounded, and that his mother was giggling.

He flushed again, until he was afraid that the whole top half of his body glowed bright red. "Unloaded, of course."

Alsa slowly got the laughter under control. "What? Oh, no, all the weapons in my house are loaded."

She bent over, plucked a misshapen lead ball from the floor, and tossed it into his lap.

He examined the pillow, but other than a small black smudge from the barrel, it was pristine. "Then...how..."

"When you're bragging, make sure you know who you're talking to."

Calder placed his hand against the pillow and focused his mind, Reading it.

His mother's voice smothered his mind, You cannot be punctured. *Every one of your fibers is a cord of steel. You only have to stop one shot. You cannot be punctured.*

She had actually invested the pillow with enough Intent to stop a bullet? With that brief of a touch?

Calder straightened himself, striving to look as dignified as he could with a burning face. And without looking his mother in the eye. "You're a Reader yourself, then."

Alsa folded her arms, still holding the smoking gun. "I'm surprised your father didn't tell you. What did you think I did for the Blackwatch?"

He had imagined her as a clerk or some kind of administrator, but he wasn't about to say that out loud.

"You're very fortunate," Alsa went on, her voice softening. "Readers are very much in demand among all the Guilds. You speak well for your age, you're obviously perceptive and intelligent, and if your talent is anything like mine...

well, when I was only a little older than you, I had Guilds lining up to bid for me. Literally bidding."

"That doesn't sound so bad," he admitted.

"There's quite a bit of variety in the ten Guilds. I'm sure you'll find a place where you fit in." She straightened and set the pistol back on the table, presumably to be reloaded later. "In the meantime, I'll have a tutor here for you before the end of the week."

His eyes rose to the other display of weaponry, the pair of swords lying below the tusk. "Will he teach me to use those, too?"

In the first genuine sign of affection she'd given him since he stepped into this house, she placed a hand on his head. "You'll learn all three of them, son. But he won't be teaching you."

He looked up at her, confused.

"I will."

In the space of a day, he had traded thieving lessons with his father for fencing lessons with his mother. His father was still missing, and Rojric's absence was like a burning hole in his chest. He would have to find a way to bring all three of them together.

He was a Reader; he could do it.

He could do anything.

CHAPTER FIVE

Calder had spent so long cleaning out the cabin for his passengers that it felt strange to be using it himself. Everything was tucked neatly away instead of lying conveniently within reach, and even the chest at the foot of his bunk had been rearranged and organized.

He dipped his sponge in the bucket of soapy water, then scrubbed at his bare chest. Jyrine had taken the time for a full bath at her parents' house that afternoon, but Calder hadn't gotten the same chance. He sponged himself off while cloth ruffled behind him: the sounds of her changing for bed.

"We could still make it out of the bay," Jerri said lightly.

"It'll be easier if we wait until dawn." He leaned to one side as she reached past him for her hairbrush. At first, it had been difficult to move around each other in such a confined space, but now they were both used to it.

"If we move out of the bay and into the Aion, the Lyathatan can keep us anchored, and we'll be farther out of the reach of any attackers. The longer we sit here, the greater the risk."

Calder stood in a wide basin, squeezing the sponge over his head to unleash a waterfall of soap and water. "I'm tired, Jerri. You're tired. Andel's tired. Even the Witnesses are tired. If I make the Lyathatan drag us out of the bay—" he paused for a moment to dump fresh water on his head— "then he's likely to leave us there. I'll be the first captain to have his *literal* ship mutiny on him."

Soft, regular strokes came from behind him: Jerri brushing out her hair. "You'll persuade it. I have every confidence in you."

Calder shook out his hair, wiping water from his eyes with one hand before he reached for a towel. "Besides, we won't be any safer until we get to deep water. Even normal ships can sail the shallow Aion; they won't even have to go through the inconvenience of hiring a Navigator. If we're not going any farther than the shallows, we might as well stay here."

"We'd still have more warning if someone comes."

He sighed and stepped past her, pulling on a pair of soft shorts. He'd learned in his mother's house that Heartlanders wore such shorts to bed, and he'd quickly grown used to them. "You really expect the assassins tonight, then?"

Jerri sat on the bed with her legs curled under her, wearing a simple white nightgown. She pulled the brush through her unbraided hair one stroke at a time. The pose exposed more of her tattoos: lines of script crawling up her left ankle, emerging over her shoulder and sneaking up her neck.

She looked up at him with a girlish smile. "I think we'd be missing out if we *didn't* get to fight assassins tonight."

Calder laughed as he sat down on the bunk next to her. With a twist of the wrist, he pulled open a latched drawer, checking that his pistol was loaded and ready inside. He would have preferred to set the pistol out in the open next to the bunk, but he wasn't enough of a fool to leave a loaded weapon sitting next to his wife's head. Not when they were on a ship that gently tossed with the motion of the waves, even if it was relatively calm here compared to the open ocean.

"If you're looking forward to a fight that much, then you should want to stay here."

"I said I wanted to see them coming so that we can prepare a real fight. It's not like I want to be assassinated." She grimaced, tugging at a snarl in her brown hair.

Next, Calder found his sword-belt and hung it from a peg above the bunk. If he had to wake up in the middle of the night and fight, he wanted his weapons close to hand. "Even Naberius said it would be okay to spend the night here. We're not in a hurry yet."

"Hmmmm. I wonder why not."

Calder opened a porthole, emptying the used water from his bath into the bay. "What do you mean?"

"Well, Cheska rushed to send us the message, and then the two of them certainly scurried to get onboard, without even bothering to meet us first. But now they don't mind if we sit in the harbor all night."

He shrugged. "We'll be leaving in the morning. That should be enough hurry for anyone."

"Maybe." She calmly brushed her hair for a few more seconds. "What kind of treasure are they after, do you think?"

That very topic had been very much on Calder's mind ever since Naberius explained their mission. He had a hard time thinking about the Chronicler's supposed treasure without finding himself blinded by greed. "It's got to be an Imperial artifact, doesn't it? It must be a good one, if he's willing to spend ten thousand goldmarks on it."

Jerri's arms snaked around his, and she rested her chin on his shoulder. "A good one, maybe. But it can't be the *best* one. How much do you think he'd pay for that?"

Calder rested his foot on his secret lockbox, chained beneath the bed. He wanted to remind himself that it was there. He turned his head a few inches and gave his wife a smile. "Too bad it's not for sale."

"I bet he'd kill for it."

Inside its darkened cage in the corner, Shuffles murmured, "Kill for it...."

Jerri laughed. "Awww, it's talking in its sleep."

With her face so close to his, he couldn't help but notice her emerald earrings, still shining in the light of the quicklamp. "Aren't you going to take those off?" He reached up to her ear.

Casually she leaned back, bringing her own hand up to thumb her earrings. "These? Oh, it's too much trouble taking them out. We're going to be up early, so I thought I'd save a step and leave them in."

In his memory, she'd never left her earrings in to sleep before. It seemed uncomfortable to him, but it wasn't like he made a practice of wearing jewelry. What did he know?

Minutes later, Calder lay on his bunk, staring at the wooden planks above him and wondering about assassins. The gentle lull of the waves eventually lured him into sleep, as he felt every inch of the ship settling into the rhythm of the water.

If anything does happen tonight, he thought, *I'll be ready.*

Through his eyes, he thought he saw a green flash.

Once, he might have jumped to his feet at any sign of the unusual, but these days he rarely had to fight for his life. Sleepily, he wondered why someone had opened a quicklamp at this hour.

It took him a handful of seconds to slide up to a seated position, looking around him. Everything in the cabin seemed normal. His sword still hung above the bunk, his chest sat right where he'd left it, and moonlight streamed in from the porthole.

Though his wife was missing.

He listened for a moment, trying to pick out anything wrong. *Maybe the assassins took her,* he thought, and then chuckled a little nervously. Killers would have no need to kidnap a woman from her bed. They would simply slit Naberius and Tristania's throats, maybe with Calder's thrown in for good measure, and then melt away into the night.

Still, on a night like tonight, he had a right to be nervous. He shrugged on a shirt and picked up his pistol. With the gun in one hand and his sheathed cutlass in the other, he creeped up and out of the cabin.

"Jerri?" he called, though he still made an effort to keep his voice down. Foster had a tendency to shoot people who woke him up in the middle of the night.

No one answered. The ship drifted gently with the water as the pale light of the moon slid over its deck.

That was when he realized something was really wrong.

Urzaia should still be on watch, and the man was incapable of remaining silent. If he didn't respond, that meant he had either fallen asleep on the job, or...

A huge body lay sprawled on the deck, hatchets inches from his hand. Calder scarcely had time to let the sight register when a flash of green fire silently exploded at the corner of his vision. He spun, pistol leveled, to see two figures locked in combat on the stern deck.

Only feet above where he had been sleeping moments before, a figure in black brandished a large-bladed bronze knife. Calder assumed it was a woman from the slight build and the hair, though it was hard to get a glimpse of her figure. She fought like a shadow, flickering forward and slashing at her opponent, dodging counterattacks by dipping impossibly low in an instant. Sparks of silver flew from her off hand: tiny daggers weighted for throwing, or perhaps needles.

Her opponent...Calder's mind tried to reject it for a moment, but truth quickly burned through his reluctance.

Her opponent was *Jerri.* Lit by the moon as if she stood in a spotlight, Jyrine Tessella Marten wore nothing more than a white nightgown, her brown hair blowing loose in the wind.

And her hands were filled with acid-green flame.

That wasn't possible. It *couldn't* be possible. No one could use powers like that except Elders and Kameira...and those humans who borrowed their powers. Soulbound.

But his wife wasn't a Soulbound. She couldn't be. He was a Reader, he would have sensed it.

Light and life, I'm married to her. There were only a handful of Soulbound on the continent, and the Empire had them all officially registered. There was no way Jerri could have kept something like that a secret.

No way.

Calder stood frozen for a long moment as Jerri struck at her opponent with a lash of flame. He would have expected any opponent of a Soulbound to die in seconds, especially one that could apparently hurl bolts of fire, but the assassin in black simply sidestepped, as though dodging a ball.

"I'm not here for you," the killer said. Her voice was low, but not a whisper. She sounded businesslike, almost bored. "I don't suppose I can convince you to go back to sleep."

Jerri kept her voice even softer than the assassin's, as though she had more to hide. "I won't let you get what you want. Time's almost up. That which sleeps will soon wake."

The assassin jerked as though Jerri had kicked her, but the words couldn't have hit her any harder than they hit Calder.

That which sleeps will soon wake.

He'd heard those words before, but he'd never expected to hear them from his wife.

Calder must have made a sound, because Jerri's eyes caught him for the first time: standing there, pistol raised, his mouth hanging open. Her burning hands froze, her eyes widened. She stared at him for a stretched instant, as though he'd caught her cheating on him with another man.

The woman in black sighed and reached down to something at her waist.

Jerri whipped back to her attacker, blazing hands coming up, but the other woman struck like a snake. One instant she was keeping her distance, and then she was pulling a needle out of Jerri's neck.

Calder shouted, his hand clenching involuntarily. His pistol sent out a crack of thunder and a cloud of black smoke, but the assassin was already out of his line of fire.

She held Jerri by the throat, pressing Calder's wife against the railing. With an almost casual gesture, the killer shoved her overboard.

Pain and shock blasted through Calder as though he'd been struck by lightning, and he reacted with the instinct of the wounded.

Through his bare feet, he plunged his mind into the ship.

The Testament came to life around the assassin. A line of rope swung at her neck, trying to catch her in a noose, but she was too quick.

She ducked, unbelievably limber, and dropped from the stern deck.

The woman in black landed in a crouch, inches in front of him. For a moment Calder looked straight at her, though half of his attention was still buried in the ship beneath him. Black hair hung down around her like a hood, and a piece of dark cloth covered her mouth. Her skin was pale, maybe Erinin, and her eyes...

As black as her hair and clothes, her eyes were flat and unconcerned. The ice-cold eyes of a woman who didn't care if she lived or died.

For some reason, that made Calder even angrier.

He tossed his pistol aside and pulled his cutlass, so similar to the dueling saber he'd trained with as a child. He'd spent even longer hours with this blade, though not recently. But a lack of practice was the furthest thing from his mind.

He attacked with a speed and fury that would have made at least one of his tutors very proud, but he didn't fight with muscle alone. He kept his Intent fixed, focused on the sword, pouring all of his anger and fear and desperation into the weapon. *You can kill her. You cannot be stopped.*

Slowly, steadily, the weapon grew stronger. Not enough to notice over the course of one fight, perhaps, but maybe enough to tip the scales.

The killer flicked her knife, knocking his sword aside, but he stepped forward, pressing her against the door of his cabin, abusing his reach. He felt a savage satisfaction flaring up as he scored a hit against the flesh of her arm. She couldn't block everything. He was overwhelming her!

More importantly, the noise had given the rest of the crew precious seconds to emerge. Foster called out behind him, and Andel's boots pounded across the deck as he ran over. He thought he even heard Urzaia groaning, but he didn't have the space to turn around and check. A little closer, and he'd have skewered this murderer through the heart. Then he'd dive into the bay, save Jerri before she drowned...

His mind had already moved on without him when the woman batted his blade aside, brought her hand up, and jabbed a needle into his upper arm.

Calder fought on for a moment more, but the strength trickled away from his arm, and she simply stepped past him.

He spun, and the motion was almost enough to send him tumbling to the deck. He grabbed at a nearby railing for support, leaning against it as he watched the rest of the fight unfold.

Andel, still impeccably dressed in a full white suit and hat, fired his pistol point-blank at the assassin.

Got her! Calder silently screamed, but the bullet tore out a crater in the wood of the deck, and the woman in black kicked in Andel's knees. How had she gotten away? It was impossible. Purely impossible.

Urzaia had indeed recovered from whatever the woman had done to him, rising up to his full height and looming like an enraged bear. He took a black hatchet in either hand and roared, charging with the force of a warhorse. The entire ship seemed to shake under his weight.

The killer didn't wait around. She turned and ran the opposite direction, toward the bow of the ship.

No. She's not running. Calder tried to shout a warning to his crew, but a strange warmth was spreading through his veins, and he was finding it harder and harder to stay conscious. Speaking seemed beyond him.

But he still clearly saw that she wasn't trying to get away—she was trying to get to her real target.

Naberius.

The man stood in the shadow of the mast, wrapped in a blanket, holding pistols in both hands. With the blinding white of his grin, and his dark hair blowing behind him, he looked more and more like an actor in a heroic play.

The assassin charged him, but he didn't even raise his gun. He only raised his eyes: up to the sails looming over his head.

"Too late," he said.

Then Tristania fell from the mast. Her coat settled around her as she landed, her bandages glowing in the white light. A dark whip unfurled from her fist, curling around her feet.

She cracked the whip once, and the woman in black hurled herself to one side.

An instant later, Calder understood why.

The tip of the whip was pointed like an arrowhead. In the air, where the point of the whip struck, a pale light exploded in a crackle of lightning.

He had seen explosions like that before, if he could only remember...

A memory drifted up, of a Stormwing gliding over choppy waves, snapping its tail to create bright explosions. For some reason, he couldn't seem to connect that thought to anything else.

Naberius' voice drifted over to Calder. He was speaking to the killer in black. "I can promise you safe conduct if you are willing to have a civilized discussion. Whatever your contract is, I can beat it."

Calder could only see the black-clad woman from the back, but she was slowly reaching one hand behind her back to grab something from her belt. A hilt. A second knife.

Once more, he tried to call a warning.

This time, he fell onto his stomach. Shadows swallowed him.

His last thought was an image of Jerri, kicking and panicking as she slowly drowned in an icy sea.

Calder woke in his own bed, with golden morning sunlight flowing in from the porthole. His arm ached from strain, and his cheeks and ribs had several bruises from where he'd collapsed, but he ignored his body's distress as he jumped out of the bunk.

He didn't see Jerri, but that didn't mean they hadn't retrieved her. It didn't mean they'd left her to drown.

Staggering over to the wall, he slammed the door open. The sails billowed away from him, the greenish skin of their canvas pregnant with wind. Urzaia sat on an upturned crate, running a cloth over one of his hatchets, an uncharacteristically grim expression on his scarred face. Andel shouted an order to Foster, who manned the wheel. He had his shooting glasses on, squinting at the horizon through his mane of gray hair. Naberius and Tristania stood over a folding travel table, discussing something on a map.

"Jerri?" Calder croaked out.

They all turned to look at him.

He walked forward, keeping an eye out for his wife. "Jerri?" he asked again. No one answered him. He spun, looking up onto the stern deck. Last time he'd seen her...

She was locked in combat, green flame in each hand. She'd been lying to him for years. She'd betrayed him.

"Where did she go?" Calder demanded.

Andel took his hat off, holding it against his chest.

Well, if they weren't going to answer him, he'd figure out the truth for himself. He leaned forward and gripped a rail, Reading the ship.

Calder focuses his Intent, trying to get one hinge to stick on the doorframe with nothing more than the power of his will. The ship needs to think of itself as one piece, or this project would never work...

Not that. Something more recent.

He gives another mental order to the Lyathatan, directing the ship forward. The ship needs to move faster if they want to catch the Stormwing in time, and he's sure not going to waste so much money on a failed venture...

His grip tightened on the railing. No, nothing to do with him. Jerri. He was looking for Jerri.

Andel called his name, walking toward him, but he ignored it.

She focuses on the stern deck under her feet. This is the ground she has to defend. Her husband sleeps beneath her, and there's a killer on the ship. She brings up her power, willing herself to be silent, mentally urging Calder to keep sleeping. There are so many reasons she needs to stop this Consultant here, before the assassin can accomplish her goal. The Sleepless have demanded it...

Calder jerked his hand away from the polished wood as though it burned, and Andel clapped him on the shoulder.

"I'm sorry, Calder," the Quartermaster said in a low voice. "The attacker got away. We spent all night searching the bay, but we didn't find any trace. Of anyone. We had to sail away the old-fashioned way before they tried again."

Calder met Andel's eyes. The other man's face, always so serious, now looked as though it belonged on a cemetery statue. "Who was it?"

Naberius strode over to answer that. "A Consultant by the name of Shera."

Stepping away from Andel, Calder moved to regard the Witness. "How do you know that?"

"I saw her many times in the Imperial Palace. She was one of the Emperor's personal assassins. A trained, deadly killer. We're lucky that any of us escaped with our lives."

His anger boiled, demanding release, demanding that he blame Naberius for something, that he pin this on the Chronicler somehow. But that would not satisfy him.

Only one thing would.

"You know her. Where will she take my wife?"

Naberius exchanged looks with Andel. "She's a murderer, Captain Marten. She does not take prisoners."

Calder envisioned grabbing Naberius by his lapels—his suit was a bright purple, today—and hurling the man bodily into the Aion Sea. *The Testament* groaned around him, ropes lifting into the air as though they were prepared to hurl the Witness into the ocean on Calder's behalf. Tristania stepped forward, one hand reaching into her coat.

He calmed himself. *"Anger is a cruel thief,"* Sadesthenes said. *"It gives one the illusion of focus, while stealing away the real thing."*

"This assassin. Shera. She didn't stab Jerri, just...pushed her overboard." He forced himself to speak rationally. "That would indicate, to me, that my wife could be alive. Somewhere."

Naberius folded his hands and tapped his thumbs together, thinking. "They would only keep her if she knew something they wanted, and even then..." He hesitated. "Even then, she would not live long. Can you think of anything she might have known that they would consider valuable?"

That which sleeps will soon wake.

"No. No, she didn't know anything."

Andel stared straight at Calder, but Calder forced himself not to meet the man's eyes. He knew. Andel had never quite trusted Jerri. For a good reason, as it turned out.

Naberius walked back over to his folding table, placing a compass next to the map. "The Consultants do not admit defeat," he said, looming over the map. "They will not stop until they have fulfilled their assignment, whether that's to see me dead or to sink this ship. We should press on."

Calder walked up to the wheel of his ship, nudging Foster away. The older man grumbled about it, but he stepped back. "I seem to recall that the headquarters of the Consultants is somewhere off the coast. Does anyone know where?"

The ship went quiet, but for the creak of boards, the slap of ocean against hull, and the distant clink of chains.

His anger boiled up again, and Calder pulled out his pistol, rapping the butt against the wood of the ship like a judge's gavel. *"Well?"*

"It's called the Gray Island," Andel finally said. "It's north and east." He stood with his arms crossed, and he obviously didn't approve. Otherwise, he would have made a joke.

Good thing Calder didn't care.

He turned the ship, keeping the rising sun slightly to starboard. The Chronicler protested as soon as the ship shifted beneath him.

"This is not the way! I assure you, this will not locate your wife."

"I'm sorry, Mister Clayborn, but there will be a slight delay before we reach your destination." And if he didn't like it, Calder could always feed him to the Lyathatan.

Naberius stepped up, beneath the wheel on the lower deck, so that Calder had no choice but to see him. The passenger's handsome face was the very picture of earnest openness.

"I sympathize entirely with your feelings. More than you realize. But the Gray Island is so named because it is shrouded in an impenetrable wall of mist year-round. More, the place is flush with tricks and deceptions. A perfectly sound-looking house could stand over a bottomless pit, so that you fall inside as soon as you take a step in the door. A field that seems empty could in fact contain traps of deadly poison. Not to mention that the island is crawling with Consultants. Even if it were empty of all human life, you could search the place for your entire life and never find where they keep their prisoners."

That speech had the distinct tune of exaggeration, to Calder's ear. There was no such thing as a *bottomless* pit, for one. Besides, he was a Reader. He'd find his wife if he had to walk barefoot across every inch of the island, sensing his surroundings with each step.

Naberius is a Reader, too, he reminded himself. *If he says it's impossible…*

The Chronicler took a step closer. "But it's not hopeless. I told you that I knew this Consultant, Shera. She is among the best in the Guild: if they've sent her once, they'll send her after us again. She knows she can't catch us at sea without a Navigator's ship, so she'll be moving to head us off. Which means your best chance of capturing her, and finding out what happened to Jyrine, is to *keep moving forward.*"

Calder gripped the wheel until his knuckles turned white. He wanted nothing more than to march straight into the Consultant headquarters, tear the walls down, and take his wife back.

But he'd tried tactics like that before. They…hadn't worked out.

"While the wise man listens to his advisors, the fool listens to his emotions." Sadesthenes again. Sometimes Calder hated the man.

"What are we looking for, Naberius?" he asked at last. "What treasure is worth this?"

The Chronicler spread his hands. "The greatest treasure the Emperor ever owned. The one thing that he never entrusted to another, in his almost two millennia of life."

"And that is?"

Naberius said nothing.

"Have it your way," Calder snarled. "What's the heading?"

Naberius didn't acknowledge his victory. He bowed and ran back to his map, looking between that and his compass.

Andel would be praying at this point, but Calder simply focused his Intent. Maybe it would change something.

Please, he silently begged. *Don't let me be too late.*

CHAPTER SIX

Yes, everyone invests objects with their Intent. It can't be avoided. If you're human and you use a tool, you will invest it.

Readers have a few inherent advantages in this process, it's true; most importantly, they can sense what changes they make and alter their Intent appropriately.

No, Readers are not more intelligent or attractive than anyone else. I should think you would be aware of that by now. Please stop asking.

– Artur Belfry, Imperial Witness
taken from a letter to his pupil,
Calder Marten (thirteen years of age).

THIRTEEN YEARS AGO

Lying on his bed, shortly after dawn, Calder rolled the Emperor's key between his fingers and thought.

The Emperor places his hand in the lock, twisting it, ignoring the pleas from the family within. 'We're innocent!' they say. 'Have mercy!' they plead. But they're not innocent, and so he leaves them to die.

With most objects, Reading took an intentional effort of will. He had to focus on the sensations he was picking up in the wood, on the Intent embedded within the physical structure of each object. If it had ever been made or used by a human being, for any purpose, it retained some of that Intent, whether a rock on the roadside or an Imperial soldier's spear.

Sometimes, it would take hours of focus to Read that Intent; to be able to enhance the remnants of human will into a physical effect. But with something the Emperor had used, for years, it took a substantial effort to not Read it.

He twists the key, but the dungeon lock sticks. It's old, though not nearly as old as the Emperor himself, and choked with rust. But he doesn't feel the resistance before his desire to have the door open, his wish to get this business done quickly, invests the key with enough Intent to spring the lock open.

'Kelarac will take your soul,' the woman growls, showing off her rotten teeth. 'Nakothi and Othaghor will share your body between them! That which sleeps will soon wake!'

If she weren't Soulbound, he would kill her now. But her powers might be useful in the future, so he twists the key again, willing it to seal the door. The lock snaps shut without a hitch.

If it had come from anyone except the Emperor, the vision would never have held so much detail.

Genuine Imperial artifacts—tools used by the Emperor in his everyday life, and thus harboring a measure of his limitless Intent—were not rare, but any Reader wanted them. A cloth used by the Emperor to dry his sweat could be a more powerful object than an Awakened weapon produced by a lesser Reader.

In the search for such artifacts, Calder had often followed trails of debris that the Emperor had incidentally brushed. A cobblestone on which he'd stepped, a sign he'd pushed past on a crowded street. With anyone else, such brief and accidental contact would leave no residue, but this was the Emperor. Anything he did left his surroundings more significant than before.

Thus armed with a library of glimpses, whispers, and half-visions of the Emperor, Calder had assembled something like a picture of the man. He was confident that he knew the Emperor as well as anyone else outside the Imperial Court.

And he was becoming convinced: the man was a monster.

He unlocks the dungeon, wishing he could leave this task to someone else. But this prison alone, of all the prisons in the world, he has to maintain personally. This is where he keeps people who have found his secrets.

Those who pass this door only do so once.

Calder didn't know how the key to the Emperor's personal dungeon had fallen outside the Imperial Court; usually, the Emperor would destroy anything that might harbor such sensitive Intent. Rojric, guided by his son, had picked it up from a dredger along with a bucketful of other junk.

If the Emperor learned of this key, he might even consider it dangerous. Having Read it might be even more of a crime than Rojric's.

He indulged himself in a brief fantasy of blackmailing the Emperor into commuting his father's sentence, but he quickly brought himself back on track. The Emperor would simply have them both killed.

That was the most frightening thing he'd learned from handling the key—the Emperor was capable of anything. And in a prison run by him, no inmates survived.

So what about Calder's father, locked in Candle Bay Imperial Prison? He was convicted of a crime against the Emperor's person, after all, though 'attempted purchase of an Imperial possession' was among the least of the crimes in that category.

Would the Emperor find out about Rojric? If he did, Calder was certain that his father would die in that cell. Perhaps it would take a few decades, but the Emperor was not the kind of man who tolerated personal insults.

Calder would have to do something.

Alsa knocked twice, sharply, and then entered without waiting. Hurriedly, Calder stuffed the key into the invested shirt pocket that had become its permanent home.

"Up!" she declared, throwing the curtains wide. "Your tutors arrive today."

He scrambled out of bed, eager to see the Guildsman she'd hired. "Tutors? I thought there was to be only one."

"In a sense, there is. I've retained the services of a pair of Witnesses. They've worked with the Blackwatch before, and they were looking for a seasonal job over the next four or five years."

She began plucking clothes out of his wardrobe, laying them out on the bed while he waited awkwardly nearby.

"Isn't that what the servants are for?" he asked at last.

She didn't look up from her work, smoothing out the wrinkles in a navy blue walking-jacket. "It's been almost ten years since I've seen my son. I let the servants choose your clothes when you were an infant, and in the years since, I have come to regret that."

Alsa gave the clothes one last pat, as though to finish them off, and then smiled over at him. "Hurry up and dress; our guests will be joining us for breakfast."

As soon as the door was shut, Calder stuffed his shirt—along with the key—into the drawer at the base of the wardrobe. He had made it very clear that the drawer was filled with his private possessions, and she had promised to honor his privacy. But he still invested the pocket every morning, just in case.

One never knew when the Imperial Guard might come around, asking questions.

Last night, Calder had expected one guest this morning—his new tutor.

A few minutes ago, when he found out about the pair of Witnesses, he had expected two.

Now, to his surprise, he found that they had *three*.

The Witnesses sat together on one side of the table, next to his mother at the head. A pair of Heartlanders, they were also brothers: Artur and Vorus Belfry.

"It is quite common for siblings to join the Witnesses together," Artur explained, lifting a forkful of fruit salad to his mouth. His shirt strained at the seam from the pressure of his bicep, which was bigger around than Calder's neck. He must have stood almost seven feet tall, and heavier than three of Calder's father.

"I am the Chronicler," Artur went on. "I Read and record Imperial history as I witness it, then I spread that knowledge to others." He patted his belt, which was packed with candles. All but one were wrapped in brown paper; the one bare cylinder of wax was snow white and half-burnt. "My brother is my Silent One, my guide and bodyguard. He covers his mouth as a symbol of his refusal to speak secrets."

From size alone, Calder would have expected Artur to be fighting as a Champion in an arena, not recording history. Except that gladiators were almost always descended from the light-haired Izyrian tribes, not citizens of the civilized Aurelian Heartlands.

But his brother...Vorus looked like a sparrow. A sparrow in glasses.

Vorus adjusted his spectacles when he was mentioned, then he tugged his scarf down to take a bite of his muffin. He pulled the scarf back up to chew. The Silent One was taller than Calder, and just as thin. Where Artur looked like he could push a bull up a mountain, Vorus looked as though he would have trouble sliding his plate across the table.

Which of them was supposed to be the bodyguard?

As interesting as the two Witnesses were, they couldn't hold Calder's attention compared to their *third* guest.

Jyrine Tessella was exactly his age, the daughter of a Watchman who had died in the line of duty.

"Her father was a close friend of mine," Alsa had said during Jyrine's introduction. *"She could never afford an education without his income, and a tutor can teach two students as well as one."*

Calder had certainly not complained. Between her tanned skin and long braid of brown hair, her dangling emerald earrings and her bold smile, she was like the genteel version of those Vandenyan dancers his father admired.

"In a few years, she'll turn heads," his father would have said. She was doing a wonderful job of turning Calder's head already.

He should thank Alsa later. By bringing him a pair of tutors and Jyrine, his mother was actually giving him *two* gifts: experts to admire his accomplishments, and a beautiful audience.

Artur took a sip of tea gently, as though he were afraid he might crush the cup in his grip. "So, children, let's get to know one another. You are both familiar with the works of Sadesthenes, yes?"

"Of course," Jyrine said.

"'Why do the petty tribes of the earth waste their time on war?'" Calder quoted. "'Don't they know that their struggles must end the same way: in a single Empire for all the world?'"

Vorus shook his head, still chewing behind his scarf.

"That's an impressive quotation from Prion the Fourth," Alsa said, her eyes on her meal. "He wrote a continent away from Sadesthenes, and a century apart."

Jyrine's earrings caught the light as she grinned at Calder. "But other than that, they might as well be the same man! Calder was clearly pointing out the similarity in their views on Imperial conquest. Both of them saw the Emperor's expansion as a natural part of the universe, decreed by Fate."

Artur suppressed his own smile, shaking his empty fork in Jyrine's direction. "That is exactly what Calder meant, I have no doubt."

Right then, Calder vowed to read more of Sadesthenes.

"We will still cover Sadesthenes, I think, simply to...enhance your familiarity. We can take a look at the foundational works of the other philosophers as well, and you can let us know if one in particular piques your interest." He speared a slice of apple, moving it to his plate. "And since the philosophies rely so heavily on Imperial history, we will study that at the same time. Of course, that's more Vorus' area of expertise than mine, isn't it?"

Artur returned to his plate, slicing his apple into bite-sized pieces.

Vorus, of course, said nothing.

After a few seconds of crippling silence, Artur chuckled. "Just a little joke, I apologize. We do tease one another."

His brother looked as though he had never heard of a joke, and would certainly never tell one.

Jyrine leaned forward, both elbows on the table. "History and philosophy are essential, of course, but I'd like to hear more from you. You two have been all over the Empire, haven't you? You must have stories like no one else!"

"Yes!" Calder piped up, eager to rejoin the conversation. "I've heard stories about the Chroniclers and their candles. Is it true that you can store memories?"

Suddenly both Witnesses turned to Calder's mother, who stared at her son.

"He didn't hear about it from *me*," Alsa said pointedly. "Calder, who told you that?"

His father had, of course, but Calder did what he always did when he wanted to deflect more questions: he smiled. "I've always been fascinated by the Witnesses, and I've tried to learn everything I could about them. Rumor only, of course, but I'm always hungry to learn more about the Guilds. Mother, didn't we speak the other day about the possibility of my joining the Witness' Guild?"

"We did indeed," she said dryly.

Jyrine's eyes widened. "It's true, then? You can store memories in the wax of a candle?"

Artur sighed, glancing at his silent brother. "It is not something we advertise, but it is also not quite a secret. There is no such thing as perfect memory, so we devised an alchemical wax that is particularly sensitive to Intent. It can record a few days' worth of memories, so that when I burn the candles later, I relive the events exactly as they occurred. Thereby, I ensure the accuracy of my own recollection."

She placed a hand on Calder's, excited. "That's incredible! I've never heard of such a thing."

As she did, Calder noticed a spidery tattoo on her left hand. The line of script, which was nothing like Imperial, began under the nail of each finger and crawled along the back of her hand, joining into one stream that vanished into her left sleeve.

He blushed, tearing his eyes away. "It is, isn't it? It's one of the reasons I find the Witnesses so fascinating."

Under her breath, Alsa grunted.

Jyrine gave her tutors a charming smile. "Will you burn one for us, sometime? I'd love to relive a battle, or a Kameira hunt, or a duel!"

Artur drained the last of his tea. "The realm has been peaceful for the duration of our career. We have only been forced to fight a small number of times, and nothing you might call a battle."

Suddenly, the Witnesses actually did seem like an interesting career choice. "Fights, you say?"

Vorus gave them a disapproving look over his glasses, and his brother seemed to agree. "I expected a young boy to be interested in battles and duels, but a young lady ought to have more sense."

"Oh no, don't hold back on my account," Jyrine said, smiling as eagerly as Calder. "Does Vorus do all the fighting, or do you fight back-to-back?"

"Today, I thought we would cover an introduction to *philosophy,*" Artur said firmly. As one, Jyrine and Calder sighed.

Alsa stood up from the table, waving at a maid to clean her place. "I have to be going. There's a Guild project that will not wait for me any longer."

As she walked past him, Alsa ruffled Calder's hair. "Try not to spend too long on your war stories, will you, Artur?"

The Chronicler drew himself up straight. "Of course not, madam. And my thanks, for serving the Empire as faithfully as you have."

Alsa waved behind her as she left.

As soon as she was gone, a question leapt from Jyrine's mouth. "She works for the Blackwatch? What does she do, exactly? I've heard such stories!"

"Don't ask me," Calder said. "I've never heard, except that it involves something called a Whispering Gaunt."

Artur shivered, and Vorus made a strange sign in the air: he drew a circle with his fingers, roughly parallel with his own face.

"It's best not to speak of such things," Artur said.

Like a cat spying a mouse's tail, Jyrine pounced. "*What* such things? My father would never tell me either."

"It's very difficult to avoid a subject when you don't know which subject to avoid," Calder joined in.

Between the two of them, Artur wilted. "What do you know about the Blackwatch?"

"They defend us from the Elders," Jyrine said.

"They worship Elders and drink human blood," Calder whispered.

Jyrine pointed at Calder without taking her eyes from Artur. "His version sounds much more colorful."

"More colorful usually means less correct," the tutor responded. "It is my job to make sure that you are operating on correct information. And I do happen to know quite a bit about the Blackwatch..."

Both Jyrine and Calder leaned forward even more, scenting weakness.

Then Artur held up a book, a copy of Sadesthenes' *From Rising Sun to Setting Moon.* "When we finish this volume, I would be happy to answer one question from each of you. Without violating any Guild secrets, of course."

Calder slumped in his chair, disappointed, but Jyrine narrowed her eyes. "What if we have more questions?"

The Chronicler grinned. "Fortunately for you, I have more books."

CHAPTER SEVEN

For a Navigator, Calder wasn't a very good navigator.

That had been Jerri's job, more than his: reading the maps and the stars, comparing them to the compass, telling him which direction to go as he steered the ship. She was the pilot, he was just the captain. Without her, he had to rely entirely on Naberius, with occasional input from Andel.

Therefore, he was effectively taking it on faith that they were headed in the right direction.

At the moment, he had focused his entire body and Intent to steering *The Testament* through the Starlight Spires—mountainous spikes of some silvery metal that stuck up from the water like a porcupine's quills. At night, the Spires supposedly lit up with spots of white light as though they were covered in stars, but Calder would rather swim through than try and navigate these turns after sundown.

Some of the silver Spires were too close to one another to squeeze through, and others didn't reach entirely out of the water. Off to port, he saw the sun-bleached remnants of a ship that hadn't cleared one of the sunken Spires, so the metal spike gouged a chunk out of the hull, leaving the corpse of the vessel impaled forever.

It didn't look like a Navigator ship, so it was that captain's own fault for venturing this far into the Aion. Still, it was a grim reminder of what could happen if Calder lost concentration for even a moment.

He couldn't rely on the Lyathatan to pull them through, either. Alien irritation flowed up through the ship, burning Calder's mind with its sullen resentment. The Elderspawn was not at all happy that it had to dodge around sunken silver spikes, so it couldn't spend the day sleeping as it normally did. If Calder called upon the Lyathatan now, he had the uncomfortable feeling that he'd end up dining with Kelarac on the bottom of the sea.

Dalton Foster stomped up the ladder to the stern deck, cradling a musket in one arm and a bottle in the other. Calder nodded to him without taking his eyes from the closest Silver Spire.

"Duster," he said pointedly. Foster had a history of forgetting his false name.

The old gunner grunted. "So. It's been a week."

Aching pain shot through Calder's gut, but he kept his expression blank. He'd tried to spend the last week distracting himself with work, and the crew had mostly stayed out of his way. He should have known it was too good to last.

"We probably have another week until we get there," Calder said, in an attempt to keep the conversation on their voyage. At another time of the year, the trip wouldn't have taken so long: the coordinates Naberius pointed out on the map was at the very edge of what Navigators called the Deep Aion. It was far enough into the sea that only members of Calder's Guild could get there, but still only a few days from shore in a straight line.

The 'straight line' part was what got people killed. This time of year, a Deepstrider migration ran parallel to the coast, and the Kameira would reduce his ships to matchsticks if he tried to drive straight through them. He'd heard rumors that Lhirin Island had drifted west, so he'd have to spend another few days looping wide enough around the island. He didn't want his crew to start eating each other, as the last Navigators to land on the nomadic isle had. And he couldn't move at full speed through the Silver Spires. All in all, it turned a four-day trip into a two-week voyage.

Traveling through the Aion Sea boiled down to nothing more than choosing between one delay, an even worse delay, and a horrible death.

Foster grunted again, looking down at the pair of spectacles hanging against his beard. "I, uh, brought you something." He held out the bottle.

Calder angled the ship to take them into a relatively clear stretch of water, and then took a hand from the wheel to examine Foster's gift. It looked like an undersized wine bottle with a white label that read, simply, 'Batch 419.'

He tugged out the cork and took a swig, expecting the bitter wash of cheap wine. Instead, he was greeted by a wash of fruity flavor that reminded him of peach.

When did we get a vintage like this?

"Alchemical wine?" he asked curiously. After a second, he took another drink. His parents would both have been offended for different reasons: his mother would have argued that he was abusing the wine by drinking it directly from the bottle, and his father would have wanted him to share.

Foster shrugged. "How should I know? I got it from Petal."

Calder sprayed a mouthful of orange wine onto the deck.

"Not good? Oh well, I'm sure she's got more. I thought, uh, you might like to hit some targets for a while."

Foster hefted the musket.

Calder ignored him, focusing on his body. Did he feel a warmth running through his veins? Was it poison? Something worse? Should he have himself locked in the hold?

"Foster...I mean, Duster. What was in that?"

The gunner frowned, confused. "Wine?"

"If Petal put nothing else in that bottle, I'll give you my share from this job."

Foster reached into his jacket, pulling out a few rolled up papers that looked as though they'd been torn from a book. "She wouldn't poison you, you know that."

In point of fact, he *didn't* know that.

He held up the papers, on which he'd drawn targets. "Where do you want me to set these up?"

Calder adjusted their course to keep them from running into a partially submerged Spire. "I'm a little busy here, *Duster.* If I stopped to shoot for an hour, we'd all be dead."

Foster shifted from foot to foot, looking at his handful of targets. "It helped me," he said at last.

Calder stopped. If anyone understood how he was feeling, it was Foster. He'd had a reputation as a world-class gunsmith, which had earned him quite a fortune among the Empire's elite. It was once considered quite a distinction to own a Dalton Foster original. Even Naberius bragged about it.

But that was before the Emperor's death.

Afterwards, until the four Regents and the Imperial Guard restored order, the Capital had spent a few months swallowed in chaos. An opportunist had found Foster, kidnapped his family, and forced him to make a gun. Every day until he'd finished, Foster's family was tortured.

Not all of them made it.

The survivors, scarred and scared, had abandoned Dalton Foster. His own wife and children. As far as Calder knew, the man hadn't seen or heard from them for years.

Calder's lips stretched into a grin.

Foster scowled, crumbling the targets in his fist. "Something funny, Captain?"

He shook his head furiously, still grinning. "No, it's...I can't...I can't stop smiling."

Out on the deck, a frizzy head poked up through the trap door to the hold. Petal looked at him with beady eyes, and then hurriedly ducked back down.

"Ah," Dalton said. "So that's what was in the wine."

For Petal, it was actually pretty good logic. If Calder wasn't happy, then slip him some sort of concoction to make him smile. He'd have to watch his food for the next few days; once she found out this batch hadn't worked, she would try a newer version.

"Thanks for trying, Foster. Some other time, perhaps." The words might have sounded a little less ridiculous if Calder wasn't smiling like a painted fool.

Foster nodded and walked off. Calder honestly couldn't tell if the man was offended or relieved.

A hand clapped him on the back, sending him crashing into the wheel.

"It is good to see you smiling again, Captain! The worse life gets, the better it is to smile!"

True to his word, Urzaia was grinning as he loomed over Calder, proudly displaying his two missing teeth. He planted hands on his hips, displaying his huge arms—one wrapped in leather, the other in gold-scaled hide.

Calder considered explaining about Petal and the wine, but decided it wasn't worth the trouble. Knowing Urzaia, he might think it was a great idea.

"A week is enough time for grieving," Urzaia said, leaning back with his elbows against the railing. "Now it is time to move on."

Calder turned his manic grin on his cook. "You think so, do you?"

"You misunderstand me, I think. Do not move on to a different wife—I have found it is best to do that slowly. Move on to the next step."

"The next step?"

Urzaia's smile was almost as broad as Calder's. "Vengeance."

Calder hadn't thought of anything else for the past week. He wasn't sure who deserved revenge the most.

The Consultant, Shera? She was the one who had attacked them while they were sleeping, taking his wife from him.

But Consultants didn't work on their own. Who had hired her? Surely, they were the ones who really deserved a lead ball in the heart.

Then there was Jerri herself.

She had betrayed him. Lied to him for years. Even as they had fought against the Sleepless, it turns out she was one of *them.* And he had married her!

The best revenge might be to leave her where she is.

He couldn't make himself believe that. If he chose to hurt Jyrine the way she'd hurt him, he wanted to see it. How could he be satisfied when he didn't even know if she was alive or dead? Besides, he couldn't leave her in the hands of the Consultants. They might hurt her.

Calder didn't even understand his own feelings anymore. He only knew that he would never be satisfied until he found Jerri.

Urzaia pulled out one of his black-hafted hatchets, laying it across his palms. "It was my fault."

Calder turned on him, surprised. Thanks to Petal's potion, he didn't look shocked—he looked delighted. "Yours?"

The Woodsman looked up, and Calder realized he was talking to a different person. Not his cheerful cook, Urzaia, but the Izyrian gladiator. Banished to the arena in the hopes that the fights would kill him, Urzaia Woodsman had managed to survive for over a year against unstoppable odds.

And a single assassin had rendered him unconscious from the shadows.

"No, Urzaia, no. If she had stayed to fight you, you would have torn her apart, and she knew that. It's why she took you out first."

Urzaia looked down at his hatchet. "There were poisoners in the arena. They tried to hide and poison me. It has never stopped me before."

"Trust me—"

The cook cut him off. "And it will not stop me now. Jyrine has secrets, even from you. This is not good, but every man has secrets. You two will talk, and you will work it out. Once I have killed the Consultant and brought Jyrine home."

Calder simply nodded, grinning like an idiot.

"A Champion does not fail. Even one in disgrace, you understand?"

Urzaia slid his hatchet back over his shoulder. "I like you like this, smiling all the time. This is how you should be. I will tell Petal to drug you more."

Only a few minutes later, he got another visit, and this one was unexpected. Tristania walked up the short ladder to the stern deck, standing by the wheel and looking at him.

Just looking.

"What can I do for you?" he asked, smiling involuntarily.

He was not surprised when the Silent One said nothing. She simply stood there, watching him. Bandages shuffled as she shifted her weight, and her coat flapped behind her in the sea breeze like a flag. Little wisps of black hair stuck out of the wrapping covering her head, and her eyes…peeking out from between two white strips of cloth, her eyes were soft and sympathetic.

Which made her silence even stranger.

He coughed politely, trying to signal her to do something, though he was afraid his alchemy-induced smile was sending the wrong message. After a few seconds of standing and looking, she reached into her coat and pulled out…a blanket.

It wasn't particularly cold out, but he wondered if she wanted to sit on the deck. Maybe make it a picnic of sorts, and stare at him all afternoon. He didn't object to women looking at him, usually, but the thought seemed quite disturbing.

But she didn't spread the blanket out on the deck. Instead, she wrapped it around his shoulders, pressing in the corners like a mother tucking her child in to sleep.

He wasn't quite sure why, until she finished, patting him on the shoulder. She let her hand linger there, squeezing as if to give him strength, and then left.

For some reason, he had to blink back tears.

Hours passed after Tristania's visit, Calder's peace was not disturbed by anything more pressing than deadly metal spikes. The sun glowed red behind him, and faint white lights appeared on the Silver Spires.

He understood the rumors now. The lights did look like stars, and they didn't seem to be simple quicklamps set into the silver. Thousands of white sparks covered each towering spire, swirling slightly like fireflies trapped in a mirror. The show was faint, competing with the setting sun for attention, but he could easily imagine that the sight would be breathtaking in full darkness.

Not that he had any intention of remaining in this maze when night fell. The Spires would light his way, certainly, but he feared they would play tricks on his eyes, driving him to impale his ship. Even worse, he could think of several creatures in the Aion that hunted by night, lured to a glow on the surface of the water. They would be swirling around the Spires only minutes after sunset, hunting.

At last, the Spires had begun to thin. Only one tilted silver spike loomed ahead of him, with another passing beneath. After that, they'd be clear.

Calder's attention sharpened. He'd learned the hard way that you had to focus most carefully when it seemed you were safe. That's where a trap would do the most harm. It helped that Petal's potion had finally started to wear off, so his lips only occasionally smiled without permission.

He scanned the water for suspicious shadows, keeping half his mind on the Lyathatan. If anything disturbed the Elderspawn, he wanted to know about it as soon as possible.

So he didn't notice Andel until the Quartermaster stood two feet away, brushing a smudge from his white sleeve.

"Sir," Andel said, by way of greeting.

"Andel."

Normally they would have exchanged jokes, but Calder was focused on navigation. It was the perfect excuse. This was the conversation Calder had dreaded, and the one that he'd known was coming for over a week.

No one ever liked hearing 'I told you so.'

"The others have all said their piece by now," Andel said, still looking straight at the darkening horizon.

"Not Petal."

"She didn't drug you. That should tell you something."

"She *did* drug me!"

"You're still standing, so it hardly counts."

Calder gave a smile that was only half potion-induced. This easy, comfortable banter reminded him of the old Andel. Maybe this wouldn't be as bad as he feared; Andel might not have a well-deserved lecture in mind after all.

"I've waited a week to speak with you," Andel went on, and Calder slumped against the wheel.

"Must we, Andel? I know what you want to say. How about we both pretend you've already said it?"

Andel Petronus was many things, but he was not easily dissuaded. "You're angry right now. I don't think you know who deserves it most."

"Thank you for that analysis. If we could save the rest of this conversation for another time..."

"I'm sorry that we don't know if Jyrine is dead or alive. I wish we could have dealt with this another way. But for your sake, I am glad she's gone."

The potion twitched Calder's lips up, and he embraced it, baring a shark's grin at his Quartermaster. He sent his Intent down, into the boards of *The Testament*, and his Soulbound Vessel responded.

The seamless wood of the ship's deck rippled under Andel's feet like the surface of a struck lake. He stumbled and fell over backwards, hat rolling off his bald head.

Calder leaned over him. "Do not say that again, Andel. Not to me, and not on my ship."

From his seat on the deck, Andel made himself comfortable. He crossed his legs under him and looked up, seemingly unmoved. "Years ago, when I was a ship's boy on a merchant vessel out of Dylia, the First Mate of that ship took me in. Raised me like a father. From him, I learned something very important. More than enforcing the Captain's orders, more than keeping the rest of the crew in line, the Mate's job is to keep the Captain in check. It's to tell the Captain when he's on the wrong course, and when he's going to get himself and everyone else on board killed."

Andel's expression was calm, but firm. He was merely stating a fact. "Captain, you're on the wrong course. You're going to kill us."

Speaking of courses, Calder reminded himself to check their heading. He busied himself at the wheel with a compass, checking their position and scanning the water for any outlying Spires. It seemed they were mostly in the clear.

Which meant he had nothing to distract him from Andel.

His emotions demanded that he shout and rail at the man, maybe use the deck to toss him around some more. The waters seemed relatively clear: maybe a dunk would teach him that Calder was the one in charge here.

But the greater part of him recognized the childlike impulse for what it was, and crushed it. Andel's advice had saved his life on more than one occasion.

What was the point of having a cool-headed advisor if you never listened to his advice?

He prepared himself with a deep breath. "I apologize, Mister Petronus. Please continue."

Andel bowed slightly, still seated. "You know that I've never trusted Jyrine. And you know that I had my reasons."

Despite his attempts to ignore it, anger still seethed in Calder's chest. Was Andel really trying to provoke him?

"Continue," Calder said tightly.

"I am setting all of that aside right now. Let's assume that Jyrine was completely justified in keeping secrets, and that her loyalty is beyond question."

"Yes. Let's assume that."

"Then we're left with a few things to consider. First, why did the Consultant take Jyrine captive? For that matter, why did an assassin capture anyone at all?"

It was a good question, but not a new one. "We've run down that road already, Andel."

"All right, then let's move past the Consultant's intentions. What are the actual results of her actions? She has someone to interrogate, so we can assume that she'll know everything about our capabilities."

Calder tried very hard not to picture Jerri's interrogation.

"And you are left in the position of wanting to recover your wife, more than anything else. More than delivering the passenger. More than getting paid. More, even, than arriving safely at our destination. One way or another, that means that you will be trying to speak with Shera. True so far?"

"True enough," Calder admitted. He hadn't thought of it in so many words, but all of his plans for Shera the Consultant involved capturing her, or else tricking her into spilling Jerri's location.

"If she had not captured Jyrine, would you care about talking with her?"

With an assassin? He wouldn't want to get within earshot of the woman. "No, I would not."

"Instead, how would you deal with this woman?"

Calder considered for a moment, letting *The Testament* drift of its own accord out onto the relatively clear ocean. The Lyathatan had begun to sink back into sleep.

"Avoid her if at all possible," Calder said at last. "I'd try to dock somewhere she didn't expect, stay somewhere she wouldn't think to check, move the crew as a whole instead of splitting up, so we weren't vulnerable. If that didn't work, I'd try to trap her. Pretend we thought we were safe, and have Urzaia and Foster ambush her."

Andel nodded, still seated. "And now, instead of doing what the trained assassin least expects, we're going exactly where she wants us to go."

Realization settled on Calder's shoulders like a sack of bricks. Andel was right. They were playing right into the enemy's hands, which he would never have done if Jerri weren't in danger.

But...they had to. This was the only way to find Jerri.

"That," Andel said, "is how you're going to get us all killed."

For the next few minutes, with Andel sitting next to him, Calder steered in relative quiet. The wind flapped in the sails, and the waves still lapped against the hull. Behind him, Naberius and Tristania chatted about something. The clink of iron told him that Foster was working downstairs, and a snatch of some Izyrian battle-song meant that Urzaia had begun working on dinner.

Calder's thoughts ran in circles. He didn't want to put the crew in danger, but he didn't want to *leave* Jerri in danger. He was making no progress when he finally sighed and looked down at Andel.

"You're right, Andel. I'll think about it."

"We've got a little time. Assuming you don't drive us straight into a reef, we're not likely to die tonight."

From up in the crow's nest, a deafening masculine voice bellowed out, "DIE TONIGHT."

Then a black shadow bobbed down, fluttering across the red-gold sky until Shuffles landed on Calder's shoulder. It turned its scowling black eyes to Calder, wiggling its tentacles.

In case he didn't hear it the first time, it shouted, "DIE TONIGHT" one more time, straight into his ear.

Andel jumped to his feet, placing the white hat on his head. In volume no less than the Elderspawn, he announced, "Danger! All hands on deck! All hands on deck! That means you too, Petal!"

Foster was already climbing up to the crow's nest, musket and powder horn in hand. Urzaia strode up to the bow, a black hatchet in each hand. Petal snuck up the ladder carrying a crate of bottles, a rat curled up on top of them like a sleeping cat.

Naberius marched over, wearing his red suit again and resting on hand on his pistol. Tristania followed him, staring through her bandages into the waters.

"What danger?" Naberius asked. "What do you see?"

"Nothing," Calder said. The Aion Sea seemed to be playing nice, for the moment.

"Then why—"

Andel jerked a thumb at Calder's shoulder. "The Elderspawn only wakes up from a nap if it thinks we're all going to die."

"And it's in a good mood this time," Calder added. "That means it's nearby."

On his chiseled actor's face, Naberius' expression of confusion looked like it had come off of a classical painting: *Portrait of a Hero in Distress,* perhaps.

Distantly, a storm of glowing, sulfur-yellow clouds began to gather on the dark eastern horizon. They pulled together, like threads of shining unnatural mist.

"Name an Elder, and he appears," Calder muttered.

"Wormcloud," Andel announced, and the crew all made some sound in acknowledgement.

Naberius cleared his throat. "What in the Emperor's name is a 'worm cloud?'"

There was no point in trying to outrun a wormcloud—it would only follow them—so Calder steered straight for it. "If I'm not mistaken, Naberius, you're about to find out."

When the worms began to rain from the sky, the crew of *The Testament* was ready.

Calder kept his three-cornered hat on and his cutlass in hand, waiting for the worms to drop onto the deck. They landed with a splat, little fat grubs the size of a man's foot, with a single needle on their heads. Yellow light, exactly matching the unnatural cloud overhead, rippled inside their squishy bodies. They squeaked while squirming across the deck, searching for the nearest source of warm blood.

He slashed one in half, spilling its luminescent yellow fluid over the deck. He crushed another under his boot, and sent a mental pulse to the ship that made the railing surge up, tossing a third worm into the sea.

"Three!" he called.

Petal moved from worm to worm with a rubber-bulb dropper, planting a single drop of acid on the back of each creature. She spoke weakly as she moved. "Four...five...six..."

"Five!" Andel announced, kicking a worm over the edge.

Urzaia did not wear a hat. He stood with a hatchet in each hand, pacing the deck with eyes on the sky. When a worm fell anywhere close to him, one of his blades left a black blur, and two squishy halves fell to the wood. "I believe that makes eleven!" he yelled, splattered with drops of luminous blood.

A musket cracked overhead, and one of the worms exploded into goo. It had been distressingly close to Calder's face.

He winced back, glaring up at the crow's nest. "Seriously, Duster? Get down here and use your boots like an ordinary human being."

Foster lifted his second musket, tracking another worm. "Sorry, Captain. Every problem is best solved with firepower."

For the first time in over a week, Calder finally let himself relax. Wormclouds weren't the friendliest things in the world, but they were among the least harmful hazards of the Aion. Over the years, he'd begun to look forward to the break.

Naberius and Tristania, by contrast, were standing back-to-back on the same cask. The Silent One held a reversed broom, and was using the wooden haft to crush any worms that got too close. The Chronicler held a pistol in each shaking hand, though at least he wasn't firing and reloading as fast as he could, like Foster.

"Is this an attack?" Naberius asked, his voice higher-pitched than normal.

Calder swept a worm from his hat and then impaled it with his cutlass. "Twelve! And no, Naberius, this is the Aion."

"I've heard that Wormclouds stem from Kthanikahr," Andel said, as he casually strolled over a pair of worms, popping them. "That when the Emperor struck him down, the Great Elder personally blighted the weather."

Calder thought about it for a moment. "That would make sense, I suppose. Wormclouds. The Worm Lord. But I thought Kthanikahr's tomb was in northern Izyria. Thirteen."

"Sixteen. And how should I know where the Great Elders died? If only there were a member of the Blackwatch around, so that we could ask him."

Calder gestured to his own expression. "I may be smiling, but don't think that means you're funny."

Petal perked up. "I can make it so that you laugh...instead..."

"No thank you, Petal, the smiling is quite enough for now."

Naberius kicked a worm off the barrel, but at least he hadn't shot anyone yet. "So these worms are...harmless?"

"Oh no, not at all," Calder answered. "They have a poisonous bite that increases your body temperature. The infected, without exception, hurl themselves into the sea within minutes."

The Chronicler glanced up nervously. "Does that help?"

Calder let his awareness drift down through the ship, along the chains that bound the Lyathatan, until he was Reading the awareness of the Elderspawn itself.

Glowing worms swirl in the water, moving in a swarm. Each individual has a row of razor-sharp teeth in its circular mouth, and their hunger presses against the Lyathatan's skin like volcanic heat. Any one of them is thicker than the mast of the ship above, and long enough to wrap the Lyathatan completely in its coils.

There are hundreds in the water.

The Lyathatan bares its own teeth, opening its spirit. Let these lesser worms, these pathetic parasites born in a world of weakness, feel its contempt. Let them feel the malice, the hunger, the hatred of centuries. They may be able to shred humans to pieces, but there's no advantage in that. One might as well brag *about swatting fleas, or crushing blades of grass.*

The worms are all but mindless, knowing nothing but the need to feed.

They still know enough to keep their distance, waiting for prey to fall outside of the Lyathatan's reach.

"No," Calder said at last. "It doesn't help."

Naberius was obviously confused, but Andel took over. "We have an accomplished alchemist onboard, with an antidote prepared. There is a gap of several minutes between when you are stung and when you start trying to throw yourself overboard. And the worms themselves are slow, stupid, and easy to kill."

"EASY TO KILL," Shuffles chuckled. It swooped down on a worm, scooping the treat up with its tentacles and returning to a perch where it could enjoy its snack.

"Twenty-six!" Urzaia yelled. "Do not worry, Naberius. There are worse dangers than these in the Aion Sea. This is simply a fun game."

Naberius recovered his composure and hopped off his cask, crushing a worm beneath him. "In that case, thirty-one."

Petal pointed a finger at him, accusing. "Cheater!"

He shrugged. "She's my Silent One. Surely our scores should count together."

"From terrified to cheating in five seconds," Andel said. "You adapt quickly, Chronicler."

"I realized that you were right. Mild peril like this should not shake my composure. Particularly not considering what lies ahead."

Calder looked up, mentally ordering his Vessel to sweep a handful of worms away from him with a length of rope. "Now, there's an interesting subject. What *does* lie ahead, Naberius?"

Naberius stayed silent for a few seconds, the odd worm still falling to the deck behind him, and then nodded. "We're close enough that I believe it's safe to tell you. We travel to the island where Nakothi herself was buried. The island was warped by her influence, until it resembles little more than a corpse itself. I have only visited the place once in person, but we were set upon by...monstrosities." He shuddered, though Calder was sure he had faked the gesture. "Children of the Dead Mother. Hideous beasts that haunt my nightmares even now.

"Mark my words. What we see on the island will make this 'worm cloud' seem like a pleasant spring rain. You will all earn your fees then.'

CHAPTER EIGHT

Certain objects share the mysterious powers of Elders or Kameira. These are usually made from remnants of the creature's body—a sword made from a Nightwyrm's claw, for instance, or a pendant made from Lyathatan scales. These items have mysterious and anomalous effects, and should be treated with caution.

However, when such objects are Awakened, a mysterious phenomenon can be observed.

Under specific conditions, a human being can be bound to these powerful objects during the Awakening procedure. Afterwards, that person can draw on that item as a source of power.

We call such people Soulbound, and such objects Vessels.

I believe that somewhere in this process lies the key to traveling the Aion Sea.

– FROM THE RESEARCH JOURNAL OF THE FIRST NAVIGATOR

TWELVE YEARS AGO

Calder had been living with his mother for more than a year now, and for most of that time she had worked on some secret project.

His questions, aimed both at his tutors and at Alsa herself, revealed very little.

"It's a secret project," his mother told him. "If I told you the details, it wouldn't be very secret, would it?"

Artur was even less forthcoming. "As you know, the Emperor formed the Blackwatch to turn the power of the Elders against them. Such knowledge is known to drive strong men insane. I would think three times before asking too many questions, and then three times again."

Vorus, of course, said nothing at all.

He'd gotten most of his information from the odd comment his mother left lying behind her as she went to work.

"Bring me my jacket, would you? The breeze off the bay is biting."

"Don't head down to the harbor today, Calder. It's supposed to be dangerous."

"Whichever Guild you choose, make sure it's not the Navigators. They're con men at best, pirates at worst."

The facts came in dribbles, months apart, but Calder and Jyrine kept their ears sharpened to catch each one.

Today, they had finally decided to do some hands-on investigation.

It was an unseasonably cold day in autumn, which gave them an excuse to wear hoods and heavy coats. Even if Alsa did spot them hovering around her workplace, she shouldn't be able to see much of their faces.

Calder, after a moment's hesitation, even belted a sword around his waist. There were so many around the Grayweather house that his mother would never notice a single one missing, and it was currently fashionable for men to wear blades in public. It made men who had grown up in the peaceful Capital look like they could handle themselves in a fight, and a swordsman could never cause too much trouble with all the Imperial troops carrying pistols.

The sword would make him look older, so no one would think to find a fourteen-year-old inside his hood. Besides, his mother had been training him. If they were caught, he might be able to fight his way free.

They snuck out of the house on the pretense of buying books down in the city, giving Artur and Vorus time to relax.

Of course, the tutors were under the impression that the children would be chaperoned by Alsa, and Alsa that they were still under the care of their tutors. That lie had taken a tricky bit of coordination, but between them, they'd managed it.

So it was that Calder found himself walking down the streets of the Capital toward the Candle Bay harbor, Jyrine on his arm and a sword at his belt.

He couldn't recall anything better happening to him in his entire life.

Jyrine's grip tightened on his arm as the harbor came into view. "Look at that," she whispered, pointing.

She didn't need to point—there was only one thing of interest happening in the harbor. A wooden scaffold covered most of the horizon, blocking off more than its share of the harbor. All the other ships were shoved off to one side, almost hull-to-hull with one another.

The scaffolding was so thick that it might as well have been a wooden wall between them and the water. Here and there he caught glimpses of rope lines, a stretch of mast, a few yards of sail.

"Are they building a ship?" Jyrine asked.

Calder stared at the scaffolding as though he could will it to disappear. "That must be a disguise. My mother hates the water. And she's certainly not a shipwright."

"But what else could they possibly be doing?"

Left with no other obvious alternative, the two of them kept walking closer and closer to the harbor. The Capital was vast, and Calder had never visited this particular harbor before. He had traveled to the Imperial prison several times, but that building was all the way across Candle Bay. This side of the bay was a total mystery to him.

Workers crawled all over the wooden frame, some shirtless and banging away with hammers, others wearing leather harnesses and dangling from climbing-ropes. A man who looked like a Magister stood on the dock, shouting something and waving a reddish staff over his head with both hands.

Jyrine squeezed his arm again. "Are you willing to get in trouble?"

They hadn't discussed the plan this far, but there was only one thing they could possibly do. He gave her a grin. "You go left, I'll go right."

Without the slightest hesitation, Jyrine split off to the left, stuffing her hands into her coat pockets and walking down to the dock. Calder moved to the right, doing the same.

There was a reason they had chosen to wear coats of solid, unrelieved black.

The Blackwatch stood around the dock at the base of the scaffolding, but not standing guard. They probably didn't need to—one could easily tell a Watchman by their black uniforms, and most people avoided the Blackwatch at all costs. They were supposed to have power over Elders, and no one wanted to risk that fate. Unsavory rumors suggested that, if you interfered with a Watchman in the course of her duties, you might find yourself face-to-face with the faceless.

All of which worked to Calder's advantage.

A knot of black-clad men and women stood around a makeshift table of stacked crates, arguing over what looked like a map.

"We need more iron," one of the women said.

"More iron? What, for ballast? Why should we keep building a trap if we can't catch anything?"

"We never will, if we don't get another Reader."

"Are the bindings in place?"

"That's Grayweather's area, but good luck finding her."

Calder's ears perked up at the mention of his mother, but he didn't show any reaction. He walked past the cluster of Watchmen, armed with confidence and a black coat. One of the men nodded to him as passed, and Calder nodded back.

Heart hammering, he ducked under the lowest wooden beam forming the box around the dock. No one tried to stop him. No one even seemed to notice.

Once he was past the scaffolding, he saw what his mother had been working on for the better part of the past year.

The ship had a hull built of smooth wood, of a green so dark that it was almost black. There were no sails, leaving the mast sticking up like a tree with no leaves. Workmen bustled around the ship's deck, nailing planks down or moving brushes over the railing. Shimmering gold leaf on the side of the hull proudly announced the vessel's name: *The Testament.*

But the most unusual aspect of the ship's construction lay on the docks.

A pair of shackles, big enough to wrap around a whole house, sat unlatched on the docks. Each shackle was bolted to an enormous chain, which slithered down the dock and vanished under the water, terminating at some point under the ship.

Far from enlightening him, the sight raised a forest of new questions. What was the point of dragging two enormous chains behind the ship? Wouldn't they anchor it in place? Were the shackles supposed to lock on to the ocean floor, or were they meant to hold something? A pair of Kameira, perhaps?

He had a sudden vision of this ship being pulled by two great sea serpents, the shackles wrapped around their necks like collars, and the idea seized his imagination. Perhaps there were no sails because this ship didn't need sails: it would move across the Aion Sea solely under the propulsion of its captive beasts.

But it didn't explain the greatest mystery.

Why does a ship like this need Blackwatch help?

He stood gazing at the vessel for a moment longer, hoping that Jyrine had managed to make it in here undetected, when he felt a metal point sticking through his coat on the back of his neck.

An unfamiliar woman's voice spoke from behind him. "You're carrying steel. You know how to use it?"

"Let me draw it, and I'll show you," he said, his mouth moving on its own.

The woman laughed and pulled the point away from his neck. "It's a duel, then!"

Calder turned, drawing his saber.

Behind him, holding a curved saber almost identical to his own, stood a woman who looked nothing at all like a Watchman. She wore no black, for one thing: a bright blue vest over a loose white shirt, a checkered scarf, and gray pants covered in more patches than original fabric. Her long hair, which she wore tied back, was the exact same shade of red as Calder's.

When she saw him, her face fell, and she lowered her blade. "Elder's *bones,*" she spat. "I'm not picking on a boy. Get out of here, kid, before I put you in the water."

Calder pushed back his hood, then raised the point of his own saber. "You have beautiful hair."

Then he lunged, intending to prick her in the shoulder. That would teach her to underestimate an armed opponent.

She slapped his blade away with hers, now grinning. "I could say the same to you." She stepped forward, testing him with a short strike.

Calder managed to turn it away. The woman was much, *much* faster than he'd expected. He needed to keep her talking. "What's your name, young lady?"

Her eyebrows rose even as she cut off a slice of his coat sleeve. "Young lady? Kelarac's balls, boy, I've got ten years on you at least."

He feinted for her neck, and then ducked low, aiming for her leg. Her arm seemed to move independently of her body, turning his blade away without her reacting at all.

"I'm Calder," he panted, already losing his breath.

"Cheska Bennett. Member of the proud Guild of Navigators, and recently made captain of *The Eternal.*" She didn't bother going on the offensive, waiting for him to take the initiative.

"Calder Marten." He took advantage of the space to give his breath to return.

A workman tried to edge his way around Cheska, but she pushed him off the dock without looking. "Who taught you to fence, your kid sister?"

"His mother, actually," Alsa Grayweather said, peeling off her gloves as she hopped down from the ship.

Calder hurriedly shoved his sword back down into its sheath, though Cheska glanced from one of them to the other. "*Your* son? Really? But he seems like so much fun."

"He takes after his father," Alsa said flatly, resting her hand on the hilt of her own sword. On her, it didn't look like a fashion statement. "I'm trying to teach him to act like an adult. By, for instance, *not* dueling strangers in public for no reason."

Cheska finally slid her blade away, still grinning. "Aw, don't be like that. I caught somebody sneaking in, and I was having a little fun with him before I sent him away. Seems like you've been slacking on the fencing lessons, though."

Alsa's grip tightened on her sword. "Would you like one of your own, then?"

The Navigator Captain backed away, hands empty and raised. "You're a hothead, Grayweather. One day, that temper of yours'll get somebody killed. See you again, Calder."

With a cheery wave, she walked off.

Behind her, a grumbling workman hauled himself out of Candle Bay.

"*Navigators,*" Alsa spat. She turned to Calder, seemingly just as angry. "I'll have you know that I caught Jyrine myself, and I have sent her straight back home. What do you suggest I do with you?"

Calder looked up hopefully. "Give me a job?"

Calder knew that, if he approached this situation carefully, he would end up locked at home under strict guard, with most of his privileges suspended.

So he decided to plunge recklessly forward.

"Surely there's something I can do to help," he said to his mother. She had escorted him some distance away from the harbor, and now the two of them sat at a small table in the shelter of a tea-shop.

Alsa pinched the bridge of her nose. "This is Guild business, Calder. Certainly, we can always use more Readers, but we haven't fallen so low as to recruit...men as young as yourself."

She sounded certain, but Calder had seen the way her eyes drooped and her shoulders fell when she came home, sometimes late at night. They were working her ragged, which meant they didn't have many Readers to choose from. Why not Calder?

And if he was working on their special project, his mother couldn't punish him for sneaking around.

"It looked to me like you can use every hand you can get. How many other Readers do they have working here?"

"The Guild is spread very thin lately. We were expected to have three more, but..."

A thought struck Calder that had never occurred to him before. "Are you the *only* Reader on this project?"

Loose strands of Alsa's hair fell over her eyes as she slumped over the table. "Two others, to begin with. First one was called off, and then the other, and they kept promising—"

The fatigue blew away from Alsa like a hat in the wind, and she stood up, stock-still. All the other voices in the shop drifted off into silence.

Not knowing what else to do, Calder stood up too.

"Guild Head," Alsa snapped, bowing crisply at the waist.

A young woman stood on the inside of the shop door as it closed behind her. Her long hair, which almost brushed the floor, was a shade of blond so white as to be almost silver. The color probably came straight from an alchemist's bottle. She wore only a long black coat that covered her entirely from the neck down, with a line of silver buttons fastening down the front.

At first glance, Calder thought she was his own age. Then he wondered if perhaps she might be even younger. But as she walked closer to their table, she carried herself with the businesslike bearing of a much older woman.

She did not sit, nodding first to Alsa, and then to Calder.

"I spoke with Cheska," she said, and her voice was high and clear, like a child's. "We had a visitor, didn't we?"

Alsa stared straight ahead, her back rigid. "Yes, ma'am. This is my son Calder, ma'am."

The girl looked at him without any recognizable expression. "Calder Marten. I am Bliss."

What kind of a name is Bliss? he wondered. And it still bothered him that he couldn't tell how old she was.

But his mother had called her 'Guild Head.'

He bowed deeply at the waist. "I'm Calder Marten, Madam Bliss. I do apologize—"

"Just Bliss. If you like, you can call me Guild Head." She squinted, as though she were having trouble seeing him properly. "Shouldn't we sit, in an establishment like this?"

In such chill and windy weather, the tea-shop was somewhat packed. Over two dozen people had turned to watch the three people in black coats, standing stiffly instead of sitting with their tea.

Calder slid into a seat next to his mother, trying not to blush. Bliss considered her chair as though she'd never seen one before, then abruptly plopped herself down. "What has your mother told you of our project down at the harbor, Calder Marten?"

"Nothing, Bliss, but—"

"Guild Head," she corrected.

He paused for a second. She had given him permission to call her by her name, hadn't she? But he continued nonetheless.

"I'm sorry, Guild Head—"

"Bliss."

"Bliss," he repeated, confused.

"Guild Head."

Now he was getting frustrated. He forced a smile. "What would you like me to call you, ma'am?"

She shrugged. "I don't care. I wanted to see how long you'd put up with it." She poured herself a cup of tea, and Calder realized that not only had his tea arrived, but she had stolen his cup.

He rushed on, trying not to show his irritation. "My mother hasn't told me anything. I snuck down here against her will, because I wanted to see what she was working so hard on. And from what I can tell, your Guild is in desperate need of Readers."

Bliss trailed a finger in her cup of tea, drawing lazy spirals in the liquid's surface. It was hard to tell if she was paying any attention.

Alsa didn't say a word. Nor did she pour herself any tea.

"I am quite a skilled Reader, as it happens," he went on.

The Blackwatch Guild Head nodded absently, sticking her finger in her mouth.

"I could work for you, on this project."

Now Bliss was blowing on the surface of her tea, watching the ripples bounce of the inside of the teacup.

"I can work hard, and I can keep a secret." He decided to play the 'sympathetic son' card. "It pains me to see my mother working so hard on something, and with me not able to help. I'm sure you can understand."

Bliss tilted her head quizzically. "No, not really." She turned to Alsa. "Will he be a security risk?"

"No," Alsa said hoarsely.

Excellent. His mother was vouching for him. If the Guild Head said he could work there, surely no one else would have any problems.

"I'm glad," she said. "I wanted to leave his memories intact."

In the cold, a drop of sweat rolled down Alsa Grayweather's cheeks. "You brought it here?"

"Of course I did, don't be silly. It's in my coat."

Slowly, it dawned on Calder that he might have jumped into a cauldron that was deeper and hotter than he had expected.

"Do you know what we do at the Blackwatch, Calder Marten?" Bliss asked. She had tilted her tea saucer up on one side and was trying to spin it like a top.

"I'm taught that you study the Elders in order to defend the Empire against them."

The saucer clattered to the table and she picked it up, trying again. "What do we *do*, though? What have you heard?"

She sounded as if she herself wasn't sure. "I imagine you study ancient texts of the Elder Days. Search through ruins, old journals, that kind of thing. I've heard that you look for Elder cults and bring them to justice."

Those were all safe guesses, fueled by Artur's teaching and Calder's own textbooks. Even when he surreptitiously Read his mother's belongings, he got the impression of a woman who spent most of her time researching and the rest traveling.

Finally, Bliss got the saucer to spin on its own. "Why would we need to search through ancient journals, Calder Marten? We can study the Elders now. Here. Under scalpel and scope."

He couldn't tell if she was joking or not, but he smiled to show her that he wouldn't be easily fooled. "I'm sure their remains still exist, but it can't be the same as when they were actually...roaming the..."

Calder trailed off. The saucer, instead of slowing down, had begun to spin faster and faster. Bliss wasn't touching it; indeed, she seemed not to notice.

With an audible 'whoosh,' one of the other diners burst into flames.

He jerked his head over to get a closer look, but the woman seemed fine, flipping her news-sheet over to read the back.

Something slithered behind the counter, dragging wet tentacles across the tiled floor. When he looked closer, he saw nothing, not even a trail of slime. Had he imagined it, in the corner of his eye? Or was it lurking out of sight?

The windows in the front of the shop shattered, spraying shards all over the room. His eyes snapped to them, but the glass was smooth and whole.

All the while, the saucer spun faster and faster. A wisp of smoke rose from the tabletop.

Bliss took a sip of her tea, and then turned the cup upside-down. Nothing spilled. "If you want to play on our side, you should at least know the game. The Elders are not gone, Calder Marten. They're not dead. Most of them are not even sleeping. They are here, all around us, and the only ones standing between you and their endless hunger are a handful of soldiers in black."

A dark fog rolled in through the walls, billowing closer and closer. He jerked back, almost knocking his chair over, and spun around to run, but the fog closed in from all directions. Something moved in the darkness, a misshapen shadow. A wet piece of meat—warm and sticky—slid down his back, and he fumbled with his coat, but then a hand reached out of the fog for his face. He jerked back, raising his arm to shield his eyes.

The saucer fell to a stop, clattering on the tabletop. Everything was normal: the fog was gone, the tea-shop spotless, the air clear and the light sunny.

Except that the other diners had vanished. Only three people now sat at the shop—two seated women and one young man, standing alone and shivering, all three wearing black.

Bliss replaced something in the inner pocket of her coat, something that looked like a spike of yellowed bone. "We can't afford to hire people part-time, Calder Marten. There are things waiting for us in the dark places of the earth, and you will either stand with us against them, or you will stand aside."

Shaking, sheathed in sweat, and trembling, Calder forced a smile. "That sounds like a challenge."

The Blackwatch Guild Head took another sip of her tea. "It can be challenging."

"I still want to help." What he wanted was to run home and curl up under his bed until he stopped shaking, but he couldn't back down now.

Bliss tossed something down on the table. It was a metal badge, a little smaller than the tea-saucer, marked with the Crest of the Blackwatch. A squirming mass of tentacles overlaid by six inhuman eyes.

"Welcome to the Blackwatch," she said. "I'm glad you got to live. I like Alsa, and I don't think she would have been happy if I had killed her son." Bliss looked around. "I don't see the shopkeeper. Should I leave payment on the table, or wait until she returns?"

"I will take care of it, Guild Head. Don't worry."

Bliss nodded precisely. "I see. Then I will pay for the tea next time, because that is fair. Now I will leave, so that your son can express his fear to you in private."

After the Guild Head left, Calder dropped into a chair. Not the seat Bliss had used; that one, he nudged away from him with his foot.

He couldn't seem to stop trembling.

"I'm sorry," he whispered eventually.

She looked almost as shaken up as he felt. "I had no idea she was even in the city. She was supposed to be gone for months, capturing a nest of Crawlers down in Erin." Alsa gathered herself, jabbing a finger at him as though she meant to skewer him with it. "And *that's* why I tried to keep you away from my work!"

"Believe me, I wish I'd listened."

There were a few more moments of silence between them.

At last, Alsa cracked a smile. "I knew you'd end up in a Guild."

When he finally returned to the house, and endured a lecture from Artur and a stern glare from Vorus, Calder made his way up to his room. Jyrine was waiting for him in the hall outside, almost bouncing with excitement.

"You made it!" she said. "I knew you would, when your mother caught me. What was it? Was it a ship? What happened?"

Mute, Calder pressed the Blackwatch badge into her hand. He ignored her gasp of shock and her string of further questions as he pushed his way through the door, crawled under his bed, and curled up in the dark. Shivering.

CHAPTER NINE

"I can't believe there's nothing here," Naberius said a week later, as they anchored outside the island.

Calder pulled on his hat, checked his pistol, and loosened the cutlass sheathed at his hip. "Don't worry, the island is disturbing enough."

It was true. The 'island' resembled nothing more than an expanse of pale, flabby flesh, with fronds of black seaweed growing here and there like patches of hair. In the distance, ten arched towers curved together in two rows of five. Between the arrangement and the yellow-white color of the towers, it resembled the rib cage of a giant.

As far as Calder knew, it could have been exactly that. He wasn't about to make assumptions when it came to an island haunted by a Great Elder.

"Everyone exaggerates!" Urzaia called. "That is what makes a good story!"

Naberius tossed his black curls behind his shoulder. "I tell you, this island and the sea around it were both crawling with abominations. I was not exaggerating. Was I, Tristania?"

The Silent One shook her head once.

"You see?"

"I could never doubt such enthusiastic testimony," Andel said. His round white hat shaded his eyes, his suit was spotless, and he had both pistol and sword buckled at his hip. The silver pendant of the White Sun hung on his chest, glistening in the noon sunlight.

Naberius smoothed out his suit, which for once was a dark, subdued shade of blue. "I suppose I shouldn't question providence. This makes it much safer to go ashore."

Calder focused on his Vessel, extending a ramp down. It hit the island's shore with the smack of wood against flesh instead of crunching against sand.

This island continued to disturb him, for reasons even beyond the obvious. Not only was it frightening to behold, there was no gradual transition between sea and land, as he had expected. The ship could get within five yards of the shore without problem. Based on what he Read from the Lyathatan, Calder discovered that the "island" actually curved up on the bottom. As though it were floating on the surface of the water instead of resting on the ocean floor.

Like a giant corpse, bobbing on the ocean.

No use worrying about it now, he thought. For the moment, the eerie island served their purpose admirably. He could get closer than he had ever dared to hope, and he wouldn't need to send the Witnesses ashore in a rowboat.

It meant that, if he had to abandon them, at least he wouldn't lose a boat.

The Chronicler and his Silent One were all the way down before they realized that no one else had followed them.

The crew of *The Testament* stood on deck, dressed for battle. All except Petal, who must have stayed below deck—Calder hadn't really expected her anyway.

"The day isn't getting any younger," Naberius said impatiently.

Andel finished lacing up one of his boots. "Neither are we."

No one else moved.

For the amount Naberius was paying, Calder supposed he owed the man an explanation. "Good hunting, Naberius. We brought you here. Now you can take as long as you need to find your artifact, and we'll be here waiting."

The Chronicler's expression darkened, and Tristania patted him on the shoulder. "What if Shera decides to attack us while we're running around on our own?"

"You should run back to us," Urzaia suggested. "As fast as you can. You get back here, and we will protect you."

"This was not why I hired you, Captain Marten."

Calder widened his eyes, adopting a surprised expression. "Isn't it? I was under the impression that we were supposed to deliver you, and then you would find the artifact on your own."

"I was under the impression that your crew would provide me with assistance and security."

"It would be difficult to assist you if we don't even know what we're looking for."

Naberius tapped his thumbs together, thinking. "I can see why you'd be reluctant," he said at last. "I have somewhat kept you in the dark, so to speak. For instance, it's possible that I may have understated the scale of this operation."

Andel stepped forward, putting a hand on his pistol. "Explain yourself."

But Calder had an idea. A premonition, maybe. He reached into his coat, pulling out a spyglass, and examined the crest of the island. At first he saw nothing except the island's grisly geography, but after a moment, a few dark spots rose up from behind the hill. Ten figures walked up from the other side, dark silhouettes in black coats.

"Light and life," Calder muttered.

Naberius sounded supremely proud of himself. "I wasn't planning to pick up a shovel and dig for myself."

The men and women in black walked closer, and Calder waited for a look at one detail: the metal crest pinned on the breast of each coat. His heart sank as the details sharpened into visibility.

A nest of tentacles overlaid by six inhuman eyes. The Elder's Eyes. Crest of the Blackwatch.

Calder folded his spyglass and tucked it back into his coat. "Change of plans. Now we're *definitely* staying on the ship."

Andel squinted into the sun, watching the black-coated strangers approach. "How is that a change of plans?"

"Before, I was open to persuasion. Now I am possessed of the firm and unyielding conviction that we need to stay aboard. If you'll excuse me, I'll be in my cabin, filling out the paperwork to legally change my name."

Minutes later, from his cabin, Calder heard muffled voices as the Watchmen and Naberius exchanged greetings with the crew.

He forced himself to relax. Andel would speak for him, and he could trust his Quartermaster to cover for him. As long as he had the presence of mind to not mention Calder's name, they'd be fine. And even if the Watchman asked... well, it wasn't like Calder knew everyone in the whole Blackwatch Guild. What were the odds that someone he knew would be on this island at this moment?

"Captain Calder Marten," a man called from outside, and Calder sighed.

"We would like to request your cooperation in this matter, sir. My commander wants to speak with you personally."

Calder emerged from his cabin with a charming smile. He adjusted his hat and ran a hand down his coat, as though he had only left to make himself presentable. "Of course, of course! I needed a moment to compose myself. Andel, gather Petal. We're headed ashore."

He was rewarded with a rare look of surprise on his Quartermaster before the man headed down to the hold to carry out his orders.

Calder marched down the ramp, his crew trickling along behind him. On the shore waited the two Witnesses and most of a dozen Blackwatch, each of them standing casually. They didn't act like an armed escort, which was a relief. At least none of them seemed to hold a grudge.

Naberius wore a smug look, arms folded. "I'm glad you decided to join us, Captain."

"I couldn't miss the chance to learn about your mysterious artifact, could I? You've been so coy about it for these past weeks, and I do *love* surprises." Calder smiled cheerily in the Chronicler's face.

The Watchman that seemed to be the leader, a white-haired man in a rumpled uniform, nodded to Calder. "Pleased to meet you, Captain Marten. I've heard a lot about you."

Calder winced. "I was afraid of that."

"Don't worry, I don't hold a young man's foolishness against him. We've all broken out of prisons."

That was surprisingly understanding of a member of the Blackwatch, even if it did make Calder wonder about the old man's past.

"So...what *have* you heard, then?"

The old man met his eyes. "That you're on the right side. Everything else is secondary."

Calder looked around the group and saw the same respect on nine other Watchmen. He wasn't prepared for the emotion that welled up inside of him at that moment—for one moment, he thought he might tear up.

How would that affect their picture of me, I wonder?

He cleared his throat. "Thank you, Watchman. I appreciate your understanding."

The old man gave him one quick nod, as though that were the only response he had expected. Naberius, meanwhile, silently worked his jaw. The Chronicler forced a smile.

"Let us abandon this beach before more Children show up. I need to speak with your commander on a matter of some urgency."

That reminded Calder of a question. "Excuse me, Watchman, but who exactly is your commander?"

A woman in a black coat spoke up. "This outpost is commanded by Alsa Grayweather, Captain Marten."

Calder wondered if he could make it back up the ramp before they caught him.

Alsa looked much the same as when Calder had last seen her: poised and controlled, with a spotless uniform, her hair combed absolutely straight and falling down her back. She might have worn a pinch more gray in her hair, perhaps a few more wrinkles, another dueling scar or two. But it had been over a year since he'd spoken with his mother; part of him had expected to be facing a stranger.

He stood before her in her own tent, as she sat back on a folding camp chair much like the ones Calder kept aboard his ship. She looked him up and down, sipping tea.

"Where's Shuffles?" she asked at last.

"It mostly sleeps during the day. I thought it would be safer if I left it aboard the ship for now. Besides, it will follow me if it wants to."

He forced a laugh, but she kept surveying him as though she expected to fit him for a new coat afterward.

"All right then," she said. "Now where's Jerri?"

The question caught him like a slap. He should have expected it, but he'd been trying to avoid thinking of his wife for so long, he hadn't prepared himself.

"I hope to find out soon," he said.

She put her teacup down on its saucer, a little too forcefully. "She ran off?"

Calder would never get away without telling his mother the story, so he sat down on the edge of Alsa's cot. "We were attacked. Naberius says it was a Consultant..."

He initially planned to tell her only the most relevant details, but she asked enough questions that she soon pulled the full story out of him. When he finished, she was squeezing her teacup in both hands so hard that he expected it to shatter.

"'That which sleeps will soon wake,'" she repeated, disgusted. "You know what it means, I assume?"

Calder nodded, anger warring with worry. He wanted to shout at Jerri and make her feel the full force of his betrayal...but in order to do that, he had to get her back.

Alsa looked as though she were ready to kick her desk over. "And I didn't see it years ago. We had our suspicions of her father, years ago, but I never..." She shook her head to clear it. "No, I'm sorry. I can't even imagine how you must feel."

Calder decided to change the subject before he broke down entirely. He and his mother had never had the sort of relationship where he cried and told her all about his feelings. No reason to start melting now.

"Something of a coincidence, isn't it? Running into you here. I was afraid it would be Bliss."

"Oh, she's coming," Alsa said in a dry tone, causing Calder's heart to sink even further into his stomach. "And what makes you think this is a coincidence? I'm the one who told Naberius to hire you in the first place."

In Calder's mind, his whole voyage suddenly took on an entirely new meaning. If Alsa was the one arranging everything, then she must have a reason. This whole time he had assumed it was his own Guild Head, who was...significantly less reliable.

"I assumed it was Cheska who got me the job," he said. "She was the one who put me in touch with the passenger, and negotiated terms..."

Alsa grimaced in distaste, taking another sip of tea. "For the time being, Cheska and I have found ourselves working together. You can imagine my delight."

Calder sat quietly for a moment, putting the pieces together. Cheska Bennett, Head of the Navigator's Guild, wouldn't be involved in anything that didn't involve the entire Guild. Or the possibility of her walking away ridiculously enriched. He assumed Naberius was working on behalf of the Witnesses, and if his mother was here with a contingent of Watchmen, that meant at least three Imperial Guilds officially represented.

What's more, Alsa Grayweather was the right hand of the Blackwatch Guild, second only to the Guild Head herself. If Alsa and Bliss were involved...

Then he remembered something Cheska had burned on the inside of his hold weeks before. "Not just for you, but for the Empire. And the Emperor."

"Mother," Calder said seriously, "what is Naberius looking for?"

Alsa leaned back in her chair. "Eternal life."

Calder waited for more, but it seemed she wanted him to ask questions. "That's very dramatic, but I was hoping for a more literal answer."

"This island, as you may have noticed, is not normal." His mother stomped the ground, which slapped as though she'd kicked someone in the ribs. "According to our records, it began as the land where Nakothi's corpse fell when she was defeated by the Emperor and Estyr Six. The Dead Mother's body landed here, after her death throes shattered the land around her.

"Over the past few years, the island has disappeared. In a way, it's like Nakothi is swallowing up the land around her, remaking it into a new body."

Calder shivered, gently pulling his heels off the ground and resting them against the legs of the bed. It was one thing knowing that an Elder had made the island look and feel like flesh: you had to expect such things, if you wanted to sail the Aion. But actually *standing* on the corpse of a Great Elder...

"So the Emperor left an artifact here?"

"Something like that. You see, after the Emperor's death, many things that were once mysterious became clear. For instance, we found the secret to his immortality for the past fifteen hundred years." She gestured to her neck, as though to an invisible noose. "He always wore a silver chain around his neck. You may remember it."

Every detail of that scene was seared into Calder's memory. A chain looped around the Emperor's neck, bright against his dark skin, whatever pendant it carried disappearing into his robes. "I do."

"When the Imperial Guard discovered the Emperor's body, they found a cage suspended from that chain. And inside the cage, a gray heart, roughly the size of your fist. It had been pierced through, in the same stroke that took the Emperor's life." She shuddered at the memory. "They brought it back to me for examination as soon as it became clear what it was: the Heart of Nakothi, the Dead Mother."

Calder began to laugh.

At last. At *last,* years after the man's death, he finally discovered that the man hadn't been the spotless avatar of all the goodness in the world. No, he was a parasite, clinging to an Elder's heart to preserve his own life.

The Luminians had suggested for centuries that the Emperor lived on because of his spotless virtue and insurmountable will. Everyone in the world believed it.

Well, Calder had seen into the man's mind before. He'd known that the Emperor was anything but pure goodness and light. Still, this...this was the ultimate justification.

His laughter died down as Alsa sipped her tea, watching him. He finally wiped tears from his eyes and caught his breath again. "Oh, you have no idea how good it is to hear that. Everybody worshiped him, and here we find out that he was little more than an Elder himself."

"I'm glad you're in such a good humor about it," Alsa said, "because we need him back."

Calder glanced over his shoulder in a sudden panic, as though he expected to see the resurrected Emperor behind him. "You can't *bring him back to life!* Can you?"

Alsa snorted. "If we could, he wouldn't have needed to live forever in the first place. He could have waited to die, and then have us resurrect him. No, what we need is a new Emperor."

It was faint, but Calder caught the scent of opportunity here. If they were seeking to raise a second Emperor, then this could be the chance he'd waited years to seize. The chance to change the Empire once and for all.

But he had to play the safe hand, slowly gathering as much information as he could. "Why so?"

"It's becoming clear that the Empire cannot survive without an Emperor," Alsa said grimly. "The Regents are doing what they can, but it's the nature of humanity to divide. If this continues for too many more years, we will have four separate kingdoms instead of one united Empire."

Sadesthenes once said, "*As it is in the hearts of men to seek authority, the path to unity can only end in one Empire.*" Calder understood the concept, though privately he didn't see the problem with having four separate empires. People already referred to the different regions separately—Izyrians considered themselves separate from the Erinin, who competed for status with Heartlanders. What would it matter if the different regions governed themselves, and then came together for the common good?

Either way, that wasn't the answer he was looking for.

"That's all well and good, Mother, but what are we looking for on this island?"

She raised her eyebrows, as though surprised he hadn't figured it out yet. "Another Heart of Nakothi. We can't very well raise a mortal man Emperor, can we?"

Disgust washed through Calder like a tide. "You want to bind someone *else* to the heart of a Great Elder? You? You're Blackwatch!"

Alsa's eyes hardened. "And this is exactly what the Blackwatch was founded to do. Turn the powers of the Elders to the good of humanity. You'd know that, if you—"

She was interrupted by a voice calling her name from the front of the tent. She pushed her way out, and Calder followed her.

It was the old man from earlier, still wearing his long black coat. He bowed slightly when he saw Alsa. "We've secured another possible candidate, Commander. Naberius wishes to have you inspect it yourself."

Alsa patted the side of her coat, where Calder knew seven Awakened iron spikes rested. "Guide me," she ordered, and the Watchman set off without hesitation.

With nothing else to do, Calder followed.

Jyrine Tessella Marten lay back on the mattress in her cell. Her imagination had failed her, in this case—the ominous mystery around the Consultants made her think that they would simply torture her and drop her body into the ocean.

They had actually treated her quite well, for a prisoner. Her cell was five yards by five, which was noticeably bigger than the cabin on *The Testament*. The mattress they gave her was thin but relatively comfortable, far from the pile of filthy straw she'd expected. They fed her twice a day, and the room was even lit by the even, warm light of a quicklamp. It was placed high out of her reach, true, but it banished the shadows far better than a candle.

She had requested two books so far, by leaning against her bars and shouting. She never saw a guard, but the books appeared in her cell within a few hours.

Say what you will about the Consultants, they know how to run a comfortable prison.

She only had one complaint about her cell: it could be easier to escape.

They had covered her head in a hood when they took her here, but they didn't bother to hide the fact that they were taking her underground. There were no windows she could conveniently slip through, no guards to bribe. She had faked illness a few days before, and found a bottle of medicine delivered with her next meal.

As she did at least once every day, she closed her eyes and stretched her mind out for her Vessel. The earring was somewhere on the island, she was sure, but not close enough for her to call its power. She kept trying, stretching her mind out for the power that she felt she could *almost* touch.

Maybe Calder could get something out of this sensation. Some vision or clue as to the Vessel's location. But Jerri was no Reader, and she eventually lost focus.

"They'll have your Vessel sealed," a voice called from down the hall. "The Architects aren't foolish enough to let a Soulbound keep her powers."

Jerri scrambled out of her cot, moving to the wall of bars that separated her from the hallway. "Is that what happened to you?"

It was a rare chance to get to know her neighbor. She intended to take advantage of it.

A smile infected his voice. "Perhaps. I'm not sure I should give too much information to the enemy."

"That hardly sounds fair. You know about my Vessel. I think I should know at least something about you."

Her neighbor went silent, and Jyrine assumed he'd given up on her. He seemed like the curious sort, to a certain degree; he would toss her a question every day or two, maybe make a comment, but he stopped responding anytime she tried to make it a real conversation.

This time, though, he'd responded. That had to be a chance.

"My name is Lucan," he said at last. "And yours?"

Jerri clung to the hope of interaction, as though merely speaking with another human being would see her free from this cell. "Jyrine."

"Jyrine. Hmm...are you from Vandenyas, Jyrine?"

"That's an astute guess, Lucan. And you...Erinin?"

He sounded amused. "Not exactly. I hear you tried to betray us to the Elders."

This time, it was Jerri's turn to go silent. How had he known that? Was she actually speaking to a guard, and this was the Consultant idea of an interrogation?

No, the guards didn't speak to her. And she'd heard Lucan moving around in his cell the past three weeks or so. Unless a Consultant was willing to stay in prison for two dozen nights in order to ask her a handful of questions, he had to be a genuine prisoner.

He must have overheard pieces of her initial interrogation, when they stuffed her in here. They'd asked normal things, mostly—who she was, what was her connection to the Sleepless, did she have any hidden powers.

So Lucan knew who she was; that could work to her advantage. She could use this opportunity to clear up some misconceptions.

"Not a betrayal, no," she said. "The Elders aren't our enemies. They're strange and eternal. Some say they have knowledge beyond the stars, and they certainly have powers beyond anything we humans can control. Shouldn't we learn to live alongside them, instead of fearing them as we do?"

Jerri hated having nothing more than his voice to go by—she longed to see his face, to judge how he was taking her speech.

"But the Elders enslaved our species, long ago," Lucan said. "Do you propose another age of worldwide slavery?"

At least he sounded curious. Unlikely though it might be, perhaps she could make an ally.

"Not at all! When the Elders kept us as slaves, we were primitives. Savages. We initially fought them with tools of bone and rock, and it wasn't until the war had gone on for years that the Emperor discovered bronze tools. How could the Great Elders, with their millennia of wisdom, work with a race like that? They had no *choice* but to keep us as slaves, as we use animals for their strength."

It felt good to have a conversation with someone that would actually listen to her, like stretching muscles long dormant. She had once held high hopes for Calder, since he lived alongside creatures like Shuffles and the Lyathatan, but he proved even more stubborn in his fear of Elders than most. Maybe if she'd tried to persuade him earlier, shown him everything she'd learned...

Well, if she survived these prisons, she would teach him the truth. Everything she'd done would directly benefit him, after all.

Lucan mused audibly from the other cell. "Hmmm. So you suggest that, in modern times, we're advanced enough to strike a bargain with the Elders."

He understood! "*Exactly!* In effect, we do it already. The Blackwatch learns more about Elder biology every day, and the Navigators need Elderspawn guides to cross the Aion. Even the Emperor..." Jerri caught herself. She wasn't supposed to know about the Emperor's immortality.

She recovered quickly. "...approved of such research. There's room enough in this world for humans and Elders both. Folk belief indicates that the Elders want nothing more than destruction, but that's clearly untrue. When they were in charge, they didn't destroy! They built a great civilization! They didn't even eliminate humanity, though they must have been tempted."

Her neighbor was silent for a minute or two. She thought she heard the scratch of a pen against paper. "I have always questioned the ancient accounts of the Elders," he said at last.

"And for good reason! Practically the only details we have of the Great Elders come from their greatest opponent!"

More pen scratching. "You're not a Reader, are you, Jyrine?"

How had he known that? "I don't see how that's relevant to the subject at hand."

"Hmmm. I'm sure you don't."

Then he was quiet, and none of her questions could coax him back into a discussion.

She sat on her mattress, leaning the back of her head against the stone wall. Idly she twisted the end of her braid in her hands—she kept braiding her hair because she had nothing better to do with her time. The invisible guards had even provided a comb after she called for one.

What do I have to do to convince someone? The conversation with Lucan had gone well, she thought, but the hatred of the Elders ran deep throughout the whole Empire. What would it take to break through almost two millennia of indoctrination?

She still remembered herself as a little girl, terrified as she followed her father to a secret meeting. She'd stared into an endless void as her father and a cabal of other men and women communicated with another power—ancient, wise, and palpably *strange*.

Jerri shivered. She almost felt as though she could feel that dry cold of another world here, in her cell. And it seemed that the light of the quicklamp didn't reach quite as far as it used to. She turned around. Were those shadows gathering against the wall?

"Lucan!" she shouted. "For your own safety, do not make a sound!"

He didn't respond, which she decided to take as agreement.

Jerri stood, her back to the bars, facing the darkening end of her cell. Cold snatched at her skin as she straightened her hair and brushed out her clothes, making herself presentable. They had given her a red shirt and pants, obviously modeled on the uniforms of Imperial prisoners, but Jerri happened to think the color flattered her.

She stood with poise as the back wall fell away, revealing an endless void swirling with colorless lights.

A voice slithered out of the dark, whispering directly into her ear. "Jyrine. The Heart has been found."

Relief drew a smile on her face. "That's wonderful news! We're on schedule, then?"

"We have gathered our forces. We must secure the Heart before the Blackwatch can bind it to one of their choosing."

"Surely that won't be difficult. They don't have a candidate ready, do they?"

The voice hissed, an invisible messenger conveying the irritation of the Sleepless cabal on the other end. "The candidate has already arrived. We do not have as much time as we wanted—the Guild Head is on her way."

The Head of the Blackwatch, Jerri was sure. Bliss. She'd heard of the woman from both Calder and the Sleepless, and they all made that particular Guild Head sound terrifying. If her presence alone was enough to force the cabal's long-laid plans off schedule, then she must be frightening indeed.

Jerri coughed politely. "I hate to ask, since I know you're on a schedule, but when can I expect to be removed from here? I can't be sure how long the Consultants will keep me alive."

She had expected to die long before this point, truth be told. She only wished they would give her Vessel back before they killed her, so that she could make a fight of it.

A dozen distant whistles sounded from the void, and an icy wind swirled out. She wondered if that signified debate among the men and women at the far end.

"You must continue to wait," the voice whispered at last. "We will soon have a powerful piece on the island. If you continue to survive, it will see to your freedom. And to your continued service."

Elders and their servants could often have strange notions of time. "How soon, exactly, could I expect—"

"Soon," the voice hissed, as the void began to shrink. "Soon...*soon.*"

The stone wall reappeared, rimed with frost. The quicklamp's light penetrated the corners of her cell unobstructed.

She heaved a deep breath, collapsing back down onto the mattress. She rubbed her eyes, fighting back sudden tears.

Calder was on Nakothi's island with the Heart, she knew it. He was on that island and in danger, without her to protect him. If he only realized how many threats she had destroyed over the years, without him ever knowing...

Now he was out there alone, unprotected. He would die thinking that she betrayed him.

And, more than likely, she would die in here without a soul to mourn her. The Empire would continue on its course of destruction. Her family would never see her body.

It was certainly enough to cry about, but she forced the tears back. Weeping never saved anyone.

And she had a job to do.

She closed her eyes, seeking her Vessel out once more. One of these days, someone would make a mistake and carry her earring closer. When they did, she'd burn her way out of this cell and teach the Consultants why they should never have captured her alive.

From the next cell, Lucan cleared his throat. "Can I speak now?"

"You're safe," she called back. If the Sleepless had known that someone was close enough to overhear their message, they would have undoubtedly sent an Elderspawn killer to eliminate the witness. It was fortunate for Lucan that he'd listened to her advice.

"What was that?" he asked, sounding fascinated rather than repelled.

She was only too happy to explain.

CHAPTER TEN

No, I will not teach you Awakening. However, I will explain the essential concept in order to satisfy your curiosity.

When you Awaken an object, you bring to that object a measure of awareness. Of 'life,' so to speak, though an inanimate object cannot move around like you or I do.

– Artur Belfry, Imperial Witness
Taken from a letter to his pupil,
Calder Marten (fourteen years of age)

TWELVE YEARS AGO

In the weeks that followed his meeting with Bliss, Calder came to a new understanding of Reading, of carpentry, and of the Blackwatch.

For one thing, he learned that none of the older Watchmen seemed at all inclined to teach him about the Guild or explain anything. At all.

"You either know what it's like to face down an Elder, or you don't," his mother explained to him. "If you don't, then nothing they teach you is going to prepare you. If you do, then nothing they teach you will tell you anything new."

"And I don't," Calder said.

"No, you confronted Bliss and her Spear of Tharlos. They all know that, so they know you're one of us."

"They could try acting like it," Calder grumbled.

But each morning, as he worked on *The Testament,* Calder understood that he had crossed some invisible line without realizing it. The men in black coats talked openly around him, making jokes about Crawlers or Children of Nakothi. He didn't know what they were talking about, but that didn't matter: they *were* talking, and he had never heard those terms as an outsider. The fact that they spoke so freely around him was itself evidence that he was trusted.

After he realized that, he noticed other things.

They were obviously used to the whims of their Guild Head. Normally the Guild required an application and interview process, but Calder learned that Bliss was prone to circumvent or overrule that procedure as it suited her. It was little more than a formality, now, and the Watchmen all reacted the same to his appointment. Upon learning that a fourteen-year-old boy had been elected to their Guild as a Reader, each and every member replied simply, 'Welcome to the Blackwatch.'

One week, every day, a different Watchman would walk up to him and hand him a foot-long iron spike, then walk away without a word. He hung them from loops inside his coat that seemed to be made for that exact purpose, though no one would tell them what the nails themselves were for. At the end of the week, his mother presented him with the seventh and final nail.

Every member of the Blackwatch stopped what they were doing, gathered around, and applauded. Then they dispersed back to their jobs.

"And that's as much ceremony as we see in the Blackwatch," Alsa said. "Sad, really. I hear that in Kanatalia, the alchemists throw a party every time one of them completes an experiment."

Calder held open his coat, revealing the seven nails. "I'm honored, really, but what do these *do?* They're obviously invested, but I can't tell how."

He didn't pick up on visions from the nails, exactly, more like a deep ocean of purpose, focused to some Intent he couldn't fathom.

"Oh, they're not complicated. Stick all seven of them into a Lesser Elder, all over its body, and it will stay bound and paralyzed."

He glanced down at the nails. "Do I have to get them in the brain?"

Alsa touched her own set of nails through her coat. "Tradition says head, heart, spine, and all four limbs. But some Elderspawn don't have heads, hearts, a spine, or limbs, so you try and do your best."

"I see. Why all the secrecy, then?"

"We're not supposed to speak to the initiate about the nails before he has all seven, but I almost warned you. I wouldn't Read them too deeply, if I were you. And for light and life, don't try to Awaken one."

"Why not?" Calder asked, suddenly desperately curious to find out what would happen.

"Because they were already Awakened, long ago. Normally if you try to Awaken something twice, nothing happens. In this case, there have been... other effects. Don't try it."

Alsa shivered, and Calder swore never to try it. Not until he knew more details, anyway.

As he warmed up to the Blackwatch, he learned more than he had ever wanted to about *The Testament.* And about using Reading as a construction technique.

For one thing, it was harder than he had ever imagined.

With most objects, you simply willed it to perform better at its given task, and the object absorbed that Intent and got better. A knife invested to cut meat would slice through a steak as if through butter, and glass invested to prevent shattering might survive a hailstorm. It was a very simple and straightforward process, though only Readers could tell what change their Intent really made without careful experimentation: most people invested their Intent into objects blindly. Calder couldn't understand that—it was like learning that most people painted without ever having seen a single color.

But the ship was an entirely different beast. Each board, nail, rope, and knot had to be invested for a specific purpose. And he couldn't focus on one purpose at a time, either; he had to take into account the Intent and significance bound into the entire ship.

So he started off by investing a nail binding two boards together, fine. Then he invested the two boards for strength, which made them too rigid and brittle. The nail driving them together wouldn't break, because of his Intent, but neither did the boards bend. Given a single tap, the whole thing exploded into splinters.

Next, he tried investing the boards for durability rather than strength. It took hours of focus and all his mental energy, but he eventually got them how he wanted them. However, he ended up with a pair of boards that would bend like rubber without breaking. Anyone who stepped on them would sink inches down into the deck.

When he finally gave up, Alsa showed him how it was done: you had to invest the two boards and the nail together, as a whole, as well as separately. It required him to focus his Intent three ways at once, which gave him such a headache that he was useless for almost two days afterward.

He returned to work with a renewed vigor. Now he could finally understand why Alsa could do so quickly what took him hours—if he practiced like this all day, he would be more skilled than a Magister by the time he'd finished the ship.

Then he saw the suicides, and they woke him as if from a dream.

He was moving his way down the railing of *The Testament,* laying his Intent into every inch of the starboard rail. He needed to focus, but he didn't necessarily need to see what he was doing, so he often found his eyes wandering up to the west side of the harbor.

To Candle Bay Imperial Prison.

Somewhere up there, his father was locked in a cell. He imagined the prison cells as dank and lined with stone, but he didn't know for sure. He'd never been able to visit.

For eighteen months now, the receptionist had turned him away.

"I'm sorry, that prisoner is under delicate medical care."

"That prisoner is being held in special confinement today."

"That prisoner is under disciplinary review, and cannot receive visitors at this time."

At first he'd tried every week, then every month, and now he was considering sending a strongly worded letter to the Candle Bay warden. From the deck of *The Testament,* he glared up at the distant windows, imagining he could see his father's red hair within.

Then one of the windows slid open, and a woman crawled out headfirst.

At this distance, she looked like a stick-figure more than a woman, but the sight was enough to destroy his concentration and ruin his Reading. What was she doing? Was she trying to climb down the wall and escape?

His questions were answered a moment later when she plunged headfirst, landing among the rocks below.

Calder's involuntary shout startled the nearby workers and Watchmen, who all turned to look at him.

He pointed straight at the prison. "That woman jumped!"

And then a second figure crawled out the same figure, falling to his death on the rocks.

A murmur went up among the workers, and there was a general shaking of heads. "Bad business," someone said, but then they all went back to work.

When a third and a fourth prisoner jumped out the window, Calder rushed around the deck looking for someone to help. He finally found a grizzled old Watchman sitting on a barrel, munching on a sandwich.

"Four people have jumped from that window in the last thirty seconds," Calder said, trying to sound calm. He pointed as another man fell. "Five, now."

The old man shook his head, letting out a sigh. "Bad business, that is. Bad business." He took another bite of his sandwich. "That's an Imperial Prison, isn't it?"

"Candle Bay Imperial Prison."

He kept shaking his head, brushing crumbs from his mustache. "I wouldn't even keep an Elder locked up in an Imperial Prison. Not in the Capital, at any rate. Emperor only knows what they do to the prisoners in there."

Calder had no doubt that the Emperor *did* know.

Back at home, in the Grayweather library, Calder recounted his story to Jyrine. With many whispers and glances over his shoulder, he told her about the Candle Bay suicides, about the receptionist never letting him see his father, and how he was *almost* sure that his father's cell was overlooking the bay.

Jyrine looked over at their chaperone, Vorus, who was silently reading *The Adventures of Soulbound Silas.*

"You know what you need to do," she whispered back. "You have to rescue him."

It wasn't a new idea, of course. He had pondered and toyed with the idea of breaking his father free since the night Rojric was taken. Once every few weeks, he'd take out the Emperor's key and roll it between his fingers, silently promising himself that his father wouldn't have to tolerate prison much longer.

But between his studies with Jyrine, his job working on *The Testament,* and his sudden appointment to a Guild he'd known almost nothing about...well, *life* had gotten in the way. It was easy to tell himself that he'd use his invested key to free his father like some hero, but it was quite another thing to give up his comfortable routine and put in the long, hard, boring work. What door would he even unlock? How would he get his father out of an unlatched cell unseen?

All that had changed when he witnessed the bodies on the stones of Candle Bay. Who knew what cruel experiments that Emperor was running on his father?

He couldn't tell Jyrine too much, though. He had to seem reluctant, as if he'd be giving this project a few more weeks of thought. "I don't know anything about the prison's layout. Maybe if they would let me in..."

"You're a Watchman now, aren't you? Why don't you, you know—" She waved her hands in the air, vaguely. "—tell them it's a Blackwatch issue. What will they know?"

Calder had considered it. There were only two problems with that plan.

"First of all, the receptionist knows what I look like. I've been trying to see my father almost since he was locked up. Second, even if I could walk straight in the door with a Blackwatch badge on, they're not about to let me walk out with a prisoner."

Jyrine nodded sagely. "I know what you need."

In spite of himself, Calder was intrigued. Jyrine often came up with unexpected bits of knowledge; he wouldn't have been surprised if she knew the exact right procedure for a jailbreak.

"A partner," she whispered. "A confidante. You need me."

Calder looked at her, in her turquoise sitting-dress and matching earrings, with her excited smile, and he almost couldn't resist the urge to let her help with the plan. He needed more help, after all, and this was a chance to work on a project together. A *secret* project.

But this wasn't a game. Failure would see them locked up in Candle Bay alongside his father, at the best. At worst, they could be killed in the attempt. Or...

An image came to his mind of Bliss, pushing a shard of bone back into her black coat. He didn't know how she'd react to hearing that one of her newest Watchmen had been arrested trying to break his father out of prison, but he couldn't imagine that she'd take it well. She might even take punishment into her own hands.

He'd rather face Imperial justice.

"I *do* need you," Calder said. "I can't plan something like this on my own. I need someone to help me gather information, to plot the escape, and to cover for me with Mother. But when it comes to the actual operation, it's better if I go by myself."

He pulled a line from a play he'd recently seen. "There are some things that a man has to do for himself," he said solemnly.

Jyrine was quiet for a few seconds, staring at the back of her tattooed hand. "I don't think my father's dead. They say he is. But he came to me one night and said that he'd be going away on important work. And he told me that, no matter what I was told, he absolutely wasn't dead."

Her eyes rose, meeting his. "Three days later, the Blackwatch came to my door and told me he had been killed in the line of duty. That the means of his death was confidential. I don't know what happened, or if he's alive, or if he knew he was about to die and he told me so that I wouldn't worry. But at this point, if I had any idea where he was, I'd go find him."

And Calder had no idea how to respond. He sat looking into her eyes for far too long.

She finally broke the contact by tossing her braid back behind her shoulder. "And don't give me that, 'A man has to do things for himself' line. I watched that play with you, remember."

At this point, he didn't know how to refuse her. He felt that he was teetering on a cliff, with the safety of home behind him and a deep unknown ahead. Until this point, his plans had remained firmly in the realm of fantasy. But if he told her he was going to free his father, he had the uncomfortable feeling she'd hold him to it.

With a deep breath, Calder took a step into the unknown.

"Let's go for it, Jyrine."

Her eyes sparkled, and she clapped him on the shoulder. "Jerri. That's what my family calls me. Anyone who lets me in on their prison break conspiracies gets to call me Jerri."

In the corner, Vorus slapped his book down on the table.

He glared at them over his glasses, raising a finger to the front of his scarf. "Ssssshhh!"

For the moment, Jerri and Calder returned to their studies.

CHAPTER ELEVEN

Calder stood in what passed for a hole on this nightmare of an island: an ugly, gaping wound the size of a crater. It looked as though the Blackwatch had gouged a warehouse-sized scoop out of the dead Elder's flesh, leaving the edges oozing red and an infected-looking green. Holes dotted the wall like empty veins, from small enough to hold a fist to openings bigger than a Capital sewer pipe. Tendons crossed from wall to wall like pinkish wires, and they'd had to duck and dodge in order to walk down to the crater's center.

There, at the center of a taut network of veins and tendons, pulsed a gray-green heart.

Six Watchmen with their black coats worn loose stood around the heart, sweating. They held pickaxes and shovels, and their clothes were covered in sickly ichor. Each of them had a haunted, dead look that Calder could well understand: he couldn't imagine the stomach it would take to dig out a mine *by hand* in a soil that looked like flesh.

Whatever his mother was paying them, it wasn't enough.

Naberius fell to his knees in front of the heart, a picture of heroic awe. "Is this it?"

Alsa held out a hand as if to Read the heart, but she shuddered before she got anywhere close. "Check for yourself."

Tristania had her back turned to Naberius, and she held the handle of her whip in one hand, though she kept the rest of it tucked into her coat. Her bandaged body was poised and alert, her eyes scanning the edges of the huge cauldron as though she expected to see a threat emerge at any second.

On instinct, Calder almost Read the crater wall to see if he could detect incoming threats, but he stopped himself before moving his hand. Alsa hadn't moved within a foot of the heart, and she still looked vaguely sickened. He didn't want to know what it would feel like if he directly Read the body of a Great Elder.

He'd seen men who were reduced to nothing more than drooling husks after Reading Elder artifacts. There were many ways he could imagine himself dying, but starving to death while lost in a hallucination was not one of them.

Naberius continued kneeling on the sticky ground as if heedless of the stains he was leaving on his knees. He cupped his hands around the heart, closing his eyes and inhaling deeply.

"It's...vast and strange," he said, in awe. "I can feel the unending life of the Dead Mother..."

Calder wondered if he noticed the contradiction. For his part, he didn't want to be any closer to the heart than he had to. Immortality had its appeals, but if he had to shackle his soul to an Elder's, he thought he would prefer death.

The white-haired Watchman had a quick, quiet word with Alsa. She turned sharply on Naberius, who was still kneeling over the heart in obvious ecstasy. "You've verified the Heart, then, Witness Clayborn. Our part here is done. Now, let's cut this free and get to shelter."

Calder eyed his mother and then Tristania, who had not relaxed her vigil. Alsa Grayweather was not prone to unjustified panic. If she wanted out of this crater, she had a good reason. "What's the hurry, Mother?"

While the Watchmen went to work trying to sever the tendons—it must have been harder than it looked, as one man swung his pickaxe into the pinkish wire with no effect—Alsa walked over to her son.

She spoke in a low voice. "Ever since we set up camp on this island, we've been under constant attack from the Children of Nakothi. I've had twice as many men guarding as digging. But these past few days, it's been slowing down. Hours before you got here, they *all* ran off. Vanished. We haven't seen skull or claw of anything all day."

That seemed like the opposite of a problem, to him. "When I land too close to an island in *The Testament,* we often find that the wildlife is too quiet. There are many things in the Aion that can sense the Lyathatan approaching."

One of the Watchmen stood over an unbroken tendon, calling for a saw.

Alsa grimaced. "I hope that's what it is. Your Lyathatan hails from Kelarac, and certain records indicate that he and Nakothi were anything but friendly. But if that's not the case, then it means they're gathering their strength."

"They would need a leader for that."

"Thus far, they haven't shown any signs of one." She shrugged. "But the more you learn about the Elders, you start to realize how little you actually know. One of the Elderspawn may have spontaneously developed the ability to command the others, or they may have established psychic contact with something higher up the ladder. Either way, I'd feel a lot safer if we were out of this crater."

Calder looked up to the bleeding edge, toward the camp where he'd left his crew. They would be safer together than he would be down here, but he couldn't help but worry. They were understaffed here, in the case of any attack. Just him, his mother, the two Witnesses, and half a dozen Watchmen with tools.

The workers cheered as the saw broke through a tendon, and the man holding it got to work on the next pink wire as the others started digging at the flesh around the heart. One man leaned, panting, on his pickaxe. Two women dug, where another man worked the saw. The white-haired Watchman leaned over toward Alsa as though to whisper in her ear again.

Calder counted one more time before he realized what was bothering him. That was five Watchmen accounted for, not counting his mother.

Five.

He pulled his gun from its holster, though he kept it pointed low and to the side. "Mother," he whispered, "how many men did you bring down here?"

"Three men, three women," she said. She paused for a moment, and then whipped her saber out of its sheath.

"We're under attack!" she shouted, and blood sprayed all over her black coat. The white-haired Watchman collapsed, missing a chunk of his head.

The musket-crack arrived a second later.

Heart pounding, muscles running with lightning, Calder grabbed his mother by the shoulder and shoved her into the sticky wall as another bullet passed through the space where her ribs used to be.

"They're aiming for you," he yelled. If the Watchman hadn't stood so close to Alsa, she would have taken the first bullet herself.

Alsa pushed him off, diving for something the old man had dropped: a musket. "Not just me," she said, taking aim at the edge of the crater.

Tristania stood over Naberius, brown coat spread like a pair of wings. Something smacked into the fabric and then fell to the ground—a musket-ball. It must be invested against bullets, though Calder had never been able to make bulletproof clothing work. Fabric wasn't a sturdy enough medium; the material pulled itself apart after taking a couple of shots.

The Silent One stood as though she never meant to move again, whip falling from her hand and coiled on the ground. Naberius took his time, walking over and scooping up the abandoned saw.

"Excellent work, Tristania," he said, and then he leaned over and continued sawing the heart free.

Alsa took a shot up the crater, wreathed in gun smoke, and for the first time Calder got a look at the enemy.

They, too, wore black.

But instead of coats, these were dressed in form-fitting suits of pure black. Many of them wore strips of cloth over their mouths, and others wore completely black masks. He tried to count them, but he found it more difficult than he'd expected—he only caught glimpses of them here and there. A black-clad elbow, the flash of a knife, the spray of blood, a half-shrouded face as one of the Consultants shoved a body into the crater.

All the bodies he saw belonged to Watchmen. Seconds into the battle, all five of the workers were down, and Naberius would have been dead ten times over if not for Tristania and her bulletproof coat. Alsa stood behind the shelter of a gash, poking her head out to fire her musket every once in a while, then ducking behind cover to reload.

She didn't seem to be doing any good.

The familiar thrill of danger charged him, and he grinned. The Consultants were here in force. At last.

He had business with one Consultant in particular.

Calder straightened his hat, keeping his pistol in one hand and drawing his cutlass with another. He drew in a deep breath, then bellowed a single word: "URZAIA!"

An animal roar answered him from the edge of the crater. A single black-clad body launched from that point, flying *entirely over* the bowl, landing on the other side with an audible crunch.

"Ah," Calder said, straightening his hat. "There you are."

Then he started running for the side. The crater was gently sloped, so he could climb his way out if he had to, but the workers had left knotted ropes dangling down to assist his ascent.

He had to sheathe his cutlass to climb up, which made him regret drawing it in the first place. A bullet struck next to his shoulder when he was about halfway up, sending up a splatter of fluid.

Calder dug his feet into the wall, pulling himself up faster.

A black-wrapped figure rose above him, pulling out a long steel knife. Calder hung on the rope, raising his pistol, desperately hoping he'd be fast enough.

But there was one other move he could try.

"Clear the way, please!" Calder shouted.

A blond cannonball slammed into the Consultant, sending the smaller man tumbling over Calder and into the pit.

Urzaia Woodsman leaned over the edge, blood splattering his scarred face. He showed a gap-toothed smile and reached one hand down. Calder took it, and the gladiator pulled him effortlessly to the top.

"I have not found the assassin woman, but there are many other Consultants," Urzaia reported. "I have killed three, but it is hard to find them, sometimes."

"I can tell," Calder muttered. A group of three Watchmen filed past a clutch of the waving seaweed, and a Consultant leaped out of hiding, killed two of them, and ducked behind one of the Blackwatch shelters before the third man noticed his companions were missing.

Calder raised his weapon as soon as he saw the disturbance, but he didn't even have enough time to pull the trigger. The Consultant was gone.

Urzaia growled, tightening his grip on his hatchets. "They will not fight me. They only hide."

It was true. After the initial attack on Alsa, the Consultants had fallen back to guerilla tactics. Urzaia and Calder were standing out in the open, but they were far enough away from any hiding-places that they remained unharmed. Watchmen were clustered together, holding guns, swords, or spikes, keeping their backs to one another in case of ambush.

Another woman in a black coat strayed too close to the back of their shelter, and she pitched over with three inches of steel sticking out of her back.

"They're stalling," Calder realized. He spun back to the crater, where Tristania was still covering Naberius. A single body in black lay near the Silent One, its chest burned and smoking, but other than that they seemed absolutely unharmed.

"Follow me," Calder ordered, and then he began to march in a loop around the edge of the crater. Urzaia followed him, looming like the world's most intimidating shadow.

If Shera wanted Naberius, she would have to strike at him from above, or else run down into the cauldron herself. Either way, Calder would be able to catch sight of her up here.

He saw a black-clad ankle sticking out from behind a seaweed frond and fired. The Consultant—a man—staggered out of cover, allowing Urzaia to finish him off. The Blackwatch shelter, little more than a hastily constructed driftwood shed, held three more Consultants that struck as soon as Calder and his cook strayed within range.

First, a tiny blade spun out from behind the shelter.

Calder swatted it out of the air with the edge of his cutlass, a little disappointed. He had been trained better than *that.* Surely the Consultants had more.

A black-clad woman leaped from the top of the shelter, a knife in each hand. Not Shera—she was taller, thinner, and her knives were well-worn steel instead of bronze.

Urzaia caught her, slamming her into the ground. Her bones snapped, and she fell limp.

The other two struck at the same time, hurling a knife and moving to flank Calder.

If he'd been alone, it might have worked.

Urzaia snatched the knife out of the air, laughed, and threw it back. The Consultant dodged, but it threw the man off-balance, and Calder slashed a line across the man's arm. With one arm and nothing more than a dagger, he managed to turn three of Calder's cutlass-strikes in as many seconds.

Calder couldn't help but be impressed as he ran the other man through.

The Consultant's death echoed through the blade, focusing the weapon's Intent. The more Calder accomplished with this sword, the stronger it would become. Like all tools, it was invested with each use.

He turned back to Urzaia only to find the man lowering his arms. A long scream, followed by the sound of impact, suggested that his opponent had just landed somewhere far away.

The Woodsman laughed, and Calder couldn't help but ask a question that had bothered him for some time. "Do you enjoy this? Or does it remind you of the arena?"

Urzaia shrugged, continuing his march around the crater and forcing Calder to catch up. "The arena was not so bad. I thought I would die many times, but that has a special kind of fun to it, you understand?"

He did. Combat terrified Calder, and he would avoid it for the rest of his life if he could, but there was something about a straight-up fight that set the blood on fire. His wife had felt that thrill, even more than he did.

Jerri will be sorry she missed this. The thought was followed by a shock of pain and anger that sobered Calder up.

He wasn't fighting for the thrill of it. He had work to do.

They circled the whole crater without running into anyone else. The afternoon had settled into a tense, quiet standoff: Alsa kneeling at the bottom, musket locked on her shoulder; Naberius sawing away at the tendons with Tristania standing over him; Watchmen huddling in clusters, watching each other, eyes pointed outward. The Consultants were invisible, but a noise here and there suggested that they hadn't yet left.

Where was Shera? She *had* to be here, if she was after Naberius. Why hadn't she…

The Chronicler's saw snapped through the tendon, and he clutched the heart to his chest like an Anthem addict with his stash.

And everything became clear.

They weren't after Naberius at all. Not anymore.

"Naberius!" Calder shouted. *"They're after the Heart!"*

And the stillness shattered like dropped glass.

Shera appeared in the center of the crater as though she had simply *ap-*

peared there. For a moment he refused to believe the sight; there was no way she could possibly have gotten down there without him seeing. And yet there she was, black hair falling around her face like a hood, mouth covered by black cloth, holding a bronze knife in her right hand as she ran straight at Tristania's back.

But that wasn't all.

At the exact instant Shera appeared, a mournful howl rose through the air, like a mother mourning the death of her child. Hideous creatures boiled up all around, rising from suddenly-opening gashes in the ground like drops of blood from a wound. Spiders the size of a man, made entirely out of bone, their heads like oversized skulls. Hairless dogs with blue-gray flesh and long, bladed tails. Four-armed giants standing head and shoulders over Urzaia, its skin pale and blue like a drowned victim.

The Children of the Dead Mother.

One more time, Andel cursed himself for straying so far from the crater. He had stayed with Petal and Foster when they visited the main base of the Blackwatch: a cluster of tents, lean-tos, and temporary wooden shelters far down the beach from *The Testament.* He'd let Calder go visit his mother, reasoning that the Captain would be safe among so many Blackwatch. And only the Emperor himself could have stopped Urzaia from wandering off.

Naively, Andel had expected them to come back quickly. He wouldn't have thought the attack would come on the very first day they arrived.

Not to mention the *second* attack.

He stood back-to-back with a Consultant who had tried to kill him a minute before, using his saber to parry the attacks of something that looked like a living vulture skeleton. Its bones were held together by nothing more than rotting strips of muscle and skin, and it struck with the needle-sharp tips of its bony wings.

Andel knocked one wing aside and hammered at the bird's skull with the edge of his sword until he heard a crack. Something glistened inside—did this thing still have a brain?

He wasn't sure, but he pulled his pistol and blew its skull off anyway.

The skeleton fell, lifeless, so he spun to help the black-clad man behind him. The Consultant had surrendered after Andel stabbed him in the leg, so

Andel had embraced one of the Unknown God's tenets—*Mercy for the undeserving*—and accepted the surrender. He had just finished bandaging the man's leg when these hideous dead creatures of Nakothi had come crawling up from the ground *inside* their tent.

Well, he'd let Kelarac take him before he let a patient die right in front of him.

The Consultant slammed the blunt end of one knife down on the head of his enemy, which looked hideously like a deformed child. Its bruise-purple skin writhed over its skeletally thin body, and it hissed through a mouth of jagged teeth. It opened its jaws to take a bite out of the man's wounded leg.

Andel skewered it through the chest, pinning it to the ground like an insect to a board. He left it there, squirming, and picked up a saber from the corpse of a Watchman.

Panting, the Consultant dropped into a chair. He gestured to the child-creature. "Are you just going to leave it there?"

"I find that I no longer have a use for that sword," Andel said. He was no Reader, but he still didn't want a blade that remembered being inside an Elderspawn. Who knew what horrible Intent the weapon would carry with it?

Foster fired his musket, shouted, and handed the gun to Petal. She poured the powder with shaking hands, spilling as much on the ground as she got in the weapon.

The gunner pulled a pistol, fired, and a splatter of liquid hit the outside of the tent. He fired again, and a third time, all without reloading.

Foster always kept the secrets of his firearms close to the vest, but Andel made a mental note to confront him about this. If he had weapons that could fire several times in combat without reloading, the crew needed them.

A shadow darkened the front of the tent.

With his left hand, Andel grasped the White Sun pendant. With his right, he steadied the Watchman's stolen saber.

A bone-white claw, like a giant crab's, slashed the front of the tent open. It peered in, and its face...Andel shuddered and had to force himself not to look away. Its whole head was a writhing mass of flesh-stalks, each capped by a disgustingly human-looking eye.

He focused on his sword. The hilt shook ever so slightly against the blade, and the weapon was a little heavy on the back-end. Something manufactured for battle, not crafted by an expert.

It would have to do. Andel would fight this disgusting crab-thing with a broken bottle, if he had to.

The Consultant stepped up beside him, a knife in one hand and a clutch of needles in the other. From the man's expression, Andel knew that they were both prepared to die.

Then a woman shouted, and the bone claw fell to the ground, leaking cloudy white blood.

The Child of Nakothi screamed like a man being tortured, falling back and flailing with its second, smaller claw. Andel could only get a glimpse of its opponent through the slash in the tent—the figure moved in a streak of black clothes, gleaming bronze, and blond hair. The two of them moved past, and Andel had to watch the rest of the fight in the shadows they cast against the tent. The woman's silhouette passed through the dark mass that must have been the bone crab.

Another scream of torment, and then the creature gurgled into silence. A small river of milky blood trickled under the tent.

The wounded Consultant shivered, wiping his forehead with the back of his hand. "Gardeners at last," he said, his voice shaky. "Thank—"

A blond-haired blur ran into the tent, and before Andel knew what was happening, a clawed hand rushed at his eyes. He brought his sword up on pure instinct, but the blade was slapped aside, and he found his throat in a crushing grip.

He fell back against something hard, maybe a table, that gouged into his spine. It was a welcome distraction from his throat, which felt as though she had tightened a noose around his whole neck.

"Wait!" the wounded Consultant yelled, moving forward. "He's not—"

He was cut off again as the pressure released from Andel's throat. Andel collapsed to his knees, coughing and desperately trying to seize a breath. He forced himself up, raising his saber. He had to fight, to do something; his attacker was moving toward Foster and Petal.

In the second it took to get his eyes on the scene, she was already done. She held Foster's musket in her left hand and Petal's hair in her right, and she was dragging the girl away from a case of glass bottles that the Alchemist strained and struggled to reach.

That was the first time Andel got a clear look at his attacker.

She was younger than he would have thought. Not yet twenty-five, he would guess. Her hair was bright blond, and cut short enough that it wouldn't fall into her eyes as she fought. She'd pulled black cloth over her mouth, and a pair of hilts stuck out from behind her lower back.

Her whole body was sheathed in black except her hands, which...Andel squinted, looking closer. Her left hand seemed to be clawed and blue-tinged, stretched slightly bigger than normal. Now that he thought of it, her pupils had the vertical slits of a lizard.

An Imperial Guard, perhaps?

All of that went through his mind as he placed his sword on the table behind him, raising his empty hands. "You really think we should be fighting each other right now?" he asked.

"You didn't do much fighting." She hefted Petal by the hair, and the alchemist whimpered.

The male Consultant limped up to her, hands spread. "Gardener. These are not our enemies. They allowed me to surrender when I was beaten, and they fought with me against the Dead Mother's Children."

The Gardener surveyed the room, her gaze lingering on the shattered skeleton-bird and the imp impaled on Andel's saber. "Looks like you didn't do much fighting either, Shepherd."

Without a word, she released Petal's hair and tossed Foster's musket back. He caught it with a squawk and began muttering to himself, fussing over the gun as though she'd tossed his infant.

The Gardener flexed her hand and the short claws withdrew, the blue tint fading back to the normal hue of healthy skin. Even her pupils had returned to a human shape. She started to walk out of the tent.

"Follow me if you want to fight Elderspawn," she said. "But I will not hesitate to kill you if necessary. Please keep that in mind."

Foster moved his musket as though he meant to turn it on her, and she *appeared* in front of him, gripping the end of his gun.

"That means you too, sir," she said.

Sir? Andel thought. A bellow cut through the sounds of battle, like an enraged bull. His gaze met Foster's.

"Urzaia," Petal whispered.

The Gardener's blond head snapped around at the sound of the name. "Your Soulbound?"

The Consultants knew about their crew. Andel supposed it wasn't so surprising—supposedly, the Consultants knew everything. But it still disturbed him to think that killers like these knew every detail of their combat capabilities.

So he decided to use a little truth to his advantage.

He smiled, just a little, and tipped his hat to her. "Our Champion."

Her eyes widened, and he was treated to a clear view as the pupils snapped from round to a vertical line.

Then she was gone, the tent flap swinging in the wake of her exit.

"What are you doing telling her that?" Foster grumbled. "And you, girl, saying Urzaia's name."

Petal muttered to herself, hiding in a veil of frizzy hair.

"They know everything anyway," Andel said. "Might as well scare them a little." He hefted his sword again.

"Now let's go see if we can save the captain."

When Shera struck Tristania's coat-shrouded back, she hit with more force than any of the musket-shots. She led with the blade of her bronze knife, striking the fabric with her weapon's tip.

The bullets had done nothing, but this blade must have been invested with more Intent than Calder could imagine: it tore through the cloth, instantly drawing blood. The force drove the Silent One forward, knocking her over Naberius, sending her sprawling on the ground.

The Chronicler staggered to his feet, clutching the Heart of Nakothi, but Calder could only hope the man stayed alive long enough to be saved. He was too busy running back to the edge of the crater, looking for the knotted rope.

The Elderspawn didn't let him get far.

Something like a severed spine on a centipede's legs slithered up to him, and he ducked as he ran, slashing it in half with his cutlass. *Death to the deathless,* he chanted silently, letting his Intent flow down into the blade. It wouldn't help too much against the Children of the Dead Mother, not unless he continued investing it for weeks, but any tiny advantage would help when he was forced to fight the living dead blade-to-bone.

The spine centipede shriveled and died when he slashed it in half, so maybe it worked.

A headless, hairless, heavily-muscled gorilla loped up to him, loping forward on pale-skinned knuckles. Calder raised his shaking cutlass.

"Urzaia!" he shouted.

The gorilla got closer.

"Now, Urzaia!"

He got a glimpse of tanned skin as Urzaia launched himself over the edge of the crater, a black hatchet in each hand and blond hair streaming behind him. He landed in a spray of fluid from the ground, only feet from Shera.

Urzaia had never taken his eyes from his prey. Admirable, in other circumstances, but this left Calder to fight a charging dead gorilla with nothing more than a flimsy piece of metal.

Light and life preserve me.

The expression had never been more appropriate.

The headless gorilla reached him, eerily silent. It raised a fist to slam his head down into his shoulders. Calder tried for a smooth, agile dodge, but he was afraid that he simply lurched out of the way. The fist struck him like a sack full of hammer-heads, sending a shock of bone-crunching pain up his left arm and sending him staggering a few steps to his right.

He still managed to keep his cutlass up, slashing the creature across the chest. Milky white fluid crept down its flesh in a line.

Other than that, it didn't react at all. It simply turned and charged him again.

As he ducked under a clumsy punch aiming for his head, slipping past the gorilla's blue-white body, he reflected on how frustrating it was to fight a headless opponent. He had never before realized just how grateful he was for the enemy's reactions: grunting in pain to let him know that he'd scored a point, panting when they were tired, screaming when they were scared, generally exchanging banter in the middle of a fight.

Engaging a mute enemy was just...unsatisfying. Not to mention terrifying, since a single connected blow meant that his bones would be nothing but powder.

He danced another round with the monstrous gorilla, trying to ignore the screams around him as the Blackwatch fought their own creatures, and the sounds of battle from within the pit. He left a scratch on the monster's back just as a deafening roar sounded from inside the crater.

Urzaia has some impressive lungs, he thought. *Maybe I should promote him. Andel couldn't yell that loud if he tried.*

He yearned to go down there, but only his own quick movements and the gorilla's clumsy attacks had kept him alive this long. If he turned his back, the monster would pull his arms from their sockets and beat him to death with them.

A streak of black passed by, and he caught a glimpse of blond hair. Then a gout of white blood sprayed from the gorilla-creature right where its head should have been, splattering on his clothes. He staggered back, more from the stench than the surprise. The blood smelled like spoiled sausages and putrid cheese, like carrion and burned hair. The faint smell followed each of the Children like a miasma, but now it was coming from his *clothes.*

He dry-heaved and tore his jacket off at the same time, more frightened of the smell than of the gorilla's flailing fists.

Only when he could breathe again did he take a look at the monster, which lay dying on the flesh of the ground.

A Consultant stood with her back to him, blond hair cut short. She held a bronze knife in one hand, and her other flexed open and closed in a vaguely disquieting manner.

"Thanks," he panted, as soon as he caught his breath.

She half-turned to look at him. "You're quite welcome."

Then she vaulted into the crater just as Urzaia had done, landing with her knees bent.

That's just not fair. Why could everyone do that but him? He scrambled closer to the rope before another dead monster could interrupt him.

Urzaia needed his help. And unless he was very much mistaken, there were now two Consultant assassins down there.

Not to mention his mother.

CHAPTER TWELVE

Calder fell from the rope into the bottom of the flesh crater, and instantly had to fight for his life.

A blue-skinned imp the size of a child hissed at him when he landed, scrambling toward him on all fours and opening its mouth wide. He jerked back, knocked off-guard by its sudden assault. Why did it seem like all these frightening monsters were so *fast?* Probability alone suggested that some of them should be slow, or maybe peaceful. But this imp snarled at him, flailing in a storm of claws and teeth, clambering to reach him.

He held the creature at bay with his sword, trying to shove his blade down the thing's throat, but it caught the steel of his cutlass in its teeth. He had to use both hands to lift the whole ensemble—sword and Elderspawn together—and slam it against the wall until the point of his blade stuck out the back of the monster's head.

Only then, panting, could he turn back to the real fight.

Tristania huddled against the nearby wall of the crater, bleeding, occasionally flicking her explosive whip at the Children of Nakothi that surrounded her. Each time she did, a white light detonated at the point of impact, and they were blown back in a spray of bone fragments and pale blood. The wrappings near the back of her ribs were soaked with red, but he supposed that was the advantage of wearing bandages everywhere: she had simply tied a few strips of cloth a little tighter to bind the wounds.

Naberius lay nearby on his stomach, holding the Heart of Nakothi in one hand and trying to crawl away. After only an instant, Calder saw the inch of steel sticking out of his left calf—it looked as though he'd tried to run, only to have one of the Consultants stop him with a thrown blade. His dark blue suit was filthy with stains, and his hair—for once—was no longer perfect. Finally, he didn't look like a figure that had stepped out of a portrait.

Alsa Grayweather had a long cut on the side of her cheek, but she fought against the Children with her back to the crater. She must have been out of ammunition, because she fought with her musket in both hands like a club; in the first instant, he saw her knock a shambling corpse to one side with the butt of the gun, drive an iron spike through the head of a hairless dog, and then turn back to the corpse only to kick its knees out from under it.

He moved toward his mother for the same reason that the Children of Nakothi were focused on her: because the other three fighters were far too terrifying.

Urzaia laughed as he fought, black hatchet in each hand. The gold hide wrapped around his arm gleamed in the sun, and his leather breastplate hung from one severed strap. He slammed one hatchet down and the blond Consultant caught the blow on her two crossed bronze knives. Her arms looked blue, almost the same hue as these dead creatures, and muscles shifted strangely beneath the skin. But she managed to hold off Urzaia's impossible strength.

Behind him, Shera flicked a blade at Urzaia's back, then turned to drive her bronze knife through one of the Children. Without looking, the Izyrian gladiator reached back and swatted the blade out of the air with his second hatchet.

The blonde saw another of those headless gorillas loping for her, and she leaped onto its shoulders, using it as a footstool to flip over Urzaia and drive her pair of bronze knives down toward his neck.

Urzaia dropped his hatchets, grabbing her by the wrists and moving as if to slam her down onto the ground, but she *twisted* somehow until she was sitting on his shoulders, legs wrapped around his neck in a stranglehold. Shera moved to drive a knife into his back, but he spun and caught her arm, hurling her into the wall. Then he fell over backwards like a toppling tree, slamming the blond Consultant into the ground. The Children of the Dead Mother, sensing vulnerability, swarmed around them.

Calder had to trust Urzaia to handle that fight, because there wasn't much he could do to help.

He hurried over to his mother, trying not to think about his growing shame and irritation. He rarely felt weak—even though he knew Urzaia was a Soulbound and an experienced fighter, the difference between them never seemed so stark. Calder was Soulbound himself, after all, and when he stood on *The Testament,* none of his crew could match his power. But seeing Urzaia here, off the ship, made him feel ordinary and useless.

As he ran past Naberius, still scrambling to crawl away, he had a sudden thought that made him stop in his tracks. *"Do not let yourself be distracted by violence. Battle is a game men play to reach an objective, but the battle itself does not matter. Only the objective matters."* Not Sadesthenes; one of the classical strategists. Loreli, maybe.

He dropped to his knees in front of Naberius and grabbed the Heart of Nakothi.

The Witness resisted—perhaps he didn't trust Calder, or perhaps he had been fighting to hold on to the Heart for so long that he couldn't comprehend releasing it to anyone. The organ squirted gray-green blood over their hands, but neither man let go.

"Naberius!" Calder yelled, trying to shock the man back to his senses. "Let go! I'm trying to help! If I can get it back to the ship, the Consultants might follow me."

The Chronicler snarled until his face twisted. If he hadn't known better, Calder might not have recognized the man. "It's *mine!*"

What was this? Was this the real Naberius, or had attempting to Read the Elder artifact done something to his mind? Calder had grown up on stories of Readers being driven insane by accidentally contacting the Elder powers, and he'd seen the results of such insanity firsthand. If this was Elder madness, then Calder had little chance of ever seeing his fee.

The thought put him in a bad enough mood that he acted on his first instinct: he punched Naberius in the nose.

Not *too* hard, but enough to startle the man into releasing the Heart. Calder ran away, ignoring Naberius and his rage, running back to the rope. If he could make it to *The Testament,* then maybe he could hold off the Consultants himself. He had no doubt that the Lyathatan would be more than a match for the Children of the Dead Mother.

He wasn't making an intentional effort to Read anything, but some hunch made him turn and raise his cutlass. It saved his life.

Shera's bronze blade scraped along the edge of his cutlass, raising sparks.

A sort of manic cheer rose up in Calder, and he lifted the Heart. "How about a trade?"

She pulled a two-inch blade from a pouch on her thigh, throwing it at him sidearm. At this distance he couldn't even try to knock it away with his sword, but he jerked to one side, catching it on the thick fabric of his coat. It still hit him with more force than he'd expected, but he managed to avoid having an artery opened, so he wasn't complaining.

Then Shera was on him, and he fought for his life.

Not for the first time, he regretted not taking the time to reload his pistol. Her eyes were dead over her black half-mask, bronze blade striking like lightning. Only fear and desperation made him fast enough to meet her strikes, and he kept back-stepping, trying to get far enough that his extra reach with the sword would matter. But if he put too much distance between them, then she would have free reign with her throwing blades.

He lived long enough to back up a few steps, and then he asked the important question. "Where's my wife?"

She swept a kick at his ankles, and he jumped. Somehow he managed to prick her just above the hip with the point of his sword as he dodged her strike, which filled him with confidence. Bold now, he stepped up and kicked her in the ribs. "*Where* is my *wife?*"

The Consultant took the kick with a grunt, then took advantage of his proximity to drive a knife into his leg. He jerked back quick enough to avoid a crippling strike, but she still sliced across his shin.

The pain flashed through his whole leg as though a shark had taken a bite from his limb, and he screamed. Form forgotten, he slashed blindly with his cutlass, trying to score a cut wherever he could.

She stood just outside the reach of his blade, crouching, her left hand behind her back as though she was hiding something from him.

He gritted his teeth against the pain, holding his sword up to defend. If she threw something, he would have just enough time to knock it out of the air and catch her as she tried to move closer. This was his chance, and he couldn't let pain slow him down.

He would take this Consultant back to the ship, even if he had to sew her back together.

As Children of Nakothi howled and screeched around them, she stayed in the same pose. Was she waiting for something? He couldn't afford to move first—if he misstepped on his injured leg, she'd see him dead.

With one smooth motion, she pulled her hand back out, and Calder realized he hadn't seen her second bronze blade. Now she held one in each hand, but his situation hadn't changed. He still needed to wait…

There was something wrong with the second knife.

The pain in his leg didn't matter—it was a shallow wound, only skin deep, though it hurt like fire. Even Jerri didn't matter, for the moment, and the lethal threat of this assassin fled from his mind. He couldn't seem to take his eyes from that battered bronze blade.

"What *is* that?" he asked, horrified. The weapon pressed on his senses from here, and he'd only seen a handful of items in his life with that much raw Intent.

An Imperial artifact? Surely not. An ordinary object touched by the Emperor escaped the Imperial Guard here and there, but they would never have missed a weapon.

But he knew he couldn't let that blade touch him.

Shera rushed him, leading with the ordinary knife in her right hand. He slapped it aside with the flat of his sword, eyes still on her left hand. Calder focused his Intent on his cutlass, chanting in his mind to focus his power.

Protect me. You can hold. You're steel, solid steel, and you are an impenetrable barrier that will shield me from harm.

She swept in, driving her left-hand blade in an arc that would take him across the stomach. He shoved his sword in the way, focusing all his Intent on knocking her weapon aside.

The bronze knife met his steel, hit with an impact that shook him like a sail in high wind, and then sheared right through. The top half of his blade tumbled off, glowing orange at the severed end.

He hadn't thought to dodge—he was only lucky that his cutlass had knocked her blow enough out of the way that he wasn't eviscerated. As it was, he lost only a corner of his coat.

Instead of backing off, the assassin stepped closer, until she was all but pressed against him. Face-to-face, Shera looked him in the eyes and spoke.

"She's dead," she said.

His breath left him.

Then she struck him in the wrist. A shot of pain shattered his arm, and his hand spasmed open. The Heart of Nakothi fell out.

She snatched it from the air and spun away, heading back to her comrade.

Calder wanted to follow, but...he couldn't. He just couldn't. He let the pain of his wounds swallow him, let it burn until he sank to his knees. Hideous creatures born of bone and flesh loped closer, now that the Consultant was gone, hissing at the scent of his blood.

He wasn't sure he cared.

Then his vision was swallowed up by smoke, and panic returned. There was something about losing his sight that struck something primal inside him, making him react even through the listless haze of depression. A pale-skinned hand reached out of the black cloud surrounding him, and he slashed it, running blindly in the other direction. A bone claw swept out, reaching for his legs, and he managed to stagger away.

The cloud of smoke cleared surprisingly quickly, and the Consultants were missing.

Just gone. As though they'd never been there.

"No!" Urzaia roared, slamming his hatchet into a bone-crab so hard that the giant creature tumbled head-over-shell for yards until it cracked into the wall. "Not again! *Not again!*"

Another tear opened up in the flesh at Urzaia's feet, and another spine-like centipede crawled out. He crushed it under the heel of one boot without seeming to notice.

Calder hadn't noticed during the fight, but now he finally realized: the Children of the Dead Mother had *never* stopped appearing. More and more crawled out of the sewer-sized tunnels in the crater, swarming closer to the humans.

A contingent of Blackwatch slid down the crater walls, many of them clutching black spikes in either hand. When an Elderspawn made contact with the Awakened iron, they fell to the ground in piles of limp bone and flesh.

His mother had told him once that it took seven spikes to immobilize an Elderspawn, but a single blow seemed to take care of these creatures well enough. Though the Watchmen hadn't been much use against the Consultants, *this* was the fight they'd been trained for: men and women in black coats against the spawn of the Elders, no weapons forbidden, no quarter given.

Calder moved to his mother. She had taken command back, as soon as the smoke cleared. "Retreat!" she called. "Back to shelter!"

He was about to follow her orders when a hand seized his injured leg and he shouted again, lifting his other foot to kick at whatever creature had grabbed him.

It was Naberius. Instead of panicked he looked desperate, as though someone had taken his child from his arms.

"Where is it?" he pleaded. "Do you have it?"

Calder tried to think of some excuse, but he was far too tired. "She has it, Naberius. She's gone."

The Chronicler's wail sounded like a man on the verge of tears.

Alsa grabbed her son by the shoulder, moving him toward the rope. "I'll have two men take him out." He looked around and saw that two black-coated Watchmen were already carrying Tristania between them, her own blood-stained coat dragging behind.

"I talked to her, Mother," Calder said listlessly. "She said Jerri's dead."

Alsa Grayweather shook him, her saber gripped tight in her other hand. "This is not the time for this, Calder. We have to move."

She was right, and he knew it.

So he moved.

It turns out the Blackwatch did have a shelter worth the name—almost a fort, it had been constructed in obvious haste by lashing thousands of logs together for walls, fences, and supports. With his leg and other, lesser wounds bandaged, Calder sat in a creaking chair next to a table piled high with weapons.

Watchmen bustled here and there, and his crew gathered around him. They were all relatively unharmed, he was glad to see. Andel had a new sword that didn't quite fit in his sheath, and his white suit bore a few new stains. Petal shivered more than usual, clutching a case of potions to her chest. Foster grumbled as he peered through his reading-glasses, inspecting the barrel of a musket.

Urzaia sat with his back to a wall, eyes closed, breathing deep and even. His hatchets were bare on his lap, and Calder hadn't gathered the courage to speak to him yet. No one had; even the Watchmen avoided him.

Outside the shelter, a thousand inhuman voices raised in a chorus of howls. The walls shuddered constantly under the force of so many blows, as though they suffered through an earthquake.

They didn't have long. Calder didn't know much about the Children of Nakothi specifically, but he knew that *The Testament* couldn't hold everyone on the island. And the ship was their only chance of escaping with their lives.

Alsa pushed hair out of her eyes, addressing the whole assembly. "We don't have long. We do have allies, and they should be coming to reinforce us soon... but if they're not here in a matter of minutes, nothing of us will remain to reinforce. I have never seen such a gathering of Elderspawn at one time."

"That which sleeps," one Watchman muttered, before the woman beside him elbowed him in the ribs.

Alsa glanced at him but didn't make a comment. "We cannot defend this location for long, but most of the Children seem to be gathered here. If we gather everything we can and punch through their formation at a single location, we should be able to make it down the beach to *The Testament.* Calder, can the Lyathatan help us?"

The Elderspawn that pulled his ship was notoriously unwilling to fight unless something specifically disturbed its rest. He had already begged it to fight the Stormwing scarcely a month past, and to a creature that existed on the scale of eons, a month may as well have been five minutes ago.

"I'll make sure of it," he said, projecting confidence. He wasn't sure he could do it, but if need be, he would appeal to the Lyathatan's master. He shuddered to think what such a meeting would cost him, but surely not as much as his life. Anything short of that was a bargain, at this point.

She nodded sharply. "Then that settles it. We need to gather—"

Naberius strode into the room, his Silent One limping along at his side. His suit was still as stained and ruined as ever, but he must have found time to comb his hair, because his dark locks tumbled down to his shoulders. Once more, he had the look of a battered hero who had survived a terrible battle.

But Calder remembered the Chronicler's face as he'd begged for the Heart. He remembered, and clutched the grip of his pistol.

But Naberius seemed in control of himself this time, waiting to be seated until Tristania pulled out a chair for him. She slid it under the table after he sat, like one of his mother's servants back in the Grayweather house. Once he was seated properly, she lifted the case of polished wood from back on the ship, placing it gently on the table.

Naberius flipped the latches and pulled open the lid.

Inside, in settings of velvet, sat eight white candles. Seven of them were whole and pristine, the eighth burned halfway down.

At last he spoke, his voice as cool and composed as ever. "What are our chances of making it out of this enclosure and all the way to the ship, do you think?"

From Alsa's expression, Calder thought she would rather punch the Witness than answer him, but her words were polite. "Some of us will certainly make it. Some certainly will not."

He nodded as though that were the answer he expected, his hand hovering over the various candles like a produce merchant selecting the ripest fruit. "With those odds in mind, I believe I may have a solution."

Some of the Watchmen around him froze. Calder hadn't realized they were paying such close attention, but it seemed the entire room held its breath in anticipation of his solution. Outside, the Children howled like a foul wind.

"Explain if you will, Witness," Alsa said in a tight voice.

"As you know, I served for many years in the Imperial Palace. My primary duties involved finances, but living around the Emperor, you find yourself exposed to certain truths. Especially as a Reader. There were techniques he designed that worked against the spawn of certain Great Elders, and failed against others."

Naberius finally seized on one of the whole candles, though it seemed outwardly the same as all the others. Calder knew that wasn't the case—he would have memories stored in that wax, weeks or even months of experience, waiting to be released until the candle was lit.

But he closed his eyes as he gripped the candle, tilting his head with the air of a man savoring a sensation. Calder thought he understood. Even if he could not relive his memories perfectly without burning the candles, the man was still a Reader, and the memory storage was essentially a function of human Intent. He would be able to Read certain details with a touch.

The Chronicler spoke as if from the depths of a dream. "In my contact with the Heart of Nakothi, I saw some...missing pieces. At last, I understood the nature of the Children. I should be able to speak their language, if you will."

Of all the people gathered, Foster was the one to speak up, though he kept his eyes on the gun in his hands. "If there's a point in there, Chronicler, you'd best get to it. I don't fancy meeting the Emperor again so soon."

Naberius shot a glance to Calder, and anger flashed across his countenance. "This would be so much easier if I *had* the Heart, but I'll work with what I have. The Children understand only death and rebirth. They want, they need, they crave to introduce the living to the sort of deadly remaking that they've already experienced. And they will only go away..." he placed the candle back in its housing and shut the case. "...if they believe they have succeeded. I can deceive them."

The room was silent for a moment before Alsa spat out, "What does that mean, Naberius?"

He offered her a dazzling smile that seemed completely out of sync with the scene around him. "That I will handle it. Tristania."

The Silent One took his case of candles, and Naberius rose from his seat. Without another word, the two of them walked toward the wall. Tristania's hair stuck out from her bandages, and her shredded and bloodied coat drifted along behind. Both of them walk with a limp, reaching out and steadying the other as they walked. Calder hadn't seen it before, but even Naberius' wound had been treated, his calf wrapped with a white bandage. As they limped away, blood soaked through the cloth.

Andel adjusted his hat and deliberately turned away from the two Witnesses. "They're dead," he said. "What's the real plan?"

Alsa nodded and looked up at the surrounding Watchman. "Everyone gather as many weapons as you can. Mobile wounded support one another. Keep the injured to the center, with the crew of *The Testament.* If you're in fighting condition, you're on the outside. We're going out the gate in five minutes, so be with us or stay and face Nakothi in person."

A few of the Blackwatch raised their iron nails in a sort of salute and hurried off to carry out her orders.

For his part, Calder kept watching the Witnesses. He had no reason to trust Naberius, but the man did seem confident about his solution. And no one knew better than Calder the sorts of desperate plans you could come up with after Reading a bit of obscure information.

The Chronicler was speaking with his Silent One as they walked. Tristania turned as though surprised, and for the first time Calder saw her speak. At least, the bandages around her lips moved. They were too far away for him to hear, and he found himself unconsciously following, using an unloaded musket as a crutch.

He couldn't deny a certain curiosity; if Naberius really knew some piece of Reading that could keep an army of Elderspawn from their gates, then that was something Calder wanted to learn. And he found himself wondering what Tristania would sound like. There was something enticing about hearing the voice of someone who never spoke.

On this side of the log wall, someone had set up a set of rickety stairs scarcely better than a ladder, leading up to a platform. The Blackwatch would have used this short tower to see over the wall, keeping a lookout when the island seemed too quiet. Tristania and Naberius helped each other up the steps now, limping pathetically until they reached the top.

Calder stood at the bottom, eyeing the stairs.

There is no way I'm doing that, he thought. Walking out here on a slashed leg was one thing, but he wasn't about to attempt stairs.

Naberius leaned over the side, and Tristania joined him, looking down at the Children of Nakothi below. The wall shook with the impact of dead fists, claws and fingers and other, stranger appendages reaching through the gaps in the logs. Calder took one prudent step back.

The Chronicler said something, and Tristania laughed.

This time, Calder heard it. Her voice was high, clear, surprisingly young, and weary. As though she laughed because she was too tired to do anything else.

While the Silent One still leaned over the wall, Naberius pulled out one of his Dalton Foster original pistols. He pressed the barrel to the back of Tristania's head.

She turned slowly, not alarmed, and Calder shouted a startled warning. His hand scrambled to his own pistol, but he got tangled in the musket he was using for a crutch. He had some vague thought of shooting Naberius before he could pull the trigger.

But he was too late.

The shot was swallowed up in the din the Children caused, no louder than their screams. Tristania's body shuddered and slumped against the wall.

Naberius stood there for a moment, the palms of his hands pressing against her shoulders. Calder couldn't exactly see what he was doing, but he could feel the flow of great Intent even at this distance.

Then Naberius reached down, grabbing his Silent One by the legs, and flipping her body over the wall.

The Children of the Dead Mother went silent.

Finally, Calder leveled his pistol, pointing straight at the back of Naberius' blue suit. "Throw your weapons down!" he demanded, his voice harsh in his own ears.

Back in the main shelter, the Blackwatch had raised a cheer. They would have heard the monsters growing silent.

With his back still turned, Naberius raised both hands. "I'm no threat to you, Captain. I just saved your life."

Calder couldn't find the words to name the questions that ran through his head, the pain he felt for a silent woman he barely knew. All he said was, "Why?"

Naberius slowly turned, his face a mask. "We still have a job to do."

"Why *her?*"

The Chronicler frowned. "Would you have followed me up here? Trusted my word when I told you to look down?"

Calder's heart flared up with rage, and he thumbed back the hammer of his weapon. "Why don't you turn back around, Naberius? Look over the side. Trust me."

A dark hand rested on Calder's arm, and he turned to see Andel standing there in his white suit. "Not the time, Captain."

As always, Andel was the voice of reason. But that didn't fit—Andel Petronus was the eternal voice of mercy, the defender of innocents. Calder usually had to talk him *out* of avenging the helpless.

"Even you, Andel?"

The Quartermaster's grip tightened on his arm, and Calder finally lowered his pistol.

"You should listen *because* it's coming from me, sir," Andel said forcefully. "We need to get out of here."

Calder took a deep breath and shoved his emotions down deep. Everything he still felt—his fear, his relief at being alive, his sickness at failing to capture Shera again, his grief. He stuffed it down, forcing his mind back to the job.

The Children were quiet for now, but that didn't mean he wanted to spend a second longer on the island than he had to.

"Ten thousand goldmarks," he said to Naberius, his voice cold.

That Elder-spawned worm *smiled.* "Lead the way, Captain."

By the time they reached *The Testament,* there wasn't a single Elderspawn in sight. Calder could sense the Lyathatan drifting beneath the island, dreaming incomprehensible dreams. He had already issued orders to have the hold emptied to fit all the Watchmen aboard. They would go hungry for a few days, and they would be forced to rely on the nearest island for resupply, but at least no one would be here waiting for the Children to return.

He was overseeing the removal of a case of dried fish when his mother walked up to him, holding out a hand.

"Spyglass," she said.

Without a word, he pulled his spyglass out of his coat and handed it to her.

She raised the glass to her eye. After a moment she let out a breath of relief, and her arms dropped limply to her sides. "Light and life, they're *early.* Bless them. Looks like you get your ship back after all."

He took the spyglass from her and took a look at the horizon himself. After a moment of searching he saw what she had: a ship approaching from the west. And not just any ship. A ship sailing on a wake of fire, with blazing red sails.

The Eternal. The ship of Cheska Bennett, Guild Head of the Navigators.

"You said you were forced to work with Cheska. I didn't know you meant this closely."

"How do you think we got out here in the first place?" Alsa turned to a pair of Watchmen who had just added a cask to the growing pile of cargo on the beach. "Change of plans, gentlemen. Get it all back on the ship."

The two Blackwatch members didn't say anything, but Calder sensed sudden despair radiating from them as they eyed the pile of crates and barrels.

Urzaia marched up to Calder, his eye on the horizon as though he could see *The Eternal* approaching with his naked eyes. He hadn't said a word since his fight with the Consultants, and his face was uncharacteristically grim.

"I have failed you again, Captain."

Calder turned to him, surprised. "Urzaia, if not for you, I would be dead. Maybe all of us. You have nothing to apologize for."

The big man shook his head, his fists clenched. "I heard her. They have killed Jyrine, and I could not avenge her."

"That's not your responsibility, Urzaia." Calder wondered if it was anyone's responsibility. Jerri had kept her own secrets, made her own choices. If they'd landed her in an execution on the Gray Island, that wasn't *his* fault.

But worry burned in his gut as though he'd swallowed coals.

"Captain, I do not mean to argue, but that isn't true. I am only strong, and I could not save her. If I can't avenge her, then what *can* I do?"

He heard the despair in the other man's voice, a depth of grief comparable to his own. Urzaia had spent years with Jerri. He must see the protection of the crew, the whole crew, as his responsibility. How must it hurt to feel like you'd failed everyone under your charge?

On second thought, Calder realized he knew exactly what that felt like.

Urzaia took a deep breath, starting again. "Good thing I will have another chance."

Calder hated to destroy the man's hopes, but he had to be honest. "They have what they wanted. We won't see her again."

"I must correct you. I have tasted the blood of the yellow-haired woman." He drew in another deep breath through his nose, like a bloodhound tasting a scent. "I can follow her as far as she runs."

A moment ago Calder had been thinking about giving up the chase.

But that was when he'd thought it was impossible.

Hope kindled in his chest, and he took a step closer to the Soulbound. "Are you sure?"

"I am sure of nothing. But yes, I can find her."

Suddenly delighted, Calder clapped the man on the back. "What can't you do, Urzaia?"

"I only have a few gifts, but I use them well." He gave Calder a wide, gap-toothed smile. "Do not worry, Captain. She can't hide from me."

CHAPTER THIRTEEN

An axe used to split wood for years, for instance, will naturally become invested with a measurable amount of Intent. It will excel at splitting wood.

Now, if a Reader decides to Awaken this particular axe, the tool itself will yearn to split wood. It gains a rudimentary consciousness related to its task. Most importantly, it can use its own store of Intent to accomplish its goal. An Awakened object will no longer gain new Intent, but it will become able to use whatever it has already collected.

This is a critical, even disturbing, point.

Readers often spend months or years studying an object to be Awakened. If you do not understand an object's Intent, you don't understand its goals. If you do not understand its goals, you will not understand its eventual powers.

– Artur Belfry, Imperial Witness
taken from a letter to his pupil,
Calder Marten (fourteen years of age)

ELEVEN YEARS AGO

Over the next few months, Calder and Jerri gathered the information they would need to break into Candle Bay Imperial Prison, retrieve Rojric Marten, and leave. Preferably without getting caught.

They perused textbooks, searched local records for partial blueprints, and even sat outside the prison for hours, watching to see if they could catch a glimpse of Rojric in the window.

But more than anything else, they plumbed their instructors for information. As subtly as they could.

On the way to work one day, sitting opposite his mother in their carriage, Calder held up his Blackwatch badge to the light. "What sort of authority do we have, as Watchmen?"

Alsa looked up in alarm. "Don't arrest anyone! You can't hold anyone under arrest, except during a Guild-sanctioned Blackwatch assignment, or in certain emergencies."

Calder glanced away from the badge. "Why would you assume that I wanted to arrest someone?"

"It's really not so uncommon as you'd think," she said. "Someone always tries it."

He squinted at her, trying to read her expression. "Did *you* try it?"

Spots of color appeared in her cheeks, but her smile was fond. "On your father."

Calder promised himself that he would get the full story from her another time. "I don't want to arrest anyone. Not at the moment. I'm just wondering what we can do."

She sighed. "A natural question. You must remember that the Blackwatch are never held in the highest public opinion, so the people will resist you, fear you, and even work against you if they get the chance."

Calder had already begun to notice that. He tried to refrain from wearing his badge and black coat until he actually arrived on *The Testament's* work site, to avoid the frightened looks and dark comments.

"Technically, you can order any citizen to do anything if it relates to an Elder or Elder magic, or if Elderspawn have been spotted in the area. Anything *legal,*" she amended. "You can even call on Imperial troops or other low-ranking Guild members to assist you in your duties, and they are bound by the Emperor's decree to comply to the best of their ability."

That sounded promising. He could simply order the staff of Candle Bay to release his father, claiming that he was suspected of Elder corruption. If they argued, he could threaten them with the involvement of Imperial troops. They would likely give him whatever he wanted.

The future was looking bright until she added, "Of course, you have to justify whatever you do to the Guild Head."

Picturing Bliss' blank expression, Calder froze.

"If you have her authorization to begin with, there's no problem. But if you're operating on your own, and she doesn't approve, you'll have to answer to *her.*"

Alsa leaned forward in the carriage, placing her hand on his knee, and looked into Calder's eyes with absolute gravity. "Calder. You don't want to answer to Bliss."

"No, I do not," he agreed.

He would have to come up with a different plan.

She leaned back, satisfied. Then she added, "And don't arrest anyone."

"Did you know my mother once worked in an Imperial Prison?" Jyrine mentioned idly, during a tutoring session.

Artur's eyebrows raised. "Oh, is that so? Well, the journal of Estyr Six only mentions the prisons this once. If you'll return your attention to the text, you'll see—"

"Did Estyr help to establish the original prisons?" she interrupted.

"As I said, her journal only mentions them once, in passing."

Calder decided to throw in his support. "But surely you have to know, right? She's one of the heroes of the early Empire, she has to be mentioned in more than just her own journal."

Artur glanced over at Vorus, who was scribbling something onto a loose piece of paper. "This is really my brother's area of expertise more than mine."

Vorus held up a sheet of paper. "Jorin designed," it read. "Estyr enforced."

Artur brightened. "Ah, of course! Thank you, Vorus. You see, the original Imperial Prison was built off the coast of Aurelia, on the land we now know as the Gray Island. It was a prototype designed and built by Jorin himself: Jorin the Curse-breaker, Jorin the Maze-walker. He gets less of a mention in history because he tended not to involve himself openly in battles, but many historians speculate that he was one of the Emperor's original companions."

Finally! An interesting story out of Imperial history.

"Does that have any relationship to Imperial prisons today?" Jerri asked, as Calder feverishly sketched notes.

"Very little, I would think. Jorin's prototype is more the sort of thing you'd find in an adventure novel—spikes, false passages, alchemical traps, stone invested to trap intruders. I suspect it was more of a hobby to him than a serious architectural endeavor."

Calder dropped his pen, disappointed, but Vorus had picked his back up. He held out another sheet of paper to his brother.

"That's right, that's right!" Artur exclaimed. "One of the most innovative bits of Reading in Imperial history, and I almost forgot to mention it. Jorin designed one device for the gates of his Gray Island labyrinth that is supposedly still in use today. Modern prisons all have an analogue, you see."

Calder tried to keep the impatience from his voice. "And? What is it?"

In excitement, Artur pounded his massive fist on the table. Everything on the wooden surface jumped six inches in the air. "A way to *detect Readers*. Imagine it! There's no difference medically in Readers and ordinary people, so there should be nothing to detect, but Jorin managed to pull it off nonetheless. I suppose he uses a structure that is particularly sensitive to unconscious Intent, but I can't imagine *how*."

"I don't understand," Jyrine said. "What good does that do? Surely they know if their prisoners are Readers or not."

"Not the prisoners. Well, yes, the prisoners too. But the staff, and the visitors, and everyone who passes through a particular doorway. You can imagine the problems back then, of course. Any Reader who was taken prisoner could simply spend his days investing a tool, even something so simple as a stick, and then shatter the lock with a touch and stroll out. And a Reader who wanted to break someone else out would have only to disguise themselves as staff and have the run of the facility. This device prevents that, both in ancient prisons and today. A remarkable bit of engineering, really."

Calder's hopes fell, dashed against reality like those escaping prisoners against the rocks of Candle Bay. If they could tell he was a Reader, they'd be watching him from the second he walked in the door.

Artur continued, not noticing his student's mood. "That brings us right around to Estyr Six. At the time, she was functioning as an interim Head of the Imperial Guard, so she made sure that the trap detecting Readers was keyed to a device in her possession. If she was alerted to a Reader trying to sneak out of—or into—an Imperial prison, she would send a squad of Imperial Guards to investigate. To this day, any prison in the Capital can requisition Imperial Guards to respond in case of an emergency."

Calder almost groaned out loud.

By contrast, Jyrine looked delighted. She glanced at him and surreptitiously pointed to herself.

When Calder figured out what she meant, he shook his head.

She pointed to herself more firmly this time.

He shook his head harder.

Two hours later, Jyrine confronted him in the hall outside his room. "It has to be me," she said, arms crossed.

"We don't even know where this 'detector' is. It could be in the front door, or it could be in the warden's quarters. Besides, I'll be able to sense it before I run into it."

"If a Reader could sense it, what good would it be?"

She made a good point.

"We just don't know enough," he said finally. "There's a lot more we need to learn. It would be best if we could visit the prison and get a look for ourselves, but they've turned me away every time. If we snuck in at night—"

"If I snuck in," she corrected. "Because you'd get caught by their magical sensor."

It burned, but she was right. He'd have to rely on her to sneak in.

Not that he had to tell her yet.

"We'll see," he said at last.

"I'll see plenty. Because I'll be in the prison, while you're outside waiting." She uncrossed her arms, smiling proudly.

Calder grumbled and started to make his way downstairs. He was halfway down the staircase when his mother called his name.

She came around the corner carrying an envelope, resting on a tray and sealed with orange wax. "Post for you," she said. By working alongside her on the docks, he had gotten to know her better, and he'd say that she sounded surprised.

Jyrine took the letter from the tray, glanced at it, and gasped.

Calder held out a hand, and she gave it over wordlessly.

Deliver To: *Mr. Calder Marten and His Current Guardian*
At the Residence of Ms. Alsa Grayweather
Sender: *Candle Bay Imperial Prison and Reformative Facility*

He tore the envelope open, taking the letter in his hands almost before he realized it. It was a single sheet of paper with remarkably brief contents.

Mr. Marten,

We are delighted to inform you that our resident, Mr. Rojric Marten, has recovered from his most recent medical procedure and is delighted to receive you. Please present yourself at the Candle Bay facility on the second day of next week, between the hours of three and four in the afternoon.

Cordially and professionally,
Ulrich Fletcher, Warden of Candle Bay

CHAPTER FOURTEEN

Every time Calder saw Cheska Bennett, her hat got bigger.

This time it was a dark blue two-cornered hat two feet tall and wide enough to serve as a lifeboat. She wore a jacket and pants to match, both blue and trimmed in gold. Everything was trimmed in gold, in fact: her boots, the buttons on her shirt, the sheath that hung at her hilt. She even wore golden ornaments in her long, Izyrian red hair.

Which was *combed*. And *styled*.

"Cheska," Calder said, by way of greeting. "Did I miss my invitation to the ball?"

She swept him an elegant curtsy, pulling out imaginary skirts. "Captain Marten, welcome to my ship." She spoiled the manners by grinning. "I know I look good, you don't have to say it."

"I'm still trying to get over the shock of seeing you *clean.* What's the occasion?"

She tipped her hat to one side to scratch her head. "Naberius should have told you. It's an emergency meeting of the powers that be."

It seemed Calder should have pressed the Chronicler for more information. "The who?"

"His *sponsors,* he'd say. We were planning on meeting up with you after you nabbed the Heart, but we got word that there was some trouble. I didn't want to miss anything, so I ran on ahead."

Calder glanced over the deck of *The Eternal.* It didn't look like a vessel prepared for battle; if anything, it looked even more scrubbed and tailored than its captain. Like *The Testament,* it was an Awakened ship, so most of its deck was made of a single, seamless, fused piece of wood. But where Calder's ship was tinged dark green, this wood was a burnt reddish orange, all the way up the mast to the bright red sails.

The two Navigator ships had sailed away from Nakothi's island as soon as possible. The day afterward, when land was out of view, Cheska had called over for Calder to join her. The two ships now drifted a few dozen yards apart, the Watchmen on both vessels calling back and forth to one another.

Cheska pulled the hat off and turned it in her hands, staring at it as though it contained the secrets of the future. "I, ah...I'm sorry Jerri couldn't be here. I'd have liked to see her face when she saw me all made up."

Thinking of his wife caused too many emotions for him to deal with at one time, so he simply nodded and changed the subject. "So where are we meeting these friends of yours?"

The Navigator's Guild Head walked over to the railing, leaning over the water. She pulled a compass out, looked at it, checked the sky, wet one finger in her mouth and stuck it up to measure the wind, then nodded.

"Here's good," she said.

Calder looked around. Other than the peaks of a few distant islands, nothing but blue in every direction. "The middle of nowhere?"

"Might as well be here, then, don't you think?"

That made as much sense as anything else Cheska had ever told him. "Guild Head, please. I've been playing with half a hand this whole time. Tell me honestly: who are we meeting today?"

She considered that for a moment before shaking her head. "Nope."

"I'm begging you, Captain Bennett." Formality had never worked on Cheska before, but maybe this time it would give him some kind of an edge.

"Nah. It's too much fun letting you stew." She put her compass back into her jacket, and then pulled out a watch from the same pocket. "Besides, they should be here soon."

Calder scanned the horizon again. This time, he saw three dark spots that might have just been sails. "It'll take them all afternoon to get here," he protested.

She walked away, waving a crew member over. "Then I suggest you get ready, Captain. They want you at the meeting. I let you know, so my job's over."

With that, she was back to work, ignoring him completely.

That was always his experience dealing with Cheska: she ran him over, moving like a whirlwind, and then moved on before he could get his bearings.

He sighed and looked for someone to row him back to his ship.

Back on *The Testament,* Calder dug through his chest of clothes, wincing as he knelt without thinking on his wounded leg. He shifted his weight to the knee that wasn't bleeding through its bandages, pushing aside one outfit after another. He didn't have anything that his mother would have called suitable, but he should be able to present the image of a proud, hard-working Navigator captain.

His hand rested on folded layers of black at the bottom.

Maybe...

He turned the coat over so that the Blackwatch crest was visible. Even through the fabric, he could feel the lines of the seven iron spikes, sensing the power of their Intent in his fingertips. His mother and the Blackwatch would be involved in this meeting, and Alsa had suggested that Bliss would be back soon. Maybe he didn't want to represent the Navigators now. The Watchmen had responded with surprising respect when they learned who he was. They might let him back in.

He had only retired on an Imperial order in the first place. Now that the Emperor was dead, who cared what Guild he supported? Maybe he wanted to show the Blackwatch that he was still one of them, still on their side, still dedicated to protecting the Empire from Elder threats.

Or maybe he just wanted to feel connected to the life he used to have, so briefly, before he'd made so many mistakes. Living with his mother, back in the Capital, studying every day with Jerri.

He lifted the coat out of the chest, and a bundle of green silk tumbled out.

Calder's eyes stuck to the emerald fabric. It wasn't any clothing, not yet—just a few yards of silk they'd picked up from a trader in Vandenyas. Jerri had always meant to turn it into a dress, just as soon as they found a worthy tailor.

This was her plan for the future, a treat that she had been saving for herself. It seemed obvious, now that he thought of it, but for some reason it hit him like a brick to the side of the head: she hadn't meant to leave. He'd felt betrayed, abandoned by her, when he found out that she had been keeping secrets from him.

Not just any secrets, he thought. *She's one of the Sleepless! She's a Soulbound, and she never told me!*

But she'd planned to stay with him. To keep living with him.

For some reason, that fact alone seemed like a monstrous revelation. He had actually considered *leaving* her to her fate.

No, he already had left her.

It was over.

And it was his fault.

When Andel came in a moment later, he found Calder sitting motionless, leaning his back against the bed, staring at the green silk lying untouched in the chest.

"I left her, Andel," he said, his voice a monotone. "Why did I leave her?"

Andel lowered himself to sit on a bench. "You didn't leave her, sir. You tried to trap the Consultant and find her. It was the best lead you had, and you followed it. Against my advice, I might add."

That sounded good, when he put it like that, but it didn't feel like enough to Calder. He should have run straight after her, not played a game of 'wait and see.' Sure, he hadn't had any idea where to go or what to do, but at the moment that felt like the flimsy excuse of a child caught in a lie.

But none of that was Andel's fault. Andel was always a clear voice of reason, and he didn't deserve to deal with a captain who locked himself in the cabin and stared at a square of folded silk. "I'm sorry, Andel, it just...hits me sometimes."

The Quartermaster looked down at his hands. "I had a...woman I was close to, once. Not a wife. She died. Imperial troops pacifying a rebellious city quarter. I was a Luminian Pilgrim at the time, so I could have stopped it. But I got home six minutes too late. *Six minutes,* Calder. Just in time to clean up the blood."

Calder stared at Andel. The man was full of lessons, advice, and dry wit, but he'd never said two words about his life before. Calder knew more about the Lyathatan's personal history than Andel's.

"That's how I ended up where I am. And this is my way of saying that I know right where you are. If time doesn't heal wounds, it certainly makes them hurt a lot less."

Calder looked back at the unborn dress. "And what about revenge? Does that help?"

"You mean the Emperor? I blamed him for years. I even planned out three assassination attempts, though I never tried any of them, thank the God. They wouldn't have worked anyway. But when I heard he was dead, it didn't help." He looked at Calder for a few seconds. "Ah. Not my revenge. Yours."

"If Shera hadn't attacked us, Jerri would still be alive." And it was more than that: it was Shera's eyes when she fought. Dead. Cold. As though she didn't care about anything or anyone, and that made it easy to kill.

If she had murdered Jerri in a fit of anger, or in self-defense, or in the heat of the moment, he would have understood. It wouldn't have been any easier for him, but at least the picture would make sense. But assassinating a stranger because she got in the way, and staying stone-cold the whole time...*that* deserved retribution. No one like that *deserved* to live.

Calder realized he wasn't making much sense, even to himself, but he shoved that thought aside.

"And if you hadn't let Naberius onboard this ship, the Consultant would never have come here," Andel pointed out. "If you and Jyrine had never met, she wouldn't have been on the ship. And if a falling star had blown the whole ship to smithereens, none of us would have been alive to realize that there was an assassin onboard."

"That's not the same thing, and you know it."

Andel looked up at the boards over his head. "I was exaggerating, but there is one point that needs to be made. We should never have let Naberius onboard this ship."

"I didn't know that at the time."

"I was suspicious. I know you were suspicious. Looking back, that should have been enough." Andel held up a hand. "I'm not blaming you, understand. It was just as much my fault as yours. I'm blaming him."

Calder nodded slowly, remembering Naberius clutching at the Heart. Naberius shooting Tristania in the back of the head. Smiling afterward.

"It's too late now, Andel. All that's left is taking him ashore and getting paid."

Andel leaned closer. "It's not *too* late, sir. I've been talking to the crew of *The Eternal,* and they told me what's happening. A meeting between you, Captain Bennett, Naberius, and his *sponsors.*"

"If you're asking, I don't know who the sponsors are either. Cheska said it was a surprise."

"More surprises," Andel said, voice dry. "I thought you'd be sick of those by now. But that's not the point. My point is, *let's be done with him.* Negotiate a partial fee, leave Naberius with Captain Bennett, and we'll be on our way."

Cheska was withholding information to manipulate him, and he knew that, but Calder still couldn't deny a certain intrigue. Who were Naberius' sponsors? How were they planning on crowning a new Emperor once they got their hands on the Heart of Nakothi? Especially considering...

He glanced at the box underneath the bed. It remained untouched, the secret card in his sleeve.

The sight reminded him of why he was *really* here. The reason Jerri had traveled with him all these years.

He rose to his feet, pulling a coat out of the chest. Anything would do; it wasn't what he wore that would make an impression on these people, but the way he acted.

"It's not about making money, Andel. It never was. I'm aiming higher than that. Naberius is involved in something as big as the Empire itself, and I would be a fool to let this chance go by." He paused. "But I would be just as much a fool to trust him, so you're coming with me."

Andel's face gave nothing away. "Did they give you permission for that?"

"You may have noticed that I don't often ask for permission." He shook himself, rolling his shoulders, shedding his weakness and leaving it on the deck. He needed to show strength at a meeting like this. Not the opposite.

He met his Quartermaster's eyes and spoke firmly. "You know where I'm heading, Andel?"

"I do."

"And are you still with me?"

Andel stood up from the bench, executing a perfect bow at the waist. His silver pendant swung freely. "To the end, sir."

Calder gathered the rest of his clothes, laying them on the bed. "Naberius has one more chance. After that, we're playing our own game."

If there was one feeling that Calder knew with intimate familiarity, it was the sudden panic of finding himself in over his head. The result of his lifestyle, he supposed; he tended to leap off every ledge instead of carefully checking first. It was only natural that a few of those ledges would turn out to be cliffs.

So when he and Andel marched into the main cabin of *The Eternal* only to find four Guild Heads sitting there, watching him enter, he was almost comforted.

One of his choices had put him in boiling-hot water—everything was right with the universe.

The majority of the main cabin was taken up by a long oval table made of the same reddish wood as the rest of the ship. Cheska sat at the far end, the head of the table, still in the same gold-trimmed blue suit and wide hat. Calder had been here before, and it was still impressive to him that the ship was big enough for a main cabin. The room looked bigger than his hold, and it was lit entirely by soft yellow quicklamps.

To her right sat a woman Calder had earnestly prayed never to see again: General and Guild Head of the Imperial Guard, Jarelys Teach. It had been ten years since he'd seen her last, but she didn't look a day older—her hair was still shaved close to the skull, but he didn't see a hint of gray, and her icy blue eyes held no hint of weakness. As always, she wore her full red-and-black plate armor, with that...*horrible* sword over one shoulder. He didn't let his eyes rest on the black hilt for too long, lest he spoil everyone's formal dress with a spray of vomit.

A man sat on Cheska's left, and though Calder had never met him personally, everyone knew him by reputation. Mekendi Maxeus, one of the most prominent instructors at the Capital's Imperial Academy, wore a painted black mask that almost blended in to his Heartlander skin. The result was uncanny, as though his face was naturally inhuman and expressionless. His staff of charred wood rested against the table, close to hand.

The Guild Head of the Magisters leaned his mask forward to regard Calder.

He didn't say a word, so Calder extended his senses to see if he could check the mood of the man's Intent.

Nothing.

That was alarming—though it was hard to Read anything without physical contact, Calder could usually get a whiff of Intent through the air, especially from other powerful Readers. But Maxeus gave off no more Intent than a stone.

It was a cold reminder for Calder, who was used to being the most skilled Reader in any room. Here was a Reader with more talent, training, and experience than anyone Calder had ever met, save the Emperor himself. Anything Calder did, this man could undo.

He wasn't planning on causing a problem at this meeting, but Calder made a mental note not to allow a *spark* of hostility in himself. Maxeus would Read it immediately.

The fourth Guild Head was, of course, an old...friend.

Bliss cocked her head to one side, examining Calder curiously. Here was another person who didn't seem to age; in fact, she might actually look younger than the last time he'd seen her. Pale eyes, pale skin, and white-blond hair made her look like a ghost, especially in contrast to her long black coat that covered her from neck to ankles. A line of silver buttons down the middle glinted in the lamplight, each etched with the Blackwatch Crest.

Something inside that coat squirmed, and she pushed it down absently. In spite of himself, Calder shivered.

Alsa stood behind Bliss, arms locked behind her back. She nodded to Calder when he entered, but said nothing. This was not his mother, but a Blackwatch Commander on duty.

The one other member of their assembly was Naberius Clayborn, again wearing his original eye-catching red suit. He had recovered every scrap of his poise, and once again looked like a dark-haired hero. His case of candles sat on the table to his right, unopened.

That was everyone in the room. Other than Bliss, none of the Guild Heads had bothered to bring an attendant.

It occurred to him now that Andel's presence would look like a childish gesture, as if he were bringing along a chaperone.

Calder stood for a long, awkward moment, adjusting his jacket—it was tight across the shoulders, and it itched—while he tried to decide what to do. He had expected influential figures in the Empire, but not *four* Guild Heads. Cheska, maybe Bliss, and a couple of clerks from the Palace.

He'd known that Naberius was into something big. But he hadn't realized exactly how big until this exact moment.

Out of sight of the table, Andel nudged Calder with his elbow. He turned his stumble forward into a walk, sliding into the round bench that circled the table. The seat looked as though it had grown in place.

Bliss slowly raised a hand and waved to Calder. "I am pleased to see you again, Calder Marten. I hear your wife has been kidnapped, or possibly killed."

At the head of the table, Cheska sighed. Alsa stiffened, but said nothing.

You belong here, Calder reminded himself. *They're not above you.*

Except, for the moment, they were. But the reminder helped him, and he managed to give Bliss a sad smile. "That's true. I'm afraid she's dead."

The leader of the Blackwatch Guild tilted her head the other way. "You imply that you have some information suggesting that she is dead, beyond her kidnapping. What makes you think that?"

Maxeus cleared his throat and spoke, in the resonating voice of a trained orator. "Lady Bliss, I think it would be appropriate if—"

Bliss cut him off by raising a finger to her lips. "Sssssssshhhh. It's not your turn yet." She nodded to Calder. "Please continue."

Maxeus massaged his temple with one hand.

Keeping one wary eye on the Magister, Calder answered. "The Consultant assassin, Shera. She said that Jyrine was...that she had been killed."

"And she had a reason to tell you the truth?"

She didn't have a reason to lie, Calder thought, but he gave the matter a little more thought. If they were actually keeping Jerri alive, why would the Consultant tell him that? Wouldn't it be safer if she lied about it? No matter what the truth was, she had no reason to tell him anything except that his wife was...gone.

It was thin, but it made him feel better than he had in three weeks.

"No, she did not," he said at last.

Bliss settled back in her chair. Though she didn't smile, her manner somehow conveyed satisfaction.

Cheska took the opportunity to control the meeting, leaning forward with her elbows on the table. "You need any introductions, Calder?"

He shook his head.

"Guild Heads, Naberius, this is Calder Marten, one of my Navigators and formerly of the Blackwatch. Behind him is his quartermaster, Andel Petronus, who is on my ship for reasons known only to him and his Luminian God."

Calder glanced over his shoulder to see Andel's reaction. Unsurprisingly, he gave none: he simply nodded at his introduction and then stood with his arms behind his back in imitation of Alsa.

"Formerly of the Blackwatch?" Maxeus asked. He turned his mask to Bliss. "I was under the impression that your Guild did not give up its members easily. What did he do?"

Calder opened his mouth to answer for himself, but the Head of the Imperial Guard responded first.

"Destruction of Imperial property," she recited. "Conspiracy to free prisoners. Theft of the Emperor's personal belongings. Abuse of Guild privileges to commit crimes."

He couldn't see how Maxeus reacted to the news through the man's mask, but Cheska gave a low whistle.

"You know, when you hear it all spelled out like that, it's actually pretty impressive."

She tipped her hat to Calder, and he responded in kind. Jarelys Teach's expression got, if possible, even colder.

At times like this, it was hard *not* to like Cheska.

Naberius rapped his knuckles on the table, drawing attention. "Ladies and gentlemen, pardon me for interrupting, but we do have business of a somewhat urgent nature to discuss."

"Not that urgent," Cheska said. "They have almost a two-day head start."

He flashed her a smile. "I'm sorry, Guild Head. I was under the impression that a Navigator ship was still fast enough to overtake them."

"That's why it isn't urgent." She waved a hand in concession. "But let's get it over with anyway. They got the Heart. What do we do now?"

"We can follow it, given time," Maxeus said. "I am merely concerned about the fate of the Heart *within* that time frame. To what use will the Consultants put an artifact of Nakothi?"

"Who knows?" Cheska muttered.

Jarelys leaned forward. "I am acquainted with two of the three currently ruling Architects in the Consultant's Guild, as well as this assassin herself. They won't try and use the Heart at all. They'll try to destroy it."

"Is negotiation an option?" Maxeus suggested.

Calder, for one, doubted it. If the Consultants were open to negotiation, they wouldn't have started by sending an assassin for their opposition. Cheska evidently agreed. "With what leverage? We can't threaten to ban them, because they're not using our Guilds in the first place. I have no idea how they're traveling the Aion so quickly without a Navigator, but Kelarac knows they're *not* using my ships. And we can't threaten war, because we can't actually wage a war against the Consultants and the Alchemists combined. They could buy everyone at this table twice over."

Bliss was staring straight up at the ceiling, so it was a surprise when she spoke. "Nathanael Bareius will do everything he can to avoid a war. Peace is good for business. But the Consultants prosper in wartime, so it stands to reason that their goals will be…different."

"There is an opening there," Maxeus mused, "if only we can use it."

Naberius gave a forced laugh. "I'm sorry, but this is like fighting a duel assuming you'll die. We haven't even discussed the possibility of recovering the Heart before it makes it back to the Gray Island."

Maxeus' mask turned to the Chronicler. "As I said before, Witness Naberius, it takes time to trace such a faint residue as the Heart of Nakothi leaves. By that time, the Consultants will already have control of the artifact."

Calder thought of Urzaia's promise. *"I have tasted her blood."* He could track the blond Consultant, Shera's partner, wherever they went. It wasn't Shera herself, nor was it the Heart, but it could be the best lead they had.

So he kept the knowledge to himself. When you had the highest card at the table, it was best to keep it close as long as you could. His father had taught him that.

"I'm sorry, I was under the impression that we had the Head of the Navigator's Guild present," Naberius said. "Surely we have enough ships between us to search manually. We know where they're headed—if we can overtake them before they reach the Gray Island, then it's our victory."

Calder's eyes whipped to Cheska. He didn't know how she treated people who spoke to her in that tone, because no one did. He wouldn't be surprised to see her pin Naberius' hand to the table with her saber.

But she did nothing. She obviously noticed—her mouth tightened to a grim line, and her eyes smoldered—but she kept quiet.

Who *was* Naberius, that even Cheska showed him respect? Calder had only known the man for a few weeks, but he didn't seem so terribly impressive.

"The Consultants would retaliate," Teach put in.

Maxeus nodded to her, recognizing the point. "Even if we were to recover the Heart, it would not immediately result in success. Naberius, how long would it take you to Awaken and bond the Heart?

Wait a second.

Naberius gave a self-satisfied smile. "On that front, I have good news. I began the process on the island, and I believe I can do it very quickly. One hour, maybe two."

The Magister's shock was obvious. "So fast? It can take years for a Soulbound to bond a Vessel. Especially a Vessel with which he has had only brief contact. How did you do it?"

"It's difficult to put into words, but this heart seemed to conform itself to my Intent. It could be due to personal compatibility, or due to my own long proximity to the Emperor."

Jarelys Teach rolled her eyes, but said nothing.

"It's almost as though the Heart was made to bond with a human."

Bliss' stretch of bench was empty, and her voice came from under the table. "Or perhaps it wants to be bonded."

The table fell quiet at that, but Calder couldn't stay silent.

They wanted *Naberius* to bond the Heart?

He pointed at the Chronicler, unable to contain his disbelief. "You want *him?*"

Far from being insulted, Naberius looked flattered. As though Calder's doubt was the exact reaction he had worked for.

Cheska sighed. "He's the only choice, Calder. None of us can take over. Guild politics. And he's got the keys to the Imperial Palace treasury."

"Not to mention a significant personal fortune of my own," Naberius said, smiling.

"He does have the potential to bond the Heart," Maxeus said. "And it was surprisingly difficult for us to find anyone remotely qualified to take the position, even if we wanted to give it away. It seems that no one wants the job."

"Nobody wants to be the *Emperor?*" Calder spat out.

Bliss' head popped up from under the table. "I, for one, don't care who the Emperor is. But we need one. And soon."

Teach nodded. "Without an Emperor, the Imperial Guard will eventually fall apart. The Regents are doing what they can, but they are no substitute for a true Emperor. And one and all, the four of them have refused the position. If something is not done soon, the entire Empire will tear itself to pieces."

Cheska jerked a thumb in Naberius' direction. "That leaves him. He's got friends in every Guild, he's a Reader, he knows exactly how the government works from personal experience, and he has lots and lots of money. Easy choice, if you're asking me."

Calder tugged at his ill-fitting jacket, trying to process his thoughts. "And what about the other side? The Consultants? Who do they want to be Emperor?"

Teach scowled, not at him, but at the world in general. "They would prefer no Emperor. A world of anarchy must look like a haven for a band of spies and assassins."

Cheska rapped her knuckles on the table. "Okay, that's enough. We'll try it your way, Mister Emperor. All ships in the area spread out and search for the Consultants. In the meantime, Calder will take Naberius and head straight for the Gray Island. Where he will wait for orders, in case we find the Heart elsewhere."

"Why him?" Teach asked.

This one, Calder could answer for himself. "Over long distances, *The Testament* is the fastest ship in the Guild. I can continue in a straight line regardless of wind or tide, you see. It's possible that if I head straight for the Gray Island, I could overtake them myself."

Cheska turned to Naberius. "You okay staying with him, *Your Imperial Highness?*"

Naberius smiled his wide, spotless smile. "I wouldn't have it any other way."

CHAPTER FIFTEEN

Awakening is a poorly understood process, though it is the method by which we create all our Soulbound and many of our most powerful weapons. Even the brightest minds in the Empire know very little about the nature of Awakened objects.

So please, I beg you, do not attempt to Awaken anything without the direct supervision of myself or your mother.

– Artur Belfry, Imperial Witness
taken from a letter to his pupil,
Calder Marten (fourteen years of age)

ELEVEN YEARS AGO

The reception room of Candle Bay Imperial Prison was just as Calder remembered it: small, cramped, and decorated almost entirely in white. The receptionist's desk took up most of the wall, and there were no chairs for guests—only stools. Small, three-legged, wobbly stools. It was as though the whole room had been designed to make visitors as uncomfortable as possible.

Alsa had offered to accompany him today, and Jerri had positively begged, but Calder has asked them both to stay at home. The support would have been welcome, but he hadn't seen his father in the better part of two years. The last time they'd seen each other was during a burglary.

Calder wanted to speak freely.

The receptionist, a young woman with a dazzling smile, noticed him as soon as he walked in the door. "Calder Marten, is it?"

"I've been here twice a month for the past year and a half," Calder said flatly. He'd stopped being polite to this woman almost a year ago.

She didn't lose her smile. "Your name is Calder Marten, correct?"

He ground his teeth. "That's correct."

"The prisoner will be available to see you at three in the afternoon," the receptionist said sweetly. "Until that time, why don't you relax?"

Calder glanced at the clock. Two minutes until three.

"Why don't we pass the time getting to know each other?" he asked, suddenly as friendly as she was. He hadn't cracked her facade in all of his previous visits, but who knew? Maybe this was the time. "What is *your* name?"

"I'm sorry, sir, but we're not permitted to divulge personal information during our hours of business."

She grinned as though pleased to have answered his question so thoroughly.

He wasn't wearing his Watchman's coat today, but he found that he missed the weight of the seven nails hanging over his chest. If he had them to hand, he'd be tempted to see if this receptionist had a brain, heart, and spine in addition to her four limbs.

"Tell me, what do you do outside your hours of business?"

She cocked her head, as if confused at the question. "During business hours, I am here at the facility. When the facility does not require my assistance, I am asleep."

He broadened his grin to match hers. "Why, that sounds *thrilling*. Do you suppose the weather will continue, or do you think the sun will blacken and shrivel up?"

The receptionist's smile suggested he'd just told a joke. "I have no opinion on the subject."

That was her favorite line: *I have no opinion on the subject.* If he had a mark for every time he'd heard that from her during his previous visits, he'd be changing them to goldmarks soon. "No opinion? I see. If I were to strip and dance naked on your desk, would you have an opinion?"

Her smile didn't shrink by a single tooth. "I would be forced to call security in that instance, sir."

Calder stopped. It was useless. He stood and let the remaining seconds until three o'clock drip by.

She smiled the whole time.

At precisely three in the afternoon, she rose from her chair and beckoned him back, through a simple white door. "This way, sir."

As he passed through the door, Calder couldn't help but wonder: *Is this the sensor? Do they know I'm a Reader? They know my name; they might know anyway.*

But nothing obvious happened. No crimson quicklamp came flaring to life; no guards rang a bell to sound the alarm. The floor didn't dissolve beneath him.

The receptionist led him down several disappointingly boring hallways. At first he tried to focus on memorizing her route, but he quickly realized that it wasn't necessary. The floor was polished stone, the walls wooden, and after a few turns he came to realize that the whole facility was a square grid. She might as well have handed him a map.

The whole time, he watched every doorframe and stretch of ceiling, looking for something that might indicate a Reader-detecting trap. He saw nothing, heard nothing, and felt nothing.

When they finally reached his father's cell, the receptionist handed him a beaten copper bell. "I will come to collect you at four o'clock. If you wish to depart before that time, or if you notice any unusual behavior in the prisoner, please ring that bell. A member of the facility staff will come to assist you as quickly as possible."

With one more beaming smile, the receptionist bowed out of the room.

The heavy cell door clanged shut behind him, but Calder hardly noticed.

He was with his father again.

Rojric Marten looked much healthier than Calder had imagined. His red beard was neatly trimmed, his hair combed. Even his bright red one-piece prison uniform seemed tailored to fit.

Come to think of it, is this really a cell?

The room wasn't pristine, but it looked like a home. The bed had a quilt on it, and a writing-desk sat in the corner, piled with books. There was even a small quicklamp bolted to the wall, with a pull-cord to activate and deactivate it.

"I think you're living better than I am," Calder said, and laughed weakly. His palms were wet, his heart racing.

Rojric smiled broadly, leaning back in his chair. "Yes, I suspect I am. Better than I ever did on the street, I'm sure."

This time, they laughed together.

"How are they treating you here?" Calder asked, waving his hand to encompass the facility behind him. "Is everything...okay."

Rojric chuckled. "Oh, better than okay. Regular meals, plenty to read, excellent medical care. I feel better than I have in my entire life."

Calder relaxed. Suddenly, the whole plan to break him out of prison seemed silly, like the games of children. When the receptionist had turned him away so many times, he had invented dark and ominous reasons, creating a fiction that his mind was more than willing to accept.

The whole time, his father had been up here reading and exercising.

Calder sat back on the bed, facing his father. "I've been living with Mother, you know."

Rojric didn't seem surprised; Calder supposed someone in the prison must have told him. "I'm glad to hear it, son. She's a wonderful woman. Everything is going well for you, then?"

Prison must have done a miracle on his father, to have him calling Alsa 'wonderful.' At most, he would have grudgingly called her 'professional.'

"As well as can be expected," Calder said. "I, ah...I found a new job. I'm a Watchman now. With the Blackwatch. You know, the Guild."

This was the news he had most dreaded breaking to his father. Rojric hated the Guilds, didn't trust them, and the Blackwatch was the most suspicious of all. But this new Rojric, softened by prison, might actually be pleased.

And pleased he was; he positively beamed at his son. "Such good news! You've got such a promising career at such a young age. And you'll be able to serve the Emperor, the light and life of our Empire."

Calder examined his father carefully, searching for any sign of irony. "You approve, then?"

"Of course! Why would I not? A good, steady income and a chance to serve the Emperor is all I could want for my son!"

Something was wrong here. Were they being watched? Was that why his father was playing the Good Imperial Citizen all of a sudden?

He lowered his voice, just in case. "Father. You once told me that the Empire would be better off eating itself alive than dying slowly under this Elder-spawned excuse for a ruler."

Rojric chuckled again. "No, that doesn't sound like me."

Calder's suspicions bloomed to full-blown alarm. Reaching out to the reading-desk, he placed his hand on the stack of books.

Rojric is in pain, he's sweating, the walls are closing in, and he has to escape. Maybe if he uses the book, he can break the window and leap into the bay. Break, window! BREAK!

Calder jerked his hand away, already gasping for breath at the brief contact.

Rojric peered at him, brow furrowed in worry. "Are you feeling all right, son? We could call a doctor. They have an excellent medical staff here, you know."

He grabbed the quilt.

Rojric twists the quilt in his fists, braiding it into a rope. If he kills himself quickly, they won't be able to hurt him anymore. "No more shots," he silently begs. "Kill me quickly."

His father's pain and fear blazed in Calder, burning away his doubts and worries for himself.

"Two days ago," he began, suddenly resolute. "I was working out in the harbor. I saw at least five prisoners open a window and plunge to their deaths on the rocks below. Why would they do that, Father?"

Rojric's smile suddenly looked as though it had been painted on, as fake as the receptionist's. "How should I know, son?"

Calder pointed at the window overlooking Candle Bay. "If I opened that window, right now, would you jump out?"

His father froze. "You can't open that window, Calder. It doesn't open. It *never* opens."

Calder walked over and placed his hands on the window as though to open it. "I'm a Reader, remember? I can open it. But only if you want me to. Only if you want to jump out. Do you? Do you want to jump out?"

Rojric choked out a single word past a frozen, paralyzed smile. "Yes."

Calder gathered his father into an embrace, fighting back tears. At that moment, if he could have planted an alchemical charge and blown the whole prison to rubble, he would have lit the fuse with a smile on his face.

Hesitantly, weakly, Rojric wrapped his arms around his son.

The cell door was locked, but Calder opened it anyway.

Two security guards hurried down the hall as he walked away, but he just ignored them and they ran past, inspecting the door to see what had gone wrong with the lock. Rojric didn't make a fuss or try to escape. In fact, Calder heard him chatting pleasantly with the guards from back in his cell.

When he reached the receptionist, he placed the copper bell back on her desk. "I found my own way back."

"That was against facility procedure," she said, smiling.

Calder placed both hands on the desk and leaned forward until he was almost nose-to-nose with her. He expected her to back up. She didn't. "I have a hypothetical situation for you. What if, when I came back, I *burned this place to the ground?*"

Her smile didn't crack. "In that case, I would be forced to call security."

Suddenly, the whole scene twisted in his mind—the smiling receptionist became the receptionist who *had* to smile. She literally couldn't make any other expression.

"What did they do to you?" he asked, hoping for a frown, for an expression of confusion to break through her mask.

The smile remained, strong and steady. "We have excellent medical care at this facility."

Calder nodded. *Of course.* He wasn't sure what else he'd expected.

Maybe that was just another scripted response, or maybe she had been trying to tell him what happened, in her own way.

It didn't matter, he supposed. If he had his way, he would leave this prison as nothing more than a hole in the ground. It didn't deserve to exist.

CHAPTER SIXTEEN

Alsa stood on the outside of the table, watching the meeting between the Guild Heads, the future Emperor, and her son.

It wasn't her place to speak—she was meant to keep an eye on Bliss, and to translate for her if she said anything particularly strange. But it was getting harder and harder to keep her peace.

Why wasn't Bliss saying anything else?

Naberius, in his red suit, rose to his feet and bowed toward the door. "Well, Captain Marten, Quartermaster, I'm sure you have many preparations to make. Please, don't let me keep you."

Andel was a difficult man to read, but Alsa knew him well enough to notice the way his mouth tightened. He didn't like Naberius, and he wasn't happy with being dismissed. That attitude would not serve him if Naberius actually did ascend to the throne.

Calder, on the other hand, smiled widely. "Of course." He dipped his head toward each member of the council in turn. "Guild Heads. Naberius. Mother."

She had stayed quiet long enough. Alsa opened her mouth to speak, but found that Bliss had twisted around on her bench to stare her Blackwatch Commander in the eyes.

Alsa hesitated, and then Calder was gone.

Naberius continued, turning to Cheska. "Captain Bennett, you have served us well as host. Now I have a few tasks for you."

She folded her arms. "Do you, now?"

"Trust me, I don't have you doing anything that you wouldn't do on your own. First, you must..."

While the Chronicler spoke, Alsa leaned down to speak in her Guild Head's ear. "Why didn't you tell him?"

"I implied that his wife may be alive, and that he should check for himself. I'm sure he got the message."

"You didn't tell him about the void transmission. That there is a member of the Sleepless on that island, that they're in contact with the rest of their cult, and so it's probably his wife."

Bliss drifted her hand through the air, as though she were tracing invisible waves. "It's all implied."

"With all due respect, Guild Head, no it isn't."

"Is that so? Hm. I will look for an opportunity to clarify, then."

Naberius was still talking to Cheska. The Navigator didn't seem too happy—Alsa had seen her smile while throwing a man overboard, and now she was scowling. Everyone was far enough away that they shouldn't overhear, and they probably wouldn't bother listening to Alsa anyway, but she lowered her voice so that even Bliss would have trouble hearing her from an inch away.

"And what about Naberius? He's obviously in thrall to Nakothi. Why didn't you say anything?"

Bliss raised a single finger into the air, staring at it as though it contained all the secrets of the universe. "Not in thrall. Not yet. Close to it, though."

"That's even worse than the old Emperor! With him, we would have had a few years left, and then now what? Weeks?"

"Anyone on the throne is better than no one," Bliss said simply. "If he can stall the Elders for a week, then that's a week we didn't have before. We can always replace him."

"Unless they finish the process, and he's all they need."

"Don't be silly. Naberius isn't strong enough for that."

The future Emperor had fallen silent, and Cheska was missing. Bliss, of course, hadn't bothered to lower her voice—the whole room heard what she'd said.

Alsa resisted the urge to cover her face with a hand, instead straightening her coat and trying to look as disciplined as possible.

Naberius' handsome smile had an edge to it. "Commander Grayweather, I'm sure you'd like to have a few words with your son before he returns to his ship. You're dismissed."

A perfect opportunity. Now Alsa could warn Calder about Naberius, and about the void transmission from the island. She bowed to Naberius and turned to walk out of the room.

A small, pale hand rested on her arm. "I'd rather she stay," Bliss said softly.

It could be frustrating, working directly with Bliss—the Guild Head often decided to follow whatever whim popped into her head, without reason or explanation, and Alsa was simply expected to adapt. So for a moment, Alsa couldn't see past her irritation.

She had *just* explained that she needed to talk to Calder. It was even Guild business! And now Bliss didn't want her to leave?

Then Alsa noticed something: Jarelys Teach and Mekendi Maxeus were staying at the table, as though they had no intention of moving. *He's dismissing the people he doesn't need,* she realized.

What business did he have to discuss with three of his four supporting Guild Heads, and no one else?

Maybe this was one of those occasions where Bliss actually *did* know what she was doing.

Naberius clapped his hands together. "Right, then. General Teach, would you remove Commander Grayweather from the room?"

Teach hesitated, looking to the Blackwatch Head.

Bliss smiled just a little. "I'd rather she *stay.*"

General Teach turned back to her future Emperor, her spine ramrod-straight even in her seat. "I will do as you command. But if the Guild Head resists, then this whole ship would be in danger."

Naberius' smile had vanished, and he gestured to Maxeus. "It's two against one."

"That won't matter if we're all at the bottom of the ocean."

Bliss began tracing designs on the table with her finger, doodling invisible figure eights.

A bead of sweat traced its way down Alsa's cheek. If three Guild Heads came to blows...Teach was right, the ship wouldn't survive. Even *The Testament,* anchored two dozen yards away, would be in danger. She had to make sure that didn't happen, even if it meant playing into Naberius' hand by missing the meeting. But Bliss wanted her there...

She was spared the decision when Naberius threw up his hands. "Fine then, Commander Grayweather can stay. It would have been easier had she just co-operated, but it's no matter. Make sure she stays under control."

Alsa's stomach sank. There were only a few reasons she could think of that Naberius wouldn't want her specifically to hear the contents of this meeting, and most of them revolved around Calder.

Sure enough, Naberius adopted a commanding pose, leaning one hand on the table and pointing the other at the General. "Load as many Guards onto *The Testament* as you can. Get the crew on deck, and then execute them."

Alsa's stomach was sucked into the void, and it left her feeling empty. She had stayed away from Calder for most of his life, and spent much of that time angry with him. But this was her *son.* And it made no sense.

Maxeus adjusted his mask, uncomfortable. "Why wait? Why not kill him now?"

"I agree," Teach said. "Make this an official execution, and let me take care of it right now."

Naberius' fists tightened. "If you plan on following my orders in the future, then now would be an excellent time to start. I don't trust Captain Bennett any more than Captain Marten. Let me remind you all that she is a Soulbound, and we are all riding on her Vessel."

"It seems to me that she will put the pieces together when she *sees* us gunning down her ally," Maxeus said.

"And what will she do then? Rescue their corpses?" Naberius waved a hand through the air. "I've given her an explanation, and orders that will prevent her from acting until it's too late. We can clarify afterwards."

General Teach glowered at the table. "I will keep Captain Bennett under control, but I don't like risking you in this." She turned her glare on Naberius. "Let them sail off alone, and I will follow on my Windwatcher. I will kill them all in a day or two."

Alsa's instincts screamed for her to pull her saber and cut her way free from the room, but she would die before her sword cleared its sheath.

Instead, she spoke. "Please, I must know why."

The Chronicler looked to Bliss, as if to say, *"You see? This is why I wanted her to leave."*

"He has proven repeatedly that he will not follow me or my orders, and I suspect he will turn on me as soon as circumstances allow. I'm simply minimizing risk."

"We need him," Alsa said. If she could establish some sort of camaraderie with this uncrowned Emperor, maybe she could get him to listen.

"We don't need him, we need his *ship*," Naberius corrected. "And I can take control of it. That's why I can't let them stay a day or two out, General Teach. That ship might well pack up and swim away."

Alsa looked from him to the Magister. "Can he do that? He has to bond the Heart, if this plan is to work. He can't do that *and* take control of *The Testament*. Can he?"

"It's technically possible," Maxeus allowed. "But it would be unspeakably difficult, and I can't imagine it taking less than two weeks."

Naberius wore a confident smile like a mask. "You must learn to trust me, Maxeus. I can do things that no one else can."

The Magister shrugged. "If he believes he can do it, then I have no further objection. Though this does seem extreme. I would think the easiest course would be to simply *pay* Captain Marten and let him do his job."

Finally! Alsa thought. *A reasonable voice.*

But Naberius turned to the Magister with a sympathetic, condescending look that dashed her hopes to pieces. "Mekendi, my friend, you have to trust me. I've spent the last three weeks on that man's ship. I have Read every inch, every board on that vessel. And I have done my best to get to know the Captain. No matter what he says, no matter what he may even tell himself, there is absolutely no chance that he will ever follow my leadership. He simply doesn't have it in him. I believe he thinks of himself as a…rival, of sorts. No, he has to go."

Reluctantly, Professor Maxeus nodded.

General Teach actually seemed soothed by the Chronicler's speech. With her concerns addressed, she rose from her seat and marched over to the door, armor clanking with every step. She leaned a head out of the cracked door, speaking softly to one of her Guards.

Alsa slumped back against the hull, despair settling over her like a cold blanket. Maybe she ought to fight for it anyway. It was somehow worse knowing what was going to happen and being unable to stop it than *trying* to stop it and dying in the process.

On her way back to the bench, Teach stopped in front of Alsa. In a rare display of humanity, she placed a gauntleted hand on Alsa's shoulder. "I'm sorry you were here for this, Grayweather. I will make it painless."

Tears welled up in Alsa's eyes, and she nodded. Sad to say, but those were the most touching words she'd ever heard out of the General's mouth.

Naberius straightened his red coat, adjusting the buttons, and then picked up his case of candles. "Well, I'd better keep an eye on my ship. Ladies, gentleman, it's been a pleasure as always."

General Teach pushed her way out the door, and Naberius swept out behind her without another word.

Maxeus sighed and leaned back in his chair. "I'm very sorry. Grayweather, is it? You should not have been allowed to hear that."

In spite of herself, Alsa agreed. It was normally her policy to face unpleasant truths head-on, rather than hiding in denial, but today...if there was nothing she could do to save her son, then what was the point of even knowing about it?

She would have to ask her Guild Head.

Bliss was missing from the bench, but that wasn't unusual. Alsa leaned over, calling under the table. "The meeting is over, Guild Head. We need to leave."

"Not you," Maxeus corrected, his voice regretful. "I'm sorry, but I must ask you to stay here with me for the time being."

Alsa's fist tightened on the grip of her sword until her knuckles flared with pain. The Magister could probably reduce her to ashes with a thought, if the rumors were true, but he was still only one man. Maybe if she were fast enough...

He sighed through his mask. "Please don't make me subdue you. It's difficult to do so gently."

Alsa gestured under the table. "Can Bliss leave, at least?"

"I have no orders to the contrary."

Alsa screamed under the table, a normally unforgivable breach in propriety. "*Guild Head!* Come out of there, now!"

Nothing. Not a sound.

She dropped to her knees, searching as if for a small child.

There was no one under the table.

She straightened, glancing to every corner of the room. Slowly, a smile crawled across her face.

The Magister's mask tilted. "What is it?"

"Where's Bliss?" she asked softly.

Maxeus looked under the table himself, and Alsa took her opportunity.

She vaulted over the table, saber clearing its sheath.

One of the Magister's hands shot out for his burnt staff, but he was too slow. She landed with her knees on the table, jerking one foot out and kicking the dark wood out of his reach. With the other hand, she pressed the point of her sword against the underside of his chin.

"I'm sorry, Professor, but I must ask you to stay here with me until my son's ship has departed."

"Fair enough," the Magister said calmly, raising both hands. "I sympathize with you, Grayweather, I really do. But this is rash."

I hope Bliss is using this time well, she thought.

If the Guild Head strolled back through this door and asked what was going on, Alsa was going to do her very best to kill the woman.

Until then, she silently begged Bliss:

Save my son.

Calder and Andel sat on the benches of a rowboat, surrounded by Imperial Guards. Calder was having a hard time relaxing.

For one thing, the last time he'd been surrounded by the Guards, it had ended in a trial. The time before that, in an arrest. So he had some understandably unresolved issues. But he had a hard time imagining anyone comfortable surrounding by such a menagerie: one of the rowers had red-scaled arms with spikes protruding from the elbows. Another had the reverse-jointed legs of a lion, and furry ears high up on her head.

A thin, pale man in a Guard's uniform stared endlessly at Calder, his eyes solid blue-white like a pair of full moons. A gaze like that could unnerve a Champion.

Andel leaned in, speaking quietly. The Guards could probably still hear him, but every little bit of secrecy helped. "We're leaving as soon as we raise sails, right?"

"As soon as Naberius is onboard, yes."

"I see. You want him to walk the plank. Old-fashioned, but I can see the appeal."

A Guardswoman with a lashing tail glared at Andel, but the Quartermaster returned her gaze evenly.

"He wants us to go to the Gray Island and wait," Calder said. "That's where we want to go anyway. We've effectively received Imperial permission to do exactly what we wanted. Why complain?"

"Because he will inevitably see us all dead."

"So long as he starts with you, I will consider myself the winner."

The shadow of *The Testament* loomed over them, even as the Lyathatan's shadow writhed beneath the water. The red-armed Guard looked over the edge and shuddered, backing deeper into the boat.

Well, it looked like Calder could do his share of intimidating.

Someone tossed a rope ladder down over the side, and Calder gripped it, pulling himself up the hull. "Is that you, Foster?" he called up.

The head that leaned over the edge was covered in quills.

"Ugh! I mean, ah, pleased to meet you, ma'am." The porcupine-woman backed up, unamused. What was the Imperial Guard doing on his ship?

When he reached the deck, he realized there weren't just a few Guards: the deck was crawling with red-and-black uniforms and mismatched body parts. He spotted Foster up in the crow's nest, clutching a pair of muskets to his chest like a miser hoarding coins.

"What's going on here, Foster?"

"You tell me, Captain!" Foster shouted back. "They tried to take my guns!"

"Not very hard," one of the Guards muttered, crossing two pairs of arms.

Calder grabbed that man by the shoulder, stopping him. "Excuse me, Guardsman. What *is* going on here?"

"The future Emperor is boarding," the Guard said simply. "We have to make sure this ship is secure."

Imperial Guards—eternally paranoid. "He sailed here on this ship. If there were any danger onboard, surely he would know it by now."

A lizard-tailed Guardsman pushed past, bending to examine a perfectly innocent coil of rope. "We're acting on orders, Captain. If you have a problem, I suggest you take it up with Lord Clayborn directly."

Andel had reached the deck by this point, and he looked no more pleased than Calder felt. And Calder didn't get any happier when the rest of the Imperial Guards from the rowboat, which he had assumed were only escorts, climbed up the ladder after Andel.

Calder walked over to the edge, peering down. Only a single Guard remained in the boat, paddling back to *The Eternal*. A figure in a red suit emerged onto the deck, accompanied by a woman in red-and-black armor. If he was keeping the Head of the Imperial Guard with him, he must be paranoid indeed.

Since when had Naberius been this concerned with his own security? He had taken a number of risks in this voyage already, including boarding this ship with no more protection than his own Silent One. He hadn't even seemed nervous sharing *The Testament* after he'd killed Tristania right in front of Calder. What did a man with such unassailable self-assurance need with an overwhelming number of Guards?

Mentally, Calder pushed the question away. The Imperial Guards were notoriously enthusiastic when it came to protecting the Emperor. Even the old Emperor, whom everyone had considered immortal, couldn't go anywhere without Guards hovering over him. It must be worse for them when their charge was an ordinary mortal.

Calder walked over to his cabin, where a scaled Guard stood with thick arms folded. "Excuse me, Guardsman. That's my cabin."

"Please stay on the deck until our inspection has concluded."

Spreading his empty hands, Calder smiled. "I just need to change my clothes, I promise I won't delay you. This jacket has never fit well. Five minutes, and I'll be a new man."

The Guard's eyes flicked over Calder's shoulder as though looking for permission. After a moment, the man stepped aside. "Don't linger. We'll need all the crew on deck soon for inspection."

What do they expect to find? Calder wondered, shaking his head.

He stepped into the cabin and peeled his ill-fitting jacket off as soon as possible. If he never wore the tight, itchy thing again, it would be too soon.

He leaned over, flipping his clothes chest open. Ordinarily he could have just walked around without a jacket, but he suspected he would need every scrap of dignity and authority he could muster with Naberius and the Imperial Guard on his ship.

There was a girl in the chest.

Covered in a long black cloak, with white-blond hair spilling down her back, Bliss lay curled on top of his piled clothes. How had she packed herself in there?

While he was still staring in disbelief, Bliss rose, stretching, like a jack-in-the-box.

"You should invest in a more comfortable storage chest," she suggested. "You never know when someone might need to stow away."

Calder wasn't sure why he was surprised. He should have expected something like this as soon as he heard that Bliss was on her way. "I try to discourage stowaways, actually."

She raked her fingers through her hair, smoothing it out. "Why?"

"It's...I'm sorry, I don't have time to explain this. I need to return you to my mother."

"I'll go back to Alsa Grayweather at some point in the future, but for now, I expect she would want me here." Bliss stepped carefully from the chest, one black boot at a time. When she was finally free, she began to stretch out her cramped legs. "She wanted me to tell you that we intercepted a void transmission from the Gray Island, shortly before the Children of the Dead Mother attacked you."

Calder hadn't been a member of the Blackwatch terribly long, though he suspected that if he *had,* then maybe he would have some idea what a 'void transmission' was. "I apologize, Bliss, but I don't know what that means."

"It means there is at least one member of the Sleepless in the care of the Consultants right now. And she contacted her comrades recently, which means she is likely still alive."

She is likely still alive.

He'd gone from certain his wife was dead to filled with painful hope in one night. This felt almost too good to be true, as though Bliss were setting him up for some huge disappointment. "How do you know it didn't come from one of the Consultants?"

"Of all the Guilds who might work under the influence of the Elders, the Consultants are among the least likely. Especially on that island, where they enjoy a certain protection. And they are culturally disinclined as well, according to many leading scholars on the subject."

Bliss had finished stretching. Now she was staring at the seamless wood beneath her. She prodded it with her foot, as though testing it to see if it would collapse.

"So you think it's Jerri?" The Guild Head's implication was clear, but he had to be sure.

"That's the most probable scenario, though I also considered the idea that the Consultants are collecting Sleepless for some reason. That seems like somewhat of a timely coincidence, though, so I consider it less likely." She sat down on the bed, her eyes now wandering over the cabin. "We rarely get to interrogate a member of the Sleepless. I would be interested in talking with your wife, should Jyrine survive."

She said it innocently, but Calder made a mental note not to hand Jerri over to the Blackwatch under any circumstances. He would kill her himself before it came to that.

"I would also like to visit the Gray Island," Bliss said. "I get the impression that several forces will soon converge there, and I should be present for the sake of observation. Naberius might not like it. Then again, he is not Emperor yet. Hm. Should I listen to his orders, I wonder?"

Calder shivered at the thought of Bliss under the Chronicler's control. "Honestly, I'm not sure why anyone listens to him. Of all the people who could become Emperor, why *him?*"

She looked at him curiously. "Do you know why the Emperor died?"

He had some suspicions, but he didn't voice them. "I was never sure, no."

"He was losing his mind," she said. "He kept the Heart of Nakothi at bay for more than one and a half thousand years, but he could not resist the Dead Mother when she began to awaken. So he was killed. I suspect he allowed it, but I cannot prove that theory. However, the fact remains that with him gone, the Elders are more active than ever. If no one directs the Empire as a whole, civilization will disappear bit by bit."

Not for the first time, Calder remembered Naberius' expression as he cradled Nakothi's Heart. "Surely there has to be a better choice."

For some reason, she waved her arms in the air as though chasing away invisible butterflies. "Whomever we select for the throne is going to be taken by the Elders eventually, but better someone like Naberius than no one at all."

Calder stood for a moment, absorbed in his thoughts. He was still having trouble picturing Naberius at the head of the global Empire, but when she put it that way, maybe he was the best man for the job. If the throne was really a sentence of insanity and death, then the Chronicler might even deserve it.

But he couldn't escape the thought that he was missing some crucial piece of the picture. Why did simply being in charge of the Aurelian Empire make him so vulnerable to corruption? Wouldn't it be the Heart? But Bliss spoke as though the authority itself put him at risk.

"It surprises me that you are so concerned about Naberius' rule as Emperor," Bliss said after a moment. "I thought you'd be more worried about his plot to have you killed."

The words echoed in Calder's mind, but it took him a few seconds to hear their meaning. "Please, go on."

The Blackwatch Guild Head slapped herself lightly on the forehead. "Ah. That's right. You didn't know, because I was going to tell you."

A fist hammered on the cabin door. "Time's up, Captain," the Guard called in. "Lord Clayborn needs you on deck."

"Naberius Clayborn is going to call you and your entire crew onto the deck, where he will have you executed. He seems to think that he is preventing an eventual rebellion." She pinched his blanket, lifting it up to examine it. "You should invest in some nice, soft sheets. A good night's sleep is healthy for the human body."

Calder stilled his shaking hands as he raced through all the possibilities. *Urzaia.* He needed Urzaia. If the Champion could keep the men off him, then Calder could eject them all from the ship. But they knew that—they would have taken precautions for the two known Soulbound on the crew. Maybe Foster could do something, or even Andel...

The Imperial Guard rapped on the door again, calling his name, and Bliss reached up to pat him on the head. "You should be calm now. I am here. Hush, baby, hush."

"...did you just call me a baby?"

"It is what mothers do to calm their children. Are you calmed?"

Not exactly. But he did feel a little better; he'd almost forgotten that Bliss was onboard. With her on their side, his crew had an actual chance of survival.

"I suggest you escape as soon as possible," Bliss said.

"It would go much more smoothly if we had your help." Rather, if she *didn't* help, they might as well feed themselves to the Lyathatan.

She considered that for a moment. "That's possible. Well then. Farewell until I see you again, Calder Marten." She opened the chest again and started to climb in."

Sweat crawled down his skin. "Bliss, please tell me that you're going to take care of this. Bliss. Guild Head. *Please answer me.*"

She put a finger over her lips, signaling silence, and then pulled the lid of the chest shut.

CHAPTER SEVENTEEN

A true Champion, of the Champion's Guild, is more than just a Soulbound.

The Champions are raised from an early age on an abusive regimen of training and actual combat. They are taught nothing but battle, raised to believe that victory is the only virtue. Along the way, they are subject to a battery of alchemical treatments to increase their physical and mental attributes.

Most of the children do not survive, but the survivors emerge with incredible gifts.

I doubt the ethics of such a system, but I cannot doubt its results.

– FROM THE OFFICIAL REPORT OF THE WITNESS
ASSIGNED TO THE CHAMPION'S GUILD

Urzaia Woodsman sat in the hold of *The Testament,* surrounded by barrels, crates, and bundles of cargo. He should have been cooking, he knew—they were about to leave, and they had all these extra passengers onboard. If he were doing his duty, he would have food ready for them before they thought to ask for it.

But instead, he sat with his legs crossed and his hatchets in his lap, breathing deeply.

It had been a long time since he'd fallen into this habit of his: before each match in the arena, he had sat and calmed himself, focusing, stripping away hesitation and thought. A practice they'd taught him as a fighter of the Champion's Guild. It was ingrained in him, after so many years—whenever he felt that he should prepare for a fight, he would sink into this state.

And now here he was.

A battle was coming.

The Chronicler, Naberius, he smiled too much. And the Captain hadn't spoken of it, but Urzaia was sure that the man had killed his own Silent One. Now Andel and the Captain had been invited onto another Navigator's vessel to meet with Naberius' mysterious backers, and while they were gone, the Imperial Guard had begun to invade *The Testament.*

Urzaia didn't hold a grudge against the Guards. They were trying to earn a living, same as anyone. But they were too tense, too off-guard, for this to really be an inspection as they claimed. He'd invited one of them for a drink, and the other man had brushed him off.

There were only two times where a Guard would refuse a drink: in the presence of the Emperor, or before a battle.

So Urzaia found himself in the hold, cross-legged and clearing his mind.

When the door crashed open, he was not surprised. He slowly opened his eyes and favored the pair of strangers with a smile.

"Welcome, my friends! Have you come to take that drink after all?"

These two were even bigger than the average Guard. One of them stood half a head over Urzaia himself, such that he had to bow deeply to slip through the doorframe. He had gray plates growing out of his skin, until it looked as though he were wearing an actual suit of dull armor. Urzaia recognized the plates of a Plainstrider from his homeland. His partner had replaced one hand with the claw of a strange Kameira—bright red and spiked like a venomous insect's fangs. In his human hand, he carried a sack that clanked with the ring of steel.

The armored man wore a pistol and a Dylian hunting knife. The other, just a pistol.

Urzaia didn't move from his seat. He'd lived through this situation many times before: the plated man would say something to get his attention, then the venomous one would slash at him to try and weaken him. If he intended to go for his pistol, then he'd have been holding the sack with the other hand. That meant he wanted his Kameira hand free, not his weapon.

To his surprise, the man with the red hand sighed and sat his sack down. It rang as it hit the ground, as though it had been filled with chimes. "We're just supposed to keep you down here for a while," he said, pulling out a flask from his chest pocket. "The Guild Head was worried that you would get fidgety and put us all in the ocean." The Guard took a sip first, to show that it was safe, then handed it over to Urzaia.

Well, it would be rude to refuse. And the man had taken a drink for himself. Urzaia accepted, tilting the flask up to his lips.

They would have been suspicious if he didn't drink at all, though it could easily be poisoned. Some Guards had a resistance to poison, and everyone knew it was easier to kill a Champion through assassination rather than in battle.

Well, of course it was easier. It was impossible to kill a Champion in battle.

"Now, why would I fidget?" Urzaia asked. "What is happening on the deck that would make me nervous?"

The plated Guard looked over at his partner, but the man with the clawed hand just took his flask back. "Nothing, nothing. I swear on the Emperor's name. It's just an inspection before Lord Clayborn comes aboard."

"You are serving the Witnesses now, then?" Urzaia asked curiously.

The armored man's eyes widened behind the plates covering his face. "You don't know? Naberius Clayborn will be the next Emperor."

Urzaia had kept a fake smile all this time. Now it became genuine. The battle was almost here. If the Guards believed Naberius was the next Emperor, then there was *nothing* they wouldn't do to protect him.

And Naberius had no particular reason for trusting this crew.

Urzaia reached out his left arm toward the red-clawed Guard. "You may scratch me," he said.

The two Guards froze.

"Your job was to poison and bind me, wasn't it? And then perhaps to kill me after?"

None of them moved.

"I accept your terms. Scratch me."

Tentatively, the Guard extended one red claw and drew a bloody line down Urzaia's forearm.

"Very good," Urzaia said. "Now, take your chains and tie me."

He nodded toward the abandoned sack.

The armored Guard slowly pulled the chain out of the sack, followed by a padlock. "These are invested, you know. They will keep down your strength."

Urzaia snorted. "I hope so. Otherwise I will snap them like...like I would snap ordinary chains."

The poison was already swimming through him, he could feel it. And he could feel the heat flowing through him, from the tips of his fingers through his chest, tingling at the back of his neck. The familiar strength, as the forces bound within his body rose to the fight.

Emperor's name, how I've missed that feeling.

He sat without resistance as they wrapped chains around him and took away his hatchets. He almost broke out right there, when he saw them take his weapons, but he forced himself to relax. The armored Guard treated the weapons with respect anyway, carrying them each in a different hand and placing them reverently on top of a nearby crate.

Very well. He would live.

The red-clawed Guard let out a breath of pure relief as he snapped the padlock shut. Then he backed off, his hands shaking. It seemed that he had believed Urzaia was going to attempt to break out.

He was wrong. There would be no attempting.

Urzaia smiled at the two of them. "So what is the plan now, my friends?"

They exchanged a glance, hesitating.

"I saw you in the arena," the red-clawed Guard said. "You fought like a madman."

"Yes, I did," Urzaia said.

The two Guards drew their guns, and Urzaia rolled chained shoulders. The poison fuzzed his vision at the edges and clouded his thoughts. The chains seemed unnaturally cold wherever they brushed his skin, drawing the energy from his muscles. The wound on his arm seemed to itch and burn.

He looked up into the two barrels and thought, *At last. A fair fight.*

"I'm sorry," the Guard said.

Focusing on the gold-scaled hide wrapped around his arm, Urzaia unleashed his Vessel. The strength and fury of the Sandborn Hydra filled him, blinding him entirely, filling him until he felt that his skin would pop, tightening his muscles as though they would tear themselves apart. The wood under him creaked under a sudden weight.

The Guards both pulled their triggers.

The rage boiled out of Urzaia in a wordless roar.

Two bullets stung him, one in the left of his chest just below his heart, the other at the base of his neck. Like stinging insects, they inflicted a little annoyance but no pain. Vaguely he noticed crumpled balls of lead falling away from his undamaged skin.

But they had tried to hurt him. They had tried to *kill* him. They had dared to lie to him, and they hadn't even bothered to lie *well.* They deserved their pain, and he wasn't going to let anyone take it from them.

And now, now *at last,* he would finally get his hands on an enemy. The Consultants were the ones who had truly earned his wrath, some part of him knew that, but the anger of the Sandborn Hydra didn't care.

Two enemies were within his grasp, so those were the enemies that would pay.

The armored Guard opened his mouth to shout for help, but Urzaia's hand snapped up and *through* the chain, tearing it like a cobweb. His hand closed over the man's mouth. One of the links from the torn chain struck against the boards overhead and fell to the ground.

"No screaming," Urzaia said, still smiling. He raised his second hand, grabbing the other side of the Guard's organic helmet and slowly squeezing his fingers together. The Kameira plate armor squealed and stressed beneath his grip.

The red-clawed guard raked at his back, trying to deliver another dose of venom. This time, Urzaia was ready for him. He was filled with power and rage, such that nothing could pierce him. Nothing could damage him.

Claws slid down his skin like chalk.

He tossed the armored Guard aside, catching a raised red hand in one of his own. He leaned in to look at the red-clawed guard from only inches away, speaking into the man's sweat-drenched face. "You get to live," he said.

Then he slammed a fist into the man's ribs, lifted him, and tossed him deeper into the hold.

Urzaia spun to catch the attack that he knew would be coming from the back. It had been years, but he could almost feel the arena sand beneath his bare feet, the weight of the sun on his back. The pattern was so simple, he could read it more easily than any book.

He held out his hands to catch a strike that didn't come.

The armored Guard still lay motionless on the ground, breathing harsh and labored. He wasn't dead, and for a brief moment Urzaia's anger almost drowned him. If he wasn't dead, then he should be up and fighting. And if he wasn't up and fighting, then he should be *dead.*

Urzaia raised one foot to crush the man's head, drawing on the Sandborn Hydra's power to increase his weight. The boards beneath his foot creaked again, but he hesitated.

Not me, he thought. *This is the Hydra.*

He forced his raised foot back down, pushing the Hydra's anger away. No matter how many times he fought in the arena, his strongest opponent was always his own Soulbound Vessel.

The Guild had given him many gifts other than his power as a Soulbound, but the Hydra was his most powerful weapon. And his oldest, never-defeated enemy.

He pushed the urges of the Hydra to the back of his mind, reaching over and picking up his two Awakened hatchets.

If he wasn't very much mistaken, the Captain and the rest of the crew should be in danger on deck. The Imperial Guards wouldn't have attacked down here if their brothers and sisters didn't have the rest of the crew well in hand. The gunshots would give them away otherwise.

In the last fight on *The Testament's* deck, Urzaia had been humiliated. A mere poison had brought him low, so quickly that he hadn't even had time to call upon the Hydra's power to block it. His alchemical enhancements had eventually neutralized the potion, but it was too late for the fight. Too late for Jyrine.

This time, he would not shame himself. The Captain would not regret giving him his freedom.

With a black hatchet in each hand, Urzaia marched up to the deck. He was calm; he was always calm, just before he stepped into the arena.

And he was still smiling.

As Calder stepped out of his cabin and saw his entire crew clustered around the mast, surrounded by Imperial Guards, he tried to appear casual.

He turned to the scaled Guard who stood outside his cabin. "I'm sorry, Guardsman, but what's going on here? Has my crew done something wrong?"

Surreptitiously, he brushed the back of his hand against the railing. He Read the ship, searching for the one crewmember missing: Urzaia.

The former Champion was beneath, sitting peacefully on the ground as two Guards wrapped him in chains. What was he doing? Had they drugged him somehow?

"...safety of the future Emperor," the Guard was saying, when Calder came out of the Reader's trance. "If you would join your crew, please, so we can see that everyone is accounted for."

Calder slowly walked over to the others, taking stock of the situation. Andel's suit was stained, his hat was missing, and they had taken his White Sun pendant. Just in case he was an unregistered Soulbound, presumably. Petal shivered and hugged herself, hiding her face in the veil of her hair. No change there. Foster sat with his back against the mast, grumbling into his beard. He wore his shooting-glasses, with his reading-glasses still dangling against his chest, but they had managed to get his guns away from him.

"Where's Urzaia?" Calder asked, as though he had just noticed.

"He caused a scene," said one of the Guards. "We had to have him confined below deck."

A roar echoed up from the heart of the ship. Just then, a shot rang out, echoing from the depths of the vessel. Or maybe several shots, overlapping. Calder let himself fall against the mast, reaching through it with his Reader's senses to get a feel for the ship.

He wanted to laugh. Urzaia was toying with the two Guards like a cat with a pair of mice.

He shook off the trance early and glanced over at the other ship, drifting a few dozen yards away. Red-and-black uniforms had clustered on the side of the deck closest him, and they all seemed to be clutching muskets in their hands, claws, or talons. The Guards on this deck had all conveniently arranged themselves so that they happened to be out of the line of fire.

Only a single figure on the other ship stood out: one man with flowing dark hair, a broad grin, and a red suit.

The scaled Guard took Calder roughly by the arm, shoving his back against the mast. One of his hands rummaged around Calder's hip and jacket, looking for his pistol.

Calder held it out between two fingers, waving it around while making it clear that he wasn't going to pull the trigger.

He called over to *The Eternal.* "Naberius! Once I'm dead, I thought you might want my pistol!"

Naberius laughed, shouting back. "Is that so? Is it worth collecting?"

The Guard froze in reaching for the pistol, hesitating now that the future Emperor had actually responded.

Calder grabbed the gun by its barrel. "It's a *Dalton Foster* original!"

Hoping desperately that Foster would get the message, Calder tossed the pistol overhand so that it would land in Foster's lap.

As the gun sailed through the air, Calder silently pleaded that nothing would go wrong. The Guards would hesitate, the bullet wouldn't fall out of the barrel in midair, and Foster would take his meaning.

In that meandering second while the gun hung in the air, a familiar weight settled on his shoulder.

Oh, good, Shuffles is here, Calder thought, as tentacles brushed his cheek. *So it thinks we're going to die.*

Dalton Foster went from grumbling and staring at the deck to a shooting crouch in the blink of an eye. He snatched the pistol from the air without looking, firing instantly into the feathered chest of a nearby Guard, and then stood. As the Guard fell, he pulled that man's pistol from its holster and leveled it at another.

The rest of the crew exploded into action at the same moment. Andel elbowed his captor in the nose with the back of his head. It did nothing, because the woman holding him had a beak, but he managed to stumble his way over to the far side of the mast, where fire from the other deck wouldn't reach him. Calder ducked and slipped out of the scaly Guard's grip, fumbling at the hilt of the man's sword, trying to pull his saber free.

As he did, he noticed Petal scrambling for freedom. Most of the Guards seemed preoccupied with the fight, so it was probably the best move.

Over on *The Eternal,* someone yelled "Fire!" Everyone on *The Testament* lunged for cover.

Everyone, that is, except for Urzaia Woodsman.

The Izyrian gladiator burst from the hold shouting, shrugging off musket shots. He plowed into a Guard with his shoulder, sending the man hurtling over the side and into the water. He threw a hatchet with each hand, burying one blade in the back of Andel's captor, and the other into the side of Calder's scaled Guard.

His scales managed to deflect the hatchet somewhat, but he couldn't stop the Awakened blade entirely. He grunted, blood leaking down his side, and staggered back to look at his wound.

And Calder managed to get the man's saber free. Many of the Guards had discarded their pistols in favor of swords, either because they didn't have time to reload or because they thought the blades would do more against Urzaia.

They were mistaken.

Blades smacked against Urzaia's bare skin and did no more damage than if they'd caught him on his hardened leather breastplate. He barreled into the first Guard, a man who tried to cling onto the Izyrian with his oversized eagle talons. Urzaia peeled him off, leaped over to the side of the deck, and hurled his opponent straight into the water.

Calder didn't have time to watch any further, because a musket-ball buzzed past his ear. A Guard leveled his pistol from a few feet away as the barrage continued from the other boat, pointing his gun at Calder's chest.

Inches from his ear, Shuffles laughed maliciously.

He held a sword in his right hand, but he couldn't fight like this. If they kept firing from the other deck, then his crew had virtually no chance of escaping with their lives. He either had to figure out a way to take out the Guards on the other ship, or...

Calder collapsed to his knees, avoiding the shot from the nearest Guard's pistol. His injured leg screamed in protest, but he forced the pain from his mind.

He placed both of his hands against the deck, Reading.

The ship yearns to fight against the intruders on its deck. It was made to fight, not to sit passively by, but it can't move on its own. It wants Calder to call it to action, so that it can fight beside its crew.

Calder let his Intent flow into the wood, giving orders to his Vessel.

And without warning, the ship listed hard to starboard.

The deck tilted, water and cargo sliding down toward the starboard rail. A Guard lost his footing, sliding closer to the ocean, only to be stopped by one of his comrades' tentacle. Everyone stumbled equally: Foster missed a shot, Andel had to hug the mast to avoid falling, and Urzaia...well, Urzaia used the slope to slide down closer to another Guard, knocking him off his feet and slamming a hatchet into the bridge of his nose.

But most importantly, the port side had risen, blocking off musket-fire. The only part of *The Eternal* still visible was the top of its mast and its bright red sails.

A Guard grabbed Calder by the shoulders, trying to stabilize himself, and Calder ran him through with his stolen saber. The body slid off, and another Guard walked up. This one had huge, clawed feet that gouged into the deck as he marched closer, not put off at all by the awkward angle. His blade was broad and thick, and he stood head and shoulders above Calder.

So Calder didn't fight him. He tucked his mind back into his Soulbound Vessel, calling on *The Testament's* power, and grabbed the man with a coil of rope. The rope hurled the Guard, screaming, closer to *The Eternal.* Shuffles flew off of Calder's shoulder, flapping in midair, mimicking the Guard's scream and combining it with triumphant laughter.

The Guard had a better chance of survival if he landed in the ocean rather on the deck, but Calder didn't care where the man ended up. Another Guard had fallen down in front of Calder from a perch on the mast, brandishing a saber in each taloned hand.

She struck with both swords in rapid succession, trying to force Calder back so that she could break through his guard.

Calder didn't back up. He knocked the first blade aside, then the second, and then he stabbed the woman just under her collarbone. She folded up, groaning instead of screaming, and slid along the deck down the port side. She wore an almost comical expression of shock and surprise.

Petal edged out from Calder's cabin, eyes wide. "Captain! You dueled an Imperial Guard! And you won!"

Calder kept an eye out for more enemies, but most of them were focusing on Urzaia. Even Foster and Andel had managed to hide behind the big Soulbound, occasionally taking shots of their own, but mostly hiding until the Izyrian cleaned up.

"I'm actually a highly trained duelist, Petal."

She hid her eyes behind her hair. "But...you never fight."

He eyed her. "I'm afraid you're mistaken. I fight all the time."

"Well, you sort of...use ropes. And the ship. And guns. And sometimes you run and hide."

"You can't simply wave your sword around all the time," Calder said, waving his sword around. "It's not tactically sound."

Andel hurried over, breathing hard, a few bleeding cuts marring his white shirt. Somewhere, he'd found his hat. "I saw that you managed to win a fight, sir. Well done."

Calder leaned forward and wiped the blood from his blade on Andel's shirt, leaving long smears of red on the white. "Why does everyone seem surprised when they say that?"

"I think I speak for everyone when I say we expected you to run away."

"I use a *variety* of tactics. It was Sadesthenes who first said, 'In most of life, to fight is to lose.'"

"Cowards everywhere bow to your expertise, sir."

Shuffles returned, landing on the top of his head this time. "COWARD!"

Even in the heat of battle, Calder sighed.

Across the deck, Urzaia laughed as he kicked the last Imperial Guard into the Aion, leaving only bodies and the groaning wounded still on deck. He turned to Calder, his scarred face practically glowing.

"What now, Captain?"

Calder considered for only a moment. If they left now, Jarelys Teach would simply catch them on her bird and kill them all. They had only one chance, and it was recklessly risky.

This will teach them to call me a coward.

"Foster," he said, and reached out a hand. The gunner wordlessly placed a pistol into his open palm.

"Urzaia, you and I will be headed over to *The Eternal,* where we will take Naberius hostage. Once we have him, we can negotiate our safe passage out of here."

The Woodsman shouted out another laugh. "Wonderful! Can you make the jump?"

"No, I'm a human being." Calder reached out and pushed a hand against the mast, once again reaching his Intent down into the ship. Through the chains. And to the Lyathatan.

There is a commotion among the tiny beings above. If it goes on for another cycle of the stars and moon, the Lyathatan may decide to get involved. But there are some dangerous tools on the other wooden vessel, and it is wary.

Calder sends his orders, and the Elderspawn agrees with a mixture of reluctance, old resignation, and tireless wrath.

He clutched a saber in his right hand and a pistol in his left, and he sent another message to the ship. Without warning, the ship corrected itself, crashing down to port until it floated evenly in the water once again.

As soon as the port side bobbed down, Calder ran and jumped onto the railing, launching himself into the air.

CHAPTER EIGHTEEN

Urzaia jumped a moment after Calder, but he launched himself with the force of a Windwatcher bursting into the air. He soared in an arc that would take him directly onto *The Eternal's* deck, clutching a black hatchet in each hand.

Calder, on the other hand, jumped off the railing and started falling toward the ocean.

The Lyathatan caught him.

Its blue, six-fingered, webbed hand burst from the dark surface of the water, rising up beneath Calder's boots. He stumbled but managed to remain standing, despite the shock of pain that ran up the cut in his leg. He forced himself to run across the pliant surface of the palm, vaulting off one of the fingers.

With that boost, he was able to make it onto the dark red deck of Cheska Bennett's ship.

The Imperial Guard reacted, but they were torn between facing Urzaia, defending against Calder, and defending themselves from what they assumed was an attack by a giant Elderspawn. Some of them rushed to the rail, some of them lowered guns at Urzaia, and only a few of them took a menacing step toward Calder.

Only two of them stood in front of Naberius, defending him with a scorpion's tail and with ominous metal claws. So they weren't prepared when Urzaia barreled straight through the first layer of Guards, smashing his way straight to Naberius. Calder simply ran through the highway he cleared, panting and desperately hoping that none of the Guards would snatch him up before he reached the Chronicler.

Naberius had managed to pull out a pistol by the time Urzaia had him in hand, one hatchet pressed to his throat. Simply for the sake of redundancy, Calder pulled his own gun, pressing it to the future Emperor's head.

"Good evening...ladies...and gentlemen," Calder panted, trying to catch his breath and still speak as loudly as possible. "If you want him...alive...I suggest... you let us speak with the Guild Heads."

Shuffles descended back onto Calder's shoulder, having taken to the air during his jump. "IF YOU WANT HIM ALIVE," it echoed.

A bleak wind passed over the deck, and everyone shivered. Goosebumps rose on Calder's skin, and he shook as though he saw his own death approaching. It was a nauseating feeling that made him want to run and hide and vomit all at the same time.

He had sensed this before, and suddenly he wondered if he'd made a grave miscalculation.

Armor clanked as General Jarelys Teach marched slowly up to them, one hand on the hilt over her shoulder. Her pale, close-shaved head almost looked bald in the moonlight, and with her eyes so cold, Calder felt as though he were staring down an Empress.

"Release Lord Clayborn and step back," Teach ordered.

Calder pressed the gun harder against Naberius' temple. "General Teach! Excellent. We'd like to speak with you. It seems that you tried to have us killed, and I'd like to know what we can do to...make that go away."

The General didn't twitch. "Your death has been ordered by the future Emperor. Threatening him will only increase your sentence."

Calder turned to Naberius. "I think I can get him to revoke that order. What do you think, my friend?"

"This is unwise, Captain," Naberius said, unruffled.

"And I'm sure allowing you to kill me and dump my body in the ocean would be the epitome of wisdom. General Teach, as you can see, I have a gun to this man's head. If you attack, I will pull the trigger. Urzaia and I will have to fight our way out, which I'm not eager to try, but trust me when I say that I can take this entire ship down with me. I have a giant Elderspawn chained up over there, and it's not happy."

"NOT HAPPY," Shuffles chuckled.

If anything, the General's grip tightened on her sword. "Captain, I could kill you and your friend from here. You'd have no chance to pull the trigger or to contact your Lyathatan. I haven't done it already because my Guards would be in danger, but the longer this discussion goes, the more I'm reconsidering the risk."

A standoff. Great. Calder *hated* standoffs. He always felt that he could talk his way out, but it somehow never worked out that way.

Before he could come up with any other ideas, a girl's voice piped up from behind him.

"You've forgotten me again, Jarelys."

Calder pulled Naberius back, keeping his gun in place, so that he could see both General Teach and the woman who'd spoken.

It was Bliss. She stood in a clear space on the deck, black coat brushing the wood, pale hair drifting behind her. Some of the Guards edged away from her.

"Bliss, *step away,*" the General said. "This does not need to involve you."

Calder had another concern. "You were just aboard my ship."

"That's true."

"How did you get over here?"

She unbuttoned two of her coat buttons and reached inside. "No one likes a man who asks too many questions."

"That actually doesn't explain anything."

From her coat pocket, the Guild Head pulled a bone about the length of Calder's forearm. A chorus of ominous cackling sounded from high up in the crow's nest, as though a coven of dark spirits had started to mock him from above. In spite of himself, Calder glanced up. Nothing up there.

When he returned his gaze to Bliss, the bone was a full-sized spear of one piece, its haft yellowed bone, its head flattened and sharpened. She leaned forward onto the balls of her feet, holding the spear with one hand near the head and one farther back on the haft.

"Clear the deck!" General Teach shouted. "For your lives, get below!"

The Imperial Guards scrambled out of the way. One shaggy-furred man popped his dripping head up over the side, having climbed out of the ocean and up to *The Eternal.* When he heard the order, his eyes widened, and he leaped back into the sea.

"Go back to your ship, Calder Marten," Bliss said calmly. "Take Naberius Clayborn with you."

Urzaia didn't need to hear anything else. He plucked the pistols from the Witness, tossing each of them onto the deck, and then threw Naberius over his shoulder like a sack of grain.

Teach bared an inch of her sword, and the force of its sheer bloodlust actually made Calder stagger backwards a step. He had to bend all his focus to close his senses, to *not* Read, simply to keep from screaming and hiding like a child. *"Stay where you are!"* she demanded.

Bliss closed her eyes briefly. When she snapped them open again, they shone with a pale light.

Roots twisted up from the boards, as though the wood had suddenly decided to bloom. The stalks flowered into leaves, then instantly burst into flame like a thousand candles flaring to life. The sudden heat flashed against Calder's skin. They burned with impossible speed, ash and smoke rising into the air, twisting around Bliss in a double helix.

The power coming off of Bliss was, in its own way, even more frightening. She radiated an eternal Intent, an insatiable hunger for *change,* a hatred of the physical world and all its restrictive laws. If it had its way, that power would shred the rules of nature and scatter them like confetti, until the world flexed and moved and changed like the sea in storm...

Calder shook it off, focusing once more on keeping his senses shut. If the two Guild Heads clashed, death and madness meeting head on, he wouldn't want to be anywhere inside a mile.

And this was the Aion, where unspeakable creatures were lured by power, conflict, and blood.

So maybe a mile wasn't far enough. Say ten miles.

He turned to Urzaia. "Time to leave."

The Izyrian didn't need to be told twice. He also didn't, as Calder had expected, immediately leap from one ship to the other.

Instead, he picked up Calder and tossed him over his other shoulder.

It was undignified and surprisingly painful, dangling with his face in Urzaia's back. The man's shoulder jabbed him in the stomach like a club, and when he got a running start along the deck, it was like being beaten in the torso with a sack of bricks.

The Head of the Imperial Guard shouted after them, but they were already in the air, Shuffles laughing as it flew alongside them.

Calder winced in anticipation of landing, clenching his stomach. This was going to hurt worse than any wound he had taken in the actual battle.

When they landed, he found that he was right.

The second void transmission caught Jerri while she slept.

She woke to an icy wind, and a feeling like thousands of ants crawling over her skin. Her eyes flew to the back wall, and for an instant, another pair of eyes stared straight into hers.

Jerri threw a fist forward, hitting nothing, flailing like a child in the darkness. She cast her mind out to her Soulbound Vessel, trying to contact her earrings. They would be in the drawer next to the bunk.

But this wasn't *The Testament's* cabin, it was a prison cell. And her earrings remained where they always were: locked on the other side of the island, out of her reach.

The eyes vanished, replaced by the familiar gaping darkness, as though the world ended in the back of her cell. If she walked back there and didn't stop, she got the feeling that she would fall off a cliff and never hit the bottom. Faint lights writhed and twisted in the shadows like tortured stars.

She rolled from the bed and tried to collect herself, prepared for the voices.

They were different each time. Sometimes she heard spidery whispers, but other times...

"HAS THE HEART ARRIVED?" the voice roared from the void.

She flinched back, hoping that no one outside the prison would hear. That could lead to awkward questions. "I'm doing just fine, thank you for asking. And yes, the Heart arrived just recently." Anyone with any sensitivity to Elder forces would have felt the Heart the instant it landed on the island. In this case, that meant she was likely the only one who'd noticed.

"WE ARE PLEASED." A shadow whipped out within the void, snuffing out a lone light. It looked like a frog's tongue taking a fly. "FORCES CONVERGE. WHEN YOU FEEL THE HEART'S POWER WAX, USE OUR GIFT."

Jerri glanced around her cell, but saw nothing out of the ordinary. "Gift?"

Something about the size of a fist hurtled out of the void like a comet, forcing Jerri to duck. It crashed into the bars with a clang of metal on metal, falling to the ground.

She leaned over, afraid to touch it. On closer inspection, it looked like a tight collar of braided black metal.

"HOLD IT AND CALL OUT FOR HELP, BUT ONLY WHEN THE TIME IS RIGHT."

Jerri brushed the back of her fingers across the dark metal, testing it. It was such a bitter cold that it stung her skin, but she'd heard that was normal for objects transferred through the void. She tucked it into a corner of her blankets, hoping it would warm up with time.

"Will this free me?" she asked.

"POTENTIALLY." The void began to shrink back into itself, dragging the unnatural chill with it. "WAIT FOR THE POWER OF THE MOTHER'S HEART. WAIT."

Then the void finally closed to one black point and winked away.

After she had collected herself, Jerri called out. "I expect you heard that."

"I can't believe the guards haven't shown up already," Lucan responded, from the other side of the wall.

"I expect the voice only sounded loud to us," she said. "Out of this room, they would have likely heard nothing."

"That makes no sense. If a voice sounds loud to us, then it's loud to everyone."

Though he couldn't see it, she smiled into the darkness of her cell. "Only one of the many mysteries the Elders have shared with us. Imagine if our Readers could craft messages that only certain people could hear."

"That doesn't appear to be the case," he pointed out. "I could hear most of it clearly. If you could actually tailor it to a specific listener, then why didn't they make it so that only you could hear the message? Or did they specify a radius..."

Lucan trailed off, murmuring to himself. That was fine with her—she left him to it. Her own father had taken advantage of her curiosity to induct her into the Sleepless in the first place, and if she could pique the interest of a few others, then she would have repaid him well. Especially if one of those others was a Consultant.

She laid back on her cot, but her mind rushed too fast to let her get back to sleep. What would happen if she tried to use the gift now? Would it do nothing, or would it simply allow her to break free and fail to fulfill whatever purpose the Sleepless had intended? Shouldn't she test it? What if she needed to use it at the appropriate time, but it didn't work?

More importantly, when would the Heart's power rise? If it wasn't in the next day or two, then the Consultants would inevitably find the black metal stashed in her blankets. They didn't inspect her possessions every day, but when they did, they were surprisingly thorough. She had hid a few innocuous items—a handful of splinters from her meal tray, a napkin, the broken tine of a fork—all over her cell, just to test, and they were always gone after inspection. There was no way she could hide something as obvious as the iron gift for long.

After a few minutes, Lucan called her name. "Jyrine, something's coming. Do not say a word. You won't hear anything, but your life may be in danger."

"Are *you* communing with Elders?"

"Not a word, I said. This is bad. She may just kill you on principle."

"Who—"

"*Quiet.* She's here."

Jerri heard nothing, but she felt another wave of cold crawl over her skin. This wasn't the same sharp, bitter cold as the void transmission, but the clammy, shivering cold of lifeless flesh. She felt it in her mind, in her connection to the Elders that she'd had since she was a little girl. It was cold loneliness, followed by the warm promise of rebirth.

The Heart of the Dead Mother. It was coming here.

As they traveled toward the Gray Island, they kept Naberius gagged and tied to the mast.

Calder found it very entertaining, though Andel didn't approve and Petal kept a safe distance. It didn't pay off in anything except personal satisfaction until the second day, when a column of slate-gray cloud appeared on the horizon.

It looked almost like a hurricane locked into place: a swirling wall of dark gray fog and cloud, raised like a barrier between them and the rest of the sea. Even after years of sailing the Aion, he'd never seen anything like it.

"What is *that?*" he asked no one in particular.

Surprisingly, it was Petal who answered, inching her way closer to him as she spoke. "That's, ah, that's the Gray Island. It's why they call it that. Gray, I mean. It's a wall of mist, or maybe fog, and it stays up all year-round. Surrounds the whole island. Nobody knows how it was done, and some alchemists...in the Guild, I mean...some alchemists try to duplicate it in their labs, and they can't."

Having said her piece, Petal scurried off.

The Gray Island. It was impressive, he had to admit. Not the most intimidating supernatural sight he'd seen on this sea, but certainly worth the visit.

Now what is it for, I wonder? The Consultants obviously weren't trying to hide the island's location: they would invite anyone with enough marks to their island any time of year. Some chapter houses handed out free maps. So what did all that mist actually accomplish?

He was still at the wheel when he saw Naberius' eyes snap open, staring straight at the Gray Island. The Witness shot to his feet, lunging in that direction.

Calder hopped off the stern deck and made his way over, reaching out a hand to Read the Chronicler. As soon as he sensed the cold, clammy influence on the man, he moved his hand back.

"That song!" Naberius cried. "Do you hear the song?"

No doubt. Naberius sensed the Heart of the Dead Mother.

"All hands on deck!" Calder shouted.

Andel spoke up from the nearby folding table, where he was idly shuffling cards. "We're all here, sir."

"What have I told you about shouting, Andel?"

"That you like it."

"That's right. Don't take that from me." The others gathered around Andel. Foster hopped down from the mast, Petal scurried up and sat on a crate nearby, and a distracted-looking Urzaia looked toward the horizon and fiddled with his hatchet.

"Where is she?" Calder asked.

Urzaia pointed straight to the island.

Naturally.

Andel clapped his hands together. "All right, everyone, let the twenty-third official crew meeting begin."

Calder sighed, pulling up a folding camp chair to the table. "I was hoping we could talk off the record, Andel."

"Rejected," Andel said. "Foster, take notes."

Foster grumbled under his breath as he switched out his shooting-glasses for reading-glasses. Petal handed him a pen and a sheet of paper.

"Please describe the situation for the record, Captain."

Calder couldn't see why they didn't just talk about it. He never consulted these logs for anything. But Andel enjoyed the formality, and it wasn't worth fighting about.

"Naberius has sensed the Heart. It's clearly in *that* direction, which is the approximate location of the Consultants' Gray Island. And now Urzaia feels the blond Consultant, Shera's partner, in that location. Isn't that right, Urzaia?"

He drew in a deep breath through his nose. "I can almost smell her from here."

Petal shivered and edged away from him.

"So—" Andel began, but Foster stopped him.

"Give me a second. I'm not a Chronicler, I can't write that fast. I don't see why we can't get Naberius to take notes."

"Really?" Andel said. "You really can't see why?"

Foster grumbled for a few more seconds until he finally caught up to the conversation.

Andel waited for his nod to continue. "We're in deep water here. This affects everyone, so we'd like to hear everyone's opinion. Petal?"

As much as Calder hated to take the time it took to consult the crowd, he had to admit that his Quartermaster was right. Landing on the Gray Island would affect everyone on the ship, for better or worse, and it would be best if everyone was willing to walk forward with their eyes wide open.

He instantly decided to act as though he had been onboard with the idea from the beginning.

Petal cleared her throat, fiddling with a bottled potion and peering out from under her hair. "Well...I think we should...at least try to get the Heart. Ourselves. The Consultants will destroy it, right? That's...probably not good. I want there to be an Emperor. But I don't want it to be Naberius, so..."

She shrunk into herself, apparently finished.

Calder was proud of her. That was the longest string of concurrent sentences he'd heard out of her this year.

"Well said, Petal."

Andel pointed to Urzaia, who shrugged.

"The Consultant women owe me a fight. I will be collecting. That is all."

"Simple," Calder said. "Effective. Easy to remember. I like that philosophy."

When Foster had finally finished writing, Andel turned to him. "And what do you think, Foster?"

Dalton Foster raised shaggy eyebrows. "Me? I think we should let the Consultants destroy the thing. It hasn't done us any good in the past."

"If they actually will," Calder pointed out. It still seemed strange to him that the Consultants would go through such efforts to *retrieve* the Heart if they simply meant to destroy it when they got it back home.

"My turn," Andel said, folding his arms. "I think we're in way over our heads."

Foster scribbled his words on the paper. "Good. That means we're in our home port."

"I also think that it will take more than the usual amount of effort to get any pay out of this."

That was a good point. Of course, they still had Naberius. Maybe they could arrange some kind of a ransom...and then escape, alive, to spend it. That was the trick.

"However," Andel went on, "I do think we need to make it onto the island. We're in too deep to back out now, and I know we'd all like to settle once and for all what happened to Jyrine."

Calder had been trying to avoid thinking of Jerri ever since the Gray Island appeared in the distance, though it was all but impossible. His wife could be on *that* island. Or perhaps her corpse was buried there.

Either way, he needed to find out.

He realized that the others were staring at him, and picked up the discussion. "I don't trust Naberius. I don't trust his sponsors. And I certainly don't trust the Consultants. If it weren't for Jerri, I would want to sail as far away from this island as possible and never look back. But if there's even a chance she's alive..."

The others didn't even move, waiting for him to finish.

"...I've got to know. But I *would* like to escape the island and get home alive. For that purpose, I believe the Heart is indispensable." He turned his gaze to Naberius. "We need something to trade for our freedom, and I don't think anything less than the Heart of Nakothi will keep us out of the gallows."

Everyone remained silent. Andel returned to shuffling his cards, which he often did simply to keep his hands occupied.

After a few moments, Andel fanned out a hand of cards, watching Calder over the tops. "It seems to me that we need advice."

"That's why I keep you around," Calder said.

"You might say that we need someone to *consult.*"

I'm an idiot. A new possibility opened up before him—he'd been overthinking everything. "I'm a little ashamed that I didn't think of that before." He hopped up from the table and hurried back to the stern deck, already adjusting the ship's position with his Intent.

Foster muttered to himself as he wrote. "Captain...jumps...to a conclusion. There. Meeting adjourned."

"One second, sir," Andel said. "As soon as we set foot on the island, we'll be in their hands. What do we have to deal with an army of Consultants?"

Calder stopped, spinning to grin at his Quartermaster. "Nothing! If they decide to kill us, they'll kill us. There comes a time when you must play the odds, Mister Petronus."

Andel cleared his throat and stared pointedly at the door to Calder's cabin. "If only we had some sort of device that would protect us from hundreds of Guild members. Hundreds of *loyal Imperial citizens* that are sworn to protect and obey."

Calder realized what the Quartermaster was getting at, and his smile slipped. He had intended to save that for a distant, ideal future. He had begun to think, recently, that he would never open the lockbox again.

He steeled himself. As the Izyrian strategist Yenzir once said, "*The winner is the one who first recognizes that the time for a battle has come.*"

"If this doesn't work," Calder said, "you do realize that we're even more likely to be killed."

"But if it does work, then this could be the endgame." Andel gestured to the cabin. "Go get it, Captain. Then let's hire a Consultant."

Calder pushed his way into the cabin, opening the drawer beside his bunk. He withdrew a small silver key, invested with his Intent. If anyone other than him picked up the key, they would feel a crippling pain in their hand.

He grabbed the key, reached under his bunk, and pulled out the lockbox. He kept it chained to the bottom of the bunk so it didn't slide around, but he had enough slack to insert the key.

If Jerri was still alive, she had better appreciate this.

CHAPTER NINETEEN

I hear that you have Awakened your mother's stand-mirror.

Upon hearing of its effects, I urged her to have the device melted down, and to hire a Luminian Pilgrim to cleanse its remnants.

Let me emphasize once again the dangers of Awakening, as clearly my previous correspondence was not effective.

Hypothetically, let us say that you tried to Awaken a mirror that once—unbeknownst to you—hung in the dungeon of a notorious murderer. Every day, his victims looked into the mirror and wished to be saved. Would it not be likely that the mirror would save a measure of their desperate Intent? And, when Awakened, that very mirror might even cry out for salvation. Why, it might do anything to be free, including distorting the minds and senses of those nearby.

Of course, we are speaking in the hypothetical sense.

– Artur Belfry, Imperial Witness
taken from a letter to his pupil,
two months after the previous message was delivered.

ELEVEN YEARS AGO

"It's supposed to be a ship for the Navigators," Calder explained. "We're going to summon some sort of Elder creature from the Aion, and it will guide the crew across the sea. With an Elder chained to the ship, the other Elderspawn won't bother them, and they'll be able to make the voyage in half the time. That's the idea, anyway."

Jyrine chewed on the end of her pen. "But will it sail?"

"It doesn't *matter* if it will sail. We won't be onboard! We can't crew a ship with two people."

"Three, once we have your father."

"Oh, I forgot! Three is precisely the number we need. I'll pilot, you navigate, and my father can *man the rest of the ship*."

Jerri threw the pen at him. It bounced off his head, and hurt far more than he felt was fair. Calder yelped, and something moved around them.

They froze. Jerri threw her scarf over the tiny quicklamp on the center of the table.

They were holed up in the Grayweather house library, under cover of night. Jyrine had returned to her family hours before, but snuck her way back to plan what she called their 'clandestine operation.'

She and Calder sat on opposite ends of a small table, papers stacked in neat piles on its surface. Shadows smothered the rest of the room, leaving them in a pool of yellow light...at least, when their quicklamp was shining. Smothered by Jerri's scarf, the illumination cast them in dull orange weaker than a candle-flame.

They froze just long enough to make sure that no one had cracked the door to the library, and then Jyrine pulled the scarf back and they both sat down.

Calder continued as if nothing had happened. "I'm sorry, but it really wouldn't work. They've prepared most of the ship, because it's supposed to go on display next week, but there aren't even any sails."

He had been sure they would add sails by now. He was no shipwright, but surely if the rest of the ship's frame was ready to display they could tack up some sails.

"Maybe it doesn't need sails!" Jerry said, undeterred. "If this Elderspawn is supposed to pull *The Testament,* then why would it require sails?"

Calder had been the one to invest the mast so that it properly flexed against the tug of a full sail. But there was an even better reason why Jerri's plan wouldn't work.

"They haven't summoned it yet," he said. "There's been an issue with the tidal forces, or something." He'd heard the other Watchmen discussing it just that morning, in worried tones. The specific creature they sought hadn't wandered close enough to shore by now, which probably meant it had fallen under the purview of a Great Elder. And no one wanted to risk incurring the wrath of a Great Elder, even one that had remained dead for over a thousand years. So far.

He shook his head, clearing it. Why were they even talking about the ship? "Anyway, that's enough about the ship. The ship won't work. There is no ship."

Jerri worked her jaws as though chewing on something, but she ultimately calmed herself by rubbing a thumb over the tattoos on the back of her left hand. "That leaves my other plan, then."

She reached into the stack of papers and pulled one out, seemingly at random. Across the top of the page, in block letters, she'd printed the name of this plan:

OPERATION "JYRINE DOES CALDER'S JOB FOR HIM"

- Jyrine disguises herself in Calder's Blackwatch uniform.
- Using her superior skills of thespianism and persuasion, Jyrine convinces the staff of an Elder-related emergency.
- She will follow this supposed Elderspawn to the very door of Rojric Marten's cell, thus insisting that it needs to be opened.

- (Remember, Calder, there will not actually be an Elderspawn present. Do not be afraid, as Jyrine will protect you.)
- With her authority as the Blackwatch, she will take Rojric into custody, suspecting that the Elders have corrupted him.
- Should the guards resist, Jyrine will subdue them with her legendary combat prowess.
- When she returns with Rojric Marten in tow, Calder will bow before her, kissing her feet and singing her praises to the heavens, as she rightly deserves.

At the bottom of the paper, she had signed her name with far more loops and flourishes than were strictly necessary.

"I tried to boil the steps down to their essence, for simplicity's sake," Jerri said, with a completely straight face. "There are some issues unaccounted for, but a good plan must allow for freedom of improvisation."

Calder sputtered for a moment before he managed to say, "You know this is completely ridiculous."

Jyrine lifted the paper and briefly scanned it. "No, I'd say that everything is in order."

"First of all, if there's not an Elderspawn present, why would you need to protect me?"

"That's the first thing you object to, is it?"

"That and the name. Other than that..." Calder swallowed his pride and distaste, nodding to the paper. "In essence, I have to admit, this could work."

She looked up, surprised. "I wrote this so that I could see you turn red."

"Well, it needs some fleshing-out, but it's not a bad idea. I could do without the repeated insults to my person, though."

"I find those aspects of this plan indispensable."

He leaned over, tracing the third step of the plan with his index finger. "From what I can tell, the receptionist has been altered to respond only as her superiors tell her to. That involves calling security in the event of an emergency. A member of the Blackwatch saying there's an Elder loose in the building surely constitutes an emergency."

"Won't we need more proof?" Jerri asked.

Calder shrugged. "What signs come along with the invasion of an Elder?"

"I don't know, screaming? Creeping shadows? Spoiling milk?"

"No one knows." If there was anything he'd learned from his few months in the Blackwatch, it was that each Elderspawn was different. Some of the

Watchmen complained about how their quarry was impossible to track, and others that the Elderspawn's shrieks had woken everyone within three city blocks. "There's no predicting the way an unknown Elder or Elderspawn will behave. Most people have to take the word of the Blackwatch that there's an Elder involved at all."

She shook the end of her pen in his direction. "If you keep talking like that, I might mistake you for a real Watchman."

He shuddered, thinking of Bliss. "Not yet, I'm not. But if you're wearing a Watchman's coat and badge, they should take your word for the emergency. That's all, though. They shouldn't release any prisoners or do anything else without an official order from the Guild or actual proof of an Elder attack."

"Then how do we get the cell door open?" Jerri asked. "Do we steal a key? Or can you invest something that will help?"

Calder took a deep breath. He had been prepared for this when he came here, but he couldn't help thinking that he was taking a terrible risk.

First, he covered his fingers in a handkerchief. Then he reached into his shirt pocket and pulled out the Emperor's key.

"I won't have to."

Skepticism was painted across Jyrine's expression. "That's it? Will it fit the lock?"

"It doesn't have to. One tap, and it will undo any lock that can be opened by a key."

The skepticism faded, but her reaction was still less than Calder had hoped for. "Oh, really? Okay, that's one problem solved. But how are we going to get him out of the building?"

He stood with the key outstretched in his hand, feeling foolish. "This is a valuable artifact."

"It sounds very impressive. But I would expect no less out of a Reader of your skill."

She was obviously mocking him, but he felt better anyway.

"I know you're patronizing me," he said, "but I still accept flattery." He placed the key down on the table. "Now, how are we going to get him out of the building?"

"Just a moment. If we're going to rewrite the plan, then I need to take notes." She pulled a blank sheet of paper out of the pile and began to write a title across the top. "How about, 'Operation: Calder Does Nothing.'"

The next morning, Calder rose early. He buttoned up his Blackwatch coat, pinned on his badge, and brushed his hair before walking downstairs for breakfast. He had to ensure that everyone down at the docks saw him at work, acting as if everything was still normal.

Because tonight, he would break his father out of prison.

The dining room was all but empty. No Artur and Vorus, no servants carrying dishes. The table wasn't even set. Only Alsa stood with her back to the door, hurriedly dropping a sheet over something that looked suspiciously like a birdcage.

"Calder!" she exclaimed, spinning around. "You're up early this morning."

She stood between him and the cage, so he leaned to the side, trying to get a clearer look. It was no good; the sheet covered the birdcage entirely. "Did you buy a bird?"

"I thought we would go out for breakfast this morning," she said, slipping into a chair. "*The Testament* is almost finished, so we won't have much to do. Which gives us a little while to talk."

Calder sat across from his mother at the foot of the table. He couldn't suppress the thrill of nerves that shot through him. Did she know? Was she going to stop him? No, if she knew anything about the Candle Bay Imperial Prison, she might even help.

All this shot through his mind before Alsa gathered herself and spoke. "It's been almost two years since you came to live here."

"I will, of course, expect a party."

"And you've accomplished so much in that time," she said. "Artur tells me you're quite taken with the fundamental philosophers, and your fencing has dramatically improved. You might even win a duel or two now, so long as you stay out of the arenas."

He straightened in his chair. "If I can beat Cheska Bennett, I'll be happy."

Alsa snorted. "If the Fates are kind, she'll drown at sea. But no, my point is... well, I know you were somewhat caught up in the whims of the Guild Head, but you did end up with a position in the Blackwatch nonetheless. The other Watchmen have been quite impressed with your enthusiasm. You've certainly made it easier on me."

He allowed himself a small smile, though he wanted to laugh with pride. "Soon, I'll be doing your job for you."

She drummed her fingers on the table. "I may be getting old, but I'm not dead."

From within the shrouded birdcage came a voice like a crumbling tombstone: "DEAD."

Calder jerked back, his hand going to the nails hanging inside his coat.

Alsa held up a hand to calm him. "One of the things you'll learn, as you spend more time among the Blackwatch, is that not all Elders are the soul-devouring, grotesque monsters from the legends. Some Elderspawn creatures are just...strange. Alien to us, in biology and mentality. But not malicious."

He left the iron spikes where they were, pointing a trembling finger at the birdcage. "Is there an Elder in there?"

"An Elderspawn, more accurately. I picked it up recently, in response to one of our more gentle summons. The Guild has already dissected a number of this species, so they were simply going to be rid of it, but I thought you might... appreciate it. To symbolize your membership in the Blackwatch, I suppose."

Calder was having trouble taking his eyes from the cage. He thought he saw something move, beneath the sheet. "What is it?"

"It is what's known as a Bellowing Horror, or more commonly, a Bellows." She stood and, with a little bow, flipped the sheet off the birdcage.

Within the cage waited a creature so malformed and poorly assembled that it took him a few seconds to figure out which end was its head. When his eyes finally traced its contours, translating its shape to something that made sense to him, the image of the creature snapped into place like a solved puzzle.

It was scarcely a foot tall, perhaps the size of a bird, and stubby. Built along the lines of a short, fat man. Its skin was greenish-black, like the wood of *The Testament,* and it had a pair of tiny wings that looked as though they belonged on a bat. A green, hairless bat. Surely wings like that were too small to support its bulbous body, but if that were true, why had Alsa trapped it in a birdcage?

Its eyes, balls of formless black, glared at him from inside its leathery face. Its mouth was invisible or perhaps nonexistent, hidden behind a mass of squirming, wormlike tendrils. Several of those tendrils now squirmed around the bars of its cage, as though tasting or perhaps chewing on the metal.

"A Bellowing Horror," Calder repeated, still weirdly fascinated by the beast. "Why is it called—"

"HORROR!" it bellowed, flaring its pathetic wings.

"Oh. I see."

Alsa laid a hand on the cage, smiling fondly down. "I call him Shuffles."

Calder couldn't help laughing. "Shuffles? That sounds like a three-legged dog."

"Well, he sort of..." she shuffled forward on the carpet, imitating its walk. "... shuffles along, you see? I thought it was appropriate."

He couldn't speak.

"And I admit that there was a cat, in my youth. Mister Shuffles."

"Ah. And this one does not deserve an honorific?"

She leaned closer to the cage. "To tell you the truth, I've never been able to tell if it's a male."

Alsa looked at her son, Calder looked back, and they both started laughing.

Finally, Calder waved a hand in Shuffles' direction. "Seriously, Mother, what am I supposed to *do* with it?"

"Oh, don't worry about that. Many in the Blackwatch keep such pets. It's like having a bird. I had one myself, until it fell into the bathtub and dissolved." She hesitated, and then added, "I wouldn't walk around with it in public, if I were you."

"I can't imagine I would choose to do that."

With a flourish of her wrist, she tossed the latch on the cage. "Let's have you two get to know each other, shall we?"

He tried to protest, but Shuffles had already pushed its way out of the door. It fluttered its wings as it jumped out of the cage, landing with a thump on the table. Its nest of tendrils quested in empty air.

Calder leaned back in his chair.

"Don't be afraid," Alsa said. "It can't hurt you." She shrugged. "At least, it hasn't hurt anyone so far."

She was right about the way the creature moved: it *shuffled* along the table like a child scuffing carpet, occasionally using its wings to hop a few inches closer to Calder. When it was a few feet away, close enough for him to look into the soulless black of its eyes, it leaped.

Its wings buzzed like a hummingbird's, and it flew at his eyes.

He shrieked like a little girl, throwing up a hand to defend his eyes. It was going to eat him! Fighting a man with a sword was one thing, but this monster was flying *straight into his face!*

A heavy weight settled onto his right shoulder, and something drew a wet line across his cheek. A scent blew over him, like copper and fresh fish.

When he opened his eyes a crack, he saw Shuffles staring back from half an inch away. Its tendrils worked in the air, occasionally brushing his skin.

"I think it wants to eat me," Calder whispered.

Shuffles leaned closer to Calder's ear, growling with the voice of a malevolent earthquake: "EEEAAAATTT."

Alsa walked over and ruffled Calder's hair. "See? It likes you!"

As Calder and his mother sat in the back of the carriage, rumbling down to the harbor, an uncomfortable thought lodged in his brain. It wouldn't go away, jabbing him with every crack of the carriage wheels on the cobblestones.

What was he going to do if he failed?

If he and Jerri were caught *before* breaking his father out of prison, they probably wouldn't see much of a penalty. At worst, it was another case of a young Watchman testing the limits of his authority, which the Guild had seen many times before.

But what if they were caught after unlocking Rojric's cell? What if they couldn't sneak him out of the facility?

Even if they escaped capture, it wouldn't be hard for the Candle Bay staff to figure out what had happened. Calder had attempted to visit his father every few weeks, after all, and he would become the premier suspect in any investigation.

Of course, he had considered all that before. But now there was a new ingredient to his thoughts, a new note to his dark daydreams.

If he were caught, what would happen to his mother?

He hadn't planned on taking his father to stay at the Grayweather house—not only would Alsa never allow it, but it would be the first place Imperial investigators would check. However, the thought didn't bother him. Rojric Marten was perfectly capable of disguising himself, finding another place to stay.

But if Calder failed, and was caught, how much blame would fall on his mother? Would she be able to keep her position in the Guild? Would the Blackwatch itself come under scrutiny, with a crime committed by one of its members? What would Bliss do, when two of her Watchmen had disgraced her so thoroughly?

And if he succeeded, his mother would eventually find out. Would she turn him in? Would she demand that he resign his post at the Guild?

For the first time, Calder was starting to realize how little he'd actually considered about the outcome of his plan.

But it was already too late.

Jyrine would be preparing herself even now. He had his own tools, invested and designed specifically for this operation, hidden inside the carriage, disguised as materials from *The Testament.*

The plan was going through, and he would free his father.

But, like a gambler who found himself trapped in a bad bet, he suddenly wondered if the stakes had risen too high.

CHAPTER TWENTY

When they pulled up to the long stone dock on the Gray Island, three people were waiting for them.

One was a pretty Heartlander woman with a long white scar down the center of her face. She wore her hair in dozens of small braids, and she had traded in her black outfit for an elegant purple dress that wouldn't have been out of place in the Capital. Two men, wearing the same black outfits as the Consultants on Nakothi's island, flanked her to either side. Their mouths were covered by black cloth, and they kept their eyes fixed on the dock.

When Calder walked up to the edge of the ship, he sent a mental command to slide the ramp down. As soon as it was in place, the Consultant gave a smooth curtsy.

"Captain Calder Marten, it's quite an honor to meet you. My name is Kerian, and I am here to facilitate your visit to the best of my ability."

Calder gave her his best smile. "Calder, but you already knew that. Should I introduce the rest of my crew?"

"That won't be necessary. I'm told you have quite a guest onboard as well. Would you mind if he joined us for our meeting?"

"Naberius?" For a moment, Calder's mind raced. What if he'd been lied to? What if the Consultants wanted Naberius to be the next Emperor as well? They could kill the whole crew as soon as they had Naberius on shore.

Kerian whispered something to the black-clad man on her left, then turned back to Calder. "I assure you, he will be far more secure on the island than on your ship. We will not let him escape, if that's your concern."

His primary concern was that Jarelys Teach could catch up to him at any moment, and if he didn't have Naberius within easy reach, she would kill him without remorse.

But he didn't see that he had a choice.

"Help yourself," he said graciously.

"Thank you, Captain."

Someone tapped him on the shoulder from behind, and he turned to see two different black-clad Consultants supporting a still-bound Naberius between them.

Calder kept his expression pleasant, bowing the two Consultants and their prisoner down the ramp. But where had they come from? How had they gotten onto the ship without walking past him on the ramp? If they could do that, what had stopped them from killing him in his sleep weeks ago?

He patted his jacket pocket, reassuring himself. *You're not a helpless target. You're in charge here. Act like it.*

Calder strode down the ramp, calling back over his shoulder. "Andel, Foster, it's time to leave."

Kerian raised her eyebrows in evident surprise. "What happened to your Champion? Urzaia, was it? And you have an alchemist too, don't you?"

"Former Champion," Calder corrected. "He decided to stay on another island about a day back. He decided to meditate in order to hone his skills, or some such Champion business. And our alchemist doesn't leave the ship if she can help it."

Kerian's face was pleasant and completely unreadable. He had no idea if she believed him or not. "I see. Well, if you'd like to follow me, we'd be happy to accommodate you in our local chapter house. I have to tell you, Captain, we expected you to sneak onto the island from behind. Not many of us thought you would simply walk in the front door."

Calder tried to look as though the idea shocked him. "We're both professionals. We should be able to settle this with business."

"That's very mature of you," she said. Her voice told him no more than her expression.

She was walking alongside him, with her original two companions leading the way, and the other two carrying Naberius at the back. He stepped forward, brushing against her elbow as if by accident.

He caught no vision—there wasn't enough Intent in her dress for that. But he received a sense of her current mental state.

Absolute focus. That was the only way he could describe his impression of her Intent. Usually, when you got the chance to read a person's active Intent, you got a sense of their background and emotions. Not so with Kerian.

She had a purpose, she knew what it was, and she was absolutely focused on that single point. There was nothing else for Calder to see.

He took an involuntary step away, though he managed to keep his pleasant expression. He couldn't even Read her. Was she human? How did anyone end up with such needle-sharp Intent?

Kerian turned her smile on him, and he tried to hide his shiver. "Please try to relax. You're a client. We will do everything we can to accommodate you as long as we're conducting business."

"Yes, ma'am," Calder said.

Andel and Foster turned and stared at him.

A staircase began at the base of the dock, winding up a grassy hill and terminating in a crown of a building. It was white and arching, almost like a Luminian cathedral, but it gave the impression of modern advancement rather than ancient dignity. Its glass panes, stained with the garden shear crest of the Consultants, flanked the polished wooden doorway. Trees and benches lined the path leading inside, though Calder was sure no one ever casually strolled outside the headquarters of the Consultant's Guild.

He glanced behind the chapter house to the rest of the island, and was surprised at how natural it looked. There were one or two shapes that may have been the tips of distant buildings, but other than that, the island was a sprawling, natural mix of hills, rocky slopes, and trees.

"I thought you would use more of the island," Calder remarked, just before they entered the chapter house.

"We do," Kerian responded. "It's more use to us in a natural state, that's all. We wouldn't want it to look like the Capital, would we?"

That's what he had been picturing: the Consultant chapter house in the Capital, which was nestled like the missing puzzle piece in the middle of a hundred crowded buildings. Now that he thought of it, there was no reason why their private island should look anything like that.

The island looked like someone had taken an especially large Imperial Park and transplanted it directly into the middle of the Aion. The only thing spoiling the view was the rolling gray background, making it seem like the sky was perpetually overcast. Only when he looked directly upward did he see a blue circle, like the eye of a storm.

Inside the chapter house, Kerian directed them straight past the reception room. Calder was unsurprised to see that it was as well-appointed as the Imperial Palace itself, with priceless art decorating the shelves and gilt-framed paintings hanging on the wall.

Five hundred goldmarks, Calder thought, passing a Cannalli original portrait. It portrayed an ancient Aurelian general standing victorious after a battle with the Izyrians. Not a single painting he passed would have fetched less than four hundred goldmarks at auction. In most parts of the Empire, that was enough to buy a house.

And he'd thought Navigators were well-paid for their travels. Maybe he should have joined the Consultants.

The woman at the desk had hair almost as pale as Bliss', and she stared at him with an iron gaze. For some reason, she kept her hands conspicuously tucked beneath the desk.

Aren't receptionists supposed to be friendly? She looked as though she'd rather kill him and deal with his corpse than listen to a single word he had to say.

Kerian kept walking without stopping, leading them down a red carpet marked with the moon-in-sun symbol of the Aurelian Empire. They finally reached a private room standing open, decorated in much the same manner as the reception room. A round conference table in the center, surrounded by padded chairs, took up most of the floor space.

There was a hat rack in the corner, but he kept his hat on. *And thus do I strike a blow against my enemies.*

Kerian gestured for them to seat themselves. "Can I offer you any refreshment? Drinks? Something to eat, perhaps?"

Foster cleared his throat. "I could use some coffee, if you have it."

"Of course."

Andel shook his head, but Calder was interested in testing this out. "I could use a light lunch, actually."

"Do you have any preferences?"

Perhaps he should have some sort of plan here, to trap them and show the Consultants that he was in charge, but he was really just curious. "Surprise me."

Kerian nodded to the back of the room, and when Calder turned to look, he found that Naberius was being supported by a single black-clad Consultant. His partner must have gone to get their order.

Come to think of it, weren't there two more of those guys? Where did they go?

Naberius was not led to a chair. They left him tied and gagged, scowling across the room at Kerian, standing against the wall and held by a black-gloved hand. Calder couldn't deny that he enjoyed the sight.

"Let's get right to business, then," Kerian said, brushing a few braids out of her eyes. She reached beneath the table, pulling out a leather satchel, which she set on the table. From inside the satchel, she withdrew a single file. "You're looking for the Heart of Nakothi and for your wife, Jyrine Tessella Marten."

Straight to the point. Calder could play that game, though it still unnerved him to think about how much the Consultants knew. If they wanted to take over the Empire, what was stopping them? Why hadn't they backed Naberius?

"I'd also like a way to keep Jarelys Teach from killing me and my crew," Calder put in. "That's a fairly important point."

Kerian made a note. "And you two gentlemen? Anything you would like to discuss?"

"We're with him," Andel said.

"And you, Dalton? I'm given to understand that there's something we could do for you." She pulled a different file out of her satchel, and Calder saw Dalton Foster's name written in a tight hand on the front.

Foster scowled at the file, no doubt upset that someone had found out who he was. "Maybe later. On my own. For now, we've got more important things to do."

Kerian gave no indication whether she was pleased or not, she simply slid the file back into her satchel. "Of course. I will take the initiative and preemptively answer your questions while you enjoy your refreshments."

Was she going to wait until the food arrived? Calder glanced over at the doorway, and then back to the table.

A pile of chicken, rice, and steamed vegetables sat in a shallow bowl just in front of him, framed by silverware, a napkin, and a glass of orange wine.

"How did you do that?" Calder asked, impressed.

The corner of Kerian's mouth twitched up, and that smile actually looked genuine. "You know, that's the most common question I get. Would you believe I never answer it?"

"I would suspect you always answer," Andel responded. "You just never tell them what they were hoping to hear."

She nodded to him, conceding the point. Foster simply sipped his mug of coffee.

"So while you enjoy that, Captain, I will lay out the situation. Your ship was attacked by an unknown assailant in Candle Bay, and your wife was taken."

Calder swallowed a mouthful of chicken. "Not unknown. A Consultant by the name of Shera."

"Is that so? Did she introduce herself?"

He waved his spoon in the Chronicler's direction. "Naberius recognized her from the Imperial Palace."

Kerian tapped her pen against the paper. "The second most common question I receive is regarding assassins. I'm afraid I have to tell you that the Consultants do not employ, and never have employed, hired killers."

Calder gripped his spoon like a dagger, forcing a grin. "Oh really? Then who do you think attacked our ship, dressed in all black?"

"I didn't say it wasn't one of our Consultants," Kerian said. "But tell me, did she actually kill anyone?"

He thought for a moment around a mouthful of chicken and rice. He didn't know anything about Consultant cooks, but Urzaia needed to take lessons from them.

"She took my wife," Calder said at last.

"Yes, she did."

Well, that was easy. She had admitted to Jerri's abduction. Now it was just a matter of negotiation.

He leaned forward, meal forgotten. "So where's Jerri?"

Kerian flipped through the file, shuffling papers. "'That which sleeps will soon wake.' Does that mean anything to you, Captain Marten?"

He took a sip of wine to buy himself time to think. "I've heard it before," he allowed.

"I thought you had. It's the credo of a group that call themselves the Sleepless. While the Great Elders sleep, these men and women stay awake and serve their interests. It's little more than a modern-day cult, and I'm led to believe that you've had some run-ins with them in the past."

"I have." The latest only a little more than a year ago.

"Then you're aware that your wife is a member of that group?"

Andel and Foster exchanged looks, but they didn't meet his eyes. What did they think about this? There was no love between them and the Elder cults, especially in Andel's case. Did they think Jerri was better off rotting in a Consultant dungeon?

"That's one of many topics I would like to discuss with her when I see her again," Calder said.

Kerian scribbled another note, and Calder found himself wishing he could see the file. "Let's discuss the Heart of Nakothi."

As far as Calder was concerned, they weren't through discussing his wife, but he played along. "The Guild Heads seem to think that you intend to destroy it."

"And by 'Guild Heads,' you mean Bliss, Jarelys Teach, Cheska Bennett, and Mekendi Maxeus?"

"I'm not going to ask how you know that, and I'll just say yes."

"Very wise. While the Guild Heads are correct about our ultimate goal, they are mistaken regarding our methods." She folded her hands on top of the file, meeting his eyes seriously. "We have a method to destroy the Heart. But doing so without taking the proper precautions, in the wrong way, could be even worse than letting it go free. Tell me, Calder, what did you think of the Emperor?"

He was going to need a file of his own just to keep track of each time she changed the subject. "I am a loyal citizen of the Aurelian Empire."

"Off the record."

"He was a suicidal captain who almost steered us into a cliff," Calder said. "He was so much older and more powerful than anyone else that he thought he was beyond human. He wrote laws and traded lives like a Great Elder, rather than a man just like anyone else. When I learned he was dead, I laughed until my sides hurt."

Kerian nodded as though he had said exactly what she expected. "This may surprise you, but many on our Council of Architects feel exactly the same way."

That did surprise him. The average Imperial citizen didn't know much about the Consultant's Guild, but two things were common knowledge. First, they would help you with anything so long as you had enough cash to interest them. Second, they were absolutely dedicated to the Empire. Even the Imperial Guard had its stories of traitors and rebels, but not the Consultants. To be a Consultant, in the popular opinion, was to be among the Emperor's most dedicated servants.

"Humankind has never governed itself," Kerian went on. "The Emperor did it for us, and as you pointed out, he didn't do so as one man ruling over other men. He borrowed the power of the Elders to stand above us as though he were a Great Elder himself."

Calder couldn't have put it any better. Maybe he would be able to come to an agreement with this Guild after all.

"So instead of letting the world develop its own leaders, the Guilds you mentioned seek to prop up an old and outdated system. Yet *another* Emperor, to rule the world for the next millennium." She spread her hands. "Why? Even the last Emperor failed us, in the end. Why try to recreate the perceived glory of the past when we can move forward into the future?"

Calder's personal dislike for the Emperor gave a little internal cheer at that, but another part of him protested vehemently. She was presenting the case as if there were only two options: another Emperor like the first, or leaving the world to stand on its own. The Elders would consume such a world in months.

There had to be another choice.

And there was Bliss' warning to consider, too: she seemed to think that a world without an Emperor would be in grave danger. He knew her well enough to suspect that she wouldn't care who ruled the world, so long as it wasn't the Great Elders. That seemed like a wise enough viewpoint to him.

Andel picked up the conversation when Calder went silent. "How do you expect the Elders to respond to an empty throne? They would feed on the chaos."

Kerian's hand moved to touch the scar on her forehead, but she visibly forced it down. "The Regents and the Blackwatch have handled the Elders for the past five years. There's no reason to suspect that the Guilds can't keep the Great Elders in hand, along with whatever world leaders rise to the occasion."

"And look what the Regents and the Blackwatch have accomplished," Calder said. "The Dead Mother's influence grew to the point that the Emperor was killed, and his successor is fighting over her Heart."

"You seem oddly well-informed," Kerian said. Her voice and expression were entirely neutral, but Calder wondered if he was in danger.

"The Head of the Blackwatch is a personal friend of mine." An exaggeration, but Bliss would probably say it was true.

"And her right hand is your mother," the Consultant finished. "I understand. Still, you have a better grasp on the situation than I would have expected."

She straightened her spine, and Calder suddenly saw past her pleasant exterior. She didn't get that scar from paperwork.

"This isn't our usual policy," she said, "but I'm going to give you some information for free. First, we will be taking Naberius Clayborn into our custody. Once we find out what he knows, we will find a place for him."

Calder suspected that their 'place' for him would be a mile under the Aion Sea.

"Second, we do have your wife. She is alive and, as far as I am aware, completely unharmed."

He missed a breath. That had been...so *easy.* All he had to do was ask, and they told him the truth? And she was unharmed! This was better than he had dared to hope—the best he'd imagined was that he would find Jerri after almost a month of torment and abuse. He had even told himself that she deserved it, for lying to him for years.

But unharmed...it was almost too good to be true.

So after his initial burst of excitement, he listened closely for the trap.

"You will be allowed a supervised visit with her, for a strictly limited amount of time. After which, you will leave this island with neither Naberius nor the Heart."

There it was.

"That's...very generous of you," Calder said. "But I'm afraid we will need a little more than that. General Teach is on her way here looking for us. If we don't have one of the two, she will see us all dead."

Kerian's smile returned. "Then we do have business to discuss! Excellent. We're more than willing to let you stay on the island until circumstances have calmed. For a certain fee, of course."

A black-clad Consultant walked up to Kerian, and once again Calder realized he hadn't seen the man enter. How did they get around like that?

He leaned over, whispering behind his black half-mask. Kerian's eyes snapped to him, and then over to Calder.

"A Soulbound has breached Bastion's Veil," she said. "You don't know any Soulbound who may have snuck onto the island, do you?"

Urzaia. They'd found him already.

Calder exchanged glances with Andel, who shrugged. This could work out for them, after all.

"It's probably my cook," Calder admitted.

Kerian shut the file in front of her. "Urzaia Woodsman," she recited. "Former member of the Champion's Guild, exiled in bad standing, forced to serve a term in an Izyrian arena until his debt to the Imperial throne was cleared, or until his death. Liberated before his term was completed by person or persons unknown. The arena was destroyed in the process, its records lost. Later surfaced as the official cook aboard the Navigator vessel known as *The Testament*."

"Ah, so you know him."

The room was filled with black shadows, now. A couple of Consultants even perched in the corners of the wall and ceiling, crouching like spiders.

"There are those who would take this confluence of circumstances as an attack," Kerian said flatly.

Calder took another bite of chicken and vegetables, then placed his spoon down and raised his palms, showing that he was unarmed. "I can't claim responsibility for Urzaia's actions. Do you really believe I could have stopped him?"

Kerian gave no reaction. "Regardless, we still have business to conclude. I rarely have to ask this question, Captain Marten, but what do you want from us?"

Calder looked around the room, which was crowded with Consultants, and considered his answer. He wasn't sure how to put it—everything had gotten so confusing.

But there were a few things he knew.

"I want to talk to Jerri. Depending on the conversation, I might take her aboard my ship, or I might leave her here with you. I want something to keep Jarelys Teach from killing us all as soon as we leave the dock. As for the Heart..." He reached into his jacket, and one of the Consultants pulled a knife.

Calder raised his hands again, showing they were empty, and slowly slid his hand into the jacket, withdrawing a gold circlet with two fingers.

The Emperor sits on his throne, considering the petitioners in front of him. He wants to give them mercy, but mercy is not what the Empire needs. Today, the Empire needs strength. Security.

"...I don't want *either* of you to have the Heart. It's not that I specifically care what happens to it, you understand, but it could get in my way. You may not know this, but I have certain ambitions."

Casually, he placed the circlet on his head.

Kerian's eyes widened. She was on the table before he could react, a bronze blade in her hand flashing for his throat.

"Stop," Calder shouted.

Everyone in the room froze. The weight of his Intent pressed on them like chains, binding them with absolute authority. With all the Intent bound in the Emperor's crown.

He still had nightmares about the voyage to recover this particular Imperial artifact.

But it was all worth it.

Kerian crouched on the table, her blade halfway to his neck.

"Kneel," he ordered.

The room filled with the sound of men and women dropping to their knees. Even Kerian didn't hesitate, but knelt, bowing her head and pressing both fists to the surface of the table.

Andel and Foster were still in their seats. Foster took another sip of coffee, eyes wide. "Holy Dead Mother, Captain. Did you know it would do that?"

"Absolutely not, Foster," Calder said cheerfully. "I fully expected to die."

"Huh." The gunner drank some more coffee.

When he first found the crown, Calder had run some tests. Like all objects the Emperor had personally used, the crown was far more powerful than a normal invested object. However, it still had its limitations. It added a little more weight to his commands, but just to the degree of suggestions...*unless* the target considered themselves a loyal subject of the Empire. Then they would listen to anything he said while wearing it.

He had considered Awakening the crown, hoping that would allow him to control people perfectly, but upon further investigation found it impossible. The crown had such a weight of Intent and a depth of history that Awakening it would take years. Even then, it might not work.

The only man who could have potentially Awakened the crown would have been the Emperor himself.

Without being Awakened, the crown wasn't nearly powerful enough to control people against their will. Even if he ordered a loyal Guild member, they could still refuse him. He had simply hoped to use the crown to help persuade the Consultants, not to take command.

So what was happening here?

"Rise," Calder commanded experimentally.

The Consultants were on their feet before the word was fully out of his mouth.

"Touch your head."

Hands went to heads all over the room.

Foster chuckled. "Make 'em dance."

Kerian's eyes were wide, and she shook slightly. With fear or anger, Calder couldn't tell, but either way he wouldn't want to meet her without this crown.

"How did you do this?" she asked.

Calder tapped the crown. "It's all in the headgear."

"No, I understand. But our oaths shouldn't—"

"Quiet," Calder said. Her mouth snapped shut on the word.

If they all survived this, he was going to have to try very hard not to encounter Kerian in the future. If looks were anything to go by, she would tear his heart out of his chest.

For now, it was time to take advantage of his newfound authority.

"Members of the Consultant's Guild, it's time to escort me and my crew to your prisoners. You are to keep your mouths shut unless you are specifically addressed. If your fellow Guild members ask you any questions, say whatever you must to allay their suspicions. Is this understood?"

"Yes sir," they said at once, even Kerian.

Calder tried to stop his smile from spreading, but he didn't quite succeed. He reached for his hat, tossing it to Andel. He wouldn't want to cover up the crown, in case that broke its effect.

Andel shook his head, but he tossed the hat under his arm.

"Let's go, then."

They were on the way out of the room when Calder noticed who was missing.

"Where's Naberius?"

A couple of the black-masked Consultants glanced at one another before one volunteered, "He ran out as soon as we released him, sir."

"And why did you release him?"

"You ordered us to kneel."

Of course. Calder nodded. No point in worrying over past mistakes; he would have the whole Guild out searching for Naberius, if he needed to.

Come to think of it, how many people would follow the crown's orders at one time? Was there a limit? Would it wear off over time?

Calder shoved the questions aside for later, and directed the Consultants out of the room. Together, the captain of *The Testament,* his two crew members, and a dozen Consultants headed out of the chapter house, deeper into the Gray Island.

"The successful man visualizes success rather than failure," Sadesthenes said. Well, Calder had imagined what a successful meeting with the Consultants would look like.

And this was *much* better.

CHAPTER TWENTY-ONE

Anyone may use an Awakened weapon, but only a Soulbound can wield power freely, as the Kameira do. It is therefore critical, when dealing with a Soulbound, that you identify their Vessel as quickly as possible.

Until then, assume that they are capable of anything.

– Jarelys Teach,
captain of the Imperial Guard

ELEVEN YEARS AGO

Calder's Blackwatch coat was not the best fit on Jerri, but she wore black underneath and covered any gaps in her costume with raw, outward confidence. She'd watched her father at work since she was a little girl, and she remembered how everyone else deferred to Watchmen. They were the guardians who stood in the gap between normal people and unspeakable threats. Or possibly they were the acolytes of the Elders, drinking blood and carrying out indescribably rituals to bring about the end of the world. Either way, common sense said to run from anyone with a Blackwatch badge.

It had confused her to no end as a child, wondering why people kept scurrying away from her father or refusing to meet his eye, but today it served her well.

She marched her way into the Candle Bay Imperial Prison with a forged document in her pocket and wearing a look of determination like a mask.

The receptionist was just as Calder had described: pretty but empty, with a smile that made Jerri want to shiver. But a Watchman wouldn't be bothered by a doll's smile. In the Blackwatch, that level of strangeness wouldn't even merit a second glance.

So Jerri slapped her fake Guild paperwork down on the desk and stared the receptionist in the eyes. "I need to speak with whomever's in charge of this facility. Guild business."

Just in case the woman missed it, Jerri tapped her badge.

The receptionist's smile remained undented. "I'm sorry. The administration cannot be reached without an appointment."

Jerri sighed as if she ran into stubborn bureaucrats every day. "Listen. I am a duly appointed representative of the Blackwatch Guild, and I have tracked an Elderspawn to this very location. We're sweeping all the buildings in the area, just in case, but I will be searching this building for signs of an Elder infestation with or without your cooperation."

The receptionist smiled down at the desk as she scanned the paper. "Elder infestation does qualify as an emergency situation. Please wait while I call security to escort you deeper into the building. Thank you for your paperwork." She pushed Jerri's fake papers back across the desk, then turned to pull a bell-cord that would doubtless summon guards.

Jerri tightened her fists in her coat pockets to prevent them from shaking with excitement. This was it! The thrill of outsmarting a prison full of guards, the tang of danger...she hadn't felt anything like it in years. Oh, sure, the Sleepless promised a life full of risk and purpose, but they delivered very little on their promises, as far as Jerri could tell.

She hadn't managed to persuade Calder to steal *The Testament,* and the Sleepless would want to see her punished, but she was past caring about their approval. This was far more fun.

Her coat bulged in the middle, rustling, but she pushed it back down before the receptionist turned around.

When the guards arrived, she didn't bother explaining the situation to them. She just flashed her badge and walked straight through the door, to the back of the prisoners' cells. The guards hurried to catch up, but they were too in awe of her to do anything else.

Every twenty or thirty seconds she would stop in the middle of an empty hallway, she would stop and close her eyes, waving her hands in front of her as though sensing arcane vibrations. "The energy here..." she said. "I can sense the residue of Elderspawn. It's very close now."

Covertly, she pushed her bulging coat back down.

The guards remained pale-faced and shaking, one of them drawing a circle in the air to ward off Elders. From what Jerri knew of the Elder races, an invisible circle wouldn't do any more than it would against a hungry tiger. But if the gesture calmed them down, that very peace might actually protect them, so she didn't bother correcting them.

Finally, they reached the cell that Calder had indicated. It looked no different than any of the others, but Jerri froze. The guards skidded to a halt around her, clearly on the verge of bolting.

Jerri spun and pointed down the hall to her right. "*There!*" she screamed.

They turned around so fast she thought their necks might snap. As they did, she reached into her coat, withdrew Shuffles, and tossed it down the hall to her left.

"No, behind you!" she called, pointing at Shuffles. The monstrosity had buzzed its wings to ease its fall, landing with a soft splat on the floor. It shuffled down the hall, surprisingly quick in its awkward gait.

One of the guards screamed, "It's a monster!"

At the sound of his voice, Shuffles turned its nightmarish head around, staring at the guard over its shoulder and one stubby wing. The tentacles that served for its mouth writhed, and its eyes glared black hate.

"MONSTER!" Shuffles echoed, and hopped down the hall after them.

The guards could not wait to scramble away from the Elderspawn, pushing each other down and grabbing at the walls in their haste to escape. Shuffles let out a disturbingly deep and masculine laugh, shuffling along the tiles for a few feet before he hopped into the air and fluttered a few yards closer.

Shuffles had disturbed Jerri at first, but now she wanted one.

From her pocket, she withdrew the copper key that Calder had lent her. She was no Reader, so she didn't need to keep it wrapped in a handkerchief. She simply pulled it out and tapped it on the cell's lock, hoping it would work as easily as Calder said.

She didn't hear anything happen, so she tapped it twice more. She still heard nothing, but when she tried the knob, the door swung open.

Rojric Marten had been sleeping, but his eyes snapped awake as she entered. He sat up with a smile just like the receptionist's.

"Hello, young lady," he said. "What can I do for you?"

He wasn't exactly the mirror image of an older Calder that Jerri had expected—he was built heavier, for one thing, and he sported a close-trimmed beard that she couldn't imagine polluting his son. But between the smile, the pale skin, and the red Izyrian hair, she had no doubt that this was Rojric Marten.

Jerri hurried inside, shutting the door behind her. Then she made straight for the window. "My name is Jyrine Tessella. I'm here to open the window."

Rojric's smile shook. "Are you going to let me jump?"

Not for the first time, Jerri wondered what they were doing to the prisoners in here. And if the Emperor knew what was happening under his nose.

He probably did. The Emperor had done a lot worse than this, in his time.

"You won't need to jump," Jerri said, in what she hoped was a soothing tone. "I'm a friend of your son's."

Like a newborn calf testing shaky legs, Rojric rose to his feet. "Calder? Is he...here?"

"He should be right outside," Jerri assured him. "So make sure you don't jump. You might land on him."

She looked for a place to tap the Emperor's key, but the window didn't seem to have a latch. She tapped the copper all around the window frame, just in case, but the window remained sealed.

From the hallway behind her, she heard Shuffles' deep, echoing laughter, and the boots of more guards hurrying her way.

It was time to improvise.

Jerri spoke in the tone she had learned from her father and his colleagues when dealing with civilians. "Mr. Marten, please turn and face the wall."

Obediently, Rojric turned and stared at the featureless wood of his cell wall. He didn't even ask questions.

Jerri took a deep breath and reached up, massaging the emerald gem of her left earring. She was no Reader, so she couldn't feel the power building in both matching pieces of jewelry as they woke for the first time in months. But she could feel them when they finally flared to life.

After all, every Soulbound could feel her Vessel.

She drew a finger down the edge of the window frame, her touch trailing green flame. Where the blaze touched, it drilled straight through the wall.

If she couldn't open the window, she would simply cut it free.

Burn it all down, her instincts whispered. *Cut loose! Be free! There are bed sheets behind you; they will burn. There is a quicklamp on the wall; shatter its glass, loose the burning fluid. The man behind you, he will burn!*

Her Vessel didn't speak to her in words, but in impressions. In impulses. In pressure to do things she had no desire to do, to use all of her power and burn the world to the ground.

But it was no more difficult to resist than hunger, or anger. Her Soulbound Vessel was part of her, and its desires were welded to her own.

The window came free, and she had to grab it with both hands to prevent it from pitching out the wall and potentially landing on Calder's head.

As she strained under the pressing weight of the window, scrambling to keep it from crashing to the ground or unbalancing her, she realized that she had never before appreciated just how *heavy* a pane of glass could be.

"Mister Marten," she grunted. "Help me."

Now under orders, he turned swiftly from the wall and gathered up the severed window in his hands, awkwardly avoiding the red-hot edges.

As the first guards pounded on the door, demanding to know what was going on inside, the two of them set the glass carefully against the wall.

Rojric leaned out of the hole where the window used to be, precariously close to the edge. The wind smelled of salt and icy winter weather, but he drew in a long, slow breath.

Jerri laid a hand on his shoulder and guided him back from the edge, just in case. "Don't worry, Mister Marten. Calder will have our ride here in just a moment."

She hoped.

When Calder's raft sank, he knew he was going to die.

He'd been *sure* the raft would hold. He spent all afternoon investing it, meditating over each board with specific Intent. It shouldn't have broken apart or dipped beneath the waves for anything short of a falling elephant. He'd even rubbed a drop of his blood on each board, to bind his Intent closer to the material.

He never figured out what he had done wrong, whether his Intent had conflicted too much, whether he hadn't focused enough, whether the Intent in each invested board had fought the power in all the others. He didn't have time to think when his raft drifted apart, leaving him to plunge into icy water.

Calder had no doubt that this was the night of his death.

First, Candle Bay was directly connected to the Aion Sea—that haunted ocean of a thousand different terrors. For every unfounded ghost story and sailor's tale of the Aion, there were five hundred monsters and phantoms all too real. This was the sea where the Blackwatch fished for Elders. They'd spent the past year trying to summon Elderspawn into *this very bay.*

He didn't know what waited for him beneath the waves, but he knew it must hunger for his blood.

So that was his first concern. His second: the water was *cold.*

When his head first dunked underwater, he almost gasped at the sheer, shocking, bone-stabbing cold of the winter water. He only avoided inhaling a chestful of icy seawater because his lungs were frozen in the grip of the frigid waves.

He pulled desperately at the waves, paddling with numb limbs, hauling his bag of invested tools along with him though it seemed to weigh as much as an anchor. All the while, visions of circling sharks and grasping Elder tentacles haunted his mind. In his imagination, the black bay beneath him was packed so full of terrors that they scarcely had room to swim.

Calder was somewhat puzzled when, five minutes later, he found himself alive and dripping on the rocks beneath Candle Bay Imperial Prison.

He raised his arms above his head in a kind of Champion's salute, and he would have shouted had his mission not required stealth. He had conquered the freezing water, and the unnamed monsters of Othaghor and his brood.

Take that, Candle Bay! Bow before me!

Then he realized that the wind was blowing through him like a frozen spear, and his wet clothes clung to his body as close as his skin. He had to admit, this *might* not be the best time for celebration.

With shivering fingers, he undid his pack. All of his tools were still accounted for, and none the worse for their dunk in the bay. Water couldn't wash away Intent, after all.

The first item, a rope made of knotted sheets stolen from the Grayweather residence, weighed the most. He wrung as much water out as he could, half-surprised that the moisture didn't freeze to slush before it reached his feet.

When the knotted rope was somewhat dry, he swung it like a lasso over his head and slapped it against the wall of Candle Bay Imperial Prison.

Calder had spent the most time on this particular item, and it bore months of his Intent. As soon as the cloth struck the wall, he focused his Intent once more, pouring it into his makeshift cloth, reminding it of its new purpose: to *climb.*

He had explained the disappearance of eight linen sheets on a particularly disastrous trip to the laundress. Alsa hadn't trusted him with the laundry since.

The cloth rope slithered up the side of the wall, directly under his father's window.

...which, he suddenly noticed, was a slightly smoking square-shaped hole in the wall. The Emperor's key hadn't done *that.* How had Jerri and his father managed to burn a hole through metal and stone? Had Jyrine gotten her hands on some weapons-grade alchemy without telling him?

The cloth crawled inside the cell, and a pair of tan, slender hands grabbed it. Jerri's head poked out of the hole, her earrings swinging and glinting gently green in the moonlight.

"Imagine meeting you here!" she whispered down.

"Have you seen an older gentleman, about my height, with flaming red hair? I seem to have misplaced him."

Jerri began climbing down the rope, which he assumed she had tied to something on her end, since she didn't collapse to her death on the rocks below.

A moment later, his father followed.

Calder couldn't help the grin that swallowed his face at that moment. They weren't safe, not by a fair shot, but they'd still *done it.* His father was out.

Jerri jumped the last story, landing a little unsteadily on the rocks beside him. He seized her shoulders to steady her, but she didn't seem to mind whether she fell or not.

"Calder, there's a little problem I may not have mentioned."

From above came the sounds of a heavy crash, followed by splintering wood. Seconds later, two heads poked their way out of the window.

"Stop! Hold it right there!"

The other man started shouting about a break.

Rojric stopped entirely. He turned to the guards, as though he wondered whether he ought to start climbing back up.

"Father!" Calder called, no longer trying to keep his voice down. "Come on!"

Rojric shook himself and started descending, recklessly fast, sliding so that he must have burned his hands, kicking the wall whenever he got too close.

As he reached the rocks below, one of the guards pulled out a pistol.

Most of Calder's invested tools hadn't proved useful, so he upended his bag over the bay and shook it out. Then he raised the last device he'd prepared that might prove somewhat helpful: the bag itself.

The pistol rang out. The ball struck the bag and rolled off, as ineffective as a thrown rock.

Instantly, the bag started to come apart with the seams. All Calder could do with his Intent was enhance the properties of the bag; the material itself was inherently weak. With another year, he might be able to make the bag permanently bulletproof, but for now it would unravel after another hit or two.

Jerri huddled under the spread bag with him. "Nice job! Where's the boat?"

"At the bottom of the bay."

She eyed his soaking clothes. "I see you've made a trip down there yourself."

Rojric was only partially covered by the bag, sticking his head out to keep an eye on the guards above. "Maybe I should just go back."

Calder ignored him, his mind churning. *A Reader's weapons are all around him,* as Sadesthenes once said. He started to catalogue everything available to him. His rope was already unraveling, intended to last only a single use and then fall apart. So he had a few wet sheets, his own soaked clothes, an unraveling bulletproof bag, his Blackwatch coat, a bunch of rocks, and water. Lots of water.

Water was useless to a Reader. Intent was carried in the structure of an object, so liquids were notoriously poor repositories. Legends were still told of Jorin Maze-walker, who spent years of his life investing a bottle of water until a drop of it could cleanse a curse. That served as an illustration of exactly how uncommon the practice was: legends were still told of a legendary Reader who managed to invest a *single* bottle of water. After *years* of work.

Panic began to swell in Calder's chest. Until this point, he had been sure that he'd be able to come up with something to get them out of any situation. It hadn't occurred to him how completely reliant they were on the raft.

Now that he thought of it, he probably should have tested the thing.

Above them, red quicklamps flashed to life. And a dozen alarm-bells began to ring.

Jyrine huddled close to him. "I know you're the Reader, but if you could hurry up and think of something, I would certainly feel a lot better."

"How long do you think it would take them to shoot us if we tried to swim for it?"

"How long does it take to load and fire a musket?"

Already, musket-barrels were emerging from all around the prison roof.

"Surrender your weapons!" A man called. "Return the prisoner! Drop the…bag!"

Second by second, the crushing weight of reality bore down on Calder. They had failed. They were all but caught. His father would go straight back to the alchemists and their experiments. His mother might lose her job, and would certainly see him as no better than Rojric. Jerri…well, they would likely return Jerri to her family. She, at least, should be safe.

And Calder would finally get what his mother had feared for him two years before: a cell next to his father.

A cell. Where he would sit, day after day, and fondly imagine throwing himself out the window.

The image filled him with new purpose, and he dropped the bag, leaving his empty hands raised in the air. "We…agree! We agree to…your terms!" He exaggerated the shivering in his voice, but not by much. "Please…just…save us!"

"Stay where you are," came the man's voice.

"Give me my coat," Calder whispered to Jerri.

"I don't know, I'm pretty comfortable wearing it." But she was already climbing out of the coat, obviously eager to see what Calder had come up with.

It wasn't much. He was going to see if he could invest enough Intent into the jacket to get it to float, and then send his father out in the bay, using the jacket as a makeshift flotation device. Since it was black, it should blend in to the night water, and his father might be able to cover his head with it and float at the same time.

It was a weak, desperate plan, filled with holes, but it was the best he could come up with. He had to try *something*.

Then Jyrine handed him the coat, and he felt his seven nails clink against each other inside.

Inspiration bloomed like light in a cave.

He fumbled through the jacket like a blind man, finally managing to extract one of the nails. When he did, he looked from Jerri's face—still excited—to his father's lost expression.

"Trust me. I'm not crazy."

Using the tip of the nail, he scraped a bloody gouge out of his hand. Jerri gasped, and his father moved forward as if to stop him, but it was too late.

Calder jumped back into Candle Bay.

CHAPTER TWENTY-TWO

Naberius shrugged off the ropes as he staggered down the hall of the Consultant's chapter house. He'd been working his Intent into the bonds since the second they wrapped the rope around his wrists, and as soon as he was ready, the whole bundle came apart like rotten rags.

With his hands free, he tore off the cloth gag in his mouth, taking his first full, deep breath in days. When he was Emperor, he would make Calder Marten and his crew *feel* what they had done. He would tear them apart.

And then he would build them anew. It was his purpose. He realized that, now.

The Heart sang to him, even here, from across the island. After so many years in the Witnesses, he thought he'd experienced just about everything life had for him. Readers could see visions of the past, goals for the future, dreams and hopes and nightmares all bound up into the objects that people used every day. He thought he knew how the world worked.

But the Heart of the Dead Mother had a song unlike anything he'd ever experienced. It drew him, tantalized him, *taught* him. Simply from the feel of it—the cool lullaby—he knew that he would unlock secrets the world had never dreamed of. Hidden knowledge of life and death. He would be the wisest man that ever lived.

With that thought, he shook days of captivity from his mind. Who cared what Calder Marten had done? In the scale of the world, the sheer scope he'd seen when he Read the remnants of Nakothi's body, Calder Marten was nothing. *Less* than nothing—the ghost of a dust mite compared to a titan.

Naberius focused himself. Even in his own mind, he hated babbling.

He straightened his coat, corrected his stride, and walked with perfect self-assurance out the back door of the chapter house. Nakothi's song guided him.

It was on the other end of the island, in the back, and a little beneath him. As though someone had taken it underground. Were they trying to hide it from him?

He smiled only to himself as he stepped into a copse of trees, seemingly natural, and found a raked path. The way was clear before him.

Soon, he would destroy this world and birth it anew. He had been promised.

Jerri was no Reader, but she still had to press herself against the back wall of her cell to escape the Heart. Its icy grasp gnawed at her like a dog with a bone, whispering promises to her that she couldn't hear.

You can be free, it said. *You can be made anew. Your husband won't understand who you are? You can change. Or you can change him. Rebirth comes for all.*

Those who listened to the Elders for too long went mad, she knew. Even those who could not Read Intent, those like her who did not see straight into the unalloyed truth, could not stand more than the briefest glimpse into the minds of the Elders.

"They are older than we are," her father once said. *"Wiser, stronger, more intelligent than all of mankind put together. That is why we must be so careful. The lies we tell ourselves are what allow us to perceive the world at all. Crack those lies, and the human mind is like an egg with a cracked shell."*

She hadn't understood her father's words until years later, and she had never experienced such an object lesson as right here, right now. The Heart spoke with the purpose of Nakothi, but the Dead Mother's intentions were strange and alien. Jerri had to learn what she could, and put that power to good use.

Right now, she wasn't even interested in learning anything. She simply wanted it gone. This was not the first time Nakothi's Heart had visited these cells—its power came and went over the past two days, as Shera carried it to Lucan for him to inspect.

Every time Shera visited, the Dead Mother's voice grew louder. And that affected more than just Jerri's peace of mind.

Whatever Reader ritual Lucan had used to mute sound, it had either worn off or vanished in the presence of Nakothi's Heart. She caught snippets of his conversation.

"...getting dangerous...can't stay. Do it now. Jorin will..."

His voice faded, but it sounded as though he was lecturing someone. And she thought she heard him mention Jorin.

That could be Jorin Curse-breaker, the Regent of the South who had taken over after the Emperor's death. He'd built the original system of prisons under this island, Lucan had told her, though the cells in which they now rested were new additions. Why would they need a Regent to get involved? Was he supposed to do something about the Heart?

Of course, it could be any other of the ten thousand people with his name. Heroes of Imperial legend tended to have generations of people named after them, so it couldn't be uncommon.

A woman responded. Jerri couldn't make out many details, but the response was flat and even.

"...not sure you should," Lucan said. "It wants...here. That's more...afraid to..."

The woman raised her voice, so Jerri could hear her clearly. "*We* have to do something. The entire island is in danger."

And Jerri finally recognized the woman's voice: Shera. He was talking to the would-be assassin who had taken Jerri here in the first place.

She pressed herself even harder against the back wall. As much as the Heart's presence frightened her, the idea of Shera remembering her scared her even more. What if Shera had only let her live this long as an oversight? And now, on the eve of Jerri's escape, the woman had finally remembered?

Jerri clutched the iron band so hard that it stabbed into the flesh of her palm. As she'd suspected, the metal had warmed up after an hour or two, and ever since it was safe to touch Jerri had worn it against her skin. She was terrified to lose it, worried that she would miss her opportunity.

Scared that she might not get to fight for her freedom.

It was strange, she thought. She was looking forward to the fight itself more than to the freedom. What did that say about her?

That I've been locked up in here for too long, probably.

A figure in black moved outside the bars of Jerri's cell, and Shera stepped up, watching Jerri curiously.

The terror gripped Jerri's heart in panic. Would it be right now? Would Shera correct her mistake here?

She clutched the metal band even tighter, such that she was afraid she might draw blood. The Heart's power had remained steady, so there was no signal, but she could try using the Elder artifact anyway. Maybe it would still work, and free her, even though it would likely anger the Sleepless.

If Shera entered, she would try it. What did she have to lose?

But the Consultant didn't say anything. She simply stood there, watching.

After a few awkward moments, Jerri forced herself to her feet, slipping the iron band onto her left wrist and casually holding the arm behind her back. The artifact was a little loose to be worn as jewelry, but hopefully Shera wasn't here for a detailed inspection.

With her other hand, Jerri combed her hair back as though that were the most important thing on her mind. It may have been too late to start playing the cool, unemotional prisoner after she had cringed and shrunk against the wall the second Shera showed up, but every bit of poise would help.

"Shera, isn't it? May I help you with something?"

Shera was silent for another second before she spoke. "Why do what you're doing? What is the point?"

Far from sounding cold and collected, she sounded...weary. That surprised Jerri even more than the assassin showing up in the first place. Every other time the two of them had spoken, the other woman had sounded as though she had a jagged black rock where her heart should be.

"I'm stuck in a cell, sleeping twelve hours a day," Jyrine responded. "Just trying to while away idle hours, I suppose. Not much point to it."

Shera sagged forward, resting her forehead against the bars. "I don't want to do this. Elders and the Emperor and living forever...any of it. I just...well, that's the way it is. So I at least want to know why. What are you doing this *for?* What's the point?"

Jerri studied her for a moment. Shera looked as though she hadn't slept for a week, and she spoke like someone about to die.

This was the ideal moment to offer hope.

"Humans are fundamentally selfish, aren't we?" Jerri said. "No matter what else we do, when it comes down to a moment for action, we will *always* act for ourselves and those closest to us. We spend our whole lives worshiping one person."

Shera didn't react. She didn't leave or argue, either, which Jerri took as a good sign.

"And where has that gotten us? Everyone agrees that it would be better if we were more charitable, more virtuous, simply nicer to our fellow man. But we don't change. We advance, we make discoveries, but the basic nature of humanity remains the same throughout the centuries."

Jerri held up one finger. "There is only one kind of truly selfless act. And that is anything done in the service of humanity as a *whole.* For all humankind. For everyone, present and future, whether or not we ever see a benefit for ourselves."

Forcing herself to maintain a calm facade, Jerri stepped forward and gripped the bars, holding herself face-to-face with the woman who had taken her captive.

"The Sleepless do not worship Elders. We're not a cult. Nor do we capture and examine them ourselves, like the Blackwatch do. Our goal is to *communicate* with the Great Elders, to establish a common understanding so that we can benefit from just the tiniest fraction of their wisdom. Not for ourselves, you understand. For all of mankind."

Jerri finished the speech with a smile. "That's not so bad, is it?"

Shera leaned back from the bars. She loosened her arms, rolling her neck, rubbing her shoulder, as though she had just woken up.

And after a few seconds, she spoke.

"So you're idiots. Thanks. That tells me what I wanted to know."

With her right hand, the Consultant reached behind her back and pulled out one of her bronze blades. Jerri stepped back, gripping the icy band of iron. Her palms were wet and clammy, and her breath was coming fast. Would she be able to complete the summons before Shera opened the door and used the knife? Would the call even work without the right timing?

But Shera didn't open the door. Her gaze lingered on Jerri for another instant before she moved off down the hall, toward Lucan's cell.

She had only taken one step when she stopped, going down into a crouch.

Lucan's voice drifted from next door. "Who are you?" he asked someone Jerri couldn't see. "What are you doing here?"

And another voice, a familiar voice, echoed through the stone hallways.

"On your knees," Calder said.

Calder had rehearsed his next confrontation with Shera, but it didn't go as well as he'd hoped.

When he and his Consultant escorts had turned the corner in the dungeon and seen Shera in the hallway, he had an instant of pure joy. He was still wearing the Emperor's crown, after all, so he ordered her down on her knees.

Everyone in the hallway knelt on command, with a few notable exceptions. Calder himself remained standing, of course, as did Andel and Foster. The man in the cell to the left, some half-Heartlander man with a cell full of books, remained seated normally. And Shera stayed where she was, balanced on the balls of her feet with a knife in her right hand.

"Shera, I order you to put down the knife," Calder said.

It might have been his imagination, but he thought he saw her hand tremble. She didn't release the knife, though.

"There, you see?" Foster said. "That's what I expected it to do. This absolute command thing is unnatural. It shouldn't work so well."

"Where did you get that?" Shera asked. Her voice had gone cold, and her eyes locked on his head.

Before he could answer, he was drawn to his left. To the cell in which the Heartlander man sat on a cot. He hadn't noticed before, preoccupied as he was with Shera, but there was something in that cell.

It wants Calder dead. It wants to use his body as raw materials, to build him up into a monstrous slave. It wants to tear apart and remake him. It wants…

Calder tore his mind away, trying not to look at the box in that man's hands. Though he was in a cage, he held the source of that malicious Intent.

The Heart of Nakothi had only grown stronger since Calder had last seen it. Now he was even more resolved to keep it away from anyone who wanted to use it—at this rate, no one would be able to resist Nakothi's will for long.

The man in the prison held up the box in one hand. "What do you intend to do with this?" he asked.

Calder started to answer, but the other man didn't wait.

He lobbed the box out between the bars.

Shera was there, snatching the box out of the air, and before Calder reacted, she had vanished into the shadows deeper in the tunnel.

"Get Shera, bring me the box," he ordered.

Instantly, all the Consultants vanished down the tunnel after her.

Calder stepped up to the bars, flanked by Andel and Foster. "And who might you be, sir?"

The prisoner leaned back against the wall, pulling a glove on. "You can call me Lucan. You're Calder Marten, I presume."

"It seems I'm famous. You asked me a question a moment ago, and I thought I'd hear your answer first: what do *you* intend to do with the Heart?"

"An answer for an answer. You tell me where you got the crown, and I will tell you about the Heart."

Sounded fair. Calder could give him just enough details to keep him interested, without giving him the actual truth. He couldn't tell a stranger the full story, after all. There was too much to incriminate him.

But a woman called out from farther down the tunnel. "Calder? Are you there?"

Behind him, Andel drew in a sharp breath, and Foster muttered something unkind. Calder barely heard them. He drifted past Lucan's cell to a second. This one was identical in construction if not in contents: one wall of bars with a door, three stone walls and a dirt floor, a cot and a small table visible from the hall. Lucan's had overflowed with books, papers, and extra small possessions, as though he had been living there for years and had slowly made the place his own. By comparison, this cell was bare, stark.

And Jerri was in it.

She wore the standard red shirt and pants provided to Imperial prisoners—the same clothes Calder's father had worn, the last time he'd seen the man. Seeing the clothes on Jerri felt like a scene out of a nightmare. Her hair was messy and unbraided, as though she'd just woken up, and she hurriedly brushed her fingers through it when she saw him.

Other than that, she was in better condition than he'd hoped. Unbroken skin. No wounds. No signs of deprivation or abuse. They must have questioned her, surely, but no one had forced any answers out of her.

Good. So she was in perfect condition to answer him.

Or she would be, if he could figure out what to say. Every question died on his tongue: *Why didn't you tell me? When did you become a Soulbound? If I get you out of here, will you tell me everything?*

In the silence, Andel took over. "Jyrine. You're looking better than I expected."

"Andel. You look exactly the same. Foster, I see you're still alive."

Foster barked a laugh, but otherwise he kept silent. No doubt waiting for Calder to take the lead.

"I'm trying to decide whether I should take you with me, or just leave you here," Calder said at last.

Andel and Foster must have taken that as their cue to exit. One of them moved down the tunnel and into the shadows, and the other back up by Lucan's cell. Presumably they were doing it to keep watch, but Calder knew they were trying to give him some space to talk.

Calder watched Jerri as she switched expressions between pleading, angry, proud, and troubled in the space of an instant. She was trying to decide which face to show him. Trying to decide which emotion she felt the strongest, maybe.

Finally, she settled on tired. "I would very much like to get out of here."

"Good. Then you can answer my questions, and perhaps we can leave together. How long have you been a Soulbound?"

Her eyes fixed on the wall behind him. "Virtually my entire life. My father made me help slaughter an Elder-tainted baby Kameira when I was little more than four years old. Its alchemically preserved heart became the jewel in one of the earrings. The other is a copy. I wore those earrings for years before I had enough of a bond to Awaken them."

That was more or less what he'd expected, though it still burned him worse than he'd thought to be hearing a *new* story out of a woman he'd known for more than ten years. A woman who knew everything about *him.*

He stopped himself before he went too far down that path and left her here out of spite. "And the…cult."

"It's not a cult. My father was one of the Sleepless leaders. He had to leave the Blackwatch because some of his fellow Guild members were getting too suspicious. We think he was eventually killed on a mission in the Aion, but we don't know for sure."

He was getting closer to the answers he really wanted and feared, as though he were circling the edges of a hungry whirlpool. "And what did they have you do?"

"Practically nothing. We were barely in contact."

Calder reached through the bars. It was hard to Read a living human being, as their Intent shifted so quickly, but he should be able to learn something about her motivations. More importantly, he'd be able to hear a lie before it formed.

She recoiled as though he'd extended a weapon.

"Tell me the truth, Jerri."

She hesitated, looking around for a way out. After a few seconds of stalling, she hesitantly clasped his hand.

From here, he could Read her current Intent. She was frightened, focused on escape, tired, and surprisingly…overjoyed to see him again. When he felt that, he almost decided to forgive her then and there.

But there was more. She also felt an old, worn guilt, and something else. She was focused on hiding something here, now. Something that she desperately hoped he didn't notice.

"My mother was worthless after my father disappeared," she went on. "The Sleepless raised me. They saw to my training and to my education. When I was old enough, they started sending me places."

"Where?" he asked, though he thought he knew.

"Alsa Grayweather's home. They wanted me to study with the Blackwatch."

Her Intent was pure, straightforward. At the moment, she intended nothing but the truth.

He closed his eyes against the seething anger. So everything, from the first day, had been engineered.

Andel warned me, he reminded himself. *'You don't really know her,' he said. 'Don't marry her.' I told him he didn't know what he was talking about.*

Yet another time he'd gotten himself into trouble by ignoring Andel's advice.

"You have to understand, Calder. We're not trying to 'destroy the world,' or whatever the Emperor told everyone. The Elders have so much *wisdom* to share, so much power. If we can establish a working relationship with them, like you have with Shuffles and the Lyathatan, then we can't even imagine everything we could learn! This world is only—"

It was too painful to listen to her. She actually *believed* everything she was saying. So he cut her off with another question.

"What was the next assignment?"

For a moment she intended to refuse him an answer, simply out of irritated anger. But then she smoothed it out and looked at him openly. "They wanted me to help you break your father out of prison."

True.

"But it wasn't just them. I—"

"And *The Testament?* Was that their idea?"

She hesitated, but he felt the truth. "They wanted the ship out of Blackwatch hands. I said we could steal it."

Calder remembered Jerri pushing for him to steal *The Testament.* He had wanted to try breaking his father out without the ship, but it had been Jerri who talked him into the theft in the first place. He'd thought it was because she wanted a more exciting story.

Now he knew.

She rushed to explain. "They wanted to take it from you, but I wouldn't tell them where we were. And when they found out you'd made a bargain with Kelarac, they worshiped you. Someone with a link to a Bellowing Horror, a Lyathatan, and the Soul Collector himself? They couldn't have *begged* for anyone more perfect. Some of them wanted to make you Emperor, Calder."

He found himself squeezing her hand painfully hard before he realized it. So he'd made an Elder cult happy, had he?

"Did they ask you to marry me?" he asked, finally.

She hesitated. "I wanted to," she said.

Her Intent was off. Not entirely straight. It was true, but missing details.

"Did they *ask?*"

"...yes. They wanted me to, but only so I could *teach* you, so I could show you the truth. They hated the Emperor too, and they wanted you to get the crown!"

He had released her already, and started walking out. "Foster, Andel," he called.

They hurried behind him, neither of them saying a word.

"Don't leave me here!" Jerri shouted.

He stopped in his tracks for a second, letting everything he wanted to say run through his head in an incomprehensible jumble.

Finally, he just left.

Jerri fought back the tears, not for her own sake, but because she didn't want Lucan to hear her crying. It was a strange sort of vanity, and she knew it didn't make any sense—he had just heard their whole discussion, after all. And they were both prisoners. But she couldn't bear the thought that he, a stranger, would listen to her weeping in her cell.

There was one good thing that had come of Calder's visit, she reminded herself. He had been so focused on his questions, and on their relationship, that he hadn't even noticed her poorly fitting alien bracelet.

The iron band didn't even feel strange anymore, but she was confident that if Calder had Read it, he would have known far more about its purpose than she did. And he would have likely interfered, somehow.

Not that she would have particularly minded. She was beginning to realize that doing what the Sleepless told her to do typically ended with her in a more miserable situation than before.

Jerri gripped the metal. She had to break out of here before *The Testament* left the island. If she forced her way onboard, she was sure that she could explain herself. She had done everything with pure motives, after all. Calder couldn't deny that.

She looked forward to seeing him realize that she was in the right all along, and that he had actually abandoned *her*, not the other way around. No matter how it had turned out, she was still glad that the truth was out there after so many years. She didn't need to hide anymore—she could openly persuade him to her cause.

But part of her just wanted him to forget everything. Wanted to forget everything herself, so that the two of them could live as Navigators and let the Elders do whatever they wanted.

She shook herself back to reality. No matter how it turned out, she had to break out of here before Calder's ship left the dock.

So she would count to five hundred, slowly. It would take Calder at least that long to get back to his ship, even if he headed straight there, and she was sure he would waste time looking for the Heart.

If the signal didn't come before she was done counting, she was sending the summons anyway.

It was past time that she checked out.

CHAPTER TWENTY-THREE

When the whispered song of the Heart led Naberius to an abandoned, empty meadow, he wondered if he'd misheard. There was nothing here but grass, flowers, and boulders that littered the meadow as though they'd been scattered by a giant child playing with a handful of marbles.

He stood there for over fifteen minutes, waiting by the boulder and listening to the reassuring sound of the Heart's whispers, before he noticed the battle.

A black-clad shape darted from one boulder to another, holding a steel blade in its hand.

He moved to investigate, then he saw a fleeing figure carrying a bronze knife. Shera.

She disappeared behind a tree, and he heard nothing. Maybe the occasional scuffle, but no clang of metal on metal, no grunt as of a man suffering a stab wound. He hurried over, checking behind the tree, and saw nothing but a few broken branches on a bush.

Maybe they had moved on…

Stay, stay, stay and be reborn, the song crooned.

So he stayed where he was. Only a moment later, a box tumbled out from between two boulders. Blood had splattered one corner of the box, and it was open slightly.

The song leaked from within.

A joyous smile spread over Naberius' face, and he reached into the box, cradling the Heart like an infant.

Run, said Nakothi's Heart. *While you sing back to me, run.*

He stumbled through the undergrowth, focusing all his attention on the Heart in his hands. Trying to get the barest sliver of a grasp on its infinite, ancient Intent. It was made for a purpose far beyond anything he could comprehend, but he had to understand at least a fraction of its significance.

Otherwise, it would never Awaken.

Calder emerged from the concealed tunnel entrance leading to the dungeons, stalking his way through the forest with Andel and Foster behind him. He couldn't seem to think straight anymore. Now, all he wanted to do was leave—he'd found out about Jerri, and Naberius had run off. Far from worrying, he was relieved; now that the Chronicler was gone, someone else could deal with him. Maybe the Consultants would kill him, maybe he would escape, but it didn't much matter.

The Heart was important. To the world, and to Calder's future. Anyone who held it could make a case for the Emperor's throne, and thus get in Calder's way—he couldn't live in a world with a second Emperor just like the first. He wouldn't do it. He would change the Empire first.

But he was having trouble remembering why that mattered.

"Which way to the coast?" he asked. The gray horizon, swallowed up by that intimidating wall of fog, kept him from getting his bearings.

"How am I supposed to know?" Foster grumbled. "I've got no idea where we are."

The instant Calder had stepped off his ship, he'd left orders for the Lyathatan to take the ship around to the back of the island. He had a feeling that they'd be making a hurried exit, and Urzaia had tracked his Consultant target to the far side, away from the docks. The plan had been to hurry and reunite with him after meeting with the Guild representatives.

Calder knelt and placed a hand against the ground.

"You think that rock has relevant information, sir?" Andel asked. On the surface, his tone was completely respectful.

There was no Intent invested in this rock whatsoever. It was as if no living humans had ever come this way. But Calder hadn't expected anything else. He broadened his senses, reaching from the stone to the island as a whole, Reading the aura of the Gray Island.

The technique was of limited use, under normal circumstances. He couldn't get any detailed visions from an object that large, and he certainly couldn't invest any Intent into everything on the island. Reading such a broad area was like listening to a crowd of a thousand people all whispering their stories at once.

But among those whispers, there were a few screams.

Calder focused his attention on one such point of intense significance. *"Join with me," Naberius whispers. "Tell me your secrets." With power like this he will be immortal—he will be unstoppable. He will be able to end all the fighting, on the island and in the entire world, and create a perfect utopia designed just so.* And overlaid over Naberius, a second voice, chanting to an unheard rhythm. *Rebirth, rebirth, join and be remade.*

The thoughts held the same icy, nauseating, unspeakably old feel that he'd come to recognize as the signature of the Dead Mother. The Heart of Nakothi was in Naberius' possession.

But that wasn't the only significant event on the island. In the distance, close to where The Testament should soon be making landfall, a building filled with ancient purpose waited underground. In that arena, two figures did battle.

One was Urzaia Woodsman, drawing on the strength of a Sandborn Hydra and carrying two hatchets that yearned to split his enemies in half. His Intent felt like a collapsing mountain: heavy, inevitable, and overwhelming. Calder couldn't imagine him losing.

But his opponent...Calder didn't believe what he felt from her. She was a killer, no doubt, but she wasn't alone in her body. Where Urzaia was drawing on the power of a single Kameira through his Vessel, she was bursting with the fury of a dozen beasts. Strong wills tore at her muscles, pressed against the inside of her skin, and shredded her from the inside. The Kameira within her seemed to fight each other as much as they fought Urzaia.

Just from what he was feeling now, he couldn't understand why Urzaia's enemy hadn't torn herself apart. She seemed to be restraining all of those Kameira with nothing more than the sheer force of her *will.*

And if she ever succeeded into focusing that power into a single direction, even a Soulbound wouldn't stand a chance.

So Calder had to go help him.

Just as Calder was going to break off the trance and end the Reading, he caught a third shout among the crowd. Something was beginning.

Close, only a hundred yards behind Calder and a little below, the Consultant prisoner was bending over a bronze blade. *The weapon's lifetime stretches back through the entire history of the Empire. There is no life it can't take, no power it can't steal, no defense it can't break. And even among others of its kind, this blade is unique. It has harvested lives of unimaginable significance, unfathomable depth... and Lucan needs it to do so again. He begs for every shred of power the blade can offer him.*

To protect Shera, he needs this knife to Awaken.

The trance broken, Calder snapped back to himself, staring up at Foster and Andel. The two of them looked away from him, weapons drawn, keeping an eye on the clearing while he gathered information.

As much information as he had managed to gather, anyway. Now he was torn. Naberius seemed to think that he could take control of the entire Gray Island if he succeeded in bonding with Nakothi's Heart. Calder believed him. If the Heart gave the Chronicler any fraction of the Emperor's power, even the Imperial crown couldn't stand against him.

But that was only if Naberius could Awaken it. Usually, Awakening an object took time and strength in conjunction with the object's power of Intent. Anything as significant as a Great Elder's heart should take months to Awaken and years to bond with. There was always the possibility that Nakothi herself was helping Naberius along, and Calder had no idea what she was capable of. Still, he had more urgent threats than Naberius.

The blade behind him, for instance, was beginning to feel very dangerous.

Calder wasn't sure what had changed to give Lucan the prisoner access to a Consultant's blade, and if he had access to a weapon, why hadn't he broken free? Especially as a Reader. There was something about that situation that Calder didn't understand, and that scared him.

On top of his own unease, Lucan seemed to think that he was on the verge of Awakening a deadly and powerful weapon, which he intended to pass on to Shera. If Calder could stop that, he wanted to. And he was closer to Lucan than to either of the other two.

"When in doubt," Sadesthenes said, *"seek first to preserve life."*

That wasn't Calder's favorite quote, but it seemed appropriate here. Rather than trying to pin down Naberius or killing Lucan, supporting his crewman came first. Especially when it might result in a dead Consultant assassin.

Calder stood, adjusting his crown. "Follow me. We're heading for Urzaia."

Foster joined him without complaint, but Andel turned and swept his hat on his head, bowing to the spot where Calder had just knelt.

"Thank you for the intelligence, rock. We are in your debt."

"Shut up and follow me."

Maybe he could arrange a way to leave Andel on the island filled with angry Consultants. It was worth considering.

Four hundred and sixty-eight.

Jerri thought someone had returned to Lucan's cell, after which she heard the edges of a whispered conversation. However, when she asked him about it, he had denied receiving any visitors since Calder.

In the moment, she decided to believe him. It didn't affect her anyway; she had more important things to worry about.

For instance, she could once again feel the power of Nakothi in the air.

The voice of the Great Elder, a voice she had learned to recognize since childhood, was screaming at her now to prostrate herself in the presence of superior power. It wanted to rebuild her, to remake her body so that she would be more acceptable to the Dead Mother. It was clearly the will of Nakothi, which meant that either the Heart was getting closer, or someone was trying to bring out its power.

She pulled the band of iron off of her arm, focusing on it. The Sleepless cabal had instructed her to use the object only when she felt the power of Nakothi wax.

Was this it? It was certainly getting stronger. Maybe she should have used it earlier. Or maybe this was one of those signals that she would know without a doubt as soon as she heard it.

Four hundred and seventy-five.

After only a moment of thought, Jerri grew frustrated at her own indecision. This wasn't like her. She didn't swing between possibilities like a broken weathervane, waiting until time made the decision for her.

Five hundred.

Suddenly resolute, Jerri sat down on her cot with her back against the wall, crossing her legs. She placed the iron band in her lap, with one hand on either side.

And closing her eyes, she focused her Intent. She had used lesser summoning objects like this three times before, and none of them had been exactly alike. But she began the ritual she had been taught as a little girl.

"I who remain awake must call to those in the dream. My power is lacking, and my wisdom is dim. In ignorance, I seek your light. In weakness, I seek your aid."

She waited a few seconds before continuing. The full sequence took about three minutes to successfully complete, and she would need to repeat it until it worked. Sometimes the Elderspawn would arrive halfway through the first sequence, and other times it waited for three or four repetitions. She knew neither rhyme nor reason to the actions of the Elders.

As she sat and chanted, she clung to one thought.

I wasn't at fault, Calder. I was right, and in time I can prove it.

Just wait for me.

Calder stood inside what seemed to be a hollow boulder, waiting for another controlled Consultant to show him the secret entrance to the arena. He knew that the structure waited beneath his feet—he could feel its heavy Intent without making a particular effort. And the whole area shook as if under heavy blows: evidence of the battle going on underneath them.

He, Foster, and Andel had wasted several minutes examining the interior of the giant boulder, finding nothing, before it occurred to Calder to shout for help. Driven by the power of the crown, the nearest Consultant had stumbled out of the underbrush and begged to help.

"Get ready," Calder said, hefting his pistol. "Urzaia's inside."

The boulder shook around them, dust drifting down from the stone ceiling high overhead.

Foster looked up at the shaking rock and snorted. "Oh, really? How could you tell?"

"Keen intuition and instinct."

A roar echoed from somewhere under them.

"I don't know where we'd be without your insight, Captain," Andel said.

At last, the Consultant finally located the secret door, tracing its outlines in the cracks of the boulder's rough wall. "Here it is. But the lock should be—"

He pushed lightly on it, and the door swung open.

"It seems that we wasted our time looking for a hidden entrance," Andel pointed out. "We should have just pushed on the rock."

"I'll be sure to try that next time, Andel," Calder said. "But until then..."

He motioned to the Consultant, and Foster bound and gagged him in a few brief, skilled motions. From the fact that none of the other crown-ordered Consultants had returned, Calder gathered that the artifact's effect didn't last terribly long once he was out of sight.

Rather than a hallway, this secret entrance led down a ladder on the wall of a shaft that reminded him of a vertical sewer pipe. Foster didn't seem to mind, but it was Andel's turn to complain, grumbling about the slick walls ruining his white suit.

From all round them, the sounds of battle echoed, as though they had been stuck inside a drum.

When they reached the bottom of the shaft, they stood on a ledge at the top of a tall staircase, looking out over a vast chamber. It looked as though someone had taken one of the great arenas of Izyria, made to seat twenty or thirty thousand people, and transplanted it here, underneath the Gray Island. Calder briefly wondered how the island itself stayed together, if its underbelly was made of such hollow chambers.

The center of the arena was hardly the wide, sand-filled pit in which

Calder had once found Urzaia. It looked like a maze—he was too far to make out details, but boxes and low walls and spiked poles littered the arena floor, arranged in a particular order that was lost on him.

Of course, it would have been easier to identify the pattern if half of the obstacles weren't in ruins.

As he watched, Urzaia swung a hatchet in an arc that sliced a pole in half. The blond Consultant vaulted over the attack, swinging a midair kick at the side of Urzaia's head. He blocked with his hide-wrapped forearm, sending up a *crack* that echoed all the way to Calder. Then he gathered his strength, driving his fist toward the Consultant.

She managed to duck the strike, leaving his punch to hit solid stone.

The low wall cracked, shaking the entire arena.

"Praise the Unknown God that we're here to help him," Andel said drily. "Quick, let's go rescue him from his mortal danger."

True, it didn't seem that Urzaia was in too much trouble. But the details from Calder's vision still troubled him.

His cook was fighting with the power of a single Kameira, focused into his Soulbound Vessel. His opponent, on the other hand, fought alongside an *army*. And she didn't feel like a Soulbound at all; somehow, she contained all that potential inside a single human body.

If she pulled herself together...well, better to be safe. Urzaia wouldn't like it, but Calder was not above shooting a woman in the back.

One of Yenzir's most famous quotes: *"While Honor has never won a single battle, Deceit wins wars."*

Calder placed his foot on the top of the staircase, and the world vanished. He found himself dragged into a Reader's trance like a leaf sucked into a tornado.

Naberius runs through the island, clutching the oozing, gray-green heart to his chest. Its beat has grown stronger with time, pulsing in rhythm with his own. It is almost bound to him, closer than his own limbs. Now the song guides him. He needs to stand in the right place, at the right time, to finish Nakothi's song. He spies a huge boulder—one that Calder knows to be hollow. There. Just beyond that boulder is a place.

"Here," the Heart cries. "Here you will be remade."

Above him, Calder felt the power of the Dead Mother, blazing cold like the fire of a dead star. But his vision did not yet return.

Lucan crouches in his cell, the bronze knife actually floating in the air in front of him. Sweat runs down his face, but he can't stop now. He finally realizes that he's been preparing for this moment for years. Everything he has done for Shera, everything that the two have shared, all of it has brought him to this moment. He shares a connection to this blade almost as deep as to his own.

The pit is ready. The wood has been prepared. All it needs is a single spark to burst into flame.

Calder still couldn't see the world around him, but he managed to speak. "Andel. Foster. I was wrong. We need to leave."

They may have responded, but he couldn't tell. His senses were swallowed up once again.

"I will be reborn. I will remake this world. I will give my life, and will receive life anew." With a great effort, Naberius brings all his Intent to bear on the Heart of Nakothi, striking a final, heavy hammer-blow.

In his cell, Lucan feels the life of the dagger taking shape, the fire beginning to flicker to life. Wisps of pale green light float around the blade, drifting like ghosts. "You are the taker of lives, the thief of secrets. You are that which turns power against power. You are the death of the powerful."

At the same instant, Calder saw a new vision. Just a flash of something he hadn't sensed before.

Jyrine sits in her own cell, only yards from Lucan. She holds in her hands a blighted circle of darkness, a twisted tool that seems to scream with anguish. But this scream will not bring aid; it is the squeal of prey that lures a predator.

Jerri grips her artifact tight. "I call out to you, my Elders, that you may hear my cry. Come to me!"

Without warning, the vision shifted.

Naberius raises the Heart into the air. "I WILL BE REBORN!"

And shifted again.

Lucan drives the blade into the ground. "You will be called Syphren, the Whispering Death!"

In Calder's mind, it was like three bombs exploding at once.

The trance forcibly broke, leaving Calder to stumble. Andel cried out and grabbed him by the elbow, hauling him backwards before he dropped off the edge.

"What just *happened?*" Foster asked, his voice shaken. Calder had almost forgotten—the gunner should have been able to sense it too.

All around them, air and earth trembled with the sound of a woman's laughter. Space twisted and distorted, shadows growing longer, trails of dust rising from the floor like wisps of smoke.

And it was getting very cold.

"We're leaving right now," Calder commanded, and leaped up the ladder.

"What about Urzaia?" Andel asked, though he followed close behind.

"I'm afraid that an interruption right now would just kill him. If he survives long enough, I'll come back for him." He left unsaid that if they stayed on the island, all they could do was die alongside him.

When they reached the top of the shaft, the three Navigators ran desperately for the shore, Calder in the lead. But they had only covered a few yards when they ran across Naberius, laughing and dancing with the Heart of Nakothi grasped in his left hand.

He no longer looked anything like the polished Imperial hero who had first shown himself on *The Testament's* deck. His hair was twisted and snarled, his face covered in scratches, and his eyes were wide with madness. His smile looked like a madman's grimace rather than a grin, and his red suit was shredded, the white shirt beneath splattered with gray-green blood.

Andel and Calder pulled their guns, ready to fight, but Foster was faster.

He clubbed Naberius over the back of the head with the butt of his pistol.

The Chronicler staggered and turned on them in anger. He began to raise his hand, and Calder sensed the burning of his malicious Intent. He had no idea what tricks Naberius could perform now that he was a Soulbound, and he had no intention of finding out.

Foster hit him again, and this time Naberius' eyes rolled up into their sockets. He fell on his chin, the Heart of Nakothi tumbling from a limp hand.

"Time was, I could have done that in one shot," Foster said, shaking out the hand holding the pistol. "Must be getting old."

Andel threw Naberius over his shoulder, and Calder used the corner of his jacket to pick up the Heart. Its malice seeped into him, even through the cloth, and he shuddered as he dumped it into his pocket. The last thing he wanted was to pick up a vision from something they'd pried out of the Dead Mother's body.

All around them, the inhuman laughter continued to echo unnaturally loud, rising into a shriek.

As they continued to run, Andel carrying Naberius over his shoulder and Calder trying not to think about the Heart, Foster spoke. "I've been meaning to ask, but who's that laughing?"

"Nakothi," Calder said, at the same time Andel said, "The Dead Mother."

"Huh. Let's run a bit faster, then, shall we?"

Calder couldn't argue with that.

The edge of the island wasn't far from the hidden entrance to the arena: it took them about ten minutes of running to reach. On the few occasions that they ran into a Consultant, Calder drove them away with the power of the Emperor's crown.

As they looked out onto the blue expanse of the Aion, and as he'd hoped, the familiar green-veined sails of *The Testament* bobbed just offshore, a shadow floating beneath the hull.

But there wasn't much of a *coast* on this coast. The island terminated abruptly in a jagged row of rocks sticking up from the cliff like teeth in a lower jaw. Calder walked up, peering through the jagged stones to the sea below.

As he'd feared: a sheer cliff, with nothing but more rocks and white surf beneath them.

"It's possible that this could pose a problem," he said.

Andel walked up and took a look for himself, leaning over with Naberius on his shoulder until it looked like he might dump the Chronicler over. He didn't seem too concerned about the possibility. "Can you call for a ride?"

Calder raised his hand purely for effect as he stretched out his mind to *The Testament.* He could sense the presence of his Soulbound Vessel even at this distance, and could still call on its power to some degree. But steering the ship or raising the sails wouldn't help him now, and he could barely feel the Lyathatan at all.

When Calder shook his head, the Quartermaster was already moving along the edge, hostage on his shoulder. "Move the ship," Andel said. "We'll meet it farther down the coast."

"It's my ship, and I think I'm the one who's supposed to give the orders."

"Then we await your orders, Captain."

"Very good, Andel." Calder sent a mental command to his Vessel. "I've moved the ship. We should meet it farther down the coast."

"If you insist." Andel had never stopped jogging in that direction.

If anything, the distortions had grown stronger since they left the cavern. Air warped in the distance, like a heat haze, and bits of grass and soil tore themselves free from the ground and rose into the air. Rather than lifting straight up, they seemed to be flying towards a point over the center of the island.

And through it all, above it all, the Dead Mother's laughter rose to a screech.

"She laughs...pretty good...for a corpse..." Foster panted.

The laughter sharpened to a squeal, like a sheet of metal tearing, but stretched into impossibility. Calder covered his ears with both hands, and still the sound made him feel as if his head would start bleeding.

Andel stopped and tilted his hat back, staring up at the sky over the island. "Light and life..." he whispered.

A bright white dot appeared over the Gray Island, directly in the circle of sky between walls of gray.

And from that spot, like roots pushing out from a seed, a nest of tentacles pushed out into the world. These weren't the limbs of an octopus, or the dark green writhing appendages on Shuffles. These tentacles were pale, the color of flesh, with bones visible through the tight skin. And instead of suction cups, the tendrils were covered in what seemed to be thousands of opening and closing hands.

The tentacles lowered to the ground like the skirt of a dress settling, and more of the gigantic creature appeared from inside the white spot. Its torso was skeletally thin, a mottled white and blue and purple, as though it was covered in a bruise. Its arms came out next, multi-jointed and longer than trees, with hands that curled into claws. Its neck, too, looked unnaturally long, and when its head was revealed...

Calder caught a brief glimpse of its head before he had to jerk away, taking deep breaths to avoid vomiting. The creature's head was a chaos of eyes, mouths, waving stalks, and cages of bone containing pulsing organs—parts that just *should not be* anywhere near a head.

As a whole, the giant towered over the island, giving the impression of a skeletal woman with a writhing, living skirt and a gut-twisting, repulsive face.

He had read of such creatures. Anyone who studied classical Imperial history would have. Sadesthenes had spoken of them in his most famous history: *"Dread of aspect and thin of frame, I would have thought these creatures Great Elders themselves had I not received testimony from both the Emperor himself and the inimitable Estyr Six. They are tapestries of flesh and nightmare, these Handmaidens of Nakothi."*

"Time to change plans again!" Calder said, his voice high and panicked. "Let's jump."

"There is no chance we'd survive," Andel responded, still calm, though Calder noticed that he was looking directly away from the Handmaiden. "That...thing isn't looking for us. Nothing has changed."

The Handmaiden let out a bobbing whistle that sounded curiously similar to the Dead Mother's laughter from a few moments before. The white light above her expanded abruptly to the size of the moon, and then shattered. The pieces, strangely, were tiny and black, and they scattered out like a parasol over the whole island.

One of the pieces landed nearby, sending up a ring of dirt and dust. It raised itself from the crash, a hideously bloated bladder of fat squeezed between a bone cage. The monster hissed as it spotted them, waddling closer and raising a stone club in its single, oversized hand.

Children of Nakothi, called to battle by their Handmaiden. And the Gray Island was covered with them.

Andel hurried for the edge. "The Captain's right, let's jump. You first, Naberius." He raised the Chronicler's body and started to sling him over the edge, but Calder stopped him.

His mind boiled furiously, just as if he were frantically looking for an advantage in the middle of a negotiation. There had to be something he could use to get out of this. Something that would give him the edge he needed. Something that he'd saved for just such an occasion.

An idea struck him, and his hand shot to the vile organ in his jacket pocket. Gripping it felt like holding a slimy bundle of insects and rotting garbage; he had to force himself to keep touching it for longer than an instant. Its song eroded the edges of his mind, prying at his Reader's senses, looking for a gap to worm its way in and drive him insane. It was so much more powerful than when they'd first arrived; it would find a way in, if he gave it the time.

Good thing he didn't need to hold it for long.

Hopping up onto one of the rocks, Calder pitched the Heart of Nakothi off the cliff and into the sea.

CHAPTER TWENTY-FOUR

There were none of the Great Elders more widely respected than Kelarac, whose name means 'Collector of Souls.' In myth and legend, he has the reputation of a shrewd bargainer whose deals more often than not spell doom for the other party.

The common understanding, in this case, comes surprisingly close to historical fact. Though no man but the Emperor remembers Kelarac's true shape, records of his rule still exist. Kelarac was the only known Great Elder without a specific domain, wandering as he did among the territories of his brothers and sisters. He gathered his power from humans, granting their wishes in exchange for an item of value: invested artifacts, personal allegiance, stolen relics of the other Elders, even blood or sanity.

Kelarac is chained to a drowned city somewhere beneath the Aion, but reports of his activity continue throughout the centuries. More contemporary legend suggests that one may summon his attention in the same way that one summons a lesser Elderspawn; namely, through focused application of Intent. However, any plea for Kelarac's attention first requires a sacrifice. An object, valuable to you, tossed into the Aion where his minions can retrieve it. There is no guarantee that such a sacrifice will warrant Kelarac's attention, only that without it, you may be assured of summoning only his apathy.

To survive a bargain with the Soul Collector, one must be exceptionally clever. And exceptionally desperate.

– Artur Belfry, Imperial Witness,
in a confidential report commissioned by the Blackwatch

ELEVEN YEARS AGO

Calder drifted in a sea of frozen darkness, blood leaking into the water around him. The rest of his body was numb with the cold, so it didn't seem fair that his cut hand still burned. Still, from everything he'd learned among the Blackwatch, the wound was necessary.

He didn't know much about summoning Elders, but between the blood and the pain and his own impending death by hypothermia, he imagined that he was presenting a feast to every dangerous predator in the whole of the Aion Sea. Any Elder that couldn't sense this was blind, deaf, and not worth his attention.

Just like Alsa Grayweather had tried for almost two years, Calder cast his Intent into the water, summoning Elderspawn.

Come to me! I summon thee! Someone help!

Readers required only focus of Intent, not speech; technically, it wasn't necessary to imagine speaking in order to invest an object. But every Reader that Calder had ever met used words to focus their thoughts.

This time, Calder didn't fully understand the summons, so he hoped the clarity of his desperation would make up for what he lacked in specificity. *Whoever you are, come now! I require your power!*

It was easier than Calder had expected.

One second, he floated in freezing black; the next, he sat on a low couch next to a blazing fire.

He was dry and warm, resting in a sitting room straight out of the ancient Empire. The walls were monuments of polished stone, supported by intricately carved columns. Every entrance was a door-less arch, and the walls were padded with tapestries just as the floor was lined with brightly patterned carpets.

He should have been startled by the abrupt transition, but he was mostly just relieved. Encounters with Elders were supposed to be nightmarish and dramatic, not plush and comfortable. If this was the typical experience of a summoner, then he should try sending summons more often.

Calder leaned forward, warming the remembered chill from his fingertips, when suddenly a voice spoke from next to the fire.

"Welcome, Calder Marten! Those who knock at my door are too often misers, but you have left me such gifts."

He looked to the right, only slightly surprised to see a seated man where a moment ago had only been empty space.

The man reminded Calder of no one so much as the Emperor. He had the dark skin of a full-blooded Heartlander as well as the poise of good breeding, and he had draped himself in shiny fabrics. A robe of cloth-of-gold was embroidered with a climbing serpent and closed with a sash of orange. Jeweled rings flashed on every finger, layers of necklaces fanned over his chest, and loops of gold hung from his ears. He was not hairless, as the Emperor seemed to be: the hair on his head was trimmed short, his beard limited to a thin goatee.

But by far his most remarkable features were his eyes. Or rather, the device that covered them.

A band of some silver metal circled his whole head, with bolts where his eyes should have been. It was as though someone had fashioned him a steel blindfold and then bolted it into his sockets.

Calder stopped staring at the man, looking for any similarity to Shuffles, and tried to recall his previous comment. *Gifts.*

Calder had no idea what gifts he was talking about, but he wasn't going to expose his ignorance at the very beginning of a negotiation. He gave his best smile, though he didn't know if the man could see it. "Of course! I would not send out such an invitation without something to welcome you."

The man spread his hands like a salesman demonstrating his wares, and suddenly a table appeared on the floor before him. Spread out on the surface of the table, arranged on cushions of velvet, were seven simple objects. Objects that Calder recognized.

One, a small hammer that he had invested to break stone. Another, a spool of thread invested to bind a man's hands and feet. They were his contingency tools, packed to help break his father out of prison and abandoned into Candle Bay when they proved themselves unnecessary.

"I must say, it was unwise of you to send such a message so broadly," the man said. "There are others of my siblings with holdings in this sea, and none of them so generous as I."

"Then I am greatly pleased that my call reached your ears," Calder said graciously. "What may I call you, sir?"

The man smiled, revealing a pair of teeth capped in gold. "I was once called the Father of Merchants, the Lord of Coin. The Gambler's Delight, they named me, and Miser's Bane. I was the Keeper of the Vaults, the Hoard-gatherer, the Seeker of Treasures. Now, I believe, men call me Kell'arrack."

"Kelarac," Calder repeated, his mouth suddenly dry.

Kelarac licked his lips as thought tasting the word. "Kelarac...is that how it is said, these days? Human language changes so quickly. It is a name I favored, though. Collector of Souls." He rubbed his hands together, a man expecting a feast. "What have you come to purchase with your soul, Calder Marten?"

Calder felt like he had slid a foot out on thin ice, only to find out that there was no ice at all. Only deep, dark seas filled with hungry sharks.

Tread carefully, Calder. Whatever you do, don't mess this up.

If he focused his Intent any harder, he would end up investing himself.

"I apologize for bothering you, Lord Kelarac," Calder said, with an attempt at a seated bow. "I was seeking a lesser member of your...entourage."

Kelarac adjusted the steel band over his eyes like a man fiddling with his spectacles. "I see. Caught a bigger fish than you expected, did you? If that is the case, I will be more than satisfied to take your gifts and walk away. Simply... throw me back."

He started to rise, but Calder threw out a hand to stop him. "Please wait just a moment, Lord Kelarac. It's possible that we can come to some sort of an arrangement."

Kelarac seated himself once more, plucking a grape from thin air and pushing it into his mouth. "You have my attention, Reader of Memory."

"Two of my companions and I are trapped on some rocks in Candle Bay. A number of armed men are closing in around us. I had hoped to call something big enough to carry us to shore."

That was what the Blackwatch were trying to do with *The Testament,* after all: summon something that could drag a whole ship through the ocean. If he called a creature that wouldn't or couldn't listen to reason, well, he always had his seven nails.

Kelarac laughed, and it was surprisingly...ordinary. The room didn't shake like an earthquake, and Calder didn't feel his brain dribbling out his ears. It was simply the laugh of a man hearing an amusing story.

"I did not realize you were so young, Calder Marten, even for one of your kind. I doubt you understand how improbable your survival was."

"I'm beginning to," he said honestly.

"Yes. I think you are." Kelarac stroked his short beard, deliberating. "I have a servant in your area who might serve you well. Yes, very well indeed. But there is, of course, the matter of price."

Calder nodded to the invested odds and ends displayed on the table. "Those are quality work. They represent months of my time and Intent. Surely, they are valuable enough to warrant this one small task."

Behind the metal blindfold, Kelarac's eyebrows raised. "These? These are the gifts you offer for the pleasure of my hospitality. If you wish to make a transaction with me, then I require something more substantial."

"Not my soul," Calder said quickly. Painful as it was to die in Candle Bay, he didn't want *that* fate hanging over his afterlife.

Kelarac waved one jeweled hand. "What is a soul? Despite the name I was given by men, I do not understand souls. I like the title because 'Soul Collector' implies that I own humans in their entirety. Minds. Bodies. Service. These things I understand."

Was it worth living, if it meant servitude to a nameless Elder beneath the sea?

If it means Jerri and my father go free, then yes.

"How much of my service might this cost me?"

Kelarac laughed again. "I collect whole objects, Reader of Memory, not pieces. To that end, I require something else that I believe is in your possession. A small copper key."

Calder's mind flashed to the Emperor's key. Jerri should have had it, which meant it should be in his coat!

"You have a deal," Calder said quickly, before the Elder could change his mind. He patted down the pockets of the coat until he located the key, holding it out for Kelarac.

The Great Elder shook his head. "We exist right now only in this dream-space. Give the key to me when you return to the cold, and the dark. Then my Lyathatan will come to your aid."

Calder stood up, buttoning his coat as though he meant to walk out into the winter wind. "A pleasure doing business with you, Lord Kelarac."

Kelarac drummed ringed fingers on his display table. "A word to the youthful, child. Alchemy is a new discipline, but we had addictive substances of our own when I walked this earth. Among the purveyors of such blends, there is a saying. I believe it has survived into this era. 'The first taste is always free,' yes?"

He smiled his gold-capped smile. "I hope you enjoyed your first taste, Calder Marten. I do look forward to the second."

Then the cold, dark water came crashing back.

Calder climbed up onto the rocks of the bay with just enough strength to breathe. Jerri hauled him up as his father stood dumbly nearby, watching.

"I hope you found some help down there," Jerri said.

He looked up at her, a little disappointed. "A little concern would be appreciated, thank you."

"You said to trust you." She smiled and placed a hand on his wet coat. "I trusted you."

If he was anything but freezing, that would have warmed him. As it was, he tried to smile through his violent shivers.

"I'm glad to hear that," he said. Then he threw the Emperor's key into the water.

She watched the copper flash as it fell into the darkness. "I take it back. I don't trust you anymore."

"Trust me."

"No, it's too late for that now."

There came the sound of something slapping against rock, and they turned. The prison guards had thrown down a ladder and were descending, pistols or batons in hand, to the rocks.

"I'm going back," Rojric whispered, and Calder couldn't tell if he sounded terrified or delighted. "They're taking me back!"

Across the bay, a huge construction of wooden planks and boards shook like a rattled cage.

Calder pointed with one shaking hand. "Lady, gentleman, I believe our transportation has arrived."

The wooden scaffolding, which had surrounded *The Testament* like a cage for two years, exploded outward in a shower of splinters. Debris the size of small trees flew halfway across Candle Bay, sending up sprays of water wherever they landed.

When the air between them cleared, the dark green ship was sailing toward the rocks. No wind filled its sails because there were no sails to fill, but still the ship slid across the black glass of Candle Bay.

Its wake stretched behind it like a bridal train, but a ripple preceded the ship as well. Almost as though something huge were swimming in front. Dragging the ship along.

When the vessel loomed over them, the guards backed against the walls of the prison in panic. They knew what haunted the Aion Sea, and nothing that dragged a ship behind it could be anything less than a monster.

Calder turned his back to the ship. He grinned at Jerri and his father.

"I'd like to introduce my friend, the Lyathatan." The ship slowly ground to a halt.

Rojric looked confused. "Is that...the name of the ship?"

"No, the ship is *The Testament*. The Lyathatan is..." Calder gestured to the bay, sure that this time his timing would be perfect.

The ship creaked as it settled in the water. A rain of droplets flowed down its wooden sides in a steady patter.

He gestured again. No Elderspawn appeared.

"There's supposed to be a huge monster pulling the ship," he said at last.

The guards decided that moment to rush the rocks. Rojric stepped forward, holding out his wrists to be shackled.

"No!" Calder shouted. He reached into his coat for an iron spike—if it worked on Elders, it would surely do something unpleasant to a living man. Jerri, for some reason, reached up to her earring.

And *finally*, the Lyathatan burst out of the water.

It lunged up like a cannon-shot, a giant creature shaped like a man and standing even taller out of the bay than *The Testament's* mast. Moonlight rippled over its fish-like scales, shining through the ridges running down its spine. Its six-fingered hands were webbed and tipped with nails like spikes. Shackles wrapped around each scaled wrist, attached to chains that led beneath the ship.

And its face...a shark's mouth with three black eyes on either side of its head. Gills flared on its short, muscular neck.

Calder's breath left him, but he forced a smile. "You...see?" he asked, teeth chattering from cold and fear. "He fights with us!"

The Lyathatan let out a hiss as loud as a roar, like air shrieking through a thousand teakettles.

One of the guards raised his pistol and fired in a puff of smoke. It did exactly what Calder had expected: nothing except to make the Elderspawn target *that* particular victim first.

Its claws closed on the guard, deceptively fast, and then the Lyathatan swallowed him whole.

"Fire!" someone yelled, and then muskets were firing from the top of the prison, all aimed at the monster.

Calder wasn't going to wait to get hit by an enthusiastic marksman or a rampaging creature. He grabbed his father, scrambling for the edge of the rocks, aiming to swim for one of the last construction materials to cling to *The Testament:* a rope ladder dangling from its side.

"No!" Rojric yelled, struggling. "Not in the water! Not with that thing!"

Calder had to admit, his father's fears were reasonable. Normally, he wouldn't want to be anywhere within ten miles of anything that looked like the Lyathatan.

But of all the things he'd ever heard about Kelarac, he'd never heard anyone say that the Great Elder ever broke his bargains.

He grabbed his father and shoved him into the water.

Calder turned to Jerri, planning to help her down, but she had already executed a perfect dive into the waters of Candle Bay. Far from showing terror, she actually stopped to tread water underneath the Lyathatan, staring up at its gargantuan body with a grin on her face.

Suddenly, his expression matched hers. He'd almost gotten her arrested, summoned a monster, and told her to swim through ice-cold water for the dubious safety of an Elder-pulled unfinished ship...and she looked like she was having the time of her life.

I'm going to marry that woman, he thought, and jumped into Candle Bay.

The climb up the rope ladder qualified as one of the most tense, frightening, and *exhilarating* things he'd ever done. Musket-balls tore finger-sized holes out of the hull, the Lyathatan raged and smashed men into rocks, guards shouted, and water rushed in a deafening cacophony. As the monster fought, the chains jerked the boat this way and that, making the ladder swing against the hull.

Rojric reached the ship first, and he simply stood around and shivered. Jerri climbed up next, heading straight for the ship's wheel.

"I don't know how to steer a ship!" she shouted, over the noise.

Neither did Calder. "Turn it! Turn it!"

She spun the wheel, and the ship turned slightly, but it couldn't fight against the monstrous strength of the Lyathatan, who simply jerked *The Testament* back into place.

"We'll need something better than that!"

Calder dropped to his knees, which felt surprisingly good. The cold and the exertion were sapping his strength, demanding that he relax, shouting at him to stay off his feet. He leaned over, which felt like collapsing, and pressed both his hands against the deck.

And, focusing his mind, he entered a Reader's trance.

Sometimes, when he Read an object, he would see a clear vision of its creation or its lifetime of use. Other times, he would merely feel impressions: echoes of its Intent.

This time, his mind plunged through the ship and into a library of sensations. His mother, perusing the plans for the ship, pointing out potential problems. Laying its skeleton, putting her time and sweat and Intent into every beam.

He felt himself, like echoes of an old, familiar song. He'd paced every step of this deck a hundred times, pouring his focus and drops of his blood into the ship's skin, its flesh, its heart. The chains, he and his mother had worked on together—turning each link into an addition to the whole rather than a separate entity, shaping the shackles until they could compel even an Elder creature to work for the good of the ship.

There were other minds here, of course. Every worker who had pounded a single nail or painted a yard of polish had invested his Intent into the ship's memory. But there were two souls here, two voices in the chorus, that stood out among the rest.

His mother's and his own.

In this moment, the wooden vessel felt more like a part of him than his own arm. He'd used drops of his blood when he worked on a particularly difficult piece of Reading, and now he could sense those pieces of him, tying the ship to him with a dozen knots of power.

And he could sense the true potential of *The Testament,* lurking beneath what he understood like a whale waiting to surface. He'd never Awakened anything before: the process was supposed to take days, even weeks of understanding the object, and even then you could never predict the full effects.

But with this ship, the project that he had helped create, it just seemed so easy.

Calder wrapped his Intent around the true significance of *The Testament,* its true power and purpose, and he pulled that power to the surface.

Around him, the ship changed.

Planks welded together as though the deck was made from a single, seamless plank of polished wood. Holes gouged by musket-balls filled in. The nails rippled and flowed until they melded with the planks, almost indistinguishable patches of iron strength. The hull merged smoothly until it looked like a green-black shell, the railings fusing together until the whole ship was made of a single piece. He could sense it all, the same way he could sense his own skin.

Sails unfurled from the yard like wings spreading from a dragon's back. These weren't made from canvas, but from a stretch of greenish skin, the material thin enough that the moon glowed through. Faintly, Calder could see veins pulsing in the sails, carrying the blood of the ship.

Through the shackles, Calder felt the Lyathatan. A being of indescribable age, vast hunger, and unknowable *strangeness.* It had its own goals, from those as simple as defending its territory to complex plots that Calder couldn't comprehend. It did not resent its servitude: this was one subtle step in a long, intricate, delicate plan that would span centuries. If it stayed in thrall to Calder for the rest of his merely human life, the Lyathatan wouldn't notice any more than a mountain noticed the dying of summer grasses. It would live on, having made another move in a game as slow and distant as the stars.

Equally, the Lyathatan felt Calder. It felt his Intent. And it obeyed.

With one clawed hand, the Elderspawn tore Candle Bay Imperial Prison open like a gutted fish.

It scraped the stone from the wall, shattering every window. Prisoners in their red jumpsuits cowered against the far wall, trapped in their tiny cells like dolls in a dollhouse. The basement was filled with one pure-white room, like a surgeon's laboratory. Alchemists in their glass-eyed masks and long aprons ran around, shouting. At the distance of his vision, Calder saw a man, naked and strapped to a steel table. A woman pulled a syringe out of his arm and ran, screaming, from the sight of the Lyathatan.

Another mental order from Calder, and the monster ripped the room to pieces.

When it was done, Calder's sight fuzzed at the edges. He sent one last, hazy thought to the Elderspawn and muttered a single word to Jerri.

"Steer," he said.

Then he collapsed.

He woke with a headache that felt like someone had tried to split his skull with an axe. Sunlight streamed in through the cabin window, and he rolled out of his bunk, clutching his head in both hands.

When he groaned and wished for something to stop the pain, he lost concentration. He got a brief glimpse of a woman stitching his blankets, hoping the pattern would please her daughter, and white-hot pain shot through his brain like a lance.

No Reading! he silently begged. *No Reading, no Reading, no Reading!*

After a few minutes, his pain subsided, and he realized that he felt something from the side of his face. Something like a snake crawling up his cheek. He raised a hand to brush it away, but the snakes only crawled onto the back of his hand.

Calder jerked his eyes over to his shoulder, desperate to see what was crawling all over him.

Shuffles stood halfway on his shoulder, halfway on his pillow, glaring at him above its tentacle-mouth. Its wings flared.

"Shuffles," Calder said weakly. He was surprised to find himself smiling, and he rubbed the Elderspawn's scaly head. "What are you doing here?"

"HEEEEERE!" the monstrosity said, and flared its wings. It shuffled down to the bottom of the bed and turned, glaring at him over its shoulder.

Calder took that to mean he was supposed to get up.

A second later, someone pushed open his door, letting in a river of sunlight. He flinched back, raising his hand to cover the sight.

Rojric Marten crossed his arms over his red prison jumpsuit and smiled. "How you feeling, son?"

"Headache," Calder grunted.

Rojric nodded reasonably. "Reader's burn. After Alsa Awakened her saber, she couldn't see straight for a week."

Calder had heard of Reader's burn, but it only happened to Readers who pushed their limits. Since he'd never felt it before, he'd always assumed that he had fewer limitations than most.

Now, his pride pounded on the inside of his skull with a five-pound hammer.

But even that couldn't dent his satisfaction. He'd freed his father! He'd actually done it!

Calder forced a smile. "You're out."

Tears welled in his father's eyes. "Yes I am, son. And I'm not going back. I keep thinking I'm going to wake up and find myself…" He took a deep breath. "You saved me. *Thank you.*"

Calder's chest puffed up like a balloon, and he felt as though he could wrestle an army. Once his headache went away, anyway.

Then Jerri shouted from above, and something landed on the surface of the deck.

No, not something. *Someone.* Someone he could feel, even through the Reader's burn, even through the ship's deck. And his heart quaked with a pure, instinctive fear.

"Hide," he whispered, and staggered out of bed.

CHAPTER TWENTY-FIVE

This time, Kelarac met him on a frozen battlefield.

Calder stood in the midst of a battle locked in a single instant, as though he had stepped into a painting. Men stood behind him, rushing forward with armor and spears to meet the charge of the monsters ahead. The humans were sweating, panting, desperate; their teeth bared in defiance, boots set against the ground. Many of them had bled through their bandages, or tried to hold their armor together with nails and bits of rope.

They faced an army of nightmares. Elderspawn of every stripe; not just the Children of Nakothi, stitched and blended together from the corpses of men, but monsters of all kinds. The giant worms of Kthanikahr, stuck emerging from their burrows as though time had stopped. The shadow-men of Urg'naut, the ever-shifting soldiers of Tharlos, the amphibious hordes of Othaghor. The monstrosities filled the earth and sky, frozen in the middle of crawling toward the men like dogs to a feast.

Black smoke hung in the sky like pillars, and the sky glowed an unnatural red.

Directly in front of Calder, Kelarac lounged on his version of a throne. Two human soldiers carried a third man, injured, on their shoulders. The injured had snatched up a spear from nearby and was beginning to turn around, as though he meant to fight with a bleeding wound in his stomach.

Kelarac sat on the wounded man's injured belly, the spearhead propping up his back. It should never have supported him, but everything in this frozen tableau was as solid as stone. He rested his feet on the helmet of one of the nearby soldiers, leaning back against the spear, and let out a satisfied sigh.

"So you come to me again, Reader of Memory," Kelarac said. "Not so young as before, but a child still."

Calder swept a bow. "Lord Kelarac. Your wisdom is matched only by your generosity, in deigning to appear before me."

The Great Elder smiled his gold-capped smile. "I have been called many things, but never 'generous.' I was compelled to appear before one of my... competitors should take your gift from me."

"You should know by now that you're my favorite customer, My Lord."

"As you are starting to become mine." Kelarac lifted the gray-green Heart in his fist, twisting it as though staring into a prism. "I tend to begin any negotiation by questioning my opponent's goods, but I suspect you know exactly how valuable this is, don't you?"

Modestly, Calder looked down. "I wouldn't disturb you for anything less than the best."

The Elder drew a sharp breath in through his nose, tilting his steel-shrouded head back. "I taste my sister's agony in this. For one whose trade was death and rebirth, she's having quite the trouble coming back to life, is she not?"

Calder and Kelarac laughed together, though the human suspected that he was missing out on quite a bit of context. One of the many things his father had taught him: people grow suspicious if you don't laugh when they do.

"On that topic, My Lord, I seem to find myself in a bit of trouble once again."

"Found out your wife was raised in a pacification sect, did you?" He managed to pull off a knowing look, even with his eyes hidden behind a band of steel. "Born and bred a slave to the *wisdom* of our race. Reminds me of an age long past, when not a one of you could start a fire without prostrating yourself before your betters for three days and nights."

Anger flared up, matched almost instantly by fear. He spoke of Calder like he was worth *nothing;* like he was a blind, stupid dog that Kelarac enjoyed tormenting for his squeals.

That was the anger. On the other hand, there was the fear—that Kelarac could do exactly that.

"That's not quite what I meant," Calder said.

"I think you'll be surprised with my perspective on pacification sects, boy." Kelarac reached out and scooped up a handful of nuts from a bowl that rested on a soldier's helmet. "What they seek is a world of harmony between our kind and yours. Admirable, if it weren't *entirely* misguided. We require totally different conditions in which to flourish. The only place for a human is not beside me, it is *beneath* me. Reaching up. Giving me gifts, in exchange for the occasional favor." He raised a fistful of the nuts to his mouth and crunched, crumbs raining down from between his ringed fingers.

While Calder searched for an appropriate response, Kelarac grinned. "That would be an excellent place for my brothers and sisters as well. I like this world, former Watchman. Slaves do not bargain. Free men do." He held up the Heart again. "And they bring *such* treasures."

Calder cleared his throat. "As I said, I came for help. Someone has summoned what I believe to be—"

"One of Nakothi's Handmaidens. And it was your wife that did the summoning, though you knew that already, didn't you? It was quite a surprise for her, I can assure you."

He was sure that he was walking straight into a trap, but Calder had to ask.

"What do you mean?"

Kelarac tossed a peanut into his mouth. "The device she used was intended to summon a lesser spawn of Othaghor, one that could lead her out of captivity and to her Soulbound Vessel. From there, she was meant to recapture Nakothi's Heart and deliver it to her sect."

The Elder leaned forward on his throne of frozen men. "But your kind understands nothing of the universe, and less of the powers you think you can use. She sent a call out while in the presence of one of Nakothi's hearts...and during the Awakening of a blade that once pierced a *different* Heart of the Dead Mother. Nakothi held so much sway over that island at that place, in that moment, that she and she alone determined what answered that call into the void.

"That she sent one of her Handmaidens means that she wants everything destroyed. The island, the blade, her missing heart, and everyone involved in the whole event. She thinks she has a better chance of victory if she resets the board."

He cackled while staring at the Heart in his hands. "Only you and I know that she's already lost."

"I need to escape the Handmaiden," Calder said, when he finally thought he could get some space to speak.

"If you want to save your wife," Kelarac went on, "you'll need to hurry. The Handmaiden will seek her out soon."

"I didn't say anything about saving my wife," Calder said, voice hot. "She dug this grave, and she can die in it. I will ensure the safety of my crew, and then I will leave."

Kelarac nodded approvingly. "Good answer. Ignore her. That's what I would advise you to do. Either way, you need a deeper link to the Lyathatan."

One of the time-locked soldiers reached out a suddenly animated hand, grabbing Calder's forearm. He tried to jerk free, but he couldn't shake the grip loose...and then it was Kelarac's hand, and the Great Elder was standing next to him with that gold-spotted smile on his face.

"I can help you out," Kelarac said, and Calder's arm began to heat up. In a few seconds, the pain moved from a sunburn to a red-hot brand pressed against his skin.

He screamed, frantically pulling at his arm as smoke and the smell of charred flesh drifted up, but Kelarac held on, unconcerned. Finally, after a minute, the Elder pulled his hand away.

The print of a hand was seared into Calder's forearm...but it looked nothing like the hand that Kelarac had used. It was surely not the mark of a human. The red, burned flesh bore the shape of six clawed, double-jointed fingers, tipped in shallow claws. It looked more like the Lyathatan's hand than any man's.

Through the haze of pain, Calder remembered stories of Kelarac devouring people who were insufficiently grateful for his gifts. He tried to stagger out a thank-you, but it came out incoherent. He couldn't stop holding his arm.

Kelarac waved away his thanks, vanishing and reappearing on his throne of long-dead soldiers. "Given the value of this offering, I will ignore your lack of any other gift. And, in fact, I think that still leaves me in your debt." He tapped a ringed finger to his lips, and then leaned closer, staring at Calder through his steel blindfold.

"I can't help but notice that you're in need of a sword."

Reaching to one side, he plucked a scabbarded saber from the grip of a nearby soldier and tossed it to Calder. He caught it on reflex, sensing the disquieting power of the weapon shivering through its sheath.

"You shouldn't use this against the Handmaiden, because she will simply counteract its effects and tear you to pieces. But against lesser Elderspawn, it should serve you quite well."

He spread his jeweled hands and dipped his head in a humble bow. "Until the next time, Calder Marten."

The whole island shook, and dust fell like an avalanche from the ceiling of Jerri's prison, but nothing came to free her. The circle of iron had crumbled to ash in her hands, and she'd instantly sensed the presence of Elders above her—more Elders than she'd ever felt before, and stronger. Nakothi's power was so strong now that Jerri couldn't help but wonder if she was about to bear witness to the resurrection of a Great Elder.

And still, nothing had broken her free.

This will free me. The cabal told me it would. I just have to be patient.

The room shook as though struck by a cannonball, and Jerri was flung from her bed. She tumbled over the floor, coming to rest on her back, a series of general aches and bruises covering her like the world's worst blanket. She blinked up at the ceiling, squinting and raising her arm to keep dust out of her eyes.

When she finally managed to make it to her feet, she realized that there was light coming in from the corner of the wall separating her cell from Lucan's. Not the bright yellow-white of sunlight, but the soft and steady orange of a quicklamp. The corner of the wall between them had fallen out, opening up a space about the size of her two fists.

Jerri heaved her cot up to the corner and stood on it, taking a look through the gap.

Lucan's cell was covered in dust and chunks of rubble. His books were shrouded in a thick layer of what looked like gray snow, his chair shattered, and his cot lying on its side. For a moment she thought he must be dead.

Then she saw the bars at the front of his cell. The door hung on its hinges, and she just caught a glimpse of a man pushing his way through the loosened door with a squeal. She could just see his back as he walked away.

"Lucan! Light and life, *Lucan!* Can you hear me?"

He was out of sight now, but he called back, "I learned a lot from you, Jyrine. I'll be back."

She pounded the heel of her hand against the wall in frustration. "No, let me out! Lucan! Come and get me! I'm a Soulbound! If you get me to my Vessel, I can fight my way free! *Lucan!*"

Except for the steady rain of pebbles from the ceiling, no sound came back to her. She was completely alone.

Calder snapped back to himself on the edge of the island, with the caged blob of skin and blubber raising a club at him. Only an instant had passed since he'd thrown the Heart of the Dead Mother into the ocean.

Yet everything had changed.

The handprint on his arm burned, and he sensed the Child of Nakothi's mind. It wasn't deep and fathomless, like Kelarac or the Lyathatan, but simple and focused.

Hunger. That was everything he sensed from this all-but-mindless creature. Not hunger for sustenance, but hunger for destruction, a deep desire to tear every living thing into a jumble of messy parts. This was the only purpose it had been given by its creator.

The monster lumbered forward, and Andel put a bullet into its belly. Milky white liquid oozed out, but the Child wasn't fazed. Foster followed up with a shot to its tiny head, which took out an eye socket. Calder could see the forest of the Gray Island through the hole in the thing's skull, but it wasn't even slowed.

So Calder raised his sword.

It was a cutlass, like the one he'd used for the past several years, but broader and straighter in the blade. More similar to the saber he'd trained with as a child, at least in shape, but twice as heavy as either of the swords he knew.

Its blade was a mottled black and orange, its hilt solid black. And just by holding it, he could sense an ancient and focused Intent.

This sword had been forged for one purpose, and one purpose alone.

When the Child swung its club, Calder felt its attack a moment before and sidestepped, slicing his blade in a shallow cut along the side of its belly.

Then he wiped the blade on the grass and sheathed it.

The Child staggered forward another step, the wound in its side turning black. Darkness spidered out from the cut, crawling over the blue-white flesh like moss devouring a boulder. In seconds, the Child of Nakothi was covered in black.

It deflated, collapsing into a mess of ash and wet black rot. The club tumbled to the ground, the bone cage landing with nothing but refuse inside.

Foster gave a low whistle, and Andel tipped his hat. "Where did you get that sword, sir?"

"Bought it."

Andel nodded as though that made perfect sense. "And the Heart?"

"That was the price."

"I thought so. Can you call us a ride now, or should we keep running?"

His quartermaster would have more to say to him on this subject, Calder was sure, but for now the man was focused on escape. There was no blaming him.

Calder raised his marked right arm and gave a mental call.

Though it has been only a moment since the Lyathatan began to rest, he hears the summons of the human who holds his leash. And this time, it comes backed by the authority of the true master.

Good. The Lyathatan hastens to obey. The more the human bargains with Kell'arack, the closer his plans will align with the Lyathatan's own.

That was too disturbing for Calder to think about at the moment, so he stored it away for another time. For now, he had to get Foster and Andel—and Naberius, he supposed—to the ship. Everything else could wait.

In only a moment, the Elderspawn stood underneath the cliff, holding up one chain-wrapped palm to the cliff. Its six black eyes were level with the rocks, its gills flapping in the breeze.

It hissed through its mouthful of needle-teeth, and Calder somehow realized that this was an expression of acknowledgement.

When Andel and Foster had stepped onto the Lyathatan's palm, carrying Naberius, Calder gave another mental order. The Elderspawn slowly sank back down toward the ocean, carrying the three men with it.

Andel stepped out onto the base of a finger, shouting up. "What are you *doing?*"

Calder hefted his sword, eyeing the Children of Nakothi slithering out of the forest. "Retrieving my crew," he called back.

And holding his new sword in his branded arm, he walked toward the monsters. "Gentlemen, I hope you're ready to return to the Dead Mother."

Something flapped loudly behind him, like a flag snapping in the breeze, and then a familiar weight settled onto his shoulder.

"DEAD MOTHER," Shuffles bellowed, right into his ear.

Calder winced. "Do you have to be so loud?"

"LOOOUUUD!" the Elderspawn shouted.

Ducking the strike of a bony tail, Calder drove his sword up into the belly of another headless gorilla. This time, it went down in one strike.

Now that he could feel their intentions so clearly, this was even easier than training in swordplay with his mother as a child. Something like a bat with skin-tone wings and the body of a child swooped down, trying to take him from behind, but he slashed over his shoulder without even bothering to turn. A hideous spider crouched in a nearby bush, radiating its commitment to an ambush, and he fired his pistol blindly into the underbrush without stopping. His new sense told him that he caught it in the eye.

If he could continue like this, it didn't matter how many Children of Nakothi stood in his way. As long as he could avoid the giant Handmaiden, standing head and shoulders over the tallest trees on the island, he could save Urzaia and get out.

Both of them, he thought. *Like this, I could save both of them.*

The prison was farther away than the arena, and he had intended to let Jerri rot. But then again, if she hadn't intended to summon the Handmaiden in the first place…

That's what I would advise you to do, Kelarac had said.

Why would he want to do anything a Great Elder wanted him to do? Shouldn't he do the opposite? And besides, he was taking Kelarac's word for everything: that Jerri had intended to summon something else, that she was in danger. He was the one who had brought up the idea of saving her in the first place.

Kelarac take me if I dance to an Elder's tune, Calder thought, and then he paused. It was just an expression, but it sunk in like it never had before.

Kelarac really *had* taken him.

For a while he simply cut his way through Nakothi's Children, still unsure. What did he even want to do?

Well, at least I can save Urzaia. I'll decide my next course after that.

"FASTER!" Shuffles shouted, flapping in place. "FASTER!"

Shuffles rarely spoke on its own without repeating someone else. If he didn't listen, it would just keep shouting.

He ran faster.

From what he'd seen earlier, there was no way Urzaia would lose in a one-on-one fight against the blond Consultant, but there was every chance they had prepared some sort of an ambush. Besides, the island was now crawling with an army of Elderspawn. There was plenty of reason to worry.

As he approached the house-sized boulder that concealed an entrance to the underground arena, he found another reason to worry.

The hideous Handmaiden was headed right for him.

Her bony arms brushed aside the tips of trees as though she forced her way through a field of wheat. She didn't make the same motion a human would as she walked, instead rolling forward on her tentacles. Calder still couldn't directly look at the Handmaiden's face, but she let out a furious wail every few seconds.

Was she aiming for Calder, now that he wore the mark of Kelarac? Or were he and the Handmaiden simply heading to the same place?

Either way, it was good reason to hurry.

A hideous abomination of stolen flesh lunged up as soon as he walked around to the boulder's entrance, flaring out into a flap of skin intended to swallow a man up like a net. Once he was engulfed in the Child of Nakothi's horrific mouth, it would slowly digest him over the course of days.

If he hadn't been able to sense all those details, it would have made for a perfect ambush.

Instead, as soon as the monster leaped up to grab him, it encountered the end of his orange blade instead. Seconds later, Calder was stepping over a stinking black mess that had once been one of the Dead Mother's spawn.

Say what you want about Kelarac, but he doesn't go back on a deal. The sword was an even better weapon than he had hoped. So much so that he began to second-guess himself.

How valuable was the Heart, that the Collector of Souls had given him two remarkable gifts? Calder had known he was overpaying, but he wondered if he should have held out for a third reward.

It only took him a few seconds to find the hidden entrance to the arena this time, and he made his way down the ladder quickly.

When he reached the bottom, he couldn't help but stare. The ancient arena lay in ruins.

As he watched, Urzaia grabbed his opponent by the ankle and hurled her into a pillar, which collapsed. For a second, Calder was convinced that he'd witnessed his friend's victory.

Then the Consultant burst from the rubble, launching a rock the size of her head with all the force of a cannon.

Urzaia shattered the missile in midair with one of his hatchets, but the debris still slammed against his face and chest, sending him staggering back a step.

...and that was all Calder had time to watch before he heard the howl of the Handmaiden above him. His time was up.

He cupped his hands around his mouth and shouted. *"Urzaia! Time to leave!"*

No reaction.

He felt like Foster, grumbling to himself as he descended down step after step, edging closer to the arena's crumbling walls. "We have to leave, Urzaia! Woodsman! *Let's go!*"

Calder sprinted down the last flight of steps. It was obvious that Urzaia wasn't listening, so he'd have to put himself in danger to catch the man's attention.

The stairs landed him at the top edge of the arena's seats. This whole side rumbled ominously, webbed with cracks in the stone benches. Urzaia and his opponent clashed at the opposite side of the arena, black hatchets and bronze knives moving in a blur that Calder couldn't track.

The Handmaiden's howl seemed to come from all around them, and Calder threw away the last remnants of his restraint. *It's too late to be careful now.*

He ran down the crumbling arena benches. When the stone shifted under his weight, seemingly ready to give way at any second, he didn't slow down. He ran faster.

More than once, he'd thought of leaving Urzaia here. If anyone could make his way out of a war zone, it would be the Izyrian gladiator. But abandoning a crewmate here would make him no better than...

...no better than Jerri, he'd almost thought. Jerri, whom he was about to abandon to her death.

"Fine, fine, I'll save her," he said to no one in particular. "Leave me alone already."

"ALONE," Shuffles chuckled. He seemed to enjoy this headlong flight down a crumbling staircase, flaring his wings to catch the wind.

"You can shut up," Calder muttered, leaping the last few steps, which had been shattered to jagged pieces. He landed in what was left of the arena's sand, crouched amid the debris of what had once been obstacles for gladiators here.

Close up, the destruction was even more impressive. Broken planks of wood lay propped against chunks of stone all around him, looking like a small town after a tornado. Each strike of Urzaia's hatchet against the Consultant's knife was louder than gunfire, and dust settled from the distant ceiling like wood smoke in reverse.

"Urzaia! Come with me!"

The Consultant planted a kick in Urzaia's armored stomach, doubling him over, and then slashed at his neck. For an instant Calder thought she had actually cut his head off, but Urzaia reacted too quickly, tossing himself down the stairs. He tumbled down every stone bench on the way down, landing with his back on a boulder.

The blond Consultant advanced on her opponent and Calder pulled his pistol almost on instinct, running forward to help his friend.

At that moment, another figure in black rushed across the arena, a bronze knife in her right hand. Her black hair blew behind her, exposing her face.

Shera.

Calder adjusted his aim and fired.

Shera ducked and rolled, and his bullet did nothing but kick up sand. But she turned to face him, knife out.

He holstered his gun and readied Kelarac's blade.

The two of them froze for a long second, facing each other. Calder stood with one foot forward, cutlass in hand, the Emperor's crown on his head and an Elderspawn on his shoulder; Shera crouched low with a bronze-bladed knife in her right hand and a tiny silver throwing blade in her left. Streams of dust drifted between them.

Her dark eyes were cold, empty, inhuman. Even the Lyathatan had more passion in his expression than she did. It was the face of a woman who would kill him without hesitation and sleep soundly afterward.

She started this.

If it weren't for this Consultant, he would have completed his assignment for Naberius and sailed away ten thousand goldmarks richer. She was the one who had taken Jerri, who had taken the Heart of Nakothi, who had drawn him all the way here.

He couldn't let her leave.

The wound she'd left in his left shin was still bandaged. He didn't think of the injury much, as it didn't slow him from walking around, but it began to throb now. If it slowed him even a step in this fight, Shera would see him dead.

The stillness was broken by Shuffles, who started to laugh. Its laughter was deep, dark, and ominous: the laugh of a triumphant villain at the end of a play. And it started quiet but grew in volume until he was cackling even louder than the wails of the Handmaiden overhead.

"KILL," Shuffles shouted, and flapped its way off of Calder's shoulder.

It served as a bell, signaling the start of the fight. Shera flicked her left hand forward, launching the steel blade at his face. He jerked to one side in time, turning the motion into a sidestep and then an advance, driving the edge of his blade down at her face.

She slapped the blade aside with her own, pulling a needle from her belt and stepping in close, reaching up to his neck. Calder had fallen for that before, so he was prepared this time.

He moved in closer, slamming his elbow into her face.

The Consultant's nose split with a crunch and she staggered back, the hand with the needle wavering. He advanced again, driving the point of his sword at her midsection.

This time, she ducked impossibly low, reversing a grip on her knife as though she meant to drive it through his foot. He shifted his weight, sliding his boot sideways across the sand, and then slammed the hilt of his sword down on the back of her neck.

At least, he tried to. She rolled to one side, slashing at his wounded leg with her blade as she passed.

It was only a shallow cut, he knew—the bandage from the last injury would slow her knife a little. But it still sent a flare of pain rising from his ankle to his hip as the new wound crossed the old, and he limped backwards in panic, instinctively trying to put as much distance between himself and his enemy as possible.

Her hand moved down to the pouch on her left thigh, pulling out another triangular blade of silver metal.

"Stop where you are!" Calder ordered, feeding his Intent into the crown on his head.

She didn't stop, no more than she had in the tunnel. But she did hesitate.

And that gave Calder enough time to lunge behind a broken wooden shed, breaking her line of sight. Crashes of thunder all around him said that Urzaia and his opponent were still in combat, and the bundle of malice and insanity that was Nakothi's Handmaiden stood directly above them now. The longer he stalled, the more likely someone or something else would interfere.

He sensed a mindless hunger approaching from behind him, and he realized that *something* was galloping toward them at great speed.

Shera didn't come around the side of the half-destroyed shed, as he'd hoped. She vaulted up to the top of it, leaping from the shed to a nearby chunk of arena stone when the shed almost instantly collapsed. A blade flashed from her hand, and he tried to deflect it with his sword.

It was only partially successful. The tiny dagger bounced off the flat of his sword, sending up sparks, and embedded itself an inch into his chest, below his right shoulder.

Pain traveled from his ribs all the way to his elbow, and he gritted his teeth to keep from screaming. He jerked the knife out, letting it fall to the ground—there was no way he could keep fighting with it stuck inside. But now his left leg and his right arm both felt as though they'd been filled with red-hot rocks.

Blood ran down in a fan from Shera's nose, but otherwise she moved as though she were completely unharmed. If she kept this up, she would kill him with a thousand tiny cuts.

At this rate, he wouldn't be able to win this fight on his own. He would have to get someone to fight for him.

He cast his mind out through Kelarac's mark, latching on to the nearest source of mindless bloodlust. There were a surprising number of Nakothi's children down here in the broken arena—they kept their distance out of fear, and the Handmaiden's lingering restraint.

Using his Intent as a lure, he dragged one of the creatures closer.

Shera crouched warily on a boulder-sized chunk of the arena, and he limped to one side, forcing her to keep her eyes on him.

In reality, he wanted to keep her eyes off the monster approaching from behind.

Shera realized what he was doing only at the last second, as the shadow of a headless, pale-skinned, shaved gorilla lunged up from behind her. She spun, bringing her bronze knife up in one hand and a poisoned needle in the other.

The Child of Nakothi's descending fist caught her on the shoulder, sending her tumbling off the rock and to the ground.

Calder couldn't let the creature run free, so he stepped up and ran it through with his cutlass, withdrawing the blade in a spray of milky white blood.

There was no point in investing an Awakened blade—it wouldn't hold the Intent. But habit made him chant silently, *Death to the deathless.*

Still eerily quiet, the gorilla collapsed and dissolved into a pile of white.

Only an instant had passed, so Shera was still twitching and groaning on the ground, her hand grasping at the hilt of her knife. He stood over her, reversed his sword, and drove it down.

A black-clad foot touched his stomach, surprisingly gentle.

The blond Consultant stared at him from a foot away, hair blowing loose. Her eyes were bright orange, her pupils vertical slits. She held a bronze blade reversed in each fist, and her face was covered in slashes and scrapes.

She snarled at him and completed her kick, launching him backwards.

The world blurred around him as he tumbled backwards. He had the presence of mind left to release his sword, as he'd been taught. If you fell, you didn't want to be clutching a bare blade, or you were likely to slit your own throat.

He slammed against stone, pain crashing through every one of his bones as though he'd been tossed out of a second-story window and landed in the courtyard. His back arched in agony and he gasped helplessly for breath. The crown flew off his head, rolling like a gold coin in front of his eyes until it came spinning to a halt a second later.

A roaring voice filled the underground arena. *"Captain!"* Urzaia shouted.

It took all of Calder's strength to turn his head.

The Izyrian's tied-back hair had come loose, blowing around his head like a storm. Blood streamed down his face like a mask, and a huge red gash in his side wept freely, but he still gritted his jaw, baring his missing teeth. His black hatchets came down on the blond Consultant like hammers of judgment.

She raised both of the knives to defend herself, but he pounded on her defense relentlessly, knocking one blade out of her hand. Seeing the instant of weakness, he shouted again, driving his second hatchet down and into her shoulder.

The sheer force knocked her to her knees, a spray of blood arching up into the air.

And something changed.

Calder sensed it as soon as it happened. Something he had seen in his Reading before, something ravenous and powerful, something newborn...a weapon entered the arena.

Lucan wore different clothes than he had when Calder had last seen him, sitting in his cell: a seamless black outfit and black cloth half-mask, identical to Shera and her partner. He ran into sight, carrying a bronze blade in his left hand.

His right went to a package at his belt and unfolded something shining a bright green.

Calder raised a shaking hand as if to stop it, but he was too far away and too weak.

"Shera!" Lucan shouted, just as Calder called out: "Urzaia!"

The gladiator kicked his blond opponent away, readying his hatchet and turning to face this new threat.

Behind him, a black-gloved hand reached out and snatched the green knife from midair.

"Behind you!" Calder screamed, struggling to his feet.

Urzaia spun instantly, leading with his hatchet, swinging with enough force to crash through an oak tree.

But Shera ducked his strike, stood up, and drove her newly Awakened blade into his chest.

Wisps of blazing green shot out from the shining knife, wrapping around Urzaia's body. Lights played like ball lightning around the gold hide wrapped around his upper arm—his Vessel. The source of his power.

Like a toppling statue, Urzaia fell over backwards. His hatchets fell from limp hands.

Shera held on to the grip of her knife, letting the momentum of Urzaia's body pull the blade free. In only an instant, the blood on the blade disappeared, absorbed into the knife.

Calder could have been imagining it, but he thought he heard the weapon sigh contentedly.

He scrambled in the dust with both hands, cramming the crown back onto his head and scooping up his blade. But now he stood facing three Consultants: a young, half-Heartlander man pulling off his gloves; a blond warrior who had stood face-to-face with Urzaia—she was injured and on her knees, but he had no doubt she could still overpower him; and Shera. She clutched her old bronze knife in her right hand and her Awakened emerald blade in her left.

They'd killed Urzaia. His anger, and his frustration at his own helplessness, kept him standing before them. He raised his sword. "Let's get to it, then," he said.

Then the Handmaiden of Nakothi tore off the roof.

CHAPTER TWENTY-SIX

'Kameira' is a tricky term. We use it to refer to any creature not of human or Elder origin that can manipulate the world in seemingly supernatural ways. The legendary Cloudseeker Hydra, according to ancient accounts, could levitate itself through the skies and uproot trees without touching them.

How? Are the Kameira powers over nature related in some way to human Intent, or do they have more in common with the strange abilities of the Elders? More importantly, what precisely are the Kameira themselves?

Our Guild has recently confirmed what naturalists have long suspected: that different species of Kameira are no more related to one another than a fox is related to a bird. How, then, do we account for their miraculous powers?

–TOMAS STILLWELL, HEAD OF THE GREENWARDEN'S GUILD

ELEVEN YEARS AGO

By the time Calder pulled on his Blackwatch cloak and staggered up to the deck, Jerri was already lying in a heap. A Kameira, a vast bird with rainbow-bright wings, circled the sun in the skies over the mast.

Calder ran over to Jyrine's body, pressing his hand to her neck and ignoring the searing pain in his head as he Read her. He let out a breath when he realized that she was completely unharmed.

Then that struck him as strange.

If she was *completely* unharmed, why was she lying unconscious on the deck?

Booted feet clanked closer to him, and he looked up to see the stranger on his ship. She towered over him, a tall woman in full black-and-red plated armor. The crest on her breastplate almost made him sick: a shield bearing the sun-and-moon emblem of the Empire.

The Imperial Guard. They'd found him, even here.

Her blond hair was cut close to her skull, her blue eyes cold. A leather-wrapped sword hilt looked over her right shoulder, and as soon as he noticed the weapon, a falling star struck Calder's skull. He screamed with the pain, clutching his head with both hands.

That weapon was older than the Empire, older than the Emperor, perhaps as old as the monster pulling this ship. And it killed. He could pilot *The Testament* through the oceans of blood that blade had spilled.

No, the blade hadn't just taken lives. It *was* a taker of lives. That was its essence, its sole Intent. And if Calder had sensed that from this distance, without touching its hilt, and while trying *not* to Read...

He was surprised the sword hadn't killed them all simply by being so close.

The armored woman spoke with the voice of an executioner. "By order of the Emperor, I have come to retrieve the criminal Calder Marten, who stands accused of destroying an Imperial prison, conspiring to set free a prisoner, and stealing a ship that is the rightful property of the Blackwatch Guild."

Having recited her piece, she leaned forward and grabbed Calder, dragging him up by the wrist as if he were a child. "Come with me."

Calder's throat was rough, but there was one thing on his mind even more important than his impending arrest. "What is that thing on your back?"

"What, you've never seen a sword before?"

She whistled and the Kameira landed gracefully on the deck, dipping its swanlike neck in a bow. Calder couldn't help but be impressed: through his bond with the ship, he could feel that its talons hadn't even gouged the wood.

Rojric hurried up the ladder to the deck, anger and fear radiating from his every movement. "Stop! I'm the one you want."

The woman glared at him. Calder felt a force pass by him, the shadow of something huge and unseen, and his father collapsed.

"No," she said. "You're not."

She bundled Calder under one arm, tossing him onto the bird's back. It was surprisingly soft, cushioned by a thick layer of glimmering feathers. The woman followed him, sliding easily onto a perch at the base of the Kameira's neck and gently patting the creature's feathers.

With a trill of birdsong, the bird soared from the deck into the air.

Calder watched *The Testament* fall away beneath him, surrounded by the vast blue of the ocean.

At last he struggled, though not very hard. A fall from this height would break his bones to gravel. "You can't just leave them there! They can't steer the ship!"

"A crew will be along shortly to retrieve *The Testament* and remove its passengers."

Calder glanced around and saw that she was right: a loose half-circle of ships drifted toward his, all flying Imperial flags.

He should have been afraid. He shouldn't have been able to think through his terror and anger and guilt.

But all he felt was his splitting headache.

"Who are you?" he asked, weakly. "Where are you taking me?"

The woman didn't turn around. "I am Jarelys Teach, General of the Empire and Head of the Imperial Guard. I'm taking you to your trial."

When Calder had pictured his trial, he'd never imagined the Emperor would be there.

The Imperial Palace was an order of magnitude more splendid than anything he'd ever seen or imagined in his life. He couldn't price the smallest floor tile, and each panel of wood in the walls must have been worth a hundred goldmarks. Here, in the center of the Imperial Palace, they had taken him to some sort of audience hall.

The floor was a single block of polished stone bigger than a ballroom—he wondered if it had been Awakened. It was lacquered with a vast panorama, the image of a battle so detailed and complex you would have to fly up to the distant ceiling in order to take it in. He knelt on the image of a painted warrior in ancient armor, holding a bronze sword and locked in combat with a shadowy, shapeless creature.

Pillars sprouted from the floor in orderly rows, each designed with a unique spiral of flame that rose from the image of battle like the fires of war. Smoke from the painted flames gathered on the ceiling, capping the room with the visage of dark clouds.

At the top of the mural, in the center of the room, stood a single figure in white armor. He stood with the rising sun, holding a bronze sword in each hand and standing against a mountainous monster of grasping claws and flailing tentacles.

Above this image of the victorious Emperor rose the Imperial throne. And on that throne sat the Emperor himself.

He looked exactly as he did in the mural, as he had in Calder's many visions: dark, tall, and hairless, with a gaze that suggested he knew your mind better than you did. He lounged on his throne wrapped in layers of pink and purple and lavender, tossing a coin in his right hand.

A simple gold circlet rested on his bare head, and this detail alone seemed off. He supposed it was natural for the Emperor to be wearing a crown in his own throne room, but none of Calder's visions had included the man with a crown. Maybe he rarely wore it, or perhaps it just didn't make much of an impression on the invested items around him. It didn't matter, in any case.

The Emperor's voice effortlessly filled the spacious room. "You found one artifact of mine. A pen. You must have found another."

Calder widened his eyes, looking innocent and frightened. The *frightened* part wasn't much of an exaggeration. "I'm sorry, Lord Emperor Most High! That was the only fragment of your greatness we ever found, though we did try. I am overcome with grief—"

"A key, was it?" the Emperor mused. He tossed a silver coin marked with his own face, snatching it out of the air. "There have not been many keys I carried personally. I can recall only a few."

Sweat rolled into Calder's eyes, but he didn't dare to blink. "A key? I don't have a key of any significance, O Lord of the Empire."

The Emperor rolled the coin across the backs of his fingers. "Was it silver? Bone? Was the key made of living flesh?"

"Ah, I'm not—"

"You weren't surprised by it, nor did you sell it. It must have been the copper key to my dungeon. I can see how you may have used it to open the cells in Candle Bay." The Emperor closed one eye, examining the coin as though he expected to find some flaw. "I sense Kelarac upon you. Why did you trade him the key?"

Panic tightened Calder's skin, froze his insides. How did the Emperor know? How did he *always know?* No one could Read minds.

"I see...with a Lyathatan to pull your ship, you could complete the binding and Awaken *The Testament*. A good bargain, for such a cheap price. Be wary of deals that seem too favorable, Calder."

Jarelys Teach stood behind the throne, arms folded, eyes forever moving around the chamber. A few more squads of Imperial Guards waited in the distant corners of the room, ready to help should the Emperor require their assistance. Something stirred behind the throne itself; perhaps a hidden guard, wearing black.

They hadn't even bothered to bind Calder's hands. He couldn't pose a danger to the Emperor with a saber in one hand and a gun in the other, even if the man had been completely unguarded.

What he didn't understand was why they needed to try him at all. The Emperor could Read everything he wanted to know; Calder didn't even need to be conscious. They could simply have taken him, put him to sleep, Read his guilt, and executed him before he woke up.

The absolute hopelessness of his situation made him bold. "My current situation seems a little too favorable, if I'm honest. I'm still alive."

The Emperor gave a faint smile. "I do prefer honesty."

"Why? It seems that you can hear the truth in any words of mine, honest or not."

"Your honesty does not help me learn the truth," the Emperor said. "The degree of your honesty, and your dishonesty, helps me to understand what kind of man you are."

Calder switched tactics. "I am hardly a man at all, my Emperor. This endeavor was a crime of passion and youth, nothing more."

The Emperor flipped his coin again. "Who is more than an infant in my presence? Should I rule with leniency on the basis of youth, even the wisest graybeard would receive clemency from me." He gripped the silver coin in one fist, staring Calder straight in the eyes.

"Five prison guards were killed by your chained Elderspawn. Ten more were injured. From the wreckage of the Candle Bay facility, we pulled a further fifteen corpses. Guards, alchemists, prisoners, clerical staff. Prisoners escaped by the score, and many of them had been imprisoned for crimes greater than your fathers. Now we have murderers, rapists, dangerous Soulbound, and black alchemists walking the streets of the Capital thanks to your reckless actions."

There was no anger in the Emperor's voice, but there was enough sheer *force* to drive Calder down into the ground. His ancient Intent filled the air so thick that Calder was sure he would feel it even without his abilities as a Reader.

Under normal circumstances, Calder would have done whatever the Emperor commanded him, bound by such pressure. He would have likely wet himself.

But today, he carried some anger of his own. "I witnessed five men and women gladly fall to their deaths on the rocks of Candle Bay. I don't know what experiments your alchemists ran on my father, but he begged me to push him out of a window. My father, Rojric Marten. He carried such pain with him that I could feel it pouring from him like heat from a bonfire. He had tried to strangle himself with his bed sheets, to shatter the window with his chair so that he could leap from his cell. And he was imprisoned for *stealing a pen*."

By the end of the speech, Calder was on his feet and shouting at the ruler of the Aurelian Empire. A ruler who seemed more interested in idly flipping his coin than in the fate of Calder's father.

"He did not just steal a pen, Calder, as you know better than most. He stole my pen. I once knew a man who killed thirty-two innocent people with a knife that I had used to spread butter. When I use an object, even for the briefest period, it is cleansed by the Luminians and then incinerated. But every once in a while, some fragment of refuse evades my notice and escapes."

The Emperor waved his hand. "But we are not here to discuss your father's crimes. We're here to discuss yours."

Standing was awkward, in this room of featureless stone, but Calder refused to kneel again. He walked over to a pillar and sat, leaning his back against the base of the stone column. "Candle Bay was a house of torture," he said. "It was better off destroyed."

He believed that. He *had* to believe that, or else confront the fact that he had been responsible for the deaths of twenty real, live, breathing men and women.

"Despite what you may believe, my Guild of Alchemists is not on trial today either. However, there is another Guild involved." He tossed the coin from one hand to the other. "Tell me, Calder, what do you know about the Navigators?"

This abrupt shift in subject took Calder by surprise. He had only ever met one Navigator, and he suspected Cheska Bennett was not a representative sample of her Guild. "Very little."

"You know that they are the only ones who can safely cross the Aion. I founded them for that purpose. What do you think makes their ships able to navigate those waters? Superior carpentry?"

"I don't—"

"*Think,* Calder!"

The Intent behind the command was enough to make the room seem to shake, and Calder rattled his brain, trying to shake something loose. "It...must have to do with Reading, somehow. The ships are invested in a particular way? Treated with a blend of alchemy?"

The Emperor tapped the edge of his coin against the throne, waiting for him to continue.

"Ah, they must navigate differently from ordinary sailors in some way. Hence the name. Invested navigational equipment?"

The Emperor leaned forward. "They have guides, Calder."

The puzzle came apart in Calder's mind. Sure, the Navigators had to be guided through the threats of the Aion, which were often caused by Elders. That was what the Blackwatch had been trying to do with *The Testament:* summon a bigger, stronger guide.

"Elders," he said. "They all have Elders bound to their ships."

"Only one ship has that distinction. The others simply have the power of an Elder bound into their ship, through bone or blood or a particular artifact.

Then the ships themselves are Awakened, bound to their captains. Soulbound."

Calder's breath caught. Soulbound were the greatest warriors of the Empire, possessing powers that came from the pinnacle of Reading. It was from them that the truly miraculous feats of history had come: Estyr Six flying over the ranks of a thousand Elderspawn to reach Othaghor, Baldezar Kern destroying the armies of the South Sea Revolution. They could call on the seemingly magical powers of Kameira, as long as they held their Vessel.

"Me? Is that what I did?"

"The Blackwatch ship known as *The Testament* is now your Soulbound Vessel, Calder. We didn't need to tow it back; the Lyathatan dragged it into the nearby harbor on its own." The Emperor leaned back in his throne. "That's why you haven't been executed."

Involuntarily, Calder's hand went to his throat.

"You're surprised. How else did you think I would deal with someone who committed thousands of goldmarks of property damage, murdered twenty citizens, and stole a ten-thousand-mark ship? You deserve execution, Calder, if anyone in my Empire does."

A small candle-flame of hope lit in Calder's chest. "But you won't execute me?"

"I will turn you over to the custody of the Navigator's Guild, who will put you to work in my service until your debt to me is cleared. Your bonds and responsibilities to the Blackwatch are hereby abolished."

Calder couldn't help the smile that started to spread across his face. "Your mercy is as limitless as the breadth of your rule, my Emperor."

The Emperor did not smile. "Bring in the prisoner."

Doors opened at the end of the hall, and two Imperial Guards marched Rojric Marten inside. He was gagged, his prison jumpsuit rumpled, his hair matted with sweat. When he caught sight of Calder, he struggled forward to try and reach his son.

But one of the Guards had an arm that looked as though it was sheathed in steel. Rojric might as well have been anchored in place. The other, whose eyes glowed a solid red, bowed before the Emperor.

From his throne, the ruler of the Aurelian Empire looked at no one but Calder. "I told you: beware of deals that seem too favorable. I do not reward criminals, Calder, not even when circumstances force me to."

The Emperor tossed something at Calder's feet, something that clinked and rang like a tiny bell. The silver coin. But now it was warped and deformed, as if under great pressure.

"Jarelys," the Emperor said.

The General stepped forward, pulling her sword out from behind her back.

Its blade was rough-forged black iron, with a core of some substance that flowed a bright, glowing red down the center of the metal. But Calder hardly saw it. His senses were overwhelmed: the smell of ash and rot, the taste of blood in his mouth, the screams of the dying, the desperately lonely fear that comes from a nightmare. All of it blasted out from the sword in a silent wind.

The Emperor stood. "Rojric Marten, citizen of my Empire, I hereby sentence you to die."

Rojric strained against his captors, pushing away, trying to escape. His eyes locked with Calder's.

Then Jarelys Teach brushed Rojric's shoulder with the flat of her blade. That done, she returned her weapon to its sheath.

With an audible shriek that emanated from nowhere and seemed to tear the world in half, the life left Rojric Marten's body. He simply sagged, his eyes suddenly glassy.

The two Imperial Guards withdrew, dragging Rojric's body behind them.

Through his tears, Calder screamed. He shouted at the Emperor, at Jarelys Teach, at his own ridiculously naive idea to break a man out of prison.

He surged forward, focused on tearing the Emperor's flesh with his bare hands.

He's a man! Calder shouted to himself. *Just a man! Like me, like my father! He will die like one!*

Jarelys Teach didn't bother with him, returning to her post behind the throne.

Instead, he was tackled by three black-clad shadows.

A blond girl held a bronze knife to Calder's throat, while a Heartlander boy about his age held his arms locked behind his back. A pale, black-haired girl—perhaps a year or two younger than he—stood in front of him, hands empty and spread in front of her.

"Relax," she said soothingly.

The boy spoke over his shoulder. "Release your Intent."

And Calder could feel the other boy's Intent smothering his own, countering the rage and lethal Intent that Calder was pouring into everything: into the stone at his feet, into every fiber of his clothes, into the weapons of these three children who dared to stop him.

But the other boy, the other Reader, was canceling it all out, smoothing the hostility like a maid smoothing sheets.

The black-haired girl yawned and scratched the back of her neck with a dagger. "Did you know that man?"

"He was my father!" Calder shouted.

She shrugged. "Then he'd probably tell you to be quiet, so that we don't kill you."

Calder glared at the Emperor, desperate to hurt the man somehow, even in the smallest way. "You keep *children* around to protect you?"

"As I said before, you're all children to me." The Emperor rummaged through his pockets, pulled out a gold coin, and flipped it. "Besides, they need their exercise. Return to your ship, Calder. You and your Vessel are now property of the Aurelian Empire."

The three black-clad children vanished, the dark-haired girl yawning as she scurried off. How did they disappear so quickly? Except for the occasional pillar, the chamber was nothing but empty, open space.

As Calder was dragged away by the Guard with the metal arm, he took one last look at the Emperor, sitting on his throne and idly toying with his gold coin.

The only one who can change the Empire is sitting right there, he thought. *So far removed from humanity that he might as well be Elderspawn himself.*

The solution hit him like a shaft of blinding light.

As Sadesthenes once said: nothing lasts forever.

CHAPTER TWENTY-SEVEN

he dome of earth rose away from the vast underground chamber, lifted by the bony hands and swarming tentacles of Nakothi's Handmaiden. The roof over the arena was hundreds of yards across, and when the titanic Elderspawn tore it away, it looked like she was tearing an island in half. Clods of dirt and chunks of rock big enough to crush horses rained down all over the arena.

The three Consultants scrambled out of the way, helping each other to shelter. Calder's first instinct told him to join them, but he had a more important task.

Urzaia. The Soulbound warrior still lay on his back only feet away, staring up at the suddenly bare sky. Calder edged closer, ignoring the ground shuddering under repeated impacts.

His first view of Urzaia told him that the situation was hopeless. He was covered in injuries, but none compared to the hole in his chest, which oozed and throbbed with blood as though his heart were trying to escape. He stared sightlessly without blinking, even as clouds of dirt fell into his open eyes.

"Captain," he said, just as Calder had convinced himself the man was already dead.

Calder fell to his knees, ignoring the pain in his leg and fighting down a sudden hope. Maybe he could still be saved…

But no, he could sense the residual Intent that Shera's Awakened blade had left behind. It stole the power Urzaia had drawn from his Vessel, turning it against his body.

Calder couldn't imagine how the man had held on this long.

"I'm with you, Urzaia. We'll see you fixed up and back on duty before next week."

The gladiator choked out a laugh. "Still undefeated."

He wanted to let it go, just to comfort the man until the end, but these were the last words of a friend. He owed it to Urzaia to understand them. "What do you mean?"

"I got her, Captain. They took Jerri, so I took…" He gasped in pain, then set his mouth into a grin. "…one of them. Meia. Her name was Meia. I took her with me."

Calder looked over to the shelter where the three Consultants huddled together. Shera kept an eye on him, working her Awakened knife in her hands, but Lucan was binding the blind Consultant's—Meia's—shoulder. She didn't look like a woman about to die; she looked angry.

"They won't be able to replace her," Calder said. "The Consultants won't recover from this so easily. You've done me proud, Urzaia Woodsman."

Urzaia laughed again, more weakly. "I told you. Never lost a fight in the arena. Not one."

Calder knelt at his cook's side, listening to the Handmaiden howling above him. Kelarac's gift, the mark on his arm, let him *feel* the Intent behind her fury: she sought the presence of something new, something deadly, something that posed a threat to her.

And she was waiting for reinforcements before she faced it.

He remained absolutely still until Urzaia stopped breathing. It didn't take long.

Then he scooped up Urzaia's Awakened hatchets, shoving them into his belt. He tried to minimize contact with the weapons, but a vision bubbled up unbidden.

Urzaia hefts his hatchets, watching the five enemies surround him. Not a Soulbound among them; this is just a warm-up match, to get the crowd in the mood. He mourns them already, but he can't allow himself to die here.

"End this quickly," he silently begs his weapons. "For them, there will be no pain—"

Calder cut off the vision before the grief and rage drowned out his reason. With the hatchets secure, he walked over to the Consultants.

Children of Nakothi surrounded them, guided by the call of the Handmaiden, waiting for their opportune moment to strike.

Good. It just so happened that he needed to kill something.

The other two stared at him suspiciously, but Shera rose to meet him, her face devoid of any human expression. Not that he expected anything else.

"It seems we have a common obstacle," Calder said. He didn't bother to hide his bitterness, in his expression or his voice.

Shera didn't react. But she didn't stab him, which he took to mean she agreed.

He pointed to her shining, shifting green blade. "Can you kill it?" He wanted to do it himself, but Kelarac had specifically cautioned him against using the blade against a Handmaiden. He'd prefer to risk Shera's life than his own, anyway.

Shera turned to Lucan, who nodded. "If we can get you close enough," he said.

Calder rubbed absently at the burning mark on his right forearm, looking up at the Handmaiden. He realized he was looking into her face, and his entire body shivered as he jerked away. It seemed less like a physical appendage, and more like a nightmare made flesh. "It's planning on attacking soon. When it does, I'll hit it as hard as I can. You'll have to find your own opening."

To Calder's surprise, Shera's expression cracked. Instead of a passionless killer, she simply looked…tired. "What are the odds that it will stay dead?"

"Based on my experience with the Elders? Abandon that hope right now."

Her shoulders slumped and she rubbed at her face with one hand, like a child up past her bedtime. "Maybe if I get wounded killing an Elder they'll give me some time off. Meia, here's your chance to stab me in the back."

Their other partner, Meia, was turning pale. She leaned the back of her head against the wall of the shed, panting and holding onto her bandaged wound. Disturbing shapes twisted and moved underneath her skin.

She didn't seem likely to rise to the bait.

Lucan patted Shera on the shoulder, consoling her. "Don't worry. I'm sure she would stab you if she could."

These were the ruthless assassins who had pursued him since he'd left the Capital? They acted like…well, like his crew. For some reason, the thought seethed with anger. What right did they have to joke with each other? They could kill his friend and still play around?

"Just do your part," he said roughly, and walked a short distance away. With his newfound sensitivity to Elders, thanks to Kelarac's mark, he reached out his Intent, seeking out one Elderspawn in particular. A simple, unfathomable, alien mind. A Bellowing Horror.

"Shuffles!" he yelled.

A familiar silhouette flapped up on top of a half-collapsed stone column, tentacles writhing over its mouth.

Calder spoke directly to his pet Elderspawn, backing up his words with intent to reinforce their meaning. "I need you to repeat everything I say as loud as you can. Do you understand? We need to reach *The Testament.*"

"TESTAMENT," Shuffles bellowed, and the entire cavern echoed with the force of his roar. Strangely, though Calder was standing next to it, Shuffles' volume didn't sound much greater than normal. By rights, a shout loud enough to reach *The Testament* should have shattered Calder's eardrums. But he only knew it was louder than normal because of the way the dust vibrated all over the chamber, echoing from the walls.

Whatever the reason, he was grateful for it. Maybe he wouldn't go deaf today.

"Foster," Calder said.

"FOSTER!"

"Ready cannons."

"READY CANNONS!"

Calder paused for a moment, giving Foster time to comply. Though the entire Gray Island seemed to shake under Shuffles' announcement, he had no idea whether the gunner heard him. At this distance, he could barely sense his Vessel's location; he had no chance of controlling the ship himself. And even though Kelarac had enhanced his ability to communicate with the Lyathatan, there was nothing the Lyathatan could do to fire a cannon.

The Handmaiden heard him and must have understood, because her Intent sharpened. Her pale tentacles, covered in hands, slithered closer, and she shrieked, pointing at him with one finger.

All the Children of Nakothi on the island swarmed down into the shattered arena, hungering for his blood. They sought Shera's blade more than anything else, but they would dismantle him on the way as nothing more than a distraction.

He turned back to Shuffles, and he couldn't help a smile. *Jerri would love this.*

"Take aim!"

"AIM!"

He waited a moment longer, forcing himself to stare the Handmaiden in the face. He began to tear up, his eyes trying to force themselves away from the sight as a purely physical reaction, but he kept looking. He wanted to see this.

"Fire."

"FIRE!"

The announcement echoed from every corner from the island.

An instant later, missiles slammed into the Handmaiden's chest, sending up geysers of white blood. Seconds after that, the sound caught up, and every cannon on *The Testament* cracked at once.

Calder grinned straight up at the Elderspawn's unfathomable face and shouted again. "Fire!"

"FIRE!"

A few seconds of delay, and two cannonballs crashed into the Handmaiden's ribs, and a third snapped a tree in half.

That was all he had time to witness before Nakothi's Children struck him like a cresting wave. He devoted himself to reading the flow of hostile Intent, lunging and dipping and dodging as he swept his cutlass through each of the dead Elderspawn.

Not one of them needed a second strike.

He kept limping along as he fought, Shuffles flapping along behind him, and occasionally shouted the order to fire.

Sword-first, he worked his way up the staircase.

He wished Shera the very best of luck, but he wasn't going to stick around to see how the fight turned out. If his fortune had turned for the better, the Handmaiden and the Consultants would kill each other.

Meanwhile, he had a date to keep.

Jerri pushed her way back against the wall as the bone-clawed crab, one of Nakothi's Children, snapped and slobbered through the bars of her cell. It strained its claw, reaching for her and falling well short.

It stood in a red mess—what was left of another prisoner, who had fled from deeper in the complex. Apparently there were more cells deeper within that Jerri had never seen, and some of their occupants had tried to make a break for it.

This one had run into an Elderspawn and been dismantled for his trouble.

Mindless minions. Useless. What good was an Elder with no wisdom? Nakothi was the one Great Elder that Jerri wouldn't mind staying asleep forever.

The bars squealed under the Child's assault, and Jerri pressed herself further against the stone. She was distracting herself, she could admit that. She just didn't want to confront the fact that in a few seconds, the bars would fold, and then she would end up just like the other prisoner: a puddle of red meat and cloth.

She shouted for help again, but of course anyone left alive in these tunnels would be locked in a cell, just like her.

If only she had her Vessel, she could protect herself. If only. But wishes hadn't freed her during her incarceration, and they wouldn't protect her now.

The crab raised up a spindly, misshapen leg that looked like it was made of nothing but skin stretched over bone. The leg wriggled in between the door, working at the twisted lock.

And the abused, weakened metal finally snapped. With a groan, the door to Jerri's cell folded open.

She forced a crazy grin onto her face, raising her fists. Whenever she'd imagined her own death, she'd pictured herself going down fighting.

Well, this wouldn't be much of a fight. But she'd take her best shot.

The corpse-crab hissed in glee, scrabbling over the stone to get closer. It moved with the eagerness of a dog, suddenly unleashed, bolting for its first meal in days.

You're late, Calder, Jerri thought.

Then the stone at her back grew much, much colder.

She almost staggered backwards as the wall behind her disappeared, but she managed to stop herself at the feeling of her heels moving out over empty air. She was standing at the very edge of a cliff.

A void transmission? Now? Whatever the cabal was going to do, they had best do it quickly.

A single piece of jewelry tumbled through the air, gleaming green and gold.

She recognized it instantly, just as she felt her own limbs, as she recognized her own face in the mirror. This close, she didn't even need to touch it to call on its powers—she'd been reaching for it mentally for days. But she caught it nonetheless.

The fury of her Vessel filled her, and she lashed out with a blade of emerald fire.

The crab's body divided into two smoking halves, each sliding around her and vanishing into the void.

Jerri gripped the earring with so much force she was almost afraid she'd crush it, fist shivering with relief. After weeks of waiting and wondering, she was finally whole.

The voice from the void, this time, was multi-layered and female, like three sisters trying to speak over one another. "We have made you wait. We apologize. The summoning did not go as we expected."

"You're here now," Jerri said. She couldn't help a surge of joy. Being separated from her Vessel was like losing her arms and legs. She stuck the earring through her right ear, sighing in satisfaction.

"Our plans have fallen apart," the voices said. "Yet we have succeeded in unexpected ways. Now we must make new plans."

Jerri started to walk toward the bars, slashing them into two red-hot halves. "Contact me when *The Testament* docks."

"Negative. Your transportation is prepared."

Jerri turned, surprised. The Sleepless cabal had never objected to her going where she wanted before.

In the swimming lights and endless black of the void, an Elderspawn floated. It looked like an octopus, tendrils swimming in unseen water, but its head was smooth and flat. Was she supposed to ride on that?

Jerri didn't sense any hostility from it, or intelligence of any kind, but she still hesitated. She wasn't so comfortable with the void that she wanted to ride into it on the back of an unknown creature.

The ceiling creaked above her, and she stepped to the side just in time to avoid a waterfall of rock dust.

"This structure is unstable," the voices said. "This is the safest way out."

Jerri still hesitated. "I want your word that you will release me. I have personal business to attend to."

"If you leave any other way, you will die."

"Give me your *word,* or I walk out of this cell right now." She had no doubt they were telling the truth about the unstable structure, but they couldn't predict the future. She would take her chances with the crumbling building if she had to.

"Our word is granted," the mysterious voice said.

Hesitantly, Jerri walked up to the edge of the voice. She glanced down, and immediately wished she hadn't: it was as though the world ended at the back of her prison cell. Colored lights and darkness swirled around at every angle.

The Elderspawn platform drifted closer, anchoring onto the stone edge of the cell with its suction cups.

"Time is short," the disembodied voice whispered.

After one more instant of hesitation, Jerri stepped out onto the creature's flattened head.

Wait for me, Calder. I'll sort this out.

She'd left just in time. Behind her, through the shrinking void portal, she saw the roof of the prison crumble.

"We told you," the voices said, smug.

Calder reached the hidden door to the prisons just as the ground caved in, like a suddenly collapsing sinkhole.

No, he thought. *No, it's not possible.*

He had agonized for so long about whether to save Jerri or not, and here he had arrived five seconds too late?

Calder jerked the door open, hobbling down the staircase on his wounded leg. The first part of the tunnel was surprisingly whole, giving him some hope. The whole island was apparently riddled with tunnels and underground chambers, after all. Maybe a different part of the network had collapsed.

When he reached the bottom of the stairs, he could see clearly that the end of the tunnel was choked with debris, but the cells on his left were surprisingly clear. Sure, Lucan's cell was covered in rocks and dust, but the door had swung open. It was nothing that would pose a threat to anyone.

Cautiously, afraid to brush against the wall lest he cause another cave-in, he edged to the next cell.

A pile of blood, bars sliced in half, and a cell filled with rocks.

For a moment, Calder's mind stopped working.

This didn't make sense. Why didn't Jerri's cell look like Lucan's? His was almost untouched; it was just a little dusty. This one was only next door. Why was it so much worse?

I was too late. After all that...too late.

The thought tore at his sanity, pulling at the stitching that held his mind together. But only a few seconds later, his reasoning reasserted itself.

He didn't *know* anything. And someone had cut these bars—the collapsing tunnel hadn't done that.

Calder reached out a hand, afraid to touch the blood and flesh. He didn't want to conjure a vision of a violent death, but he had to know if it was Jerri.

The Reading was vague, as the death hadn't occurred long ago. There was very little Intent clinging to the remains, and none in the surrounding rocks. But he sensed panic, and fear, and finally desperation.

Along with a familiar, mindless hunger. The Children of Nakothi had been here.

He reached his hand farther into the cell, seeking a vision, probing for Jerri's presence.

Jerri looks at the Child trying to force its way into the cell...

Joy surges in her chest as she finally feels complete for the first time in weeks...

She needs to break open a hole between her cell and Lucan's...

The transport doesn't look reliable, but she's determined to live...

He was getting brief flashes of Intent, a few fractured visions, but they were all broken. Weak. Out of sequence.

If he could only learn a little more...

A crack ran down the wall behind him, and he grimaced to himself. He was out of time. All he knew for sure was that Jerri had made it out of the cell.

One way or another.

He turned away from the rubble-filled hallway and almost lost his head.

A bronze blade flashed at his neck, and only years of training let him bend backwards, narrowly missing the edge on the skin of his throat.

The blond Consultant, Meia, panted as she leaned with one hand against the wall. "You...will not...escape," she panted.

Her skin was pale, her face covered in scrapes and cuts, her body trembling.

She looked worse than Urzaia had when he died.

At that thought, Calder steeled his resolve and drew his sword. "You should have checked behind you," he said.

She didn't even blink, her eyes hardening.

Then Shuffles flapped up behind the Consultant. "BEHIND YOU!" he declared, tentacles waving.

Meia spun on the Elderspawn, but she was too slow. Calder clubbed her on the back of the head with the hilt of his sword. She didn't lose consciousness, not entirely, but she did collapse. That was good enough for him.

He confiscated her two obvious knives, the bronze ones she kept buckled to her back, and stuffed them into his belt next to Urzaia's hatchets.

Meia struggled weakly as he tossed her over his shoulder, just as Andel had carried Naberius. The wound in his chest screamed in pain, but he was getting used to ignoring agonizing injuries. Just as he was getting used to holding captives. At this rate, he would soon have more prisoners on *The Testament* than crewmen.

Shera's not the only one who can take prisoners.

Taking Meia hostage wasn't the best idea he could have come up with, but he was more comfortable improvising. It was likely the years of practice.

But he couldn't help thinking, as he carried Meia and Shuffles back to The Testament, that he may have possibly made a mistake.

CHAPTER TWENTY-EIGHT

Are all seven of the known Great Elders malicious? I do not think so. I think that most Elders think of themselves as benefactors. Their ways are simply so alien, so absolutely incompatible with humanity, that the kindness of the Great Elders will very likely kill us all.

Nakothi likely believes, in her way, that she is improving humans by warping their bodies into the monstrous Children.

Kthanikahr cares not for humanity, but he is interested in preserving this planet as a habitat for his worms.

Urg'naut works for peace, as he sees it: the true peace of nonexistence.

Tharlos prefers a world of constant, endless change.

Othaghor wants, above all, to preserve life.

Ach'magut seeks knowledge at all costs.

Kelarac could say that he grants wishes.

– Artur Belfry, Imperial Witness,
concluding his confidential report to the Blackwatch

ELEVEN YEARS AGO

Bliss stood on the top branches of the leafless tree, peering out of her greenhouse. From a vantage point like this, she could see the Capital spreading out all around her: ancient spires and gleaming clock-towers rising like fresh shoots from the soil of shingled townhouses. With a view like this, she could almost forget that she was surrounded by walls of glass.

The Spear of Tharlos squirmed within her coat, knocking against the fabric like a fist against an oak door. It didn't speak to her, not today, but she understood its pleas nonetheless. It thought those towers should be volcanoes, the clocks should be filled with muscle and skin instead of cogs and gears, and the townhouses should be solid blocks of ice.

Tharlos was getting far too predictable. He *always* wanted *everything* to change. So boring.

So what if he turned all shoes into ducks? If shoes were constantly turning into other things, then it wouldn't be anything special when they eventually started quacking. No one would even notice.

Change was only interesting when everything normally stayed the same, and Tharlos could never understand that. That's why he would never beat her.

The image struck her again, of people walking around with ducks strapped to their feet, and she almost giggled. She thought about giggling. She *imagined* herself letting loose a nice, girlish giggle, and that was just as good as the real thing.

A gust of wind picked up the end of her white-blond hair, drawing it behind her like a streamer, and it took her a few seconds to understand why that was odd.

There's not supposed to be any wind in a greenhouse, she reminded herself. *Wait. Is there? No, definitely not.*

She smacked the Spear of Tharlos through her coat. It must have been up to its tricks again, making her see things that weren't actually happening, but for once the Spear felt quiet.

So she was sensing something herself, and this was her unconscious mind's way of warning her consciousness. Or was it?

She didn't know, but she hopped down into the tree nonetheless, swinging down from branch to branch until she could drop to the soil. Something was coming, and she'd rather face it up close. It might be interesting.

The doors swung open, and a pair of Watchmen walked in, escorting Alsa Grayweather.

They didn't look happy about it, but neither of them appeared quite so miserable as Alsa. Her face was gray, her hands tied in front of her, and her eyes were red and puffy. That meant that she had been crying. Or that she hadn't gotten much sleep. Or that someone had sprayed an irritant in her eyes. Or she had imbibed any number of alchemical substances, both harmful and recreational.

After a moment's consideration, Bliss decided that weeping or exhaustion were the two most likely possibilities.

"Are you under arrest, Alsa?" Bliss asked, before one of the other Watchmen could say something useless.

Alsa tried to speak, cleared her throat, and tried again. "My son had his trial this morning. As a result, my former husband was executed, Calder was exiled to the Aion under the supervision of the Navigators, and I was...remanded to your custody."

Bliss tried to fit Alsa's story together with her memories, but found too many pieces missing. "A trial? Calder Marten? What did he do?"

Alsa's eyes widened. *An expression of surprise, or shock, or fear, or anger. Probably surprise.* "I'm sorry, Guild Head, I thought you would have been informed."

One of the Watchmen stepped forward. "Guild Head, we've left several—"

She stared at him until he fell silent.

"He broke his father out of prison," Alsa said wearily. "In the process, he stole the ship we were preparing for the Navigator's Guild, binding himself to it as his Vessel. And the prison itself sustained irreparable damage. Many of the prisoners have not been recovered."

"Which prison?" Bliss asked.

From what Bliss had observed of typical conversation, her question must have seemed out of context, but Alsa answered immediately. "Candle Bay Imperial Prison."

That was why Bliss liked Alsa. No matter what else changed, Alsa Grayweather still did what she was supposed to.

"Candle Bay Imperial Prison," Bliss repeated. She knew the place.

She knew what happened there.

Kanatalia, the Guild of Alchemists, performed experiments on the inmates of many Imperial prisons, especially those who had committed higher crimes. They would attempt to increase docility, prevent a return to prior behavior, and generally improve the prisoners by means of altering their bodies and minds.

By means of poking and prodding. By means of needles, and potions that burn, and tools that cut memories like paper. They'll take their subjects apart, stick them back together, and then cut them apart again. Over and over.

Bliss had been born in just such a facility.

She hadn't said anything in a long time, so Alsa spoke to fill the silence. "That's right, Guild Head."

"Candle Bay Imperial Prison," Bliss said again, but this time she finished the thought, "belongs at the bottom of the ocean."

Bliss grabbed the chains between Alsa's manacled hands and let a trickle of her power change them. It was such a simple change that it took no effort; after all, there was no real difference between manacles locked and unlocked.

The cuffs clicked open, and the mass of metal fell to the ground.

One of her escorts sighed. "Guild Head, we were ordered by the Emperor himself to keep her in Guild custody. That means we have to move her to a secure facility. We only need your signature."

Bliss so rarely felt anything like anger, but something inside her had been scraped raw, thinking of Kanatalia and their experiments.

It had put her into what Nathanael Bareius would have called a *mood.*

She unfastened two of the silver buttons holding her coat together, reaching inside. Her fingers closed on ancient bone.

She pulled the Spear of Tharlos from its resting place.

Foot after foot of old, yellowed bone came out of her coat, until it became clear that the spear was longer than her pocket could have possibly contained. Until it was longer than she was tall. It rushed out of her coat almost without her guidance, leaping into the air, where it spun in a quick circle before she reached up and caught it.

The ancient Spear stood six feet tall, with a straight shaft that flattened into a sharp, spade-like blade at the top. The weapon had been carved in the Elder Days, by one of the Emperor's companions, from the corpse of Tharlos, the Formless Legion.

It took all of Bliss' willpower to keep the weapon from driving everyone else insane.

Even with her restraint, the plants in the greenhouse twisted and danced, as though driven by a thousand shifting winds. Her coat flapped in a wind that didn't exist, her hair blowing in the opposite direction. One of the Watchmen shielded his eyes, shouting as though the sight of the bone burned him, and the other covered his ears.

Alsa shook like a sail in high wind, but she kept her eyes fixed on Bliss.

"As the Head of the Blackwatch, I hereby decree that Alsa Grayweather is under my personal supervision," Bliss said. "If you would like to protest, file a complaint."

The two members of her Guild staggered away, leaving their captive behind.

The power of Tharlos wriggled under Bliss' skin, trying to *change* her, but she liked things the way they were. She turned to Alsa. "Do you think they'll really file a complaint?"

Alsa struggled to speak. "No," she said at last. "No, I don't think they will."

"Good. I don't like paperwork."

Bliss turned and examined the bone spear, struck with a new problem. Now that she had given the Spear a taste of freedom, it would be all the more reluctant to go back to sleep. Maybe she should have let it consume the other two Watchmen; they had annoyed her anyway.

She pulled the butt of the Spear off the ground, walking over to the leafless tree at the center of the greenhouse. Alsa followed, though it must have been difficult for her to push against the power of Tharlos.

"The Spear is restless," Bliss explained. "I must feed it to calm it down."

She leveled the Spear of Tharlos, driving its bone point deep into the trunk of the tree.

The tree shook like a struck drum. Bliss turned and walked away, pinching Alsa's wrist between two fingers as she did and dragging the taller woman along with her.

"We should stand back."

When they were far enough away, Bliss turned to watch the show. The bark was already shot through with pale purple flesh like cracks in a window. Flesh spread through the tree, bringing wood to life. The lowest branch drooped like a melting candle as it *changed* from a stiff bough to a limb of skin and flesh.

Soon, all the branches were purple-white tentacles, flailing in the air like a squid trying to escape a trap. The trunk was a solid, bulbous mass of throbbing flesh, firmly rooted in the ground by its own sticky weight.

Bliss clapped quietly, politely, like an audience member at the opera. There was no better show than watching reality *change* before her eyes.

When she stepped up to the newborn creature's trunk to retrieve her Spear, the waving tentacles parted to let her pass. She pulled the sharpened bone out, leaving not even a wound behind.

The Spear of Tharlos sat easy in her hand, warm and sated. It wasn't difficult to compress it down to the size of a thighbone and tuck the weapon back into her coat.

Alsa Grayweather stood staring at the tentacle-tree, but something about her expression was off. Perhaps she didn't seem disgusted enough, or she didn't show much emotion at all. Either way, it was not the expression that Bliss had come to expect from someone witnessing the Spear's effects.

Bliss took that to mean that something else was troubling her.

Probably her son's trial, she reasoned. *That event must have caused a good deal of stress.*

"What will you do with me now, Guild Head?" Alsa asked, still looking at the tree. "The others were telling the truth. The Emperor did order me confined."

Certainly, Bliss did not want to oppose the Emperor. She knew, better than most, how powerful he really was.

But Bliss was not weak herself. Her experience suggested that the Emperor would likely overlook anything she chose to do, as long as Alsa didn't make any more trouble. "You'll stay with me, under my personal supervision. You will be very secure. And you may be able to help me with some investigations of my own."

She had started to hear some disturbing rumors.

Navigators and their passengers had spotted Children of Nakothi swimming around the Aion. The island over the Dead Mother's corpse was shaking, sending unseasonable waves into even the shallower islands. And more than a few sailors had reported contact with Kelarac, the Soul Collector.

Even more disturbing than the rumors were the silences. If Nakothi and Kelarac were stirring, then the other Great Elders should be as well. But from the tombs of Kthanikahr, the desert temple of Othaghor, and the ruined city over Urg'naut's corpse, she heard nothing. Not a whisper.

Bliss had always found stillness more disturbing than screams.

But those were longer concerns. In the short-term, Bliss knew that *she* would feel better if she could just get Alsa to relax.

Exercise was supposed to alleviate stress, but Alsa would probably not enjoy a fencing match in her current state. Alcohol relieved stress in some, but seemed to increase it in others. Bliss couldn't take the risk. That left, to Bliss' knowledge, only companionship and sugary foods.

Bliss took Alsa's hand in her own and proposed a solution. "Let's go buy some pie from a restaurant. It is my turn to make the purchase." That was only fair. "Tell me, do they accept gold coins?"

Alsa's demeanor was already more pleasant, which pleased Bliss. She had done something good today, after all.

"Yes, Guild Head. I expect they will."

PRESENT DAY

The Eternal was waiting for them only a day's trip out from the Gray Island.

Calder saw the red sails and bright alchemical flames on the ocean long before the ship actually hailed him. There was no point running; they had surely been spotted, and whenever Jarelys Teach returned on her Kameira bird, she would be able to overtake *The Testament* no matter where he ran. So he had no choice but to confront the Guild Heads dead-on.

Which left him with several hours between spotting *The Eternal* and reaching her. He stared out over the port railing, thinking. He was in no hurry, so he left Dalton Foster at the wheel, pulled forward by nothing more than the power of the wind.

Andel joined him, leaning white-clad elbows on the edge. "I'm sorry we didn't get her back."

The words threatened to cut a bundle of emotion free, but Calder choked it back. "I had my chance, and I left her there."

"You went back."

"Didn't matter much in the end, don't you think?"

The quartermaster rubbed his silver pendant. "I think...I think we don't know yet."

Calder eyed him. "Don't know what?"

"Many things. For instance," Alder turned around, leaning back against the railing and staring at the center of the deck. "What are we going to do about him?"

The first of their prisoners knelt tied to the mast, still wearing his torn red suit. Naberius had spent an hour of the first night screaming about what he was going to do with their parts once he'd killed them, how they would be more useful after they died.

After that hour, Calder had stuffed a foot of rope into his mouth. Now he mostly grunted and spat.

"That's a good question," Calder said. He walked over to Naberius, pulling the wet length of rope out of the man's mouth. "What do you think, Naberius? What should we do with you?"

The former Chronicler coughed and swallowed for a few seconds, working enough moisture into his mouth to speak. At last, he said, "Beg me for forgiveness."

As expected. A week before, Naberius would have been cunning enough to at least lie to his captors in the hope of freedom. The Heart had taken even that shred of sanity from him, leaving him lost in delusion.

But Calder was sure of one thing. "They're not crowning *that* Emperor."

Andel walked over, circling the bound Witness like a shark circling prey. "I would hope not."

"Trust me. I have the crown."

"It will do nothing for you," Naberius spat. "I will be remade. And you will be remade. The Empire will be torn to pieces, and from those remnants I will create a masterpiece..."

He kept on mumbling to himself as Andel dropped to his heels in front of the man, looking him in the eye.

"Tell me, Naberius," Andel said. "Is there any part of you left? Anything that does not bow to the Dead Mother?"

The Chronicler's raving didn't even slow. "...death is not the end, *life* is the end. We are all children, waiting to return to the mother."

Andel nodded, as if Naberius had said something completely reasonable. "I see. If we left you on an island, what would you do?"

What was the point of this test? Naberius was clearly not in his right mind. He would give nothing but nonsensical answers, and surely Andel had to see that.

But, trusting his second-in-command, Calder said nothing.

Naberius grinned. "I would call to the Dead Mother for claws and wings. And I would fly to you. And I would tear out your heart."

Then he spat in Andel's face.

Andel's expression didn't change. He nodded again, wiping his cheek with the back of his hand.

"There's no cure for what ails him," Calder said at last. They could hand him over to Cheska; she would make sure that Naberius got back to his family. Or to a mental facility equipped to deal with him. Or an abandoned island; Calder wasn't particularly bothered.

Evidently, Andel disagreed.

"There's one," he said.

Then he pulled out his pistol and shot Naberius in the forehead.

The shot floated over the deck like a ghost, and the Chronicler's body slowly slid sideways. Andel gripped the man by his suit, heaving him up and carrying him to the railing. A second later, a splash indicated that Naberius had made his way to the Aion.

Calder's shock made him feel like *he* was the one who had just taken a bullet to the head. He'd seen men die before, but he didn't...*execute* people. And for Andel, of all people, to have done it...he was having trouble adjusting his thoughts.

"Too many chances we couldn't take," Andel explained, wiping down his gun with a handkerchief before he tossed the weapon up to the gunner. "Reload that for me, Foster."

Dalton Foster desperately snatched the gun out of the air. "Don't go throwing guns around! Loaded or unloaded, I don't care, don't do it." He glanced over at Calder, then added, "But good job with the dead weight. Would've saved us some trouble to put a bullet in his crown three weeks ago."

Calder didn't bother to respond. He had more important things to deal with—he was the one who had to explain to the Guild Heads what had happened to Naberius, not Foster. And he would have to do it today, which meant he had to wear that same itchy jacket again.

He lifted the dark blue jacket, staring at it. It was rough, tight, and it looked just as uncomfortable as it felt.

Seized by a sudden inspiration, he opened the porthole and shoved the jacket out.

Naberius was dead, and Calder couldn't tell if he felt more disturbed or relieved. They had a Consultant prisoner in the hold, they still hadn't gotten Jerri back, and Urzaia was gone. His crew was down to Andel, Foster, Petal, and himself. Even with his control over the Vessel, he was shorthanded.

It was time to stop holding his cards back, and put everything on the table.

He marched into the main room of *The Eternal* without a jacket, carrying with him a wooden case and an all-but-empty sack. The bandages over his chest would be visible through the shirt, and he still walked with a limp, but he thought the injuries made him look rugged and battle-scarred.

The only wound he wanted to hide was Kelarac's burn on his right arm, which was covered by his sleeve. No telling how Bliss would react to *that*.

General Teach sat at the far end of the table, her red-and-black-plated arms crossed. She had returned only minutes after he'd set foot on deck, and it had taken all of his and Captain Bennett's combined persuasive power to prevent her from killing him on the spot.

Cheska Bennett was no longer dressed for a ball: her hair was tied back with a bandana, she wore clothes almost identical to Calder's own, and she leaned back against the wall, propping her boots up on the table. She faced Calder wearing a cocky grin, evidently more amused by his actions than upset.

And then there was Bliss, alone at the other end of the table. She looked... exactly the same as always, staring at a tiny butterfly of blown glass as though she expected it would attack at any second. His mother was conspicuously absent, but Bliss had explained that Alsa was, "Somewhere else." He didn't expect any more detail.

Also missing was the Head of the Magisters, Mekendi Maxeus. His Guild was stretched thin as it was, and apparently he had decided his skills were of more use in the Capital than floating in an unmarked stretch of the Aion.

Calder entered on his own, but he didn't sit. Before Cheska could welcome him or anyone else could say a word, he bowed to Jarelys Teach. "General Teach, I apologize once again for the unfortunate circumstances of our last meeting."

"What about the meeting before that?" Teach asked, eyes flashing.

"...I apologize for the unfortunate circumstances surrounding *each and every* one of our meetings, and I hope we can be more friendly in the future." He turned to Bliss. "Guild Head, it's a pleasure to see you again. Thank you for your recent support."

Teach gripped the table at the mention of Bliss' *support,* but Bliss only nodded vaguely, still fixated on the butterfly. It slid slightly as the ship bobbed, and the Guild Head jumped as if she thought the movement signaled an attack.

At last, he nodded to Captain Bennett. "Cheska. You looked better last time."

If anything, her grin widened. "Carve it into your memory, Captain. You'll never see anything like it as long as you live."

Calder placed the wooden case onto the tabletop, setting the sack next to it. "Before you make a decision regarding me and my crew, I would like to submit a few facts for your consideration. First, Naberius Clayborn is dead."

General Teach's hostile Intent scorched him from across the table. Thanks to the sword she wore, he physically shuddered. At this distance, it was entirely possible that she could kill him just by *wishing* hard enough.

"Details," she demanded.

"It was an unavoidable casualty of battle," he said smoothly. "Naberius' mind was eroded completely by the Heart of Nakothi. Before he died, he said nothing without ranting about death and rebirth."

Bliss sighed. "Shouldn't have tried to Awaken it on his own. It was dangerous enough sleeping, but when it...hey! Get back here!"

The butterfly slid across the table, and she used her hand to stop it before it fell to the deck and shattered.

Cheska shut her eyes and let her head flop back. "There go months of planning. And *so much money.* Do you know how much I invested in him?"

Calder cleared his throat. "I may be able to help with that."

He flipped open the case, revealing rows of white candles.

Teach nodded slowly, and Cheska opened her eyes a crack. When she saw what he'd revealed, she whistled and pulled her legs off the table.

"He claimed that all the riches of the Imperial palace, and all the details of the accounts, were somewhere in here," Calder said. "If a Reader—say me, for instance—burns them, we should be able to learn something. At least we can get your investment back, Cheska."

"I should hope so," she said, but she sounded much more hopeful than before.

"That doesn't address our most important concern," Teach said irritably. "We still have no candidate for the throne. If we're forced to anoint Nathanael Bareius the leader of the Aurelian Empire, I just might kill him myself."

"Just so I'm clear," Calder began, "what were the qualities you were looking for in our new Emperor?"

Cheska and Teach exchanged glances.

"He should be a powerful Reader," Teach began.

"Well-connected," Cheska continued.

"We were looking for a man. If Estyr Six were willing to sit on the throne, perhaps the people would accept an Empress, but without her... there's only so much change the common rabble can take at one time."

"Rich," Cheska added.

"He has to be well-educated and dignified," Teach continued. "And, of course, I have to approve."

"I'm still stuck on rich."

"He must be someone the people can approve. The public need stability, now more than ever."

Bliss finally looked up, adding, "I'd like it if he were sane, but I will work with what I can get."

To each of their points, Calder nodded. When they were finished, he placed one hand on the case of Chronicler's candles, and one on the sack to his left.

"With all that in mind, I would like to propose a new candidate." Pinching the burlap sack between two fingers, he picked it up.

The Emperor's crown tumbled out, rolling slightly as it landed on the table.

Jarelys Teach's breath caught, and she unconsciously reached a hand out. Cheska gave a low whistle. Bliss tilted her head, interested.

"Where did you get that?" Teach whispered, but Calder ignored her. She probably wouldn't appreciate the story anyway.

"I like to think of myself as a powerful Reader, I am reasonably well educated, and I can be dignified when I put my mind to it. Hopefully," he patted the candles, "I will be coming into some money soon. I'm reasonably sane. If you three approve, that would qualify me as well-connected. And even my harshest critics don't doubt my gender."

Calder finally let his true feelings bleed into his voice—the ambition he'd hidden for years. "And I'm *not* immortal. I don't need to be bound to the Heart, or to anything. Let me live a normal span of years and then die. A regular, mortal, *human* ruler who will be replaced by an heir after my death...and hopefully, that won't give the Great Elders enough time to turn me into a puppet."

He picked up the golden crown and placed it on his head, striking a pose. "So, what do you think?"

There was an instant of stunned silence before Cheska burst out laughing. Bliss raised her eyes to him. "Is it appropriate to call you by title, or should I keep using your name?"

Only Jarelys Teach seemed to object, scowling at the sight of him wearing the crown. "More than anything, we need a willing person to sit on the throne. As far as *that* goes, you qualify."

His hopes soared. Part of him had wondered if she would take his head off for even attempting this.

"But you are quite possibly the worst candidate when it comes to patching relations with the other Guilds. The Consultants are undoubtedly after you as we speak. How will you handle them?"

Calder tried to project absolute confidence and an air of mystery. "In fact, I've already taken steps. Trust me. I have held one card in reserve."

When he climbed up the ladder and onto *The Testament's* deck, no one was at the wheel. Andel was nowhere to be seen, and a pile of ropes sat at the base of the mast.

Foster hurried up to him, blood running down into his beard from a split lip. The gunner spoke only two words:

"She's loose."

The End

OF THE ELDER EMPIRE: FIRST SEA

Next time, follow Calder in...

Of Darkness & Dawn

The Elder Empire
Second Sea

Coming Soon!

For updates, visit *www.WillWight.com*

turn the page for a glossary and
excerpts from The Guild Guide

AM'HARANAI The ancient order of spies and assassins that would eventually become the Consultant's Guild. Some formal documents still refer to the Consultant's Guild in this way.

ARCHITECT One type of Consultant. The Architects mostly stay in one place, ruling over Guild business and deciding general strategy. They include alchemists, surgeons, Readers, strategists, and specialists of all types.

AWAKEN A Reader can Awaken an object by bringing out its latent powers of Intent. An Awakened object is very powerful, but it gains a measure of self-awareness. Also, it can never be invested again.

Jarelys Teach, the Head of the Imperial Guard, carries an ancient executioner's blade that has been Awakened. It now bears the power of all the lives it took, and is lethal even at a distance.

All Soulbound Vessels are Awakened.

CHILDREN OF THE DEAD MOTHER Elderspawn created by the power of Nakothi out of human corpses.

CONSULTANT A member of the Consultants Guild, also known as the Am'haranai. Mercenary spies and covert agents that specialize in gathering and manipulating information for their clients.

Consultants come in five basic varieties: Architects, Gardeners, Masons, Miners, and Shepherds.

For more, see the Guild Guide.

DEAD MOTHER, THE *See: Nakothi.*

ELDER Any member of the various races that ruled the world in ancient days, keeping humanity as slaves. The most powerful among them are known as Great Elders, and their lesser are often called Elderspawn.

GARDENER One type of Consultant. The Gardeners kill people for hire.

INTENT The power of focused will that all humans possess. Whenever you use an object *intentionally*, for a *specific purpose*, you are investing your Intent into that object. The power of your Intent builds up in that object over time, making it better at a given task.

Every human being uses their Intent, but most people do so blindly; only Readers can sense what they're doing.

See also: Invest, Reader.

INVEST Besides its usual financial implications, to "invest" means to imbue an object with one's Intent. By intentionally using an object, you *invest* that object with a measure of your Intent, which makes it better at performing that specific task.

So a pair of scissors used by a barber every day for years become progressively better and better at cutting hair. After a few years, the scissors will cut cleanly through even the thickest strands of tangled hair, slicing through with practically no effort. A razor used by a serial killer will become more and more lethal with time. A razor used by a serial-killing barber will be very confused.

KAMEIRA A collective term for any natural creature with unexplainable powers. Cloudseeker Hydras can move objects without touching them, Windwatchers can change and detect air currents, and Deepstriders control water. There are many different types of Kameira...though, seemingly, not as many as in the past. The Guild of Greenwardens is dedicated to studying and restoring Kameira populations.

Humans can borrow the miraculous powers of Kameira by creating Vessels from their body parts, and then bonding with those Vessels to become Soulbound.

MASON One type of Consultant. Masons are craftsmen and professionals in a particular trade, covertly sending back information to their Guild. There are Masons undercover in every industry and business throughout the Empire.

MINER One type of Consultant. This secretive order is in charge of the Consultants' vast library, sorting and disseminating information to serve the Guild's various clients.

NAKOTHI, THE DEAD MOTHER A Great Elder who died in the Aion Sea. Her power kills humans and remakes their bodies into hideous servants.

NAVIGATOR A member of the Navigator's Guild. The Navigators are the only ones capable of sailing the deadly Aion Sea, delivering goods and passengers from one continent to the other.

For more, see the Guild Guide.

Reader A person who can read and manipulate the Intent of objects. Every human being invests their Intent subconsciously, simply by using ordinary objects. However, Readers can do so with a greater degree of focus and clarity, thanks to their special senses.

Readers often receive visions of an object's past.

Shepherd One type of Consultant. The Shepherds are observers, thieves, and saboteurs that specialize in infiltrating a location and leaving unnoticed.

Soulbound A human who can channel the power of an Elder or a Kameira. These powers are contained in a Vessel, which is *bound* to a person during the Awakening process. Soulbound are rare and powerful because they combine the focus of human Intent with the miraculous power of inhuman beings.

Bliss, the Guild Head of the Blackwatch, is a Soulbound with the Spear of Tharlos as her Vessel. Therefore, she can borrow the reality-warping powers of the Great Elder known as Tharlos, the Formless Legion.

A person becomes a Soulbound by having a personally significant object Awakened. If the object has a strong connection to an Elder or Kameira, and if it is significant *enough,* then it can become a Soulbound Vessel.

See also: Vessel.

Vessel An Awakened object that becomes the source of a Soulbound's power. Not all Awakened items become Soulbound Vessels, but all Vessels are Awakened.

In order to become a person's Vessel, an item must fulfill two criteria: it must be *personally linked* to the individual, and it must be invested with the power of a Kameira or an Elder.

1.) Personal link: A ring that you bought at a pawnshop three weeks ago could not become your Soulbound Vessel. It has not absorbed enough of your Intent, it is not significant to you, and it is not *bound* to you in any way. A wedding ring that you've worn for fifteen years and is significant to you for some reason—perhaps you pried it off your spouse's bloody corpse—could indeed become your Vessel, assuming it fulfills the second criteria as well.

2.) Power: A spear made of an Elder's bone could allow one to use that Elder's power of illusion and madness. If you bonded with a necklace of Deepstrider scales, you might be able to sense and control the ocean's currents as that Kameira does.

See also: Soulbound.

WATCHMAN A member of the Blackwatch Guild.

For more, see the Guild Guide.

A brief guide to the Ten Imperial Guilds of the Aurelian Empire, written by a licensed Witness for your edification and betterment!

The Am'haranai

Also known as Consultants, the members of this mysterious brotherhood work behind the scenes for the good of the Empire...or for anyone with enough gold to pay them. Consultants are more than willing to provide strategic advice, tactical support, and information to the Empire's rich and elite, so long as it doesn't destabilize the government they've worked so hard to build.

Believe it or not, the Am'haranai were the first Imperial Guild, having existed in one form or another since long before the birth of the Empire. The next time you walk by the local chapter house of the Consultants, know that you're in the presence of true Imperial History.

The Consultants' local Guild Representative would not give us a definitive response to the less savory rumors surrounding this particular Guild. Juicy speculation suggests that—for the right price—the Consultants will provide a number of darker services, including espionage, sabotage, and even assassination. We can neither confirm nor refute such rumors at this time.

Consultants in the field are known to refer to each other by code names, to conceal their true identities.

Shepherds are their expert scouts, trained to watch, remember, and report.

Architects are the leaders of the Am'haranai, and typically do not leave their island fortress. They're the strategists, alchemists, tacticians, and Readers that make the work of the Consultants possible.

Masons are a truly terrifying order, though once again the Guild Representative put off most of my questions. They go undercover as everyday folk like you or me, living ordinary lives for months or years, and then providing information to their Architect leaders. Your best friend, your neighbor, that street alchemist across from your house...any of them could be a Mason secretly watching you!

Other, less credible reports suggest the existence of a fourth brand of Consultant: the **Gardeners.** The job of a Gardener is to "remove weeds." They are the black operatives, the pure assassins, the knives in the dark.

The Guild Representative had this to say on the matter: "There is not now, and never has been, an order of the Am'haranai known as the Gardeners. That's simple speculation based on our Guild crest, which is actually derived from our origin as humble farmers. Having said that, if you do have someone interfering with your business, it is possible that we could help you bring the situation to a satisfactory conclusion...for an appropriate level of compensation, of course."

Since the Emperor's death (may his soul fly free), I have no doubt that business has been very good indeed for this particular Guild.

Guild Head: **The Council of Architects.** No one knows much about the leadership of the Consultants, but it seems that the Architects collectively vote on Guild policy, coming to decisions through careful deliberation and long experience.

Crest: Gardening Shears

The Blackwatch

Thanks to generations of legends and misinformation perpetuated by the Luminians, many of you have certain preconceived notions about the Blackwatch. They're hated by many, feared by all, and I urge you not to heed the rumors. Every Watchman I've ever met has been professional, focused, and inquisitive--very few of them actually worship the Elders.

Let me put a few of your unfounded fears to rest: no, they do not eat human flesh for power. No, they do not conduct dark rituals involving blood sacrifice. No, they do not kidnap babies from their cradles.

Yes, they do use certain powers and techniques of the Elders. That's no reason to treat them like cultists.

The Blackwatch was originally founded by the Emperor for two purposes: watching over the graves of the Great Elders, and studying the Elder Races to twist their great powers for the good of the Empire. It is thanks to the Blackwatch that Urg'Naut or the Dead Mother have not risen and devoured our living world.

Members of this Guild are known as **Watchmen.** They respond to calls for help and reports of Elder activity. Each Watchman carries seven long, black nails invested with the power to bind Lesser Elders for vivisection and study.

The goals of the Blackwatch often bring them into conflict with Knights and Pilgrims of the Luminian Order, who hunt down Lesser Elders with the goal of destroying them completely.

If the two would only work together, it's possible that Aurelian lands would never be troubled by Elder attacks again.

Guild Head: The current head of the Blackwatch is a young-seeming woman known only as **Bliss.** Her origins are shrouded in mystery, though tenuous evidence suggests that she was born in a Kanatalia research facility.

Like every Blackwatch Head before her, she carries the **Spear of Tharlos,** a weapon supposedly carved from the bone of a Great Elder. I have never interviewed anyone who witnessed the Spear in battle and survived with their sanity intact.

Crest: the Elder's Eyes (six eyes on a mass of tentacles)

The Champions

I doubt there is a single child in any corner of the Aurelian Empire who does not know some story of the Champion's Guild, but I will still labor to separate fact from romantic fiction.

The Champions as we know them today rose out of an old Izyrian tradition. In ancient days, before the Empire, the continent of Izyria was divided into a thousand clans. When two clans had a dispute, instead of going to war, they would send two representatives into a formal duel. The winner's clan, of course, won the dispute. These clan champions were often Soulbound, strengthened by some secret alchemical technique, and highly skilled fighters.

When the Emperor (may his soul fly free) originally crossed the Aion Sea with the aim of enfolding Izyria into his fledgling Empire, he created his own collection of duelists to defeat the natives at their own cultural game.

Thus, the Champions were born.

Champions became, as we have all seen, the best fighters in the Empire. They singlehandedly quell rebellions, reinforce Imperial troops in the field, and put down dangerous Kameira. And sometimes, when the Empire still needed to fight its own duels, the existence of this Guild ensured that the Emperor never lost.

Since the death of the Emperor, this Guild has become—dare I say it—a dangerous liability. Each Champion has largely gone his or her own way. The Guild still trains initiates according to the old traditions, but it doesn't have the organizational stability or control it once did.

Guild Head: **Baldezar Kern,** an undefeated duelist and the man who singlehandedly pacified the South Sea Revolutionary Army. Though he is known as a gentle man with an easy sense of humor, when he straps on his trademark horned helmet, he becomes a force of carnage on the battlefield like none I have ever seen. I had the opportunity to witness Kern on the warpath almost fifteen years ago, and the sight of this man in battle will haunt me until the day of my death.

Crest: the Golden Crown

The Greenwardens

While the Greenwardens do protect us from wild Kameira and keep the Imperial Parks that we all know and enjoy, you may not be aware that they were originally intended to save the world.

The Guild of Greenwardens was founded at a time in our history when alchemy was first coming into its own, and we were afraid that a combination of alchemy, then-modern weaponry such as the cannon, and unregulated human Intent would tear the world apart.

Greenwardens were created to preserve Kameira, preventing us from driving them extinct, and to monitor and repair the effects of alchemical and gunpowder weapons on the environment. They each carry an Awakened talisman, which for some has become their Soulbound Vessel: a shining green jewel that they use to heal wounds and promote the growth of plants.

Guild Head: **Tomas Stillwell** is a practicing physician and a fully inducted Magister of the Vey Illai as well as the Guild Head of the Greenwardens, proving that no physical infirmity can prevent you from contributing to your Empire. Though he lost his legs in a childhood encounter with a wild Kameira, he never let that experience make him bitter. Instead, it drove him to study Kameira, their habits, and how they function. He is now one of the most famous natural scientists in the Empire, and he has done much to prevent the extinction of species such as the stormwing and the shadowrider.

Crest: the Emerald

The Imperial Guard

I trust that all of you understand the purpose of the Imperial Guard: to protect the Emperor's person, and to shield him from attack and unwanted attention. Some suggest that they failed, that the death of the Emperor proves that the Guard were unequal to their task.

I can assure you that this is not the case.

Through a secret alchemical process known only to the Guild of Alchemists, the Imperial Guard replaces some of their original body parts with those of Kameira. Some Guardsmen have patches of armored Nightwyrm hide grafted onto their skin, or their eyes substituted with those of a Cloud Eagle. The process is said to be long and unbearably painful, and it results in guardians with the appearance of monsters.

However, in the twelve hundred years that the Emperor reigned, not a single assassination attempt reached his person. We owe that fact solely to the power and extraordinary sensitivity of the Imperial Guard.

I know that many outside the Capital are wondering what the Guard are up to, now that they have no Emperor to guard. Well, in the words of their Guild Head, "We may no longer have an Emperor, but we have an Empire. That, we will preserve until the sun rises in the west."

The resolve of a true patriot, gentle readers.

Guild Head: **Jarelys Teach,** a General in the Emperor's military and Head of his Imperial Guard, does not at first strike you as an imposing woman. I have met her on many occasions, and found her to be singularly devoted to her job. Popular legend says that she swallowed the blood of a Nightwraith, thereby absorbing its powers, but that's little more than speculation. It's a matter of Imperial record that she carries Tyrfang, the Awakened blade used to execute the Emperor's rivals over a thousand years ago.

Crest: the Aurelian Shield (a shield bearing the sun-and-moon symbol of the Aurelian Empire)

Kanatalia, the Guild of Alchemists

As I write this guide, I sip a glass of enhanced wine that slowly shifts flavor from cherry to apple to lemon. A cart rumbles by my house, with a hawker loudly announcing his remedies for sale. A quicklamp provides my light, glowing a steady blue, never smoking or flickering like a candle.

Truly, one cannot escape the advances of alchemy in our modern society.

Though alchemists have existed since long before the Empire, Kanatalia is one of the more recent additions to the Ten Guilds. It was the first organization to unify the previously contentious brotherhood of alchemists, allowing them to collectively achieve what they never could separately.

Matches, quicklamps, potions, invested alloys, healing salves, enhanced soldiers, vaccines...practically every scientific advance in the past century, including the advance of science itself, can be traced back to Kanatalia's door.

Just don't ask too many questions. A true Kanatalian alchemist can be very protective of his secrets, and you might find yourself a drooling vegetable if you get on the wrong side of an experienced potion-maker.

Guild Head: **Nathanael Bareius** did not become one of the richest men in the Empire by relaxing on his inheritance. After receiving a substantial fortune from his late father, Lord Bareius went on to receive a full education at the Aurelian National Academy. He graduated as a licensed Imperial alchemist and a member of Kanatalia. At that point, he wagered all of his capital on a single risky investment: alchemy. He opened his vaults, spending every bit he had to make sure that every corner and crevice of the Empire had a licensed Kanatalian alchemist there to provide illumination, potions, medical care, and Guild-approved recreational substances.

Lord Bareius has personally earned back triple his initial investment over the past ten years, and is now poised as the most prominent leader in the

Capital. Even more significantly, he seems to have won the battle of public opinion—I haven't seen a street in the Capital unlit by alchemical lanterns, and no one has died of dysentery or plague since before the Emperor's death. No matter what you think of his politics, Nathanael Bareius has made great strides in moving our Empire forward into this new century.

Crest: the Bottled Flame

The Luminian Order

Ah, the Luminians. A more versatile Guild you won't find anywhere: they're responsible for building cathedrals, policing Imperial roads, hunting down Elders, and generally acting heroic.

Luminian Knights, the martial arm of the Order, march around in their powerfully invested steel armor, fighting deadly monsters chest-to-chest. Their swords are bound with light so that they reflect the sun even in the dead of night, burning through creatures of darkness.

The trademark representatives of the Luminian Order are **Pilgrims,** humble wanderers in simple robes. They are each Readers—some of them Soulbound—charged to remove harmful Intent and the maddening influence of the Elders.

The Luminian Order and the Blackwatch have each held a knife to the other's back for hundreds of years, arguing over the best way to protect the populace, to prevent the rise of the Great Elders, and to keep the Empire whole. Perhaps if one of them would learn to compromise, we would all feel safer after midnight.

Guild Head: **Father Jameson Allbright** is an old man, but his vigilance has never dimmed in the fight against darkness. He is one of the oldest Soulbound on record, wielding his shining Vessel to bring the purifying light to Elder worshipers and malicious Readers alike.

Crest: the White Sun (usually on a red banner)

The Magisters

Magisters are the most accomplished and educated Readers in the world. You probably grew up with a local Reader, who invested your knives and cleansed your graveyard of harmful Intent. Most small-town Readers are powerful and possibly even quite skilled.

But they aren't Magisters.

A Magister is a Reader who has received an extensive education inside the Vey Illai, an extensive forest in the Aurelian heartland, inside what was once the original Imperial Academy. They can use their Intent with a degree of focus, subtlety, and precision that an ordinary Reader could barely comprehend.

Magisters are in charge of regulating Readers and the use of human Intent, in much the same way that a father is in charge of preventing his children from misbehaving.

It's impossible for all Readers to study at the Vey Illai and become Magisters, because there are simply too many people with a talent for Reading. And of course everyone invests their Intent into objects, to one degree or another.

But the best and most powerful are called Magisters.

Guild Head: **Professor Mekendi Maxeus,** one of the most distinguished researchers at the Aurelian National Academy, retired from his lecture tour to the "relaxing" position as head of one of the largest Imperial Guilds. He isn't seen outside much these days, having received several disfiguring facial scars in the Inheritance Conflict five years ago, but he still lends his overwhelming power of Intent to the construction of new public monuments in the Capital. He carries a black staff, and I have personally witnessed him use it to blast a collapsed building off a pair of trapped children. I have met few heroes in my career, but this man is among them.

Crest: the Open Book

The Navigators

When I call the Navigators a Guild, I use the term loosely.

Navigators are the only sailors who can cross the deadly, shifting ocean at the heart of our Empire: the Aion Sea. We therefore rely on them for communication, trade, exploration, and transport between the eastern continent of Aurelia and the western continent, Izyria.

It's too bad that they're the most shifty and unreliable collection of pirates, confidence artists, mercenaries, and outright criminals the Empire has ever seen.

No one knows how they cross the Aion, with its hundreds of deadly Kameira, its disappearing islands, its unpredictable weather, and its host of lurking Elders, but anyone else who sails far enough out into the ocean either vanishes or returns insane.

The best way to recognize a real Navigator from a faker is to ask to see their Guild license, which is unmistakable and cannot be reproduced. Unfortunately, that only tells you which sailor is truly able to cross the Aion: not whether he can be trusted.

Guild Head: **Captain Cheska Bennett** is one of the few reliable Navigators left in this world. She owns *The Eternal,* a most striking ship with billowing red sails and a wake that trails flame. She commands truly shocking prices for her services, but if you hire her, you can be certain that every splinter of your cargo will remain secure between one continent and the other.

Crest: the Navigator's Wheel (a ship's wheel with a single eye at the center)

The Witnesses

I am proud to count myself among the honorable Guild of Witnesses, the final entry on this written tour of Imperial history. Witnesses are the official record-keepers of the Empire, having chronicled the entirety of the Empire's history since our inception. We also observe momentous events, record battles, produce educational reading materials for the general public, and notarize official documents.

As Sadesthenes once said, *"The Witnesses are the grease that allow the wheels of Empire to turn."*

Generally speaking, Witnesses travel in pairs:

As a **Chronicler,** I am a Reader with the ability to store my memories inside a special alchemically created candle. I burn the candle while I write, and as the memories flow out, I can record my thoughts without any margin of error even years after the events I have witnessed.

Always, I am accompanied by my **Silent One,** a trained warrior and my bodyguard. Silent Ones bind their mouths to symbolize their inability to betray secret or sensitive events, but contrary to popular belief, we do *not* remove their tongues. We're not barbarians. They are capable of speech, they are simply discouraged from doing so in the presence of outsiders.

Guild Head: The Heads of my own Guild are the twin sisters **Azea and Calazan Farstrider,** natives of exotic Izyria. Though they are young, having risen to prominence after the Emperor's untimely demise, I have never met anyone so dedicated to accuracy and neutrality. Azea works as a Chronicler, and Calazan as her attendant Silent One, though I can personally confirm that either sister can perform either role. Azea is a remarkable fighter in her own right, and Calazan a skilled Reader and clerk.

Crest: the Quill and Candle

And now…

A preview for the parallel novel

OF SHADOW & SEA

Follow Shera as she works for the Consultants, trying to stop Calder while following the Emperor's last command.

CHAPTER ONE

FIFTEEN YEARS AGO

When they had to kill a grown man, the children worked in pairs.

The Bait, usually a girl, would lure the target in by faking some sort of crisis and begging for help. When the target isolated himself, the Knife would drive their blade home.

By mutual agreement, Mari was always the Bait. She had long, curly hair and big eyes that looked like she was always ready to cry. Sometimes adults would stop her on the street and ask her what was wrong, even when she wasn't trying to lure anybody.

Shera was the Knife.

The two of them dressed poor, but not too poor. They couldn't look like homeless beggars, or the target would never stop. Maxwell had provided a faded dress and cheap blue ribbon for Mari, and a boy's pants, shirt, and cap for Shera. No shoes.

Some of Maxwell's older children complained about how they hated waiting; the long, boring stretch of hours between the time you set up your ambush and the time the target wandered through. Sometimes the target would never show, and you wasted your whole afternoon.

Not Shera. This was her favorite part.

As Mari sat on one side of the street with her chin in her hands, waiting for the target to pass by, Shera leaned against the wall of an alley, eating chunks of meat from a stolen skewer. The noise of the Capital blurred into a soothing lullaby, and she found herself drifting off as she watched the people pass her alleyway: a tourist couple carrying their luggage; a shirtless Izyrian hunter with a musket over one shoulder and a rabbit in his hand; an alchemist with her mask hanging down around her neck, biting her lip and scribbling on a clipboard.

Shera could watch the crowds all day. You saw all kinds of people in the Empire's Capital.

The familiar sights and the droning music of the city lulled her to sleep, tugging her eyelids down. She curled up against the alley wall, hugging the skewer to prevent its one remaining piece of meat from falling to the ground.

She so rarely got the chance for a nap. And now they could be here for hours...

Shera opened her eyes again at the sound of Mari's voice. "Please, I don't know what's wrong with her," the girl choked out, through her sniffles. "She's fallen asleep and won't wake up!"

Why can't she let it go? Last time, Mari had brought the target around the corner and found Shera fast asleep, knife still clutched in her hand. That had required some fast talking—and some fast work with a blade.

The sun had all but set while Shera napped, leaving her blanketed in the shadows of the alley. Perfect. The target wouldn't be suspicious when he failed to see her.

Shera rolled up to a crouch, hiding behind a crate of empty bottles. She tore the last piece of meat—now cold—from the skewer and tossed the empty stick away. Still chewing, she pulled the knife from the back of her pants.

"I am no physician, girl," Kamba Nomen said, his voice shrill and precise. "I can promise nothing for your sister."

Maxwell made sure that his gang of children knew their targets better than they knew their own reflections. Before Shera could see Kamba, she knew him: a short, dark-skinned man with a limp, walking with the aid of a cane. He was a Reader, but not the sort who cleansed battlefields of lingering resentment and invested scythes so that they cut wheat more efficiently.

"He's a different breed of Elder-spawned filth," Maxwell had assured them. *"He lays curses for hire, and as the whim strikes him. A woman sold him a bad piece of fruit, and within the day her cart collapsed. Sent her to the physicians with two broken legs and a cut neck. Last week, a neighbor of his burned up in an unexplained fire. The Empire has no use for this man, children. He deserves his fate."*

The silver-capped tip of Kamba's cane appeared around the edge of Shera's crate, and she tensed her grip on the knife. He wasn't supposed to see her before she struck. She was going to have to fight.

Ice grew in her heart, cold spreading inside her like frost on a winter field. If she had to fight Kamba, so what? Either he would die, or she would. Her hand steadied on the knife, and her body loosened.

But Mari hastily ran up and grabbed Kamba's other hand, directing him to the other wall of the alley.

"Not there! Over here."

Kamba leaned over, looking into the shadows where Shera and Mari had placed another bundle of clothes. In the darkness of the alley, it should look enough like a little girl crouched under a blanket.

The Reader nudged the bundle with his cane. "This doesn't look like—" he began, but he never got to finish the sentence.

The Bait had done her job. Now it was time for the Knife.

Shera leaped, kicking off the nearby crate and latching onto Kamba's back like a monkey.

Maxwell had warned them about the dangers of confronting a Reader. *"His jacket might be invested. It could turn your knife, so don't risk it."* Shera didn't. She stabbed him in the throat, where his jacket couldn't cover. Blood sprayed onto the alley wall and trickled over her fingers.

She dropped back to the ground as Kamba staggered around, flailing his arms. One of his spasms jerked his cane back, catching Mari on the shin.

Mari muffled a shout and fell backwards as Kamba finally quieted, twitching and bleeding on the alley stones. Shera quickly dragged him behind the crate—no one on the street would look twice at a suspicious stain on an alley wall, but even the Capital's indifferent citizens might come investigate a body in a rich man's jacket and pants.

Then she walked over and knelt, examining Mari's leg. "Is it cracked, do you think?"

"It hurts," Mari said, real tears welling up in her eyes. "And he almost found out. If you had taken one more second..." She shuddered. "I'm still shaking. Aren't you?"

Shera wiped her knife off on the dead man's coat and stuck it back down the waistband of her pants. "Shaking? It's not cold."

Mari sniffled, wiping tears from her eyes. "Not from the *cold.* Weren't you scared?"

"Of what?"

Shera glanced around the alley, in case she'd missed the sight of an Imperial Guard or some monstrous Elderspawn. Something to be scared of. Surely Mari couldn't have meant she was frightened of Kamba. The man had walked into an alley, and they'd stabbed him. Where was the threat?

Through her tears, Mari let out a long-suffering sigh. "Sometimes I want to be more like you. Other times, I think you'd get yourself killed in a week without me to take care of you."

This spoken by a girl who might have been ten years old. Shera wasn't sure about her own age, but she knew Mari couldn't be that much older. But for some reason, the other girl liked to think of herself as the mother.

Shera looped an arm around Mari's shoulder, helping her to her feet. "Who's taking care of who?"

Together, the pair made their way back to Maxwell's safe house, leaving a corpse behind them.

The safe house for Maxwell and his brood of adopted children rested underneath an *actual* house, a residence across from Gladstone Imperial Park that his family had owned for generations. The two stories above street level were furnished the way a single man living alone might keep them: dishes piled up on the table; a whiskey cabinet perpetually open; only two chairs in the sitting room.

But if you pushed the piano aside and rolled up a cheap Vandenyan rug, you found a trap door.

The three floors beneath formed the home where Shera and the others spent most of their time. Now that Mari and Shera had arrived, with Shera helping Mari down the ladder, they found the safe house in a state of panic.

A girl ran up to Shera, hauling a pillowcase stuffed with odds and ends. "*There* you are! Maxwell says he won't leave without you."

Shera exchanged confused glances with Mari. "Where is he going?"

The girl almost dropped her pillowcase in her excitement. "You haven't heard? Oh, that's right, you've been away. Well, Benji and Keina didn't report in at sunset. When Maxwell went to look for them, he found them *missing*. So he checked the traps in the upstairs house, and they've all been disarmed!"

Shera still felt like she was looking at a puzzle with half the pieces gone. "So...Benji disarmed the traps and ran away?"

A few children ran every few months. Sometimes Maxwell brought them back and dealt with them himself, as examples. Other times, he came back empty-handed. He called the losses, "acceptable costs of doing business."

"You don't get it?" the girl said. "We're under attack! Somebody found us! They might be here right now!"

She seemed more excited than terrified, hurrying down the hall with her pillowcase over her shoulder.

This time, Shera didn't need to look at Mari's face to know what she was thinking. They hurried downstairs together, Shera helping the hobbling Mari along.

As they shuffled down the hall, Shera heard a clatter and glanced back over her shoulder. There was no one else in the hallway. Only a fallen pillowcase, spilling its treasures all over the ground.

Of the girl, there was no sign.

The safe house was simple, and simply decorated. White walls, bare stone floor, and functional rooms with the bare minimum of cheap wooden furniture. The children slept in beds packed one against the other, sharing straw-stuffed pillows and scratchy woolen blankets.

Shera considered it the most comfortable home she'd ever had. With her real mother, she'd be lucky to have a single blanket in a filthy alley.

The pair hurried through the safe house, passing a steady stream of boys and girls bustling around and clutching their meager belongings. After Mari asked directions three times, they finally found their way to Maxwell: waiting for them in the discipline room.

The discipline room was lined with metal cages, where Maxwell's unruly students found themselves locked for days at a time.

He'd given up using that punishment on Shera after the first time, when she'd simply curled into a ball and slept from sunrise to sunrise.

Maxwell himself stood at the far end of the room, his sleeves rolled up, carrying a cage away from the brick wall. When he heard them enter, he staggered a few steps to the right, dropping the cage in a clatter of iron.

Some students saw Maxwell as their father and called him such, but he never insisted. Personally, Shera had never seen him as family at all.

He always wore black pants and a black shirt, with a white rose tucked into his shirt pocket above the heart. Some of the older girls giggled about how handsome he looked, with his curly brown hair down to his shoulders and his compact, muscular figure. Again, Shera found it difficult to think of him in that way.

He was just Maxwell.

When he turned and saw Shera, he gave a relieved sigh. "Shera. At last. I was worried that they would...never mind. Did you see anyone in the upstairs house?"

Mari moved away from Shera' support, stepping gingerly on her good leg, and answered. "We saw no evidence of any intruders, Maxwell."

"Of course you didn't see anyone. They're too good for that." He rubbed his hands together, invigorated, but his face still looked drawn and tight. It was the same look he wore in the first day or two after a child ran away and he couldn't bring them back.

He raised his boot and kicked another cage out of the way, and Shera finally saw what he was doing. A low metal grate rested in the middle of the wall, leading into a dark tunnel.

Maxwell nodded to the tunnel. "The other children are trying other means of escape, but this is where we'll be going. Rebel soldiers used this to move from base to base in the Kings' War."

"Should we gather anything from the house, sir?" Mari asked.

He didn't look at her. "Shera, what have I taught you about weapons?"

"A warrior is never unarmed," she said.

Maxwell gave her a proud smile. "Good girl. The others know where to rendezvous, but I didn't want to risk you getting lost. Come on, now."

Mari hesitantly raised her hand, as though asking for permission to speak. "What about—"

"Yes, yes, both of you. Into the tunnel, quickly. If they're who I think they are, we don't have much time."

Shera grabbed Mari by the shoulder again and began helping her toward the tunnel, but Maxwell held a hand out. His eyes sharpened. "What happened to Mari's leg?"

He directed the question at Shera, but she waited for Mari to answer. "I... the target hit me with his cane, Maxwell. It isn't bad."

Their leader shook his head. "Mari. There's too much at stake this time, girl. The Empire is sick, and we are the cure. But if these *hirelings* have their way, we'll never get to spread our good work."

He turned from Mari, picking up a crowbar to pry away at the grate. "Ordinarily I'd wait for you to recover, but we don't have time for that now. You'll slow us down."

Shera had completed the assassination of Kamba Nomen without a single instant of fear, but now a worm of doubt and uncertainty crawled its way into her heart. Instinctively, she stepped between Mari and Maxwell.

"Shera," Maxwell said, without turning around. "When do we kill?"

"When the target has earned his fate. When the target serves no useful function."

He gestured in Mari's direction with his crowbar. "Today, Mari serves no useful function. Quite the opposite. Finish your work."

Mari turned to Shera, eyes wide, tears streaming silently down her cheeks. "Shera..."

Shera looked between Mari and Maxwell. In the back of her waistband, the knife felt freezing cold.

She didn't want to kill Mari. *Why not? Because she's my friend? That doesn't matter. If she's useless, she's useless.*

But Mari was the one to shake Shera awake when she overslept. Mari made fun of Shera for being lazy. Mari told her when she should be afraid, even if Shera didn't feel it.

"She does serve a useful function," Shera said. Mari stared at her, hopeful.

Maxwell turned fully around, gripping his crowbar like a sword. "Then what is it?"

"I can't...I don't have the words for it. But I have a use for her."

Their leader blew out a breath, running his empty hand through his hair. "Children. I sometimes forget that they're children." Gently, he placed the crowbar on top of a nearby cage.

Then he pulled out a pistol and shot Mari in the chest.

Gun smoke filled the tiny room, the shot echoing like a collapsed wall. Shera couldn't take her eyes from Mari, who staggered backwards in her red-stained dress, clutching at a nearby cage for support. She finally collapsed, her mouth working for a few more seconds before she stopped trying to suck in a breath that wouldn't come.

Maxwell tossed his pistol aside. "What have I taught you about mercy, Shera?"

There is no such thing as mercy. There is only hesitation.

But this time, she didn't say it. She remained silent, thinking about Mari.

Her friend was dead. Shera confronted death every day, but she rarely thought about it. Death wasn't personal…except, this time, it was. It hurt like a knife to the chest, and she couldn't quite understand why.

And with the pain, her thoughts grew cold.

Maxwell had grabbed his crowbar again and resumed his work on the grate, prying it away from the brick wall. "No one else has learned my lessons better than you have, Shera. The Consultants think they have the best, but they won't be able to compete with you."

Shera stood behind Maxwell, her knife in her hand, thinking of Mari.

She cocked her head, aware of something she had never thought of before. Maxwell engineered the deaths of dozens, perhaps hundreds of people. *He deserved his fate.* And as for his 'useful function'...

"I have no use for you," she said.

He was starting to turn around when she drew her knife across his calves. He fell to his knees, screaming, and she plunged her knife into his back. Five times, to be safe.

The other children soon arrived, drawn by the sound of the gunshot. From the doorway, they each saw Maxwell, facedown in a pool of his own blood, as well as Mari's body slumped against a cage.

Some of them cried. Others screamed, and still others remained silent. A few looked as though they'd finally been released from prison.

But when they saw Shera, sitting on top of a cage with a bloody knife, none of them entered the room.

Kerian stood in the hallway of Maxwell's safe house, watching her fellow Consultants work. Or rather, watching the *results* of their work.

It was rare, even for her, to catch a Consultant in action.

A twelve-year-old boy raised a shaking pistol with both hands, pointing the barrel at Kerian—the only target in sight. She didn't bother moving.

A black shape passed across the boy and he was gone, pistol and all. A nine-year-old girl, who happened to be turning the corner at that exact moment, gasped and dropped a bundle of clothing. Before she could run off, a pair of black-clad arms reached down from the ceiling and pulled her up through the trap door.

Idly, Kerian fiddled with the leather satchel that hung from her shoulder. She had prepared for any number of contingencies, and thus far none of them had materialized. She couldn't help the boredom. Gardener missions were many things, but they were rarely boring; even if you had to lie perfectly still under a flowing river for six hours, breathing through a reed, assassinations had a thrill all their own.

She was the only Gardener on this mission, for which she was glad. Certain instincts could be hard to suppress, and they wanted these children back alive. The clients had specified as much, for understandable reasons.

The clients were the parents of these missing children. And they had finally offered such an obscene sum of money that the Consultant's Guild could not turn them away.

As glad as she was that she didn't have to rein in a team of Gardeners, she could never get used to working with Shepherds and Masons. The Masons weren't suited for real stealth work: they relied on their disguises to see them through, and they couldn't see that disguises served them nothing. A Mason hustled into view now, dressed as an old lady in an apron, chasing a girl down the hallway.

It doesn't matter if you look harmless. If you're a stranger, these children will run. It seemed, sometimes, that Masons left common sense on the island with their Consultant blacks.

Shepherds were a little better; at least they wore black. They were so *skittish.* Kerian had personally witnessed a Shepherd running from an eight-year-old boy with an undersized saber. Shepherds had been trained for so many years to minimize risk that they didn't recognize a harmless target when they saw one.

These children, on the other hand, had been raised like Gardeners. Or as close as Maxwell could come to it, having never seen the Garden himself.

Kerian strolled down the hall, searching through her satchel with one hand as she walked. *An extra pair of knives...useless. Climbing gear...unnecessary. An invested hammer in case we have to break through a wall...well, that one might come in handy.*

She still hoped someone would attack her. A mission didn't feel right without the risk of danger.

When she heard the pistol-shot ring out through the safe house, Kerian's spirits soared. Here, at last, something was happening.

She made her way downstairs, catching snatches of the reports from Shepherds who had—*of course*—already checked out the noise and returned.

"...Maxwell dead."

"...shot one of the girls. Don't know..."

"...looked like he was trying to escape."

A crowd of children clustered around the door to the room full of cages. They were facing the same way, so it was easy for Kerian to slip around them unnoticed and into the room herself.

The scene inside looked like the aftermath of a sloppy Gardener's botched mission.

Cages had been hauled away from one wall, revealing a metal grate that was halfway peeled away from the brick. The tunnel beyond it was Maxwell's "secret" escape route, an underground road dating back to the Kings' War. Five Consultants waited in hiding at the other end, prepared to take Maxwell when he emerged.

But he hadn't made it that far. Maxwell lay facedown as though drowning in blood, five or six stab wounds in the back of his shirt. His killer had been shorter—they'd slashed him across the legs to bring him down so they could reach. One of his children, then, had turned on their master.

Perhaps this girl over here, the curly-haired one with the bullet in her chest. Tears had worn tracks down her cheeks and she still had a blue ribbon in her hair.

Not her, then. She'd died surprised and unarmed.

Kerian glanced around the room before she spotted the killer: a girl, probably less than ten years old, with her black hair spilling out of a cheap cap. She was curled up on a cage, a bloody knife still gripped in her hand.

Asleep.

The Gardener snapped her fingers twice and two Shepherds appeared, black-clad and black-masked, bowing their heads and awaiting her order.

"Finish collecting the rest of the children," she ordered. "Then bring them to the chapter house for the clients."

She nodded to the sleeping killer. "I'll bring this one myself."

The story continues in…

OF SHADOW & SEA

WILL WIGHT lives in Florida, among the citrus fruits and slithering sea creatures. He graduated from the University of Central Florida in 2013, earning a Master's of Fine Arts in Creative Writing and a flute of dragon's bone.

Whosoever visits his website, *www.WillWight.com*, shall possess the power of Thor.

If you'd like to contact him, say his name three times into a candle-lit mirror at midnight. Or you could just send him an email at *will@willwight.com*.

(This paperback is made from 100% recycled troll-hide, for a sturdier finish.)

Made in the USA
Charleston, SC
26 May 2015